Acclaim for BEST OF ENEMIES

'A feisty follow-up to their smash novel SPLASH . . . Kept me reading far too late into the night'   Maureen Lipman

'Spicy, sharp but sympathetic insider's view'
Celia Brayfield

'Flashy, trashy and lots of fun, this book sashays as confidently as its authors through the media circus'   *Daily Mail*

'An entertaining account of boardroom battles and family rivalries'   *Woman's Journal*

'A page-turner . . . great fun'   *The Times*

'Enjoyable blockbuster'   *Sunday Times*

'Sizzling'   *Ideal Home*

Val Corbett began her career in journalism in her home city, Cape Town, then came to Britain to work in Fleet Street, where she was a feature writer and a columnist on national newspapers and magazines before switching to television. She has produced several acclaimed television programmes, including 'Living with the Enemy' for BBC1; she was also co-writer of the comedy series 'Life without George'. She gave up a directorship of a leading independent television production company to concentrate on novel-writing. She is married to Robin Corbett MP and has a daughter and two stepchildren.

Joyce Hopkirk was the launch editor of British *Cosmopolitan*, women's editor at the launch of the *Sun* newspaper, women's editor at the *Sunday Times*, assistant editor on the *Daily Mirror*, editor-in-chief on *She* magazine and launch editor of *Chic* magazine. She has twice won the Magazine Editor of the Year Award. She is married to Bill Lear, an executive of De Beers; they have a daughter and a son.

Eve Pollard was fashion editor at *Honey* and wrote features for the *Daily Mirror* before becoming women's editor on the *Observer* magazine. After launching American *Elle* in New York, she became editor of the *News of the World* colour supplement, then of *You* magazine on the *Mail on Sunday*. As editor of the *Sunday Mirror* she won the Editor of the Year Award in 1991, the year in which she became the first woman in recent years to edit a broadsheet as editor of the *Sunday Express* which, after its format was switched to tabloid, won both the Newspaper of the Year and the Sunday Newspaper of the Year Awards. She is married to Sir Nicholas Lloyd and has a daughter and a son and three stepchildren.

Best of Enemies

Val Corbett,
Joyce Hopkirk and
Eve Pollard

HEADLINE

First published in 1996
by HEADLINE BOOK PUBLISHING

First published in paperback in 1997
by HEADLINE BOOK PUBLISHING

A HEADLINE paperback

10 9 8 7 6 5 4

ISBN 0 7472 4968 7

Typeset by
Letterpart Limited, Reigate, Surrey

Printed in England by Clays Ltd, St Ives plc

HEADLINE BOOK PUBLISHING
A division of Hodder Headline PLC
338 Euston Road
London NW1 3BH

To Elizabeth, Walter, Veronica and Mimi

ACKNOWLEDGEMENTS

Our thanks to: Jennifer Clinton, Wendy Oberman, Diana Goodman and all the other first and second wives and their husbands who shared emotions, encounters and experiences; Jennifer Goodwin from Somerset House for details about adoption procedures; Dr Tony Gaze for medical advice; Robert Cox, assistant public affairs director, Scotland Yard; the Hertfordshire Child Protection Unit; officers at Hemel Hempstead police station; solicitors Tarn Hodder and Chris Brown; David Webster, deputy chairman of the Argyll Group and John Minshull Beech of Chelsfield plc, all of whom gave invaluable advice about multimillion pound takeovers and trust funds; Sally Ann Voak for advice about nutrition and weight loss; solicitor-turned-divorce-mediator Valerie Kleanthous; Police Sergeant Jim Traversh; DCI Peter Dumpleton; computer doctor Pete Venes, who calmed nerves while sorting out bytes; computer whiz Sean Solle, who miraculously found crucial hidden files; Judy Wade, Jeffrey Archer, Lynn Pemberton, Shirley Conran, Maggie Goodman, Heloisa Mulhall, Lord Thurso, Champneys and all their staff; Brenda Porter; Sue Cracknall, who fussed over us in France and her counterpart Sheila Bower in Mallorca; Barry Myers; Lucy Purdy; our husbands Bill Lear, Robin Corbett and Nicholas Lloyd for love, support and bathdrawing; our children and step-children Justin, Rachael and James Lloyd, Susannah Magal, Victoria Hopkirk,

Claudia Winkleman, Polly Corbett, Nicholas Lear and Oliver Lloyd; Al Zuckerman in New York; Don Shea; and, as ever, our agent Carole Blake and editor Marion Donaldson.

THE FAMILY

The Rt Hon Philip Lockhart	Member of Parliament
Vanessa Forrester Lockhart	his first wife
Amy and Louise Forrester Lockhart	their daughters
Charlotte (Charlie) Mills	Philip's second wife
Miranda Lockhart	their daughter
Cecily Toscani	Vanessa's aunt
Dorinda Cazalet	Vanessa's best friend
Peter Cazalet	her husband
Angus McKinnon	the unknown quantity

THE BUSINESS

Walter Threadgold	Chairman, Forrester Group
Anne Grover, Hugh Purcell	Directors, Forrester Newspapers
Paul Salter	Chairman, Salter Foundation
Kyle Salter	his son

THE MEDIA

Tony Burns	Assistant Editor News, *Daily Chronicle*
Fergus Canefield	Proprietor, Chronicle Group
Imogen Ferris	writer for *Sussex County Magazine*
Kevin Jamieson	Chief Reporter, *Daily Chronicle*
Tom Levin	American Broadcasting Network

Prologue

The woman felt deeply embarrassed. She was by now quite naked. Within the last five minutes the fine wool jacket and sheath dress had been peeled off, slowly revealing her breasts slightly overfilling a black underwired bra.

Seconds later that, too, had been removed, along with the flimsy matching panties, taut suspenders and sheer tawny stockings.

He had started mentally undressing her from the moment they had met and his expression made no secret of exactly what he was doing. And what he was imagining.

She had selected the navy outfit carefully to make her look businesslike. Self-consciously she touched her shoulder to reassure herself that her dress was still in place. His eyes remained fixed on the swell of her breasts. The swishing sound of the silky hose as she nervously re-crossed her legs increased the tension and goaded her into saying more than she intended.

The stranger was tall and attractive in an intense, Italianate way. At ease in the best corner suite in The Ritz, he felt excitement building, and not just because of the deal. He had not envisaged that this new ally, this spy in the enemy camp, whom he had privately and without much originality codenamed 'Deep Throat', would so physically unsettle him.

As he sat behind the ornate desk, the late winter sunlight streamed in behind him and fell harshly onto her attentive face, just as he had planned. This was the first international deal he had handled alone on behalf of his father's empire. What they needed was privileged, inside information to help clinch the takeover. This was the reason the woman was here but she was not the type to be motivated by personal aggrandisement or financial greed; there was something else she wanted, and he could provide it.

Her voice was hoarse. 'I need this takeover to succeed so what can I say? I accept.'

The man leaned back. His private investigator had been one hundred per cent accurate. He had defined, precisely, the weakest link in the Forrester chain and had given him what he needed to get her on board.

'Good. I'm glad you feel able to help,' he replied formally and opened his briefcase. 'Here are the private numbers you'll need. I anticipate this should all be over quite soon.' He stood up and they shook hands. 'It's been a pleasure to meet you.'

The woman recognised that this could be construed by the others as dirty business. But she had never dreamed of having such power. Over both families. She would use it well.

No adulterer could have left the suite as she did with such a heady feeling of guilt, delight and remorse.

Chapter One

There was nothing like a death in harness to make the pre-Christmas House of Commons buzz with more incredible rumours than usual.

In this case the insider gossip was that an MP was to be plucked from the back benches to become the new Secretary of State for Transport. With less than eighteen months until an election, the Prime Minister, the Right Honourable Edward Saunders, 'Steady Eddie' as the tabloids called him, needed a bold initiative. Something to prove he could still come up with bright people and ideas and demonstrate there was life in his government yet.

Few gave the rumour much credence. The last time a PM had promoted someone straight from the comparative anonymity of the back benches into the Cabinet was nearly twenty-five years ago and it had ended in political failure. Along the corridors of Westminster, senior journalists in the parliamentary lobby predicted that the PM would wait until after the Christmas recess to fill the job and also take advantage of the vacancy to reshuffle his ministerial pack. The hot money was on a couple of high-profile backbenchers for junior posts and a pugnacious junior minister for the plum post in the Cabinet.

The tipsters were wrong.

The day after the House rose for the holidays, Philip Lockhart, MP for London Heathgate, chairman of the Commons Transport Select Committee, one of the party's deputy chairmen and also chief executive of the Forrester Newspaper Group, was quietly summoned to 10 Downing Street.

He was shown into the geranium-red hall and ushered towards the balustraded staircase, lined with the portraits of prime ministerial predecessors, all male with one exception, then into the book-lined study on the first floor. For generations this room had been used as an office by the Prime Minister and First Lord of the Treasury for Great Britain and Northern Ireland.

The Premier, a small, stocky, slightly balding figure, rose from one of the pair of maroon and pale blue damask sofas and offered a welcoming hand.

'Thank you for coming to see me, Philip.' His manner was friendly. 'I've called you in because I've been watching your performance in the House and more importantly at party headquarters. I've noted your skills as a negotiator.' He sat behind the magnificent mahogany desk and rested his elbows on the surface. When next he spoke, a note of formality entered his voice. 'I've been impressed. Most impressed.'

My God, thought Philip, he's going to make me a junior minister at last. 'Thank you, Prime Minister,' he answered, trying to keep his excitement in check.

'So I'm inviting you to join my government.' He paused. Philip was about to accept but the Prime Minister had not finished. 'In fact, I want you in my Cabinet. As the new Secretary of State for Transport.'

The PM affected not to see the stunned surprise on Philip Lockhart's face.

'Transport,' he went on smoothly, 'won't give you an easy ride.' He coughed. 'Do excuse the pun. The current Road Extension Bill is in deep trouble, very unpopular in the country, but it's vital to get the public on our side before it goes through the House. We need a good communicator who can explain what we're trying to do. I think you're the right man for the job.' Saunders looked at him. 'You have youth and vigour on your side.'

Was there just the smallest hint of envy from the ageing politician? Saunders had won two previous elections and Philip was aware that he was eager for a third victory and a postponement of his retirement to the Lords.

'That's extremely kind of you, sir. I'm very surprised but, of course, delighted. As you know, I have some strong ideas about what needs to be done.'

'Yes,' said Saunders drily. 'I read what you said about that in your constituency. Well, now you can put those ideas into practice. We've let the Opposition make far too much of the running. I'll be looking to you to make the right stand, let them know from the beginning there's a new, firm hand on the tiller.'

Could he only speak in clichés, thought Philip. But he said, 'I'm grateful for the trust you're putting in me, Prime Minister. It's a huge challenge, just the kind I've been waiting for.'

Saunders nodded. 'This job won't be a cul-de-sac, Philip.' He tutted at himself and apologised for making yet another pun. 'Do this task well and, all things being equal, you won't find me ungrateful.'

'I won't let you down, sir,' responded the new Secretary of State.

The PM held out his hand and Philip shook it firmly, still hardly believing what had happened.

'My private secretary will contact you when you get back to your office, I should say your old office, to discuss arrangements. Good luck and I'll see you at the first Cabinet meeting in the New Year.'

Philip emerged slightly dazed from Number 10 and ran his fingers distractedly through his unruly dark hair. Turning up the collar of his coat against the cold December evening, he walked jauntily down a near-deserted Whitehall back to the Commons. A six foot, rugged-looking man with a broken nose, a remnant of his varsity team's bobsleigh race, he was euphoric about his change of status. Not bad for a builder's son, a scholarship boy with a brain described by his tutors at Cambridge as 'not first-class but wily'. He would have to use all his guile to persuade his wife that his health could handle it.

So what if it was close to a general election and the job might not last long? He had been talent-spotted. If they won, he would be in the next Cabinet. If the government lost, he would be in the Shadow Cabinet preparing for power.

But as he crossed Whitehall, an unpalatable thought struck him. Cabinet ministers had to give up all outside business interests. With growing unease, Philip began to work out the ramifications of his sudden promotion and, as he did so, his steps slowed.

'Shit,' he said out loud. 'What a way to ruin Christmas.'

Chapter Two

Vanessa was dreading the party. She poured a large gin. Not for herself but for her pot plant.

An American gardening fanatic had once told her it was a certain way to stunt the growth of prized narcissi once they had reached the required height. She poured a smaller gin for herself.

The dress of indigo blue silk, carefully chosen for tonight's occasion, was lying on the bed. It was more expensive, better tailored, more forgiving than anything else in her wardrobe but Vanessa was aware it still would not disguise her over-generous curves. At five foot seven, she would look better if she weighed twenty pounds less. But although she regarded herself as finally being back on the marriage market, she did not yet have the impetus to stick to a diet or give up the too frequent glasses of alcohol.

She sighed. These days, she had to admit, she was not a party animal. After three years of being on her own, she often thought she would like to marry again but living without a man, she seemed to have lost the knack of flirting, of making amusing small talk. Not that she did not try. She smiled wrily at the memory of her terminal error at last week's dinner party. One of the guests, an attractive man, had idly asked where everyone had been the night President Kennedy was shot.

'I was at my eleventh birthday party,' she said to the latest prospect. 'And you?'

He looked amused. 'In my mother's womb.'

It was unfortunate that, minutes before, she had lopped eight years off her age. She hoped he was no better at maths than she was.

The trouble was, invitations out to dinner were rare. Her women friends preferred to 'play safe' by inviting her out only at lunchtimes. Now she was eligible they thought of her as a predator, a risk to their marriages. It was so unfair. In any case, who the hell would want *their* husbands?

Vanessa breathed in deeply, looking at herself critically in the bedroom mirror. At least her fair hair was thick and luxurious-looking, and it was no coincidence that the colour of the dress enhanced her lavender-blue eyes.

To boost her morale for the party she had bought a pair of extravagantly expensive silk stockings to flatter what her ex-husband used to call her Shirley MacLaine legs. She placed the graduated heavy pearl ropes, a gift from her grandfather to her mother, round her neck and told herself that tonight's dress with its discreet décolletage would, she hoped, draw attention to her cleavage instead of her hips.

Louise, her gangly twelve-year-old daughter, burst through the door, long blonde hair still trapped in the snood required by the local riding school. She made a running dive on to her mother's king-sized bed, her dilapidated sneakers just missing the antique white pillowcases.

'What's the river running through Florence called, Mum?

It's for my geography test.' She started fiddling with her mother's clutch bag.

'The Arno. And keep your filthy paws off that, miss,' Vanessa remonstrated mildly. 'Is Tansy still in her basket?'

'Yes, she's asleep.' Louise put on a wheedling tone. 'Why can't I come with you tonight?'

'Because you're not old enough, Lou-Lou,' said her mother patiently. 'When you're Amy's age you will. Which is what I told you yesterday and again this morning.'

Louise watched her mother walk into the bathroom and lean towards the tall, bevelled mirror spanning the double sink installed twenty years ago as a wedding present from her in-laws.

Peering at her naked face, Vanessa began to apply camouflage. Perhaps this mixture of foundation, mascara and powdered shading would help mask her insecurity.

Vanessa had married early and, encouraged by her former husband to stay at home full time, she had never had to earn her own salary. Sometimes she wondered if her marriage would have survived had she led a more independent life. Now at the age of forty-three, unskilled, untrained and reliant on alimony, she filled the hours when her children no longer needed her by helping to organise charity events and working in her well-stocked garden. Since the divorce she had made a conscious effort to overcome her shyness and sense of rejection. The tapestry she was working on bore testament to her efforts: 'Optimists are wrong as often as pessimists,' it read. 'But they have a lot more fun.'

She inspected her face critically, gratified that a few strokes of blusher could work such miracles.

Her grosgrained high heels still had mud splatters from an

earlier outing. Damn. Now there was no man in the house, shoe-cleaning had become a forgotten activity. She made an ineffective rub at the heels with a slightly damp tissue. That would have to do.

'Mrs Prescott doesn't need to babysit me,' pleaded Louise. 'Not while the dogs are here.' It was an old argument.

'Yes she does. Tansy needs another pill about now, doesn't she, darling?'

Louise sprang up, tripping over the Persian rug and narrowly missing the huge Victorian wardrobe, its carved doors spread wide to reveal shelves spilling over with scarves, belts and rifled underwear, testament to a futile search for a favourite evening bag. Signs that her mother was making an effort.

The clutch purse was a compromise choice. Vanessa picked it up from the bed and walked across the landing to check Amy's progress. But there was no sign of her elder daughter in the jumble of her blue and white gingham bedroom, sofa obscured by piles of clothing looking as though an Oxfam sale was about to take place.

In her unaccustomed high heels Vanessa walked carefully down the curved staircase with its rows of original water-colours lining the walls and past the bottom steps, a transit dump for items meant to live upstairs – books, trainers, laundry and spare loo rolls which seemed to linger well past their move-by date. Absent-mindedly she picked a dirty glass up off the leather-covered Regency desk in the drawing room and hurried with it into the kitchen.

This, too, revealed more detritus of an all-female house-hold. There were collections of old catalogues, torn-out coupons, gymkhana rosettes, notices advertising the local

point-to-point, pine drawers so overweighted with magazines containing recipes never again consulted that they
were almost impossible to open or close.

The shelves were adorned with a proud eight-year-old's
version of a papier-mâché sea lion, a ten-year-old's attempt
at a pottery plate depicting bacon, eggs and sausages, and a
more recent piece of sophisticated handiwork of a ceramic
tube of toothpaste.

Vanessa found it hard to criticise daughters who had
clearly inherited her untidiness gene.

In the middle of this comfortable clutter stood Amy
wearing every nineteen-year-old's favourite accessory, a
cordless phone attached to her ear. It had been a term since
Vanessa had seen her daughter in anything other than jeans
and sweatshirts and she was taken aback at how glamorous
Amy had become since going up to Cambridge. The black
panne velvet dress had earlier been carelessly tossed on the
counterpane of Amy's bed. In its unstretched state, it looked
no bigger than a handkerchief. Now the dress extended to a
close fit on the nineteen-year-old's lean, perfectly-contoured
body. In her neat ankle-gripping boots she towered above
her mother.

A ring at the door heralded the arrival of Mrs Prescott,
closely followed by their regular taxi driver to take mother
and daughter to the party in nearby Brighton.

To Vanessa's consternation the jacket of her dress, which
had seemed to fit so well only days ago, now gaped and
strained when she buttoned it up. Too bad. She would have
to wear it open.

The two women had just settled into the back seats and
the taxi was performing a U-turn in front of the Rectory

when Louise burst through the front door waving her arms frantically.

'Muuum,' she screamed. 'Come quickly. Tansy's staggering about in the kitchen.'

Vanessa and Amy climbed out of the taxi and hurried back into the house where the ageing Labrador was making a valiant effort to stand on legs which kept crumpling beneath her. The dog was nearly fifteen and although the family had not expected her to live much longer, the sight of their beloved pet trying to gulp air was highly distressing.

The vet took only twenty minutes to arrive. He was adamant that the animal had to be put out of her misery at once and the three of them tried to comfort each other in the hall while the vet did the deed quickly and efficiently.

Vanessa closed her eyes, party make-up ruined, as the tears streamed down her face. She was remembering the small ball of fur curled up at the dog breeders all those years ago and Amy's excitement as her father pretended to make up his mind. Vanessa could still hear Amy's squeal of glee as Tansy, the only one of the litter to lick her hand, made the selection for them.

Now the dog was dead and another link with the past was gone.

Vanessa sighed, took her mirror from her handbag and began to repair her make-up, wishing yet again that she could be rescued from this most wretched evening of the year.

Chapter Three

Charlotte was dreading the party. Although she was in a rush it was with reluctance that she cut short her precious playtime with Miranda.

Mother and toddler enjoyed an evening ritual where 'Itsy Bitsy Spider' was followed by 'This Little Piggy'. Tonight, however, with an eye on the clock, Charlie was having to truncate the number of piggies. To make matters worse, her husband had told her only an hour or so ago that she would have to make her own way down to the coast.

Charlie tried to shut herself off from the sound of the nanny saying, in an over-loud voice on the phone, '. . . so I can't come to the party. No. I have to work tonight. Yes. I know. But what can I do?'

Not for the first time, Charlie had a fleeting moment of doubt about the upbringing of her child. She could find no fault with the way the tall brunette from New Zealand looked after Miranda. Helen Brickhill was conscientious and affectionate but there was a coolness between her and her employer.

In her darker thoughts, Charlie wondered whether it could be due to jealousy, a feeling of rivalry, but she dismissed the idea. This was the first time she had ever employed anyone in her home and, if she was honest, she disliked having someone else in the house. She never felt truly private. And if she did think she could do a better job herself, her work as a producer for an American television channel made it impractical. Like every working mother Charlie believed that her child would fare better if she could devote more time to her. If only they were not paying so much for her husband's first wife. If only they did not rely on Charlie's salary.

Like many wives with partners whose jobs kept them out of the home for long hours, Charlie felt she had the major responsibility for Miranda because her husband had so many other calls on his time and his emotions. It did not help that the two of them were travelling along wholly different stages of parental experience. This was her first baby but his third. The problems which panicked her he dismissed as commonplace. Similarly, some of the baby's glories, which entranced her, he took for granted.

Usually she was too busy for such introspection and though sometimes she felt lonely as his wife, she shivered when she remembered the dark six months they had tried being apart when he was still attempting to make his first marriage work. Living as part of his life was still better than living, she would say merely existing, with none of it.

In the study her husband's phone and fax kept up a constant clamour for attention which Charlie ignored. What she needed now was a swift injection of caffeine. She was always shattered these days. With a hot towel wrapped round her head heating up some revolutionary product which claimed to straighten the most stubborn curls, she went into

14

the kitchen, placing Miranda in the high chair.

The old scullery and pantry had been knocked into one comfortable room where the family spent most of its time. The walls were sponged alabaster and Charlie had rediscovered the original oak floor underneath layers of matted carpet and linoleum.

The five-bedroomed, high-ceilinged Edwardian apartment was bigger than many town houses and the mortgage was horrendously high, but Philip had insisted on the space so his children could have their own rooms when they came to stay. Charlie had enjoyed modernising the flat, giving it a transatlantic spaciousness which reflected her time in America. Its uncluttered look was greatly admired by guests ranging from the popular American ambassador to the capital's leading playwrights.

On a small budget she had achieved miracles. Lining the hall were inexpensive watercolours found at country auctions and mixed with witty, old political cartoons by Spry which her husband had begun to collect. One of the most successful presents from him to her was hanging in their lavatory. In copperplate hand it read: 'An alcoholic is someone who drinks more than their doctor.' Using that yardstick, guests joked, they had plenty of leeway. In the reception rooms were a few pieces of lovely old furniture which they had picked up at knockdown prices because they were too big for most modern rooms.

As she made herself a cup of coffee, Charlie noticed a small paper bag with a chemist's imprint that she had noticed the nanny bring in earlier. Idly she opened it. With a mixture of interest and dismay she saw that it contained two packs of three condoms. Extra-sensitive.

There had been no evidence so far that the girl was sexually active. Helen Brickhill was an intensely private person who dressed plainly, wore almost no make-up and always came home at a reasonable hour. In the six months she had worked for them there had never been a mention of a man in her life, nor had Charlie ever heard her speaking to one on the phone. Obviously, appearances were deceptive. But six condoms? No wonder Helen was miffed at missing the party.

As she was on her way back to the nursery, holding Miranda in one arm, Charlie's work phone rang and without thinking she picked it up.

It took only thirty seconds to ruin her weekend. New York wanted her to do an extra shift on Saturday. How was she going to persuade Helen to give up Saturday as well? She would not even try.

Several goodnight kisses later Miranda was tucked into her cot and Charlie began to dial her mother's number to plead with her to help out the next day. Whenever possible Susan Mills was ready to drop everything to help her daughter and spend precious hours with her only grandchild. But this time Charlie was unsuccessful. Susan's own mother was too ill to be left alone and at the weekend there was no nursing cover. She would have to ask Miranda's godmother, her friend Jane, who was around this weekend. Now she would have to hurry and get dressed.

Charlie's spacious, walk-in closet held an impressive array of clothes, arranged in colours and fabrics for seasons and occasions, another idea she had imported from America where such organisation was commonplace. Everything had its place. Her maternity clothes were stored in canvas zip-up bags and above was a giant hatbox which she remembered with a pang of yearning was filled with the best of Miranda's layette.

After three years of marriage she wanted another child but she suspected her husband was not so keen. Although he had not discussed it with her, when she had become pregnant with Miranda she was certain he had been worried about the reaction from his first family to the birth of another child. But whatever his feelings during her pregnancy, there was no disguising his adoration of Miranda and it gave Charlie hope that he could be persuaded that they should have another baby.

She selected an amethyst-coloured tight-fitting dress for tonight's event, a Royal Command performance. It was elegant, understated and would, she hoped, kill 'em dead in their tracks. Like they said on Fifth Avenue, 'brash not trash'.

She slipped a necklace off the latticed jewellery rack. Her husband teased her that this complicated structure was an over-reaction against the wardrobe in the small flat which he had shared with his first wife. He and Charlie had moved in there briefly before buying the flat in Pimlico. Charlie had not changed a thing. Except for the mattress, the lavatory seat and the telephone.

A matching pair of shoes boosted her five foot five inches by another four inches. Her dark hair, which was never totally tamed by any treatment, was almost dry now, and her face never needed much make-up. Charlie was blessed with the sort of skin which looked sunkissed all year round and her full, generous mouth gave life to her expression even in repose.

Since her pregnancy, she had re-trained herself to follow a regime of vigorous regular exercise and careful eating as she was certain her American bosses would think she had gone native if she did not stay a trim size ten even after the birth of her daughter. When she had to meet potential interviewees or organise visits for bigshots from the New York head office, she had to look well-groomed, on top of things and, above all, slim. But it was her husband's wellbeing that motivated her most. She tried, without too much success, to set him an example and involve him in her strict eating and exercise habits. But, as yet, she and his doctor had failed to convince him that poached fish and sparkling water should be his staple diet and only interspersed with treats like claret and steak. So far his predilection was in the reverse order.

To the outside world, Charlie seemingly had it all, an absorbing job working as a senior producer for an American news television channel and a successful husband. It did not harm either of them that her prestigious job brought invitations from all strata of London society. The only shadow in her life was that the first wife still had the capacity to upset their harmony. Whenever she was in any predicament – her car breaking down, fixing the drains to the roof gutters, a possible intruder in the garden (which turned out to be a fox) – Vanessa contacted, not the repair man or the pest control operative but her ex-husband. If the woman had friends, she never seemed to ask their help. And because of his guilty conscience, Philip never complained, simply dismissing each problem as a minor irritant even when it was extremely inconvenient.

Charlie, who had been lauded for her tough interviews with statesmen and her ability to draw out confessions from hardened fraudsters when she had presented a current affairs programme, still found herself intimidated by a woman who, by her own admission, preferred animals and plants to people. Sometimes she had the maddening feeling her spouse thought she was paranoid about his first wife. Which was not true. Not at all. Throughout their married life the subject of her husband's first wife could never and had never been discussed honestly between them. Charlie had discovered early on that she could talk about virtually everything with her husband but this. She could be as critical as she liked about her predecessor but he refused to join in. Inevitably these one-sided conversations soon ground to a halt.

He would admit that whenever his second wife mentioned his first, he would cocoon himself with invisible ear muffs. Like many divorced husbands he had put the conflict between his two wives into the compartment marked 'I can't change it, I can't help it, so I won't think about it.' He imagined that he had the relationship with his first wife under control and felt too guilty to want to probe it any further, reasoning that as they would never agree, what was the point in talking about it with Charlie?

She turned away from the mirror, confident in her appearance at least. From her white-tipped nails to her immaculate shoes she had the ability to make the most ordinary outfit look special and yet appear as if it took no bother at all. And she seemed to emanate energy. She was bouncy, feisty, extrovert. In a recent interview, Philip had described how he had fallen for her. 'Her intensity makes me feel alive,' he was quoted as saying. 'She's passionate, opinionated, exciting, exuberant and has a fierce intelligence.'

19

An embarrassed Charlie had accused him of going over the top, but it was true he thought of her as someone who never whined and had a 'positive approach to life. She always believes we'll find a parking spot,' he had told the interviewer. 'And we usually do.'

But her demanding schedule – working wife, mother, constituency wife and stepmother – meant she found it harder and harder to be the girl with whom her husband had fallen in love. Bubbly personalities did not stay bubbly when they constantly worried about the overdraft which grew ever larger because guilt at leaving a wife and family had resulted in over-generous alimony payments.

None of this had mattered until the family company had bought a news magazine which turned out to be a money-eating machine. The dividends paid to shareholders annually had to be cut. She and her husband had economised. His first wife had not.

Still he refused to reduce the payments paid to his first family. They were frank with each other about everything. Everything except his bank account. He did not like her to know how well or badly the family budget was doing as there were constant out-of-pocket expenses for his first family. A school trip, piano lessons, a new bicycle, a replacement pony for Benjy who had died and later a car for the eldest daughter. The list was never-ending and as the girls grew, so did the demands.

Charlie understood that her salary was vital to maintain their standard of living. Most of the time she accepted all this as the penalty of marrying a man with past baggage.

She picked up her purse, checked that there was enough money for the train fare, and went in to see Helen.

'I've put Miranda down and she's nice and sleepy.' She hesitated, noticing the girl's mutinous expression. If only she realised how much her employer yearned to swap places with her right now. 'Helen, I'm really sorry about tonight, I will make it up to you.'

Helen's response was a cool nod.

With an eye on the clock, Charlie promised to make her usual check call later and rushed towards the front door, grabbing her door key on the way. She wished yet again that she could be rescued from this most wretched evening of the year.

Chapter Four

From her crowded corner at the party, Vanessa Forrester Lockhart sensed that her successor had arrived.

Without moving her head, she slid her eyes towards and then away from the panelled doorway. Vanessa did not miss a beat. No one but her best friend would have guessed how the entrance of her rival had affected her.

'God, look how she's sucking up to those old men,' Dorinda Cazalet murmured under her breath.

Vanessa suppressed a smile. 'That's rich coming from someone who's left a trail of broken pacemakers all over the county.'

Dorinda, who had a penchant for discreet extra-marital affairs, gave her friend a playful push. 'They died happy,' she retorted.

As ever, Charlotte Lockhart's appearance on Vanessa's territory aroused a conflict of loyalty among the other guests, many of whom had been employed for years by the group started by Vanessa's grandfather Elliot Forrester. The newer recruits to the expanding newspaper group followed what they saw as the power trail and greeted Charlie with grandiose gestures of affection. Even staff Vanessa had known for years made accommodation for Charlotte Lockhart, the new Queen.

The two women were at opposite ends of the room. Their eyes met and they nodded coolly to each other.

Vanessa covertly observed the meet-and-greet rituals and despised herself for the feeling of resentment which engulfed her.

'Look at that shower, fawning around That Woman.' Dorinda was scathing. 'They're being so obvious, it won't do them any good.'

The company's Christmas party had always been held on the top floor of the elegant Georgian building with its coveted sea view. The narrow structure was at odds with the twentieth-century requirements of a modern media group but they held on to it for sentimental reasons. Since the company had purchased a national news magazine, most of the workforce had been transferred to new headquarters which could accommodate the extensive cabling required for computers and other electronic equipment. The granite skyscraper in London's Docklands with its ostentatious mission statement in the atrium was peopled by those who preferred talking to each other on the Internet than face-to-face. Although *The Citizen* had brought the group financial headaches, it had also given the family national recognition.

Despite the move, Vanessa and other old-timers had made sure the firm's Christmas party stayed in its traditional home in Brighton. They felt at ease here, with the waves in front and the famous pier twinkling in the distance. The place had a slightly musty, unused air these days. This floor was once the haunt of the group's directors and Vanessa could remember her grandfather and Philip working here, taking over local paper after local paper, buying printing plants and local radio stations, building the business up, up, up. It had all been so exciting then.

Tonight, the support in the room for her was almost tangible. The warm feeling gave her the courage to cope with this, for her, the worst night of the year. Her presence was her way of showing that, despite everything, she and her daughters were involved with, and attached to, the business. Vanessa should have been enjoying this familiar evening. The reality was she hated being there simply because she was older and fatter than Charlie. How stupid. What a childish obsession for a grown woman. Even so, she hoped she had repaired the worst of the ravages caused by Tansy's death.

Anne Grover, the group's human resources director, gave Vanessa a sympathetic smile as she passed her a glass of chilled champagne. 'This may help take your mind off Tansy,' she said. A dog-lover herself, she had been the first person Vanessa had told. Her twenty-odd years of service with the firm gave her a certain familiarity with the founder's family and, like many of the long-serving employees, she had been upset about Vanessa's divorce. She had never truly accepted the second Mrs Lockhart though she was wise enough not to show it.

Divorce was almost like a hobby in this Sauvignon and Saab belt of Sussex. Some of the women regarded Vanessa as a bad luck omen. 'There but for the grace of God go I,' they thought. If they were honest, many of them blamed the marital split on her. Looking at her tall but fulsome figure, they censured her for not working at keeping the curves of middle-age at bay. They also believed she should have had the sense to turn a blind eye to Philip's little adventures, as they had learned to do in their marriages. Philip was, they had long since decided, like many of their own spouses, emotionally and sexually in the child-man bracket.

Dorinda decided it was time to divert her friend's attention from her rival. 'I saw that delicious estate agent again at the Templetons',' she confided. 'The spark's still there.'

'Don't tell me,' Vanessa smiled. 'I suppose you'll have to check out lots of empty houses with him.'

'Hmmn, I hope. My only problem is how to give the heave-ho to my lawyer friend.' He had been Dorinda's lunchtime sex partner for some six months, the optimum duration of these liaisons.

Vanessa looked wistful. 'I can't get men and you can't get rid of them.'

'You must send out the right signals,' advised her friend. 'I've told you what to do. It's easy. You look them straight in the eyes and you think: "Fuck me. I want you to fuck me. I want you to fuck me right now." '

'I've tried that,' replied Vanessa, 'but by the time I'm halfway through they've moved off across the room.'

'Practice makes perfect. It's just like cooking an omelette.'

'Even if I managed the flirting, Dorrie, I can't go on to the next step. I can hardly bear taking my clothes off in front of a mirror, let alone some new man. Just look at this.' And she discreetly grabbed a fold of flesh on her waist. 'I must lose some weight. The trouble is I get so ravenous.'

'Well, I've found the perfect diet for us.' Dorinda was triumphant. 'It goes like this. If you eat something and nobody sees you, it has no calories. If you drink a Diet Coke and then eat chocolate, the calories are cancelled out by the drink. Broken biscuits don't contain any calories at all. The process of breaking causes calorie leakage.'

Dorinda was enjoying her friend's amusement.

'Best of all, foods the same colour have the same calories, for example spinach and pistachio ice cream, mushrooms and white chocolate.'

Vanessa smiled. 'If only it were that easy.' She gazed enviously at Charlie's slender back. She was in animated discussion with a group of sycophants. 'If I was slim I could try being as uninhibited as you,' Vanessa said ruefully.

'It's just a trick. You could learn it if you wanted to. But,' she paused, 'there comes a moment when you still have to take off your knickers.'

'I presume you also have to quite like the man,' said Vanessa with an ironic smile.

Dorinda lifted another glass from a passing tray. 'Well, you know what they say, "Love is blind but lust don't give a damn." ' She sipped at her drink, thinking how attractive Vanessa looked when her face was lit up with laughter.

'And talking about knickers,' she went on, 'Charlotte the Harlot's manless tonight. Where's Philip? Aren't the loving pair usually joined at the hip?'

'I don't know where he is but she keeps looking at her watch and at the open door. Something must be up.' The lateness of her ex-husband brought back savage memories for Vanessa. She remembered the countless times Philip had been tardy, times she was now convinced, not always correctly, that he had been pleasuring himself with Charlie in bed.

Vanessa had been known to use that well-worn cliché, 'A leopard never changes his spots.' Perhaps Charlie already had a rival after only three years of marriage.

Vanessa caught sight of Amy's reflection in the glass of the huge portrait of her grandfather which dominated the room. Her daughter, despite careful re-application of eye make-up, showed evidence of copious weeping. Vanessa walked over and gave her a squeeze. 'She was a darling dog,' she murmured, 'and we must try and remember her in her best days. Everyone's complimenting me on how lovely you look. I'm so proud of you. Let's try and enjoy ourselves.'

Amy smiled wanly. It was the first time she had volunteered to attend this party and Vanessa revelled in the compliments about her demeanour and beauty. 'Doesn't she look the spitting image of you, Mrs Lockhart?' was the often repeated comment. And in truth she did, being a taller, slimmer version of a young Vanessa.

In spite of everything, Vanessa began to relax. This was, after all, her patch.

Charlie would rather have sat in a dentist's chair having root canal work than be at this Christmas party.

This was her second appearance as wife of the company's chief executive and she hated every single thing about it, most particularly meeting the ex-wife face to face. The glazed smile and that little flicker from Vanessa as she eyed her up and down, monitoring what she was wearing, made Charlie clench her jaw with suppressed irritation. In an unguarded moment Louise had once remarked, 'Mummy says you spend a fortune on your clothes, much more than she does.'

In the middle of the Yuletide buzz, because she was so uncomfortable Charlie felt abandoned. She and Philip had spent some time on the phone conjecturing why the Prime Minister should want to see him so urgently. 'Whatever it is,' he had told her, 'I can hardly say sorry, PM, my wife doesn't want to be alone at my company's party, some other time perhaps, can I?'

As she looked at the throng over the rim of her champagne glass, Charlie suspected that the older staff felt she was an interloper. Worse, was the rather oleaginous manner of the newer staff. To Charlie, this was especially alien. Like her, they worked in the media. She had met one or two of the news magazine people through her work. Why did they fawn over her? She would prefer it if they looked upon her as a colleague rather than the boss's wife. It was strange that Vanessa, who had never had a byline in her life, nor a paid job, seemed to be much more at ease with them. Charlie, used to big city life, felt she would never understand the loyalties of the Sussex men and women.

She watched Vanessa darting from one group to another, organising drink refills, steering trays of canapés towards the far end, playing the perfect hostess. For the millionth time Charlie wondered what on earth Philip could have ever seen in a woman who delighted in small talk and had such bland views that Charlie's mother had nicknamed her 'Vanilla'.

Why was he taking so long, knowing how much she loathed this ghastly shindig? Once more she checked her watch, once more registering the gleam of interest in Vanessa's eyes. There was no doubt the bloody woman was revelling in her discomfort.

Vanessa's kind of woman rarely entered Charlie's world. Charlie could not remember exchanging anything more than curt greetings with her predecessor on the few occasions they had been forced to see each other. However careful Philip was to censor comments from his ex-wife on the occasions they had to arrange to pick up the children, there was no doubting the bitterness Vanessa felt towards the woman who had taken her place.

Would things ever improve between them?

Chapter Five

In the car driving down to Brighton, Philip, one of his greatest ambitions fulfilled, was singing to the music. He felt terrific and almost persuaded himself that Charlie would support him despite her misgivings about his high blood pressure. She had taken Dr Murray's gloomy prognosis far more seriously than he had. The heat and a shellfish dinner had disagreed with him one evening on holiday, that was all. It did not mean his heart was about to pack in.

No, Charlie was not the difficult one. It was Vanessa, that was the downside.

He stopped the tape.

His pleasure at being promoted straight into the Cabinet so unexpectedly was tempered by what lay ahead. The decision he would have to make. It would mean yet another battle with his ex-wife. Philip sighed. She would certainly expect him to hand over Amy and Louise's large share portfolio in the Forrester business to her. But how could he do that? The woman was hopeless with money. Always had been.

At eighteen, Vanessa had dissipated all but a few thousand pounds of the legacy her widowed mother had left her. Her grandfather never forgave this profligacy and never again trusted her with any financial dealings. Which is why he had instructed in his will that Philip should manage the family's share portfolio in the media group, except for Vanessa's personal holding. Of course Elliot Forrester, who had built up the business with Philip, had not contemplated that he and Vanessa would divorce.

Their split was all the sadder because the marriage had started so well. They had looks, money and health and they had known each other since childhood. Philip was born two years before Vanessa, in the next village. His father was the local builder, employed regularly by Elliot Forrester first to extend the Rectory then to erect warehouses for paper storage.

From an early age Philip used to help his father during school holidays and in that way became acquainted with the entire Forrester family. He endeared himself to Vanessa's grandfather by absorbing details of the business, which presses were too old and needed constant care, which buildings were strong, which needed strengthening. He and Elliot Forrester formed a close and enduring bond.

Awarded a scholarship to the local direct grant school, Philip then went up to Cambridge to study economics. It was during his last year at Trinity Hall that Vanessa, recently back from Europe, was invited to the 'Tit Hall' Ball by a cousin. Philip was among the guests at Vanessa's table. Their affair was serious from the beginning. Philip liked the idea of being romantically involved with a Forrester and, even better, Elliot's grand-daughter. Vanessa, always seeking approbation, was aware that her grandfather doted on Philip. Elliot was delighted when the couple announced their engagement.

In the early years of their marriage Philip worked as political correspondent for one of the national newspapers in London, a job he liked mainly because of the contacts he made in high places. Later they would help him join the most exclusive club in Britain, the House of Commons.

Two years after the wedding Elliot, aspiring to family continuity in his business, persuaded the young couple to return to Sussex by promising Philip an equal share of the reins, a 'power base' as he put it. With an energetic, vigorous new man at the helm, the group expanded fast; regional newspapers were added, then a local radio station. Profits increased. So did the Lockhart family with the birth of Amy, then Louise.

When Philip was first selected and then elected MP for his London Heathgate constituency, they were euphoric. They did not realise how much of his life would be spent away from home on motorways travelling to the House of Commons or his constituency advice bureaux. With Elliot living nearby and reliable help available for the children, Vanessa still managed to spend time with her husband at constituency engagements and looked forward to their nights alone in his small flat in Heathgate. But with the increasing demands of growing daughters, she began making excuses about accompanying her husband to political functions in London, preferring to be home with the children, the garden and the dogs. She was also frankly bored with the relentless workload of an MP's life. The annual round of constituency fêtes, committee meetings and dinners fascinated her in the first year, interested her in the second and gave her a sense of déjà vu by the third.

Evenings together in the London flat became rarer and eventually they gave up these trysts and settled, like many other parliamentary couples, for separate weekday lives. At various stages both tried to keep the excitement of their relationship alive but rarely at the same time. So many of their friends seemed to have similar marriages, Vanessa thought it was just part of growing older.

There were few rows and more silences as their marriage deteriorated and they settled into an almost platonic contentment. When she complained about feeling lonely, unattractive and unloved and questioned the state of their marriage, he placated her, but to himself pondered their future. He tried to be at her side every weekend and they always had long holidays with the family. Outwardly they appeared content. But Philip was not.

He dutifully phoned from the House each evening, but as Vanessa lost the finer threads of the thrust and parry of the political world, she substituted her conversation with domestic trivia like the washing machine breaking down and trite local gossip, arguing that an MP needed to keep his feet on the ground. But this did not absorb his interest. Without his realising it, his phone conversations with Amy and Louise became far longer than those with his wife. He told her less and less of what he had been doing because it often needed lengthy, time-consuming background explanation. At weekends it seemed easier not to discuss his job with her and it was relaxing to talk of other subjects, but it also meant Vanessa was omitted from the main passion of his life, his pursuit of political power. Even when he was promoted to be a vice chairman of the party, Vanessa remained uninvolved in his career.

The first time Philip was invited to a conference at Number 10, he phoned her immediately afterwards, in jubilation. But instead of recognising the importance of his inclusion, she merely asked, 'What sort of food did they serve?'

It was after this that Philip started having unimportant but exciting affairs with the young women who regularly frequented the House of Commons. These lobbyists, researchers or personal assistants always seemed available to an attractive MP. At first he felt guilty but soon made up his mind that they did not harm Vanessa. Nor, he convinced himself, did these short-lived flings affect his family life. On the contrary, a little frisson here, a surge of lust there, put him in a better mood and made him less critical of his wife when he was at home.

Sub-consciously, however, they put him in the frame of mind to fall in love.

He had met Charlie at the beginning of the last election campaign. At first, she had been for him merely part of the travelling media caravan which trailed up and down the country; it was the most mundane of reasons, her station's budgetary restraints, that brought her to his attention. To save travelling costs her researcher was instructed to select a London MP to interview as part of a TV programme on British constituency politics. Philip was hardly able to concentrate on her questions; he was mesmerised by her air of vitality, suppressed energy and vibrant enthusiasm. He found himself staring, rather rudely she told him later, at her mobile, expressive lips. When she asked him, testing a voice level, what he had had for breakfast, there was a silence while he gave the question some thought. 'Two journalists, lightly roasted. Isn't that what every politician should have?' he said and smiled straight into her eyes.

The interview went by like a flash. He barely remembered what he had said and as the crew was dismantling the lights he whispered quietly, 'You know, it's essential for this election that I see you again, soon.'

He did. Although her station was not remotely interested in any further coverage of the whereabouts of one London MP her sudden need to build new political contacts found her at a party press conference the following evening. A quick drink afterwards turned into a slow one as they could not bear to part. The atmosphere was so highly charged that when he accidentally brushed her sleeve he saw her shiver.

'Are you cold?' he asked solicitously, taking her hand.

She shook her head, a slight smile playing on her lips.

'I shouldn't be feeling the things I'm feeling,' he said, testing the water.

'Nor should I.'

And the look in her eyes made him call for the waiter. 'The bill please,' he asked hurriedly.

He still could not remember how they reached her flat. If she had refused his offer of a lift home, that might have been the end of it. But as it was, it marked the beginning. He could remember every detail of their lovemaking even now, the taste, the smell, the feel of her.

She told him later that everything about him pleased her, his hands, his eyes, his body, everything except his wedding ring.

Right from the beginning, it was serious. It was never just another fling. Neither of them slept that night. But that was not the reason they stayed in bed all next day. Love at first sight is always defined as lust, need or magic. Whatever it was, neither of them looked at anyone else again. Sex became a higher art form. Simple passion turned the touch of fingers, hands and lips into caresses of excitement. Their taste, their fit together, their minds made what was ordinary, extraordinary.

It was a delight to discuss politics with her. She was on the inside track and so he was able to use shorthand. Even when they watched political coverage separately he would phone and say, 'You said he'd try and wriggle out of that. Didn't he make a hash of it?'

They were metropolitan people, liking the same films, jokes, newspapers, hating the same political pundits, on both sides of the Atlantic, for, like all serious politicians, Philip kept up with events in the United States.

Charlie was a completely different animal from Vanessa, who was so much happier away from London. Philip began to long for Mondays.

For a while real life passed them by but inevitably Philip began to feel the strain of leading a double life. It was easier to field the occasional troublesome question from his wife than to deal with the increasing pleas from his daughters to spend more time at home. And Amy, at fourteen, had been asking quite intrusive questions like, 'Why weren't you in your office when I phoned you after the six o'clock vote?' Once she pointedly told him he had not been sitting in his usual place at Prime Minister's Questions. Where had he been? It was easy to deflect her but Philip wondered uneasily whether it was the girl's natural curiosity or if her mother was behind the questions. He also worried occasionally that if news of the liaison leaked to the press it would harm his party. He was not well known though the papers would still capitalise on the affair. But the need to see, and be with, Charlie overrode his fears.

Charlie, too, hated the situation. While she accepted that Philip no longer loved his wife, she could readily appreciate the familial responsibility and loyalty that bound him to Vanessa and the girls. Indeed, she respected him the more for it.

After several weeks of agonising they tried to cool down their love affair. For forty-eight long hours they did not have any contact until Philip cracked at 6 p.m. on the third day. At the sound of his voice, all Charlie's steely resolutions dissolved.

So began an on-off cycle of misery and happiness. Marriage was discussed and dismissed by both of them. Philip was reluctant to leave his daughters and it was not in Charlie's nature to be a home-wrecker.

After enduring months of this, Charlie decided that as she was the problem, she would provide the solution. Without discussing it with Philip, she arranged with her office for a transfer to the New York bureau. Only after committing herself to the new job did she announce her decision to him.

'You must give your marriage another chance,' she told him tearfully. 'I'm sure if I was out of the way you and Vanessa might try and make a go of it. You can't leave your family. If you do, on my account, you'll end up hating me and I couldn't bear that.'

Charlie was so determined, he was forced to agree, reluctantly acknowledging that of the four females in his life, she was the strongest emotionally.

During the following six months, he and Vanessa tried to

patch up their marriage and failed miserably. It was when they had had yet another row that Philip could take no more. He moved into his constituency flat for what his spokesman described to the media as a 'trial separation'. Apart from one stilted phone call when neither said what they were really thinking or feeling, he had had no contact with Charlie, although he thought of her every day.

In New York, Charlie was in mourning. The job which until recently had immersed every waking moment was less satisfying because Philip was not there to share in her triumphs or difficulties. She felt as though she was walking through a never-ending tunnel. Friends complained she had lost her sparkle and they were right. She never turned down invitations, believing it a 'good thing' to be occupied all the time but her date was never clever or funny enough and as for sex, she could not bear to be touched.

As the months passed, Charlie began to wonder if she would always feel this grey, this empty. Until that wonderful day in April.

She was in the newsroom which was as usual exploding around her. Five phones were flashing simultaneously on the console in front of her. Luck, fate, she did not know what it was, made her pick up the one with Philip Lockhart at the other end.

'It's me,' he said without preamble. 'Don't say anything until you hear me out.'

Which was fortuitous because, hardly able to breathe, she was not able to speak.

'Vanessa and I are divorcing. I've moved out and I cannot live another week without you. I'm sending you a one-way

ticket to London. If things have changed with you, tear it up.'
His voice sounded anxious but he did not falter. 'In any case
I'll be at Heathrow to meet that flight. I absolutely adore you
and I want you to marry me as soon as we're able.' He
stopped. Then, 'My love, I hope those are tears of happiness . . . Charlie? Please say yes.'

The Concorde ticket arrived by special delivery an hour
later.

The introduction of a special woman into Philip's life took
some time to become apparent to his family. It was Amy
who suspected first. Squashed into their father's small flat in
London, she spotted Charlie's jacket hanging in a cupboard
and occasional oddities like female-sized razors around. And
when Charlie 'popped in' for lunch or tea, she seemed to
know her way around the minute kitchen.

When Amy eventually asked him outright if he and
Charlie were living together, he finally admitted that 'from
time to time' Charlie stayed with him. 'Now I'm a bachelor
again,' he said lightly, 'it's handy having someone to cook
the odd meal or sew on a button.' When Amy protested that
at fifteen she could manage those things for him, he
deflected her by saying she should concentrate instead on
her exams.

Urged on by her elder sister, Louise told her father that
from then on when they came to see him, they would prefer
it to be just the three of them. Charlie had to endure months
of moving every scrap of evidence of her existence out of the
flat when the girls were due to arrive.

Neither of the children mentioned their father's girlfriend
to their mother. Without ever discussing it with him they

realised it would hurt her and although Amy had warmed to Charlie originally, later she became jealous of her. Despite their father's obvious happiness, which they assumed was due to Charlie, both girls hoped their parents would get back together again. They dreamed about this up to the day of the divorce.

When, after more probing from Amy, Philip eventually plucked up courage to tell Vanessa about Charlie, she asked him three questions.

'Did you leave me for this woman?'

His answer was unequivocal. 'No.'

There was a pause.

'Are you going to marry her?'

'We're not that far yet although it is on the cards.'

'I see.' Her voice was flat. 'Have the girls met her?'

'Yes, a couple of times.'

'They didn't say anything to me.' He could hear the anger building. 'Why have you made them keep secrets from me? They're all I have left now. It's so cruel of you, Philip. I suppose they thought they were being kind to you, and to me.'

'Oh Vanessa,' he said contritely. 'I should have told you long ago but I didn't want to hurt you more than I have done. I'm so sorry the way things have turned out. I want you and me to be friends and not just for the girls' sake.'

Vanessa was trying to cover up her tears that day when her daughters returned from school. Amy noticed at once that her mother had been crying and soon elicited the reason. From then on there was a coolness between her and her father which took months to overcome. They refused to attend his wedding, for which Philip blamed Vanessa. The

41

truth was more complex. Though the girls felt loyalty to Vanessa, they also burned with jealousy that their father preferred to live with a new woman rather than with them. It was not until the birth of Miranda that there was an eventual rapprochement. Both girls seemed genuinely fond of their little half-sister.

The new Secretary of State for Transport shifted his tall frame in the seat of his dark blue estate car as he wrestled with the problem of his daughters' shares. This was a particularly difficult time in the publishing world. The right thing to do would be to put the shares in the control of a safe, experienced pair of hands. And there was only one person he could trust with that job.

Oh God, he thought, as he drew up outside Forrester's Georgian building. However carefully he presented his decision, Vanessa would never understand, never agree and never forgive him.

Chapter Six

'You what?' Charlie's eyes were wide with anger. 'After all we talked about? Philip, how could you accept a post in the Cabinet in your state of health?'

Philip had rarely seen his wife's lovely face so contorted with exasperation and his disappointment that she felt none of his excitement was sharp. Before joining the party, he had asked the company chairman, Walter Threadgold, to extract his wife from the throng so that he could share his news with her privately before making it public.

'You think Dr Murray's exaggerating, don't you?' Charlie went on angrily. 'You think that collapse you had last summer was due to the heat. Can I remind you that he said you were a heart attack waiting to happen? And now you've agreed to take on one of the most stressful jobs of your life. If you couldn't think of me, kindly remember that you have a tiny daughter and she needs you to be around as she grows up.'

What Philip hardly dared admit, even to himself, was that he would rather be dead than turn down such a powerful political job.

'Calm down, darling. It'll be all right. I'll have a whole

department to help me, it's easier than being an MP,' he lied. 'And of course it means I'll have to stand back from all this.' He looked round the Forrester office. The adrenaline which had been pumping in overdrive since he had entered Number 10 made him less sensitive. 'You can take over from me here. That'll cut down my workload.' He laughed, trying to lighten Charlie's mood. 'I'll end up with less to do.'

This last salvo rendered her speechless. He watched the colour drain from her face and cursed himself for his inept handling of the situation. He started to soften the impact with conciliatory muttering when they were interrupted by Walter Threadgold, anxious to usher the host, now over an hour late, into the reception.

'Darling, it's going to be all right,' Philip repeated.

Charlie pursed her lips, and he saw that she was far from convinced.

The noise of the party had reached the decibel level where medically it could do damage to the ears. Two hundred and fifty people were squashed into a room built to take half that number. So far, few had gone to the canteen to collect the extravagant buffet, a proud tradition of the event. The canteen had been decked out in Christmas reds and greens and would be doing duty as a disco later.

Despite keeping a keen watch on the door, Vanessa missed Philip's entrance and only noticed him when he emerged with Charlie from a director's office. The couple looked flushed and self-conscious. Surely they could keep their hands off each other at the office party. Vanessa was indignant.

Unbidden, a sharp memory of a naked Philip looking

down with passion at her outstretched, responsive body flashed into her mind. What That Woman had taken away from her.

It did not matter how much or how often Philip had protested that Charlie had not broken up their marriage, that she had been out of his life, out of the country, when they separated, Vanessa still blamed her. She refused to believe that his other sexual escapades had been symptomatic of a failing marriage. For her it was always the scheming Charlie who had lured him from her side.

She would never forget the day Philip had come home exhausted, complaining that he had almost fallen asleep at the wheel of his car, and said he could not continue with the marriage. It had been hard explaining to their friends that no one would be cited in the divorce. It was easier to blame another woman and when Charlie reappeared in Philip's life Vanessa felt vindicated, convinced she had been manipulated all along.

She watched Philip now talking earnestly to Walter Threadgold. Her ex-husband was still handsome; in fact he was better looking than he had been when she first met him. His dark eyes had more intensity now. His body had thickened but he had not run to fat. Sophistication and better tailoring had done wonders for him.

As soon as Amy had caught sight of her father, she rushed up to him and Vanessa could see by his sad expression that she was telling him about Tansy's death. He immediately left Walter and Charlie and walked swiftly towards her, gripping both of her hands in his.

It was the first time he had touched her since their separation and she was reassured how little it affected her.

'Vee, I'm really sorry. She was a great dog and we had a lot of fun with her.'

He sounded as though he really meant it and Vanessa nodded, grateful for his sympathy. For a moment it was like old times with Amy hanging on to his arm, the three of them together.

'I suppose Louise is inconsolable. Tansy's been around ever since she can remember. I'll give her a ring tomorrow.'

'She'd like that, Dad. The good thing is Tansy didn't suffer long,' Amy told him, blinking to keep back the tears.

'I'm glad. Now,' he smiled. 'I want you two to be in the front row to hear my news.'

They moved forward and Philip stood on a chair and asked for quiet. It took a few moments for the din to subside.

'Sorry I'm late, folks.' He paused for an instant and looked around for a waiter. 'Who do I have to charm in this place to get a glass of champagne?'

There was a laugh around the room and a glass was quickly passed to him. Carried along by the groundswell of support from the employees who had known him man and boy, Philip relaxed.

'As I'm here surrounded by great editors and assorted hacks and paps,' loud cheers, 'I thought it was only right that you should hear this news from me rather than from the wires or your mates in the lobby – or heaven forfend, from the newsdesk of our own *Brighton Gazette*, if someone's minding the store down there.'

The laughter quickly died when they saw his expression turn serious.

'The reason I was delayed was that I've just come from Number Ten. The Prime Minister has been kind enough to think it might help him if I were to join his Cabinet.'

The crowd erupted but Philip waved his outstretched arms for silence.

'My appointment as Secretary of State for Transport was announced by Downing Street two minutes ago so you can understand why I wanted to tell you first.'

Congratulations flowed from all sides. 'Well done, boss,' was shouted from around the room while Walter raised his glass and proposed a toast to the new minister.

As the cheers died away, Philip thanked them. 'And when you see me driving the new Jaguar, remember I'm just hard at work testing it out on your behalf.'

They laughed, appreciating his humour. Not for nothing was Philip known for his skill at handling a crowd. As the Prime Minister's spin doctor put it, 'He plays well,' and then, the ultimate compliment, 'especially on television.' It had clinched his appointment.

'I know I will always be able to rely on the support,' he went on with a smile, 'from this corner of Britain at least. Now, to return to my usual Christmas script. It's been a tough year and only our second one as a national media group. Who said we couldn't survive? The *Express* sneered, the *Mail* snarled but we're still around and, what's more, editorially the *Citizen*'s kicking at their heels.'

Applause and cheers from those who worked on the magazine, good-natured boos from those on local papers. The difference in salaries and lifestyles between the two sets of employees was huge and most media conglomerates did not mix them at gatherings like this. But Philip relished owning a national news magazine and could not resist having them and the regionals under the same roof at Christmas.

'Meanwhile,' his voice was triumphant, 'once again the local papers and radio stations have done remarkably well against tough competition.'

This time applause came from those working for the locals and hisses from those on the national magazine.

'I see we've returned to the traditional rivalry so it only remains for me to say that . . .'

Vanessa was conscious that on the other side of the semi-circle round Philip's chair, Charlie had been ushered to the front and she was uncomfortably aware of the couple's eye contact as Philip wound up his speech.

'. . . I and all the other directors thank you for your efforts. We appreciate the sacrifices you've made this year and the support you've given us and we wish you and yours the happiest of Christmases and a safe, healthy and prosperous New Year.'

Listening to the warmth and humour in his voice, the pain of separation once more came back to Vanessa. She risked a glance at Charlie. Why was she looking so bloody miserable? What did she have to worry about? At least Amy seemed oblivious of any undercurrents and was gazing at her father with unadulterated joy and admiration. Vanessa envied the young their resilience. She was thankful that she had always taken care not to criticise Philip in the girls' presence at least.

Philip was about to climb down from the chair when the strident voice of the group's chief paper buyer boomed out the question the political cognoscenti were already asking among themselves.

'Just one thing, Philip.'

He paused and straightened.

'Will the PM allow you to stay on here as chief executive?'

Once again Vanessa witnessed the swift exchange between husband and wife. Without knowing why, she suddenly felt threatened.

There was an almost imperceptible hesitation then Philip gave a decisive nod. 'Yes, I wondered if that would come up,' he replied slowly. 'As many of you will know, there are clear guidelines about business when one joins the government. Like everyone else in this position, I shall have to put my shares in trust and appoint someone else to take my place on the board.'

There was a collective intake of breath from those who had not realised this.

One of them was Vanessa. The full implication of his promotion was beginning to penetrate. What would happen now at those board meetings she so looked forward to? Not only did she have a chance to see Philip but once or twice they went to the local pub and had a snack to discuss the children, lunches she gleefully suspected were kept secret from Charlie. Although her position as the only grand-daughter of the founder and a substantial shareholder gave her automatic access to the board, a new chief executive might sideline her.

'Nothing's written in stone,' Philip was saying, 'and I've had less than two hours to think about it. Naturally I want someone on the board whose judgement I respect, someone I'm able to rely on totally because you know all the problems we are facing as well as I do.' He ticked them off one by one. 'Cross-media ownership. The price war. Satellite and cable opportunities. Changing ownership rules. Soaring newsprint costs . . .'

Vanessa who, with the board, had been hearing about these difficulties for years, felt her heart soar. Perhaps he was referring to her. Maybe he was going to give her the responsibility for the children's shares.

'I shall, of course, have to speak to the other directors about the new appointment and to all the family members and sort this out over the next few days,' added Philip, 'but an announcement will be made shortly. As far as the group is concerned, nothing's going to hold us back. So once again, have a marvellous party, a merry Christmas and the best ever New Year to all of you and your families.'

As he looked at Vanessa's upturned face full of expectation, Philip realised the enormity of the decision he had made and its inevitable repercussions. If he could, he would certainly wait until after Christmas to tell her.

Peter Cazalet pushed through the over-excited crowd. For him and many of the Forrester employees, Christmas had started early.

Peter Cazalet of Cazalet, Cazalet & Dove, respected solicitor and Commissioner of Oaths in the City of Brighton, with a head office in London, would rather have stayed at home recovering from his hangover, but this function was organised by his most important client. A local dinner party the night before, with all its complexities and intricate drinking rituals, meant he and his wife Dorinda were both suffering the effects of too much claret – and the killer, after-dinner port.

Tall enough to see across the room, Peter's creaseless brow and tranquil expression reflected the ease with which he had adapted to a life of comfort provided by the successful firm built up by his father. He was a contented man. The joys of his life included a maroon Daimler Sovereign, a Queen Anne house and what he considered a settled, fifteen-year-old marriage which had produced an attractive, obedient daughter now twelve.

His only worry was his receding hairline – follicly challenged, as Dorinda called it. He was enormously proud of his petite, blonde wife. She was always the best-dressed woman in their circle and he did not begrudge a penny of her generous clothes allowance – primarily because he was able to write it off under miscellaneous entertaining in the books.

The babble around him was now based on only one topic, Philip Lockhart's elevation.

'My God, do you think Philip could end up as Prime Minister?' asked Dorinda.

'Well, he's never struck me as that brilliant. Of course, that's probably an advantage. And I daresay he makes more effort at the Despatch Box than at parties like these.'

'I wonder how Vanessa's reacting to all this,' pondered Dorinda. 'Where is she? I haven't seen her for ages.'

Her husband grabbed a glass from a passing tray, justifying it on the basis of the 'hair of the dog' theory. 'It's one thing to be ditched by a common or garden MP, quite different to lose a Cabinet minister. The car, the driver . . . the status.'

'Oh, you know that has nothing to do with anything,' she chided. 'She's pretty low anyway. That old dog of theirs has gone and died on her tonight of all nights.'

'How inconvenient of him.'

She ignored this. 'There's one good thing that may come out of this,' she continued. 'Vanessa's always moaning about

51

money and maybe she'll get a hike in maintenance. This'll nearly double his MP's salary, won't it?'

He nodded. 'Yes, but he'll lose his chief executive's pay at Forrester's, which is far more. I wonder who'll be appointed in his place.'

'Oh dear, Vanessa will hate somebody new joining the family firm. Since the divorce, that company's been her life-line. Vanessa still hasn't got over him, you know.' Dorinda's green eyes surveyed the crowd. 'She's not mooning about him. It's being part of a couple she misses.'

'You mean she misses being a missus.' He smiled. 'If she wants to get married again she'll have to come off her high horse. Look how she treated old Jeffrey at that dinner party you took such trouble to fix. I was sure they would hit it off.'

'Don't be ridiculous.' Dorinda was scathing. 'I wish I'd met your old school chum before the dinner party. I'd never have put them together. He plainly hadn't had his overcoat cleaned since he left university and the subtle aroma of a multitude of curry takeaways didn't help, however much Givenchy aftershave he slopped over it.'

'But old Jeff's funny. Rich, too.'

'Not enough in either direction to make up for such a total lack of presentation.' She was still looking for her friend. 'She does need to get out more but she can't see the point of coming to all the local dos. There's never anyone there for her.' Only for me, she thought wickedly.

Peter Cazalet was completely ignorant of Dorinda's little sexual adventures and how much pleasurable exercise his stay-at-home wife indulged in at lunchtimes.

She hesitated. 'Peter, darling, what do you think about

Vanessa coming to us at Christmas?'

A wary look crossed his face.

'The girls are going to stay with Philip and she keeps saying that she's going to bed to watch old movies. We won't be stuck with her for ever,' she assured him. 'She'll have the girls back again next Christmas.'

Her husband still made no comment and she took his silence for assent.

Vanessa had no recollection of how she had managed to manoeuvre Philip away from the admiring circle and into his old office though she had a clear memory of Charlie's anxious face as she closed the door.

She had a dizzy sense of elation anticipating that Philip would ask her to assume the duty of controlling his and the girls' shares. But he did not seem to be pleased at being pulled away from the party.

'Do you really need to talk about this now?' he asked rather crossly when she put the question to him. 'Wouldn't it be better if we sorted it out after Christmas?'

'Whenever you try to postpone talking about something, it's never good news for me,' Vanessa retorted. 'Why can't we talk about it now?'

'Because I've not made up my mind a hundred per cent,' he replied cautiously. 'Of course I intend to talk to you and the other directors. Soon.'

Vanessa's joy evaporated. That familiar feeling of anxiety began its tentative build-up. '*Talk* to us? No, you mean *tell* us. Knowing you as I do, I'm sure you've already made up your mind. You have, haven't you?'

He looked uncomfortable. 'Vanessa, this is a party, for

God's sake. Nothing's going to happen this week. It can wait until after the holidays.'

'No, Philip, it can't.' Vanessa could feel herself flushing. 'The shares belong to our daughters. Don't you think that I, as their mother, should have the final say? And why should that decision wait?'

'We've gone over this same ground so many times,' Philip responded wearily. 'If your grandfather had thought that, he would have left the shares in your hands, not mine, until they were twenty-five.'

'But that was then and this is now. Everything's changed. Philip, I can cope. Now I'm on my own I have to.'

Anxious not to have an argument, he repeated gently that they could discuss it in a few days and tried to leave but she caught his sleeve.

'I have changed. You must be able to see that.' His silence made Vanessa more suspicious and she erupted. 'What the fuck are you playing at?'

That stopped him. Philip had rarely heard her use that word.

Seeing his hesitation she went on, 'It's outrageous. You can't possibly make this decision without discussing it with me. It's my grandfather's company! You wouldn't be here if you hadn't married me.' Vanessa's voice was rising. She jabbed at his chest with her finger. The champagne she had consumed on an empty stomach kicked in. 'You'd probably be scrabbling around like your father in the building trade. Or be a failed teacher with your average degree.'

Philip tried to extricate himself. 'Vee, I promise you we'll discuss it after Christmas. We really must go back to the party. Come on.'

Vanessa was incensed by his evasiveness. Always in the past it had meant That Woman was involved. She had an awful premonition.

'You're not thinking of giving the shares to that wife of yours?' When he made no reply she felt panic. 'You're not, are you?' she asked almost pleadingly.

Instantly he was on the defensive. 'She'd only be managing them.'

Vanessa was stunned by this admission. In the few minutes since his speech she had visualised herself as one of the most powerful persons on the board. Her twenty-five per cent shareholding, plus the children's twenty-six per cent, would make her a force to be reckoned with. She had tasted the power, lived it, been there. Now she felt hostile and powerless. Yet again Philip was rejecting her. Another bitter thought struck her. 'You're putting her on the board in your place.'

It was not a question and when, again, he was silent, she was certain it was true. Her pain was clearly visible but she kept her voice as steady as she could.

'My family worked their brains out for this business. What gives you the right to bring in an outsider, and such a scheming one, because it suits you? Well, it doesn't suit me.' Vanessa's eyes were blazing. 'There are dozens of people better qualified than she is who could do the job and who would be an asset to this company. No, hundreds.'

He made no attempt to try to quieten her down, knowing from past experience it was better to let the volcano erupt and work itself out.

'You think I'm just a stupid housewife, a dope, someone you could fool for years while you were playing around with *her*.'

Philip thought wearily, how many times have we rowed about this? She used to go through my diary convincing herself that any time I wasn't available, I was with Charlie. And I wasn't. His denials always fell on unyielding ground. 'Vee, I'm trying to do the best I can for all of us. I know it won't be easy but although I'm not supposed to have anything to do with the business, it would be madness to imagine that anyone in my position wouldn't still take a keen interest in it. With Charlie on the board I can keep myself completely up to date with major events. She can be my ears and eyes.'

Even after years of increasingly spiteful quarrels, Philip could still find words to pierce her thin, self-made layer of emotional protection.

'And I can't?' She almost choked on the words. Words of a supplicant. Words of a loser.

Philip's day had been long and emotional and this made him less than diplomatic in his response. 'Vanessa, it's years since you spent a day working in a newspaper office and you've never worked in a TV studio. The truth is you'd hate getting more involved. Charlie has experience of both of those, she lives and breathes the business. She reads every newspaper every day, she knows which buttons to press and whose strings to pull.' He realised how patronising he sounded and made his final remarks in a gentler tone.

'I don't want to be unkind but Charlie's American contacts and her news-gathering experience have already been invaluable to us. How do you think we secured the Karnak contract or that CBS news deal?'

He attempted once more to move towards the door. There was silence from Vanessa and he looked at her anxiously.

She seemed too upset to speak.

'We should put on a united family front tonight,' he said quietly. 'Think what sport our rivals would have if they heard we were fighting over this.'

His words incensed Vanessa more. Had she not spent all evening trying to put on a facade of unity, even though she had been so upset at Tansy's death? She felt the dangerous pricking of tears behind her eyelids. It was frustration that made her want to cry but he would see it as weakness, another reason why she would be deemed by him 'unsuitable' to be given extra power.

She looked him straight in the eye. Her one-time lover. Her husband. The father of her children.

The bastard.

'I warn you, Philip,' she said fiercely, 'I'm not going to be a pushover this time. This is not the end of the matter.' With that she marched out.

She was devastated. Her grandfather would have been as incensed as she was at Philip's action. She would not, could not, sit back and allow Amy and Louise's birthright to pass into the hands of That Woman.

Vanessa wanted, needed, a few moments' respite before rejoining the noisy throng so she made for the only sanctuary she knew, the small powder room, tricked out in chintzy style for the first female executives employed by Forrester's and rarely used these days because most of the new staff did not know of its existence.

It was already occupied – by Charlie. For some seconds they faced each other in silence.

Vanessa had never been alone with this woman but she had imagined the scene a thousand times. She would be cool, distant, choose her words carefully. But as she faced the woman she blamed for bringing her so much unhappiness, her hurt and despair threatened to overwhelm her.

'What more are you going to take from me?' Her voice emerged as a whisper but her eyes blazed. 'First you take my husband, now my children's shares. What more do you want? My watch? These pearls? My wedding ring?'

Charlie backed away from her, her face pale. 'Vanessa, please calm down. I didn't ask for any of this. Don't blame me.'

'Oh, but I do blame you. You always get what you want, don't you? It's been that way from the beginning. You went after him and you got him. Now you want the shares as well.' Her voice was breaking but she was determined not to cry in front of this woman.

Like a cornered animal Charlie edged against the washbasin, looking round for escape but Vanessa was between her and the door. 'I don't want your daughters' shares. The last thing I need in my life is more work on top of everything else.'

Vanessa was coolly vicious. 'Oh, you're so hard done by, aren't you? Well, if you think I'm going to stand back and let you come into the firm my grandfather started and get anywhere near my daughters' inheritance—'

'You have to believe me,' Charlie broke in. 'I had no idea Philip wanted me to take control of the shares. In fact I haven't decided whether or not I'll do it.'

Vanessa felt burning anger. With a loud smack she brought her hand down sharply on the basin. 'It's not your bloody decision to make. Those shares belong to my daughters, not to you. Never to you.'

'Well, now that I know you feel so strongly about it I'll discuss it with Philip.'

'Don't patronise me. I don't want you to interfere any more. If there's any discussing to do, I'll do it with Philip myself.' Her tone was withering. A nervous Charlie pushed past her and darted for the door. In a second she was gone.

Vanessa looked at her distraught face in the mirror and now the tears, grey with mascara, fell unchecked into the washbasin. She longed to go home but it was her duty to return to the party.

After a few minutes she dried her tears and repaired the damage to her make-up as best she could. This was where she belonged and she was damned if she would let That Woman usurp her.

Neither the first nor the second Mrs Lockhart had noticed that one of the cubicles was occupied, by someone changing into party gear. She had been listening to every word. Sitting uncomfortably on the lavatory seat, only one leg into her tights, she heard Vanessa's sobbing subside, then the sound of splashing water followed by the tap-tap of heels across the tiled floor and the click of the door.

Imogen Ferris, social editor of the successful *Sussex County Magazine* and one of the secret tipsters for a national newspaper, decided to play it safe and remain inside the cubicle for a further five minutes before struggling into her dress.

How could she use this, not just as a journalist, but to ingratiate herself with the *Daily Chronicle*'s assistant editor? Dare she ring him at home at this hour? He was, after all, married and her new lover. Why not? This was good. This was great. This was the truth behind the colour supplement trio. The Lockhart women were at war.

What a story.

Chapter Seven

The scene in the suburban bedroom was a familiar one to any journalist. Newspapers and magazines were piled high on one side, his. A hardback romantic novel on hers. A huge double bed, larger than kingsize, coped with her problem, a bad back. The telephone, next to a large luminous clock, helped cope with his problem, total marital boredom.

The phone rang for the second time since they had gone to bed.

'Sorry to bother you at this hour.'

Tony Burns was instantly alert. This was not a voice he had expected to hear in this bedroom.

'But I think I have a good story and I don't know if it will hold.'

Where the hell had she found his home number? He would string up the bastard who'd been stupid enough to give it to her. He feigned disinterest and distance in case his wife was not yet asleep.

'OK, Miss Ferris, spill the beans.'

'Well, I've just been to the Forresters' Christmas party in Brighton and in the loo I overheard Philip Lockhart's ex-wife having a screaming row with wife number two.'

'You mean Lockhart as in new Cabinet minister?'

Tony Burns, number three on the *Daily Chronicle*, sounded more awake and interested and Imogen proudly repeated every word of what she had overheard in the cloakroom, using the hastily-scribbled shorthand notes she had jotted on toilet paper with her black eyebrow pencil.

'Sounds quite good,' Tony replied, looking at the clock, 'but if you've got it to yourself, we can work on it tomorrow. Thanks for thinking of us,' he said rather peremptorily for the benefit of his wife. 'I'll talk to you in the morning.'

At thirty-three Imogen was old enough to know better but she liked to deceive herself that sex with Tony equalled love and romance. Her new adventure was all the more satisfying because it was doubly forbidden. Not only was he married, he worked for a rival organisation.

Carefully she put her scribbled notes into a polythene bag for safekeeping. She had taken the precaution of transcribing them into her reporter's notebook. She had not mentioned to Tony that she had already fixed an interview with Vanessa Lockhart in her capacity as *Sussex County Magazine*'s social editor, ostensibly to publicise Vanessa's chairmanship of the Harlequin Charity Ball, the major fundraising event of the year for the National Cancer Charity.

Imogen had never exchanged more than brief pleasantries with Philip Lockhart although he was head of her newspaper group, but she and Vanessa had been on nodding terms for years. They had attended the same school though at different times. Somehow she would have to manoeuvre the interview from menus and flower displays to divorce, shareholdings and cat fights. It would be quite a test of her journalistic ingenuity but just because she worked for a local county magazine did not mean she could not do her stuff. She would show Tony, and the Forrester Group, she could bring off a great story.

She would have to tell Tony about the interview. She would phone him tomorrow in his office and take the risk of being recognised. Working with him would be a bonus but until she could move jobs she had to make sure the story did not have her fingerprints on it. Maybe she could use a codeword.

She giggled as she thought of a description which Tony might recognise as applying to her.

'I think we're going to have trouble with Vanessa,' Charlie said as lightly as she could. She and Philip were in the car going home from the party. Charlie was reluctant to change the mood especially in view of their earlier quarrel. Philip was still on a high. His new job had been the evening's main topic of conversation and he was basking in the delight of being seen as the coming man. But she had to tell him about the fight before Vanessa gave him her version.

'We're always going to have trouble with Vanessa,' he responded. 'Leave her to me, darling.'

'Too late. She's already had a go at me. She found me when I was alone in the loo. She was in quite a state about the shares.'

Philip seemed unconcerned. 'The woman's always in a state. She'll get over it.' His tone of voice suggested he wanted no more discussion on the subject but Charlie was not to be deterred.

'I'm not sure she will get over it, darling. I didn't say anything to her but she really was overwrought. Exactly

63

what did you tell her? Did you mention me?'

'Not in so many words but she worked out I wanted you to take my place.'

'I think my going on the board will cause a great deal of trouble with Vanessa. She was really angry.'

Philip reached for her hand. 'Charlie, I'm afraid she wants me to give her carte blanche with the girls' shares, not to mention mine, and that's not on. You know I can't rely on her. It's difficult enough trying to deal with her because of the children. Can you imagine the grief I'd have if I had to discuss business with her as well?'

It was so rare that he criticised Vanessa that Charlie was silent.

'You and I'll decide what's in the best interests of the company in general and the children in particular. Not Vanessa. Agreed?'

Charlie was about to make another half-hearted attempt to tell him about the argument but she stopped and tried another tack.

'Quite apart from the Vanessa problem, wouldn't it be better to choose Walter or someone like him instead?'

'No.' He was emphatic. 'I've worked bloody hard to build this company up and Walter's not strong enough. I need someone I can rely on totally, someone intelligent who'll keep in close contact. And it won't be hard keeping in close contact with you,' he added with a smile. 'Besides, this parliament has only eighteen months to run. If we win the next election I'll make a permanent appointment for the company. If we lose, we revert to the status quo. So whatever happens, you won't be on the board for long.' He looked at her sideways.

'Please, do this for me, won't you, darling?' he said pleadingly. 'I'm sure Dr Murray would approve of me passing on my work to you.' He smiled. 'Thank God I have you to rely on.'

She gave a mock sigh. It signified agreement. Charlie could never refuse him anything.

Vanessa hurried up the stairs at the Rectory to Amy's bedroom hoping that her daughter would be in and awake. But the room was empty. It was one o'clock. Amy had mentioned staying on for the disco. Needing to talk, too wound up to sleep, Vanessa decided to wait up for her daughter.

Since the divorce, she reflected, Amy had never regained her early uncritical admiration of her father. Which was just as well because now she needed to enlist Amy's help against him. It was still not going to be easy.

The last time she had been this upset was the night of her grandfather's funeral when she had been truly convinced that the fabric of her marriage was unravelling. At the age of ninety-four, Elliot Forrester's death had not been unexpected – he used to make jokes about who he was going to meet in Heaven, anticipating that few of his friends would be there. But still Vanessa took his death particularly hard. Her father had died when she was very young and her mother, a dominant woman who had never remarried, suffered a fatal heart attack when she was only eighteen. Vanessa had been close to her grandfather and had come to rely on him.

Elliot's send-off was exactly as he had planned. Cars had been nose to tail on the road to Pridlington, a village on the fringe of Brighton, off the Sussex motorway from London.

The local florist had not been able to cope so a number of the wreaths had been driven from London. The most imposing, a huge circlet of Arum lilies tied with dove-grey ribbon, had been ordered from the Côte d'Azur by Cissi Toscani, as she then was, a daughter of the founder and a shareholder in the company. Cissi had not come herself; she was certain Elliot would understand completely her hatred of both funerals and the dank Sussex countryside in winter.

There had been at least three hundred mourners at the church, many of them unknown to Vanessa. It was Philip who greeted everyone by name, local MPs, the lord lieutenant of the county, the colonel of Elliot's former regiment and various aristocratic patrons of the many charities he had supported. The old man, fit until the end, had died in harness and had remained on good terms even with businessmen he had bested, most of them much younger than him. Mingling with local Rotarians were Forrester employees and two elegantly dressed older women arriving separately whom Vanessa could not place. She never discovered who they were because although most of the guests had come back to the Rectory after the graveside interment, they did not. She wondered what their roles in her grandfather's life had been.

The funeral spread was impressive. Hundred-year-old cream damask tablecloths starched and laundered for the occasion enveloped gargantuan trestle tables, carried in from the church hall. There were creamware dishes heavy with homemade game pies, three differently-cured hams, one studded with cloves, smoked salmon sandwiches, thinly-carved roast turkey and Elliot's favourite sultana and raisin cake.

Philip knew how much Elliot would have appreciated the

deals that were done in the conservatory over venison pie and especially the adulterous liaisons which had their beginnings in a stroll to admire the summerhouse.

Habit ensured that Vanessa and Philip fulfilled their respective roles at the wake to perfection. The knowledge of who would get the glasses, open the bottles, look after the young and charm the old was seamless. To watching eyes their marriage seemed harmonious.

At last everyone was gone, including the catering help, the vicar, and Amy and Louise who had asked to sleep at the home of friends. As early evening shadows lengthened, Vanessa, who felt a little tipsy, went round the house picking up stray glasses. Philip's long back was leaning over the sink, rinsing glasses. He looked so vulnerable. Watching him, she was reminded of old times, before he became too busy to help with domestic chores.

Suddenly the finality of her grandfather's death hit Vanessa. She felt the need for bodily warmth and wrapped her arms round his waist. Philip tensed. She pretended not to notice and laid her head against his back. Neither of them moved. It was only a moment but Philip stayed silent, motionless and Vanessa, embarrassed, moved away.

He dried his hands and with slow deliberation, as if he realised she was upset, put an arm round her.

'You did well today, missus,' he said smiling.

Vanessa was not reassured. She felt his embrace was placatory rather than affectionate and tried hard to remember when they had last made love properly, not perfunctory married sex with the lights out (and that was weeks ago) but taking time to linger sensuously and be passionate with one another. It was long enough ago to worry her.

After they had cleared up the debris, they sat seemingly contented in front of the glowing log fire, watching television. Where once they would have been forced to talk, the television had become the third partner in their marriage, absorbing the stress and strain.

The funeral service had made Vanessa conscious of her own mortality. She did not want any more passionless years. To waste any more time. It was this instinct that impelled her to initiate something tonight before they reached the bedroom and their usual night-time routine of teeth cleaning, alarm checking, taking out of lenses, five-minute exercises and shutting the dogs in the kitchen.

Now was the time, in front of the fire. It might make lovemaking more exciting. Who knew when they would be alone again in the house? These days there was always someone around, children, neighbours, people from Philip's office.

Kicking off her shoes, Vanessa cuddled up to him as they watched the news. Philip automatically put an arm round her shoulder but she felt that the local vicar who had made the same gesture that afternoon had done it with more warmth.

During the advertisements she stroked his cheek. He smiled, took her hand and rested it on the sofa between them.

'Aren't you hot in that sweater?' she asked. 'I certainly am in this.' She began to unbutton her cardigan and enough of the buttons of the silk blouse underneath pulled apart to show off her still attractive breasts. Her hands were trembling.

Philip kept his gaze on the newscaster's face.

'Funny thing about death. Makes me think about age,' she

said quietly. 'Philip, do you still think I'm attractive?'

'Of course,' he replied without moving his eyes from the screen where a Guatemalan river had once more broken its banks.

Vanessa put her hand on her husband's thigh and started gently stroking backwards and forwards with her fingers.

A lunchtime conversation with two girlfriends came unbidden into her mind. 'Darling, if it had a pulse, men would screw it.' But not Philip. At least not now. Not with her.

She wondered if she should undo her skirt and felt a sense of panic. 'Darling, why don't you look at me?'

'It's been a long day, Vee,' he said at last. 'I've probably had too much to drink.'

Vanessa was almost crying. 'But I only want a real cuddle.'

It seemed to take for ever for him to hold out his arms. She nestled against his chest. It was like being embraced by a father or a brother. Sexless.

Vanessa began to cry. 'Philip, what's happened to us?'

'Vee, I'm sorry. It's been a hell of a day.'

'Yes, but it's not just today, is it?'

'What do you mean?'

'You don't love me any more.'

'Of course I do. We're happy, aren't we?'

'You never seem to want me.'

He was silent.

At length she ventured, 'From what I read men always seem to be needing to have sex with somebody.'

He laughed. 'That's all exaggerated. We're not as young as we were. Anyway, we're friends, companions.'

She was not reassured. 'You're not answering my questions.' She gazed up at him in the firelight, her clothes in disarray.

She did look rather attractive and he wished he could make love to her to make this nightmare go away. But he realised with dismay that for the first time in his life his body was reacting totally faithfully – but not to his wife. He bent over and kissed her on the lips. Once upon a time that was all he had needed.

Nothing.

Her face, which had lit up when he leaned towards her, was an image of misery as he drew away from her. 'We're fine. We're fine. Let it go, Vee.' He seemed to be almost pleading. 'We're together, aren't we?'

Vanessa was stung. 'Not most of the time.'

'But I'm away working. You must have understood how much of our lives politics would take up.'

She looked at him carefully. 'Philip, we're not old. It's not natural to live like brother and sister most of the time.'

Philip shifted uncomfortably. 'Funerals always make us try and take stock. Where we're going, what we're doing. You were fine last week, you'll be fine next week. Take it easy and don't analyse everything so much.' With that he got up and headed for the door. 'It's late. I'd better go and see to the dogs.'

He had known her for over twenty years and he thought again what a handsome woman she still was. If only his body could respond. It surprised him that Vanessa still cared so much. He had thought that she was satisfied with their semi-platonic relationship, that the children, the privileges and the success filled in the fissures where passion used to be. Her tacit acceptance of his many nights away from home had reassured him that his wife was happy with what their marriage had become.

'Have you ever been unfaithful to me?' Her voice was husky and her face was barely visible in the shadows of the desk light and the embers of the fire.

He turned to face her, his hand on the door. Her question dismayed him, and he did what adulterers always do. He lied.

That started the downwards spiral. During the following months Vanessa was incapable of leaving alone the subject of their marriage and his suspected infidelity, continually reintroducing the subject like picking at a scab. The wound would not heal but she could not resist it. Philip's own efforts at patching up the marriage were based on trying to re-fit Vanessa into the main passion of his life, politics. Vanessa hated standing around aimlessly waiting while constituents took the chance of enlisting the help of their MP. Philip, in turn, was irritated when he constantly had to explain what was happening and apologise to Vanessa for how time-consuming his work was.

Re-introducing her to his world added yet another problem. It opened up a million opportunities for her to be jealous. Having ignored his career for years, every time Vanessa now saw him talking to an attractive woman at political meetings it aroused her suspicions further. Ever since she had known him Philip had been a flirt. He was a man who loved women and happily admitted, 'I flirt with all of them, nine to ninety-year-olds. None of it means anything.'

In the end it was physical exhaustion that killed the

marriage. Philip only had to be half an hour late for his wife to suspect the worst, particularly as their infrequent couplings did not work for her and she suspected provided only temporary relief for him. There was no trust or lust. When challenged over and over again, Philip finally admitted that he had succumbed to one or two flings in the past. He assured her they had nothing to do with their relationship and the last thing he wanted to do was to break up their marriage. He swore he would never be unfaithful to her again but however much she wanted to believe him, doubts kept surfacing.

Miserable, Vanessa tortured herself and him with constant references to his adultery. Surrounded by an atmosphere of tears, too much drinking, too much eating, trying to behave normally in front of their two nervous daughters, the months rolled by in torment.

It was 5 a.m. when Vanessa's maternal ears pricked up as she heard Amy tiptoeing across the landing, too late to have the kind of talk she needed with her daughter. It would have to wait till later in the day.

This was one of the moments when Vanessa doubly cursed Charlie for the absence of a supporting partner. She longed for someone who could help her enforce some sensible rules for her strong-willed daughter.

When Amy finally appeared in the kitchen shortly before noon, Vanessa plunged straight in.

'You'll never believe what your father's done,' she said. 'He's lied to us. To all of us.'

Amy looked at her guardedly.

'Always going on about how much he loves you both.

Huh. He has a great way of showing it. It's disgraceful. Everything has to be done to suit him. He's like a dictator.'

Amy waited for her mother's tirade to finish. Although she was used to hearing her rail about her stepmother, criticism of her father was rare.

'What did he lie about, Mum?' she asked, shaking a spoonful of bran flakes into a bowl.

'Your shares. And Louise's. He's handing them over lock, stock and barrel to That Woman.'

'I don't understand. To Charlie? Why? Can he do that?'

'Of course he can. He has the power.'

'I can't believe Dad would go for that. Not without talking about it to me first. When did you find out?'

'Last night. You know in his speech when he said he'd have to give up running Forresters and that he would consult all of us, the board and the family? Well, I found out he's already made up his mind.'

Amy's lips tightened. 'Does Louise know?'

'No, I wanted to tell you first. I've not seen her this morning. She's out with the horses as usual.'

'I'll never hand over my shares to Charlie, and Louise won't either.'

Vanessa was pleased at her daughter's determined reaction. 'It's not what your grandfather would have wanted, I can tell you,' she said. 'He asked your father to look after your shares, not some woman he didn't know.'

'Well,' retorted Amy, 'I was only little when he wrote that will. I bet if Great-Grandpa was still alive he wouldn't make me wait till I was twenty-five to have them. They're *my* shares and I'm going to fight for them.'

'I'm sure you're right but that's not everything. Your

father didn't say it in as many words but I get the impression That Woman will go on the board as well, in his place.' Vanessa shuddered. 'I'll have to face her at every meeting.'

'Oh Mum, how horrible for you. It's so unfair.'

They discussed little else until late afternoon although Vanessa omitted any mention of her argument with Charlie in the cloakroom, too embarrassed to admit to her daughter that she had lost control.

When Louise returned from riding to be told about the shares, she was as indignant as her sister. Various options were pored over. Vanessa might raise the issue at the next board meeting but that would take weeks. They could try and enlist the support of Walter Threadgold but they decided it was too risky. It would be far more likely he would be Philip's ally than theirs. Eventually they decided the best approach would be for Amy to tackle Philip directly.

'I'll have three days over Christmas to talk him out of it,' she told her mother. She sounded confident. Her father never refused her anything. If anyone could manipulate him, she could. The brand new Mini Mayfair standing in the drive was testament to that.

The nineteen-year-old was pleased she was being allowed into battle. Since she had been old enough to notice these things, she was aware that Philip was increasingly impervious to her mother's crying and recriminations. Amy saw that her stepmother used very different tactics, charm, humour and patience. The girl had already made up her mind not to remonstrate with her father but cajole him instead. She would impress upon him how sensible she had become and how she could be trusted to handle her own shares. With his help, of course.

She was determined to change his mind. If he passed control of her shares to her stepmother, he would be demonstrating once again that when he had a choice, he chose Charlie.

Chapter Eight

Charlie had a feeling of foreboding quite at odds with the glimmering, shimmering gaiety of Christmas in Knightsbridge.

Demands from New York had kept her unexpectedly busy all morning. It was rare that they wanted so much on a Saturday, usually a slow news day. A bright overnight researcher, as she had once been, was getting everything ready for Charlie's 'special' to be transmitted by satellite, part of a survey of an end-of-the-year financial forecast around Europe.

She had had little time to reflect on last night's bitter row. Seeing the enmity in Vanessa's eyes had unnerved her more than she would admit. She was plunged into gloom at the thought of the endless strife ahead if she took Philip's place on the board. However much, in the beginning, she had made allowances for Vanessa's hurt and bitterness, in the five years she had been part of Philip's life, relations between them had worsened rather than improved. If only they had found some points of contact, they might have been able to avoid this destructive rivalry. She was depressed at the thought that she would be manacled to this woman for years ahead.

Still recovering from the trauma of last night's scene, she had to confide in someone and she could tell from Philip's expression at breakfast he did not want it to be him. So as soon as she had arrived for her stint in the ABN offices she had phoned her mother.

Susan Mills assumed Charlie's call was to have a familial gloat about Philip's promotion so she was perturbed by her daughter's despondent voice.

The history of money troubles caused by Vanessa's financial demands and her seemingly constant intrusion into her daughter's marriage made Susan a highly prejudiced listener. After hearing the details of Vanessa's attack at the party, she was forthright.

'I know I shouldn't say it but the woman must be unhinged. I can't see why she's blaming you for this share business. It's Philip she should be attacking but I suppose she wouldn't have a go at him. He's her Mister Moneybags.' There was a snort down the phone. 'I just don't know why she doesn't get on with her own life and leave you alone. She's not the only woman to be divorced. There are millions of people much worse off than she is.'

'Philip's caught in the middle,' said Charlie. 'He's trying to be a great father to Miranda at the same time as concentrating on the other two. It's hard for him.'

'It's just as difficult for you,' retorted Susan. 'And you're both stuck. Vanessa knows she can get exactly what she wants while the girls live with her. You'll just have to grit your teeth until they're independent.'

'That'll be a few years yet, Mum,' replied Charlie.

'In the meantime you won't solve the problem by avoiding it. Don't you think you should have a straight talk with

Philip? Put your point of view just this once?'

Charlie gave a hollow laugh. 'Fat chance I'd have. You know how touchy he is about her. I have to be careful what I say.'

'What about talking to Amy? She's old enough to understand.'

'Amy?' Charlie said the name so loudly a colleague turned round to look at her. 'I've not been able to get more than two or three words out of that young woman lately. Louise is easier but when Amy's around she becomes really stroppy. It's as if she doesn't want to be seen fraternising with the enemy.'

'I'm sorry for the girls,' Susan said. 'These problems between you and their mother don't make things easy for them.'

'And it's all so unnecessary,' Charlie interjected. 'And so frustrating. I just wish I knew how to change it.'

Charlie and her mother had often discussed the way the children had become a frayed rope in Vanessa's tug of war with Philip. Simple things like going on holiday with the girls or a modest trip to the Zoo became minefields of diplomatic manoeuvres.

Like the rendezvous arranged at Gatwick Airport after the girls had been on holiday with their mother. Philip and Charlie arrived on time, only to discover the plane had landed at the more accessible Heathrow. And that summer beach holiday when Charlie had opened the girls' suitcase to find it full of thick sweaters, Wellington boots and little else. It had meant taking the two girls shopping at the hideously-expensive seaside boutique. She wouldn't have minded but the clothes had never been seen again.

In Charlie's mother's eyes Philip's guilt manifested itself in allowing his emotions to be governed via his wallet. She understood that her daughter was aware of this but she was too canny to comment out loud.

Philip had excused the suitcase incident as the flailings of a rejected woman hitting out in any way she could. 'She's just trying to punish me and sometimes the children get in the way,' he told Charlie.

What Charlie did not discover until months later was that, after a particularly upsetting farewell with the girls, Philip had stopped at a lay-by. To regain his equilibrium, to focus his pain, he had gripped a coin so tightly in the palm of his hand that the imprint stayed for hours afterwards.

When Charlie relayed this to her mother she echoed Philip's words, 'I'm sure it'll get better with time. Just be patient.' Patient? After five years?

'If only you were going to be there for Christmas, Mum. I'm dreading the whole thing.'

'You know how much I'd love to, darling, but Grandma's still not well enough to travel and I can't leave her alone. I had to give the nurse time off over the holidays.' Susan had moved her ageing mother into her home after her husband, Charlie's father, had died three years ago.

'Oh well, thank God for Miranda.' Charlie was trying to be more cheerful for her mother's sake. 'The girls do seem to love her, especially Louise, but,' she could not help giving another heavy sigh, 'I don't think I'm any good with teenagers.'

'Start practising,' retorted Susan, 'for the day when that sweet angel of yours turns into a rebellious monster from hell. And pray she's better than you were and doesn't come home with bright purple hair.'

Susan promised to phone on Christmas Day and once again Charlie wished she could see more of her own family instead of concentrating on Philip's. As an only child herself, unused to the world of children, Charlie found it especially difficult to cope.

The trouble with step-relationships, she decided, was that they were unnatural. She and the girls were members of the same family but they never had time to allow any closeness to grow. Just when she felt she was making some headway with either of her stepdaughters, the visit came to an end. When next they met, things were back to square one and the immense effort to re-inject some of the previous warmth had to start all over again. It was bloody hard. Divorce had damaged the girls more than most because it had been so unexpected, protected as they had been from the worst aspects of their parents' marriage. The main problem was that they were still at the stage of accepting without question their mother's interpretation of events. Vanessa's apparent demonisation of the woman she blamed for 'stealing' her husband meant that, if the girls ever seemed to be enjoying themselves with Charlie, they felt guilty about their mother, alone at home.

The only bond between the three was Miranda. Both girls loved seeing her excitement when they came through the door and Miranda toddled into their outstretched arms. She was the perfect ice-breaker.

Charlie had tried to share Philip's excitement when Vanessa had, at last, agreed that the girls could spend Christmas in Chelsea Mansions. Amy had agreed to accompany her sister because, despite the age gap, the shared pain of the divorce had driven them to rely on each other. It would be hard but Charlie was determined to make it perfect, especially since Miranda was now old enough to share in the thrill of the preparations.

Buffeted by determined-looking shoppers weighed down with carrier bags and gift-wrapped parcels, Charlie battled her way up Harrods' escalator. The rest of her Christmas shopping had been bought with care and a firm eye on the cash register but today, desperate for inspiration for her stepdaughters' presents, she made the decision to throw money at the problem.

At the top of the escalator she found herself in an alien world. How was she going to choose from such a bewildering display of compact discs? She did not understand their music any more than she understood her stepdaughters. In the accessories department, she brightened when she saw striking fake elephant tusks used as a clasp for thick black leather belts. Surely Amy would love one of those. She winced at the price then decided it would be worthwhile if the present evoked a rare smile in her direction.

In the hour squeezed out of the office, she picked out silver baubles for the tree, the special Christmas pudding – she would add her collection of old sixpences to it before serving – and trinkets for stockings since Philip had assured her even nineteen-year-olds expected Father Christmas to call. 'In fact, darling,' he had smiled, 'forty-somethings like them too.'

As she was paying for her purchases, Charlie smiled to herself. Harrods prided itself on being able to get anything a customer wanted. If only it was possible to order a husband for Christmas, she would have him gift-wrapped and delivered to Vanessa.

Her precious sixty minutes had raced by. She had to get back to work.

It was seven before Charlie left the office and when eventually she turned the key of the door to her flat, the first thing she saw was a gorgeous bouquet of pink daisies awaiting her, banishing her troubles for a while. Although Philip had many engagements that day, he had made time to order her favourite flowers. Inside was a card: 'Remember, dull it ain't. My love, as always, P.'

As she took the flowers carefully out of the cellophane, Charlie recollected her mother's sound advice on how to choose a husband. 'If ever you meet a man who loves flowers and his mother, nab him quickly. Liking flowers means he has sensitivity, an enjoyment of colour and the pleasant things of life. And loving his mother gives him a sense of responsibility which will stand his wife in good stead.' In Philip's case her mother had been proved right.

Pushing the stems on to heavy metal pins, Charlie decided it was time to discuss with her husband the fact that, despite all the impracticalities, she longed for another child.

In his suite at The Ritz, Kyle Salter picked up the phone. It was his direct line which circumvented the hotel operator and whose number he gave to only a handful of close associates.

When he recognised the voice, he felt a glow of satisfaction. Deep Throat was certainly keeping to her side of the bargain. 'The daughters' shares?' He listened intently. 'How very useful. So they're not being broken up? Thank you. And thank you for getting back to me so quickly. It's much appreciated.' She really was an attractive woman. 'Are you free for lunch next week? I think this needs more analysis.'

When Kyle replaced the receiver he allowed himself a gratified smile although he was under no illusion. Lunch was all he was going to get and he dare not jeopardise their new relationship. This deal meant far too much to him.

His father's supermarket empire, reaching from Orlando in Florida through Chicago and Washington to Philadelphia, had recently bought a large regional group of stores in Britain which were in danger of dying. With them came a sheaf of giveaway magazines and local newspapers in the area abutting the Forrester Group's regional chain. This media toehold in the UK suited the Salter company's long-term strategy to cut their publishing teeth in Britain before purchasing a newspaper group back home, and it suited Kyle. He had become fascinated by the media and less interested in the supermarket side of the business, unlike his father who was solely a bottom line man and not interested in the creative side.

Kyle sat pondering this new development concerning the Forrester shareholding, a transfer which none of his advisers had predicted. They had anticipated every move in connection with the takeover, but not this one. Well, how could they?

Was it worth waking his father in New York? No. Better to wait until tomorrow. That would give him time to work out all the possibilities this new angle presented. Still, it could not make his task more difficult.

Chapter Nine

Tony Burns made a thirty-second peremptory phone call to Imogen Ferris in her flat on Sunday afternoon. He assured himself that she had not talked to any other paper and that the story about the fight in the cloakroom was the *Chronicle*'s and theirs alone.

They agreed she would discuss it in future only with him and no one else on the paper. Then he asked her never to contact him at home again and gave her his private number at the office. Imogen was elated.

Tony took care not to mention that he envisaged it as a major story. The ingredients encompassed everything needed for a tabloid splash, a great human problem, first wife versus second wife, and the political challenge, the undermining of a new Cabinet minister, which was in line with the paper's political stance. A double whammy. Telling Imogen how good the story was would only give her rarefied ideas of how much she would get paid for it. In his opinion she would have to do a lot more to prove she was worthy of a staff job.

An unexpected bonus was provided by the deputy picture editor. He phoned every photographer who had covered top drawer events in London and the south east over the last twenty years, asking them to trawl through their libraries. Twenty-four hours later this produced a black and white picture of a nineteen-year-old Miss Vanessa Forrester dancing close with the then most eligible man in the country – the heir to Britain's throne, the Prince of Wales.

This was the photograph which would trigger a long-forgotten memory in an Edinburgh nurse and so begin the slow torture of Vanessa Lockhart and her family.

After several transatlantic calls, Kyle Salter at last tracked down his father. He was in his helicopter en route to New York from their East Hampton duneside weekend home.

The younger Salter was well aware of the need to be at his most eloquent. His father had never been wholly convinced that the Forrester Group was worth pursuing, and this new development increased his reservations. 'Remember Salter's Law,' he said. 'When you're doing a takeover, if the unexpected happens and you can still walk away, unless it's completely in your favour, walk.'

'But Dad, the shares aren't being broken up,' protested Kyle. 'The daughters' and the father's shareholdings are staying together.'

Paul Salter was sceptical. 'Listen and learn. We're not ready to bid yet. The money isn't lined up. How the shares are divided isn't the point. What matters is that some new guy will come in to take over from Philip Lockhart. He'll waste no time showing the world what a swinging dick he has. He's gonna make changes so everyone knows he's there. If he gets it right, the group does well and becomes harder to buy. If he gets it wrong, all the analysts will come to the same conclusion we did and we might end up in a fight for control with someone else.'

Kyle was silent.

'I know how much this deal means to you.' Kyle could hear the familiar voice almost as clearly as if he was in the helicopter with his father. 'But this is outside influences. You must be realistic. I know, I've done this before. I've only ever bought when they've wanted to sell and nobody's wanted silly money. Changes at the top always mean everything else changes, one way or the other.'

Despite his father's objections, Kyle was determined not to let his first international deal slip away. Their City advisers had warned them that the Press in Britain was considered a mature industry which made investors reluctant to pour in money.

Kyle had persuaded his father how much fun they could have trying to manipulate politicians rather than sorting out the lowest prices for baked beans.

Paul was amused to be used as a chess piece by the twenty-eight-year-old, who saw himself as a fledgling Citizen Kane. Well, Rupert Murdoch anyway.

'Dad, it's early days. Let me keep the options open for just a while longer.'

His father's voice rose. 'Kyle, this Forrester Group's not the only one we could buy. There are other media groups in Britain. I've been looking at the *Despatch*. They own two nationals. Great opportunities there. Also I hear United might be up for sale.'

Despite his anxiety, Kyle was smiling. He appreciated that his father was trying to humour him. Both of those companies would cost a great deal more than the Forrester Group.

'Dad, you know you've always told me never to give up. So far it hasn't cost us any more than getting our analysts to put a microscope over the company. Let me stick to my hunches for a bit.'

'Just promise me you'll take a look at some other media groups, OK?' Kyle could hear the reluctance in his father's voice but then Paul changed the subject. 'Say, that was a good looker you were pictured with in *Town and Country*.'

'Oh, she's history. The new one's more your type, a blonde. She's an Oxford grad and has started doing a bit of modelling.'

'Brains and a body? Deadly combination. Watch out.'

After he and his father had finished swapping news of the latest Big Apple gossip, Kyle wasted no time in phoning Deep Throat. He had been careful to gloss over the fact that when a takeover was successful, inevitably that meant change among executives, many other less senior personnel and a revolution in work practices and company culture.

She was silent as he outlined his father's anxieties. After a pause there came a low laugh.

'Don't worry,' she murmured in that distinctive voice. 'This will be a dick-free zone.'

Tony Burns was ready for battle. He had taken great pleasure early that Monday morning in purloining the spread, normally the exclusive preserve of the assistant editor features, his equal but also his rival.

As he had carefully outlined the story to the editor before the eleven-thirty conference, the headline was clear in his mind: 'Battle of the boardroom beauties' with a strapline, 'Wives one and two of new minister fight over shares.' Now all he needed was some zingy copy and those much-heralded pictures. But at conference the momentum slowed when Diana Grocott, the City editor, pleaded for a stay of twenty-four hours.

'After you told me about the Lockhart ladies, I phoned Walter Threadgold on Sunday evening,' she told him. 'Of course, I didn't tell him what it was about but when I asked to meet he offered to buy me lunch tomorrow. I think it would be stupid to pass up the chance for a face-to-face talk. And anyway, as there hasn't been a whisper of the story in any other newspaper, I took the chance you'd agree with me to hold fire until tomorrow.'

'Far be it from me to stop you having yet another meal at a five-star restaurant, Diana,' said Tony sarcastically, 'but this is just delaying things. Call me old-fashioned but I used to go round to interview people in their offices.' He was only half serious. He was well aware that the chairman of a rival group of newspapers would more likely unbend after a glass or two of fine wine with a respected City commentator than reveal all to one of his foot-in-the-door reporters.

The picture editor pointed out that the old black and white picture of Vanessa Lockhart and the Prince of Wales could not only be coloured up but would reproduce better if they waited for the original to arrive by courier from the veteran photographer's collection, rather than be wired. This tipped the balance.

Tony was mollified by being assured that when everything came together, it would not only make a great two-page spread for Wednesday, it would also provide a fabulous blurb for the front. His only worry was keeping the story under wraps.

★ ★ ★

Vanessa cursed her lack of organisation. If only she planned ahead she would have known that 20 December was not the day for cheerful interviews. But Imogen Ferris had been insistent. This month the county's glossy magazine went to press earlier than usual because of the office shutdown over Christmas and Vanessa did not want to miss an opportunity to publicise the charity ball. She still had tickets to sell.

The interview started well. Imogen had brought a bottle of vintage champagne which was swiftly opened. Vanessa was nerving herself to ask the journalist not to smoke although Imogen had once told her she would much rather have a cigarette than a meal. It explained why she was nervy and reed-thin. But after the first glass, Vanessa relented and allowed her relieved guest to smoke.

Imogen appeared to be interested in every detail of the work of the chairman of the charity ball and showed a great understanding of the vitally important role Vanessa had played in the Harlequin Ball's survival. She seemed to be fascinated, too, by the most minute aspects of organisation from the colour co-ordinated floral arrangements to how the seating had to be arranged, every particular being noted down assiduously in her notebook, recorded, as the journalist said, for posterity.

'Posterity and *Sussex County Magazine*,' Vanessa amended.

They had both smiled at that.

Vanessa was wary when Imogen steered the conversation round to the Forrester Group and the sad news that Philip Lockhart had to give up his post as chief executive.

'That must be a great blow to all his colleagues,' Imogen

prompted, fiddling nervously with her long auburn curls.

Vanessa was highly suspicious of what relevance this could have to an article for a social diary. She simply said, 'I've found it more prudent never to comment on any aspect of our business.' It made her sound stiff and pompous but she softened when Imogen confessed she was only pursuing these 'difficult questions' on her editor's insistence. He was trying to give a harder edge to the magazine and she felt privately it was also to feed his own curiosity.

Vanessa laughed. 'Well, he'll have to accept that I won't answer any of them,' and she politely refused to reveal any of her thoughts with regard to the shareholdings.

Imogen tried for a direct hit. 'If Mr Lockhart can't administer your daughters' shares any more, who will?'

Vanessa pursed her lips and sidestepped the question by lifting up the empty champagne bottle and going down to the cellar for a bottle of wine.

Imogen acknowledged that she was getting nowhere and decided to come at these questions from another direction. As she continued to show interest in Philip's future career, Vanessa wondered if Imogen had been one of his past conquests.

The two women were very different. The journalist dressed to please men, worked hard to keep her schoolgirl figure, always wore a Wonderbra and never went round the corner in anything less than four-inch heels and artfully applied make-up. They had little in common but their alma mater, St Mary's.

When Vanessa returned from the cellar, Imogen ostentatiously put away her notebook and with a mixture of attentiveness, humour and alcohol set about crossing the bridge that divided Vanessa's acquaintances from confidantes.

Vanessa relaxed. She had been several years ahead of Imogen at St Mary's but many of their recollections were the same, teachers, meals, even the antics of the school cat.

'Do you remember how they told us constantly we were the brightest, prettiest girls in the whole country?' Imogen asked.

'Mmm.' Vanessa was hesitant.

'They repeated it so often, we didn't think to question, we just accepted it,' Imogen went on. 'And who would have thought it, here we are, two model pupils.'

'Until life proved otherwise,' said Vanessa so softly Imogen barely heard it.

'Both alone,' murmured Imogen.

Although husbandless, Vanessa had until that moment never acknowledged that she was now in the same position as a spinster like Imogen. The title of Mrs Philip Lockhart had been like a security blanket even though nowadays there was a new one. She felt as though someone had roughly dragged the cover away from her and she shivered.

Unaware that the journalist had another agenda, in her slightly maudlin state Vanessa slowly let down her guard.

Leafing through the family photograph album, Imogen had spotted a picture of a radiant Vanessa, aged fourteen. Casually remarking what a beautiful young woman she had been at that age, and how much she looked like Amy, Imogen was puzzled when Vanessa remarked bitterly, 'That must have been the only photograph of me smiling that entire year.'

It was true. There were no other pictures of her fourteenth and fifteenth year in an album that had chronicled the minutiae of her life until she had become Mrs Philip Lockhart.

After opening up about her schooldays, Vanessa just as quickly clammed up about that part of her life. She wanted no further questions about why she was suddenly absent from the well-groomed hockey field, the stone-clad library and the medieval chapel. The reason why the wrought-iron gates of St Mary's had clanged behind her for ever when she was just fifteen was known to only a few.

Skilfully Imogen guided the conversation away from schooldays until Vanessa began to relate how she and Philip had known each other as teenagers, but then had seen little of each other for several years until they met up again in their early twenties. She described it as if it was only yesterday.

Try as she might, Imogen could not inveigle her to speak ill of Philip or about the divorce, his new wife or the shareholding problems.

She sighed. All she had winkled out of this woman was information about the bloody ball. This would not interest Tony. He was looking for the hard stuff not the emotional ramblings of an ex-wife past her sell-by date. Mentally she relegated her interview from the national paper to her county magazine.

But her patience did not go unrewarded. As she was leaving, Vanessa apologised for her emotional state, saying she should have re-scheduled the interview. 'Sorry to have been so boring,' she said quietly. 'I'm just a bit down. Today always has bad memories for me.'

'Oh?'

'Sorry, I can't talk about it.'

'Well, it might help to share the burden and obviously this

won't be for publication,' said Imogen, mentally crossing her fingers.

Vanessa hesitated. 'Well, today always focuses my mind on a decision I made many years ago which I still regret.'

Imogen waited, hoping Vanessa would say more, but she did not and eventually the journalist was guided courteously to the door.

An hour later, when she had sobered up, Vanessa remembered the journalist's thoughtful expression. Had she given away too much? She re-ran the events of that morning like a slow video through her head. If only she had not opened that second bottle of wine. Although she had taken only one glass from it, it had been enough to make her dip her defences.

Sad anniversaries were always bad, particularly when they could not be shared, when they had to remain secret. But she had not been secretive enough, had she?

She sighed. She was dreading Christmas alone without the two girls. Vanessa felt middle-aged. Unsexy. A dumpee.

Chapter Ten

Over the years Diana Grocott, the *Chronicle*'s City editor, had grown close to Walter Threadgold. Her previous job as the share tipster of a Sunday broadsheet meant that she and Walter had been regular conspirators. She felt she had done a great deal to help him and the Forrester Group with a judicious piece here and there, specifically during their takeover of the news magazine only eighteen months ago.

Like many City commentators, she did not dig too far below the surface for stories. If a chairman or managing director boasted about company profits, unless she had concrete proof to the contrary she used the information. In common with most of her peer group, she felt no guilt that many financial scandals had passed her by. It was not for journalists like her to rock the boat. The deal was straightforward. In exchange for a good bottle of 1991 La Chablisienne Chablis plus the odd bite of caviar, Walter would insinuate advantageous gossip about himself and the Forrester Group into the conversation and try to poison the well for his opponents.

Walter actively encouraged all of his journalistic contacts to hope that he might offer them the editorship of his magazine in the future. This enticed them into giving ideas and helpful criticism which allowed Walter, an accountant, to keep one step ahead of the editors in his employ. Not for nothing was he known in the City as Walter the Weasel.

During the year Diana had enjoyed two or three lunches *à deux* with Walter Threadgold in the Savoy Grill but she was a little nervous today. Straying from her financial brief into the personal area was not to her taste.

When the wine had been well and truly sampled and the traditional jousting about sales figures, circulation wars, and libellous gossip about media executives was behind them, Diana raised the real purpose of the day's lunch.

'Look, Walter, this is not really my territory, it's more in the purple prose department, but I've been given the three-line whip by my editor.'

Walter put down his glass expectantly.

Diana was not used to 'fronting up' her victims unless it was about money, hirings, firings or other financial facts. She plunged straight in. 'I was wondering how you got on with Mrs Lockhart the second.'

'Oh?' Walter's antennae told him something unpleasant was in the wind.

'I hear she's joining the board.'

No one was privy to that information except four people. Himself, Philip, Charlie and probably Vanessa. 'The board hasn't made any decision yet,' he replied after the slightest of hesitations. 'I think you've been misled.'

'Sorry, Walter, my information comes from a good source.'

For a moment Walter was at a loss for words. Who could have leaked this and why?

The journalist continued, 'I hear there were some fisticuffs in the ladies' loo after your Christmas party. Apparently when the ex-Mrs L found out about the new plan, we're reliably told she went nuclear.'

'Really? News to me.'

Diana took a sip of wine and decided to turn the screw. 'Look, Walter, we have some freelance who was in a cubicle in the cloakroom and wrote down every word the two women said. Of course I haven't seen the copy, it's only been verballed to me, but I gather the women actually hit one another and the first Mrs L called the second one a whore. This is pretty hot stuff when they're fighting not just over shares but a Cabinet minister.' She smiled, noting her host's startled expression. But, she had to hand it to him, he recovered well.

'I haven't heard a word about this,' said Walter smoothly.

'At the moment, as I say, it's a freelance who's come up with the story but if we don't print it they could sell it to someone else. Because of our friendship I persuaded the editor to wait till I met you today but they won't hold out much longer. It'd be better if I handled it rather than one of the hacks who won't understand how sensitive these things can be in business.' Diana was almost purring.

Walter's face was impassive and he allowed her to continue without interruption.

'We think it's important to put your side of the story, Walter, so can you get back to me by four o'clock? That'll just make my deadline.'

Walter was far too wily an operator to be drawn and, used to manipulating the media, all he said was, 'It all sounds highly improbable. I'll get back to you as soon as possible.'

If the story about the argument in the loo was true, some swift action needed to be taken fast to squash it. Or, if the worst came to the worst, dampened down so it merited little attention. He had to tread carefully. A change in the Forrester share ownership had already rated press interest. But on the City pages. An inter-family squabble on the board would warrant much more coverage. Hot stuff, as the journalist had said.

Tony was at the art desk drawing up the centre spread. Next to the picture of the nineteen-year-old Vanessa dancing with the Prince of Wales were two wedding photographs, one of a radiant, white-veiled Vanessa, and the other, from Philip's second outing as a bridegroom, was of Charlie, looking more demure in a pink suit. Below it was a new, highly flattering professional campaign portrait of Philip and his three daughters.

To accompany the main story the women's department had produced an instant look at another festering war between first and second wives that had been played out in a court case recently. They had dredged up some fashionable guru to analyse the psychological effect on two women battling for the bloke, the booty and, in this case, the boardroom.

It was all great stuff, and they also had 'psycho facts' on the husband and on the children from marriage one and marriage two, all broken down into boxes, what the professionals called a 'magpie read'.

'Bloody good-looking family,' said Tony to the art director. 'It's just right for a Christmas week read. The message is simple. The average married man may be dreading his mother-in-law coming down, he may have noticed that since the office party his wife's not speaking to him and he may think that the bank manager will have a fit if he puts any more skid marks on his plastic cards but look at this lot. They're rich and they're not having it easy either.'

'Perfect.'

At the bottom of the spread was a large box outlined in a heavy black rule. It said: 'Do you know any warring stories about first and second wives? Write, fax or phone' – and it gave the address and contact numbers at the newspaper. 'We're very interested in hearing from YOU. We'll pay for the ones we print.'

In the business this was known as a come-on. Pity his ferret – the nickname Tony had given Imogen Ferris not because of her reporting skills but because she appeared to love ferreting down the bed and she used her mouth brilliantly – had not been able to glean any more juicy facts from the prime source, but then he had not really expected her to. She had just got lucky being in the right place at the right time.

'Yes, Minister, we can certainly arrange that for you.'

Philip had heard all about the usual intractability of civil servants but at his first inter-departmental lunch he sensed he was receiving the full new boy treatment.

It was a delicious moment. Each suggestion he made, however tentative, was seized upon for action by members of his private office, particularly Christopher Bennett, his chief aide. Nothing seemed to be too much trouble for him and Philip wondered how long this uncritical support from battle-hardened veterans would last. He was only too aware that he was being assessed. After this lunch, there would be just two questions among them: 'Is he manageable?' And 'Will he give us any trouble?'

Well, they would find out soon who was boss. He well understood the pitfalls of allowing himself to be so drenched with paperwork that decisions were made by the permanent secretary instead of the minister. The department had had an easy time with his predecessor who was more interested in image than substance. But Philip was determined to work hard, assiduously plunder his Red Boxes and make a real difference. He wanted to use this appointment as the spring-board to a seat at the Cabinet table much nearer to the Prime Minister.

His euphoria was punctured by the buzz of his personal mobile. It rang very rarely these days; the number was known only to five people, all of them private and uncon-nected with politics. It must mean trouble.

Walter Threadgold understood at once that Philip could make no response in a room full of people so he made his briefing succinct and clear enough for Philip to have no need to comment. Walter omitted no detail of his lunch with the *Chronicle*'s City editor.

'Try and find out from Charlie exactly what happened,' he said. 'And get back to me as soon as possible.'

In front of his audience, Philip was noncommittal. 'I suppose if all else fails we'll have to try our Canadian friend.'

Walter understood this to be a reference to Fergus Canefield, proprietor of the *Chronicle* newspaper group. Philip was sug-gesting a personal call to get the story squashed. There must be some truth in the tale, after all, Walter thought, and that could mean a hairy ride. They did not want or need a mud-slinging war.

Philip tried to quell his mounting panic. Only four days into a new job and his private life was about to be splashed all over the tabloids. He recalled Charlie mentioning something about a row at the party but he could not remember the details. He had better find out as fast as possible.

Although Philip's face remained impassive, Chris Bennett seemed to be aware of his boss's change of mood. 'Anything I can assist you with, Minister?' he asked smoothly.

'No, thank you,' said Philip briskly and to escape as soon as he could he told the assembled group, 'I'm not a pudding or a cheese man.' He often rued the fact that he was never offered them again.

In his private office, Philip waited impatiently for Charlie to answer her phone. Once again he searched his memory, trying to remember just what she had said on their way home on Friday night. His only recollection was that she had told him Vanessa had been overwrought. He felt sure the story had been grossly exaggerated by *Chronicle* reporters looking for any kind of tittle-tattle to embarrass the government and their newspaper rivals.

When Charlie picked up the phone, she was aghast to discover that a reporter had been listening to Vanessa's tirade in the cloakroom. 'What are they saying happened?'

With increasing trepidation Charlie listened as Philip recounted what Diana Grocott had told Walter.

'How accurate is that?' he asked her.

Like many stories before they reached print the Lockhart v. Lockhart tale had been exaggerated and embellished. It virtually had the women wrestling in mud.

'Well, the idea that she hit me in the face is ludicrous, doubly so since we both went back to the party. Also she didn't say half the things the reporter is claiming. And she did not call me a whore.' She sighed. 'But I have to admit that the rest is accurate. Do you think it could have come from Vanessa? Would she talk to some journalist?' Charlie could not resist suspecting her predecessor of organising a vendetta. It had become second nature to doubt Vanessa's motives but rarely had she been so candid about her to Philip.

'I can't see what good it would do Vanessa,' replied Philip tersely.

Even now he's standing up for her, thought Charlie gloomily.

'In any case,' he went on, 'Walter was definite about the source. It was some woman sitting in a cubicle eavesdropping on every word. I blame myself. I should have been more vague when I talked to Vanessa about the shares.'

Charlie was frank. 'Whatever you did, the result would have been the same. I've always said I don't think it's wise for me to be at the Forrester party. She's always seen me as a rival in her territory and, let's face it, putting me on the board is bound to lead to more trouble.'

'You know what I think about that,' said Philip abruptly. 'I need you there, end of story. I just wish I'd known about the rumpus when it happened.'

Charlie heard the anxiety in his voice. 'Darling, I'm sorry I didn't tell you the full details. I didn't expect it to come out and each time we talk about Vanessa it ends up in a row. On Friday night you were so happy and I didn't want to spoil your mood. Anyway, we planned to discuss the whole share business over Christmas so I thought I'd tell you then when we were both more relaxed.'

Philip was well aware that his wife kept to herself her intense irritation at some of his ex-wife's actions. He admired her for it.

'So how are we going to handle this?' Charlie asked. 'You've hardly had your feet under the desk. We'd better talk about it later. You don't want the civil servants gossiping that you spend most of the day on the phone to the little woman.'

They laughed weakly.

'We have to look like we're in control,' Charlie continued. 'The news of the change of shareholding should appear to come out through us, not the bloody *Chronicle*. Vultures. You go back to work. I'll talk to Walter and get things moving with the PR people.'

'And I'll have to talk to the Chief Whip,' Philip said, 'so the Prime Minister can be briefed before anybody makes political capital out of the story. Great, just great.'

Philip tried not to speculate at the delight this would bring, not only to the Opposition, but even more to his rivals on the back benches of his own party. His elevation had been so sudden that there were many raw, unfriendly egos out there. And in the Cabinet there were already signs that some of those nervous about hanging on to their portfolios might be less than co-operative in the future.

Philip sighed. 'Dull it ain't.' It was his favourite saying when the bullets were flying and even now it made Charlie smile.

Vanessa, too, would have to be warned about the impending story. While she remained in ignorance, she could be a loose cannon.

There was no reply from her number and for the ump-
teenth time Philip cursed that she had thrown his answer
machine out with the rest of his belongings. Apart from not
being able to leave messages for his daughters, he thought
an answer machine might have been helpful in promoting
Vanessa's marriage prospects, something he wanted desper-
ately for both financial and emotional reasons. In a cynical
understanding of his own sex, Philip had estimated that men
who phoned forty-something divorcees might not phone
twice.

The Chief Whip took Philip's news in his usual stoical
manner. 'Just get it sorted out quickly and quietly,' he
advised. 'I will, of course, tell the Prime Minister so keep
me in close touch with developments.'

Philip was impressed with the Chief Whip's detached
style. No censure, just calm acceptance of the facts. He
would have been less sanguine had he overheard him a few
seconds later speaking to his deputy.

'Fucking ministers,' he raged. 'Hasn't been in the job for
more than five minutes and can't even stay out of the manure
over Christmas.'

Philip's next call was from Walter Threadgold. He had
spoken to Fergus Canefield in his New York apartment
overlooking Central Park. He was friendly but unhelpful; he
told Walter that he had 'no control' over what his editors
published. Both of them appreciated the fact that he was
lying. But the unfortunate story which Philip's magazine had
splashed of his son's dalliance with a male pop star had not
been forgotten. Or forgiven.

To draw the poison from the *Chronicle* story Walter,
Philip and Charlie arranged to issue a statement through the

Press Association. Without embellishment it would simply announce Charlie's appointment to the Forrester board in the light of Philip's promotion. The PA statement ended: 'All members of the Lockhart family are united in their wish to see the company progress and will work closely towards that end. The recent circulation successes of both the *Citizen* and the local papers augur well for the future.'

Following the announcement, the press consultants released Charlie's impressive CV which reaffirmed what an asset she would be to the Forrester board. Walter and their PR man had also spent a furious hour briefing as many editors and City journalists as they could track down, to spoil the *Chronicle*'s so-called exclusive. In doing this, Walter and the press office had to strike a fine balance, careful to make the story interesting enough for City coverage while downgrading the personal elements so it would not sound too fascinating and merit a news story elsewhere in the paper too. Talking to journalists off the record, they dismissed any suggestion of a row as being no more than the coughs and splutters that plagued all families, particularly after a divorce. And uttered at a boozy function, they were of even less account. To male journalists Walter laughed and mixing his metaphors added, 'It's only two birds squawking in a teacup.'

By the time Philip finally got through to the Rectory, his call was answered by Amy. He was dismayed by her lack of warmth, so unlike his beloved daughter. Her manner went from cool to Arctic as he gave her a sanitised version of what might appear in the following morning's *Chronicle*. The worse scenario, he told her, was a story on the City pages and another in the diary column. All other papers would probably carry something from the PA statement which was being put out by their press office. 'But that'll only make the City pages and won't bother you or your mother,' he concluded.

Amy made no response apart from saying she would tell her mother when she returned home. Philip would normally have attempted to jolly her out of her bad mood but right now he was in too much of a hurry to deal with what he thought was a teenage sulk.

Wrong tactics. As she replaced the phone on its cradle, Amy recognised instinctively that she would never be able to persuade her father to give her the shares if she carried on like this. But she was feeling too raw to be civil. Far more serious was that Charlie, the media queen, seemed to have gone to the papers with this stupid story about some row she'd had with Mum.

She waited restlessly for her mother to come home.

The telephone was busy elsewhere, too. Minutes before the PA announcement, Kyle Salter received a preview of its contents from Deep Throat.

It was a happy son who informed his father that the shares were to stay in the family. 'We don't have to look elsewhere, Dad. I'm going to bring this little baby home to you.'

His father laughed. 'What the hell, just see she doesn't wet all over you.'

Chapter Eleven

'Put your computer on to PA.'

The excited voice of the *Chronicle*'s news editor boomed out of the squawk box on Tony Burns's desk. One look at the screen and Tony yelled, 'God Almighty. We've been shafted. Get me the City editor. Right now,' he barked into the telephone console.

Two seconds later his secretary put her head round the door. 'She'll be with you in a minute. She's on an important call.'

Tony went ballistic. He levitated to the door. Staff only half-jokingly flattened themselves against the wall. As he flung open the City editor's door, she gesticulated to the receiver in her hand and mouthed, 'Walter Threadgold.'

Through clenched teeth he hissed, 'Just give me a moment.'

Fearful, she covered the mouthpiece. 'He's just explaining—'

'That fucker just stabbed us,' Tony cut in, his face thunderous. 'Have you seen PA? He's done a statement about the shares. I was sure the bastard wouldn't do the *Chronicle* any favours. I'll make sure the story goes on page one now.'

Before slamming her door, his parting shot to Diana was, 'And take a course in real journalism, will you?'

As he strode quickly towards the editor's office, he vowed it would be the last time he would ever let City handle any news story. We should have done it yesterday, he chastised himself, a sentiment he repeated to the deputy editor, along with his ardent wish to put the story on page one.

On his return to the newsdesk, Tony fired off reporters in all directions to corner the Lockhart trio, Philip, Charlie and Vanessa. 'I want quotes out of this lot as soon as possible but remember, they know the boss so try the hearts and flowers approach first and don't be fobbed off by that guff on PA.'

All the reporters were doubled up with a snapper. An angry face on the front would help the story along. It was a dull week and there was nothing going on elsewhere except for the pre-Christmas sales and the usual foreign famine stories. Falling circulation figures showed that compassion fatigue among readers had set in early.

The *Chronicle*'s trackers failed to get anywhere near Philip who was protected by his aides, nor could they find Charlie. When she realised they were waiting for her in the entrance hall, she left the American Broadcast Network building by an unwatched back exit. But the hunters did manage to corner Vanessa as she was returning home alone in the gloom, Christmas tree squashed in the back of her Volvo estate, completely oblivious of the day's developments.

As she climbed out of the car she was surprised by the sight of a dark saloon in the drive, occupied by two large men. Who would be waiting for her outside the house like this? Her instant fear was that it was the police. There had been an accident.

Then one of them shouted out at her, 'Mrs Lockhart, do you have any statement to make about the boardroom fight?'

Vanessa immediately felt relief: there had been no accident, and she had too much printer's ink in her veins to be fazed by the question.

'About the fight you had with your husband's second wife.' The *Chronicle* reporter, aware he must be polite, had emerged from the car and lowered his voice.

Vanessa stared at him and at that moment she was blinded by the photographer's flashgun, which provided a picture of a flustered-looking Vanessa for page one.

Shaken, Vanessa still had enough schooling in the wiles of the press to realise that a 'No comment' quote could be used to build up a story. So she remained silent and hurried towards her front door.

'Are you happy about Charlotte Lockhart joining the Forrester board?' the reporter shouted at her retreating back.

That halted her for an instant.

'It's on PA, you know, it's all official,' he added.

So everybody knew.

At that moment Amy opened the door and thankfully Vanessa rushed into the hall and slammed the door.

Her daughter looked as upset as Vanessa felt. 'Those two have been here for ages, Mum,' said Amy. 'I didn't know what to do to make them go.'

In the face of her daughter's worries, Vanessa forced herself to remain calm and drew the curtains in the hallway.

'Let's close every curtain in every room. Remember, darling, as you pull, stand to the side so they can't take any more pictures.'

When the house was closed against the outside world,

Amy told her mother about her father's earlier phone call. 'Apparently the *Chronicle* has some story about you and Charlie having a fight and because of that he says they've had to announce she's going to be on the board.'

Vanessa was appalled. 'You mean he's put Charlie on the board already?' The words were hardly out of her mouth before she was punching out Philip's number.

'How dare you issue a statement about Forrester's without talking to me first?' She attacked as soon as she heard his voice.

It had been a long, hard day and Philip wanted to relax with his wife and baby daughter and not have to deal right then with a fractious ex-wife who was the cause of all the trouble.

'Look, we had no choice. It was a damage limitation exercise. We kept on trying but we couldn't get hold of you and in the end we had no other option.'

'I can't see why it couldn't have waited another day,' stormed Vanessa. 'Obviously you and Charlie are trying to ease me out, that's the reason for the rush.'

Philip was incensed at the injustice of it all. 'Just hang on. Remember it was because of your bloody lack of self-control that we've landed in this bloody mess. Some woman was listening in the loo to your tirade and sold it to the *Chronicle*. They're threatening to publish every spit and comma of it tomorrow.'

'Oh my God.' Vanessa was momentarily jolted but recovered her sense of outrage almost immediately. 'Well, it was your fault it happened. If you hadn't sprung all that on me at the party, which is always a very difficult situation for me now, I wouldn't have behaved like that. How do you expect me to react when I'm told my children's shares are being given to That Woman?'

'Look, Vanessa, there's no time for any of this. I've been trying to reach you to warn you not to say anything at all to the reporters.'

'You're too late,' Vanessa snapped. 'They're already outside and they've taken a photograph of me.'

'What? You let them take a picture?'

'Let them? I don't have secretaries and assistants to protect me like you and Charlie do. I'm here all on my own. What did you expect would happen? They're still outside,' she told him, wanting to prolong his anxiety as he seemed so worked up at the idea of her talking to journalists. 'If I asked them in for a cup of tea, do you think they'd tell me exactly what their story says?'

'Vanessa, don't you dare.' He could hardly get the words out.

Her voice was steely. 'Why not? You're not worried about bad publicity for me or for Amy or Louise. All you're thinking about is your new job and what the Prime Minister's going to think.'

This was so near the mark that Philip was speechless for a second. 'Vanessa, of course that comes into it but my main concern is for the welfare of the Forrester Group. How do you think it will look to the other directors and the staff and our competitors if they think there is such disharmony at the core of the company?'

He was right but she would not let him off the hook so easily. 'Philip, can't you understand how I was that night? Without any discussion, you decided to hand over control of our children's future to a stranger and put her on the board.

Do you think my grandfather would have wanted that? And what about Amy and Louise? They're both upset, particularly Amy. I think you're going to have trouble with her. Poor girl, she's had a terrible afternoon fending off the press on her own.'

Philip adopted a more placatory tone. 'Vanessa, I'm sorry about that but we did what we thought was best for all of us. I still think that and I hope you'll come to agree eventually.'

'Never,' she almost shouted. 'And if you think I'm just going to sit back and accept what you've done, you're quite wrong.'

Philip heard the familiar sound that regularly ended his conversations with Vanessa. *Bop*. The slamming down of the phone.

The Rectory was under siege and the women were nervous.

'It'll be awful if Lou-Lou has her picture taken too,' said Amy. 'Maybe she could stay the night with Mrs Prescott. Shall I ring and ask her, Mum?'

'Yes,' Vanessa agreed distractedly. 'Good idea.'

Then the phone calls started. Young reporters who had only heard of the Forresters since they had taken charge of the *Citizen* were pulling up library cuttings on their computers to try and build up a story based on the PA announcement.

After Amy had fielded two of the calls, saying that her mother was not available, they decided to take the phone off the hook. This only made them feel more vulnerable and isolated.

Vanessa gave Amy a fairly truncated version of the argument she had had with Charlie and then launched into a diatribe against her and Philip. 'How could your father have done this to us? He must have realised when he spoke to you what would happen, that you were going to be besieged. Poor baby, he knew you were here on your own. I'll never forgive him for this.' She began pacing up and down in agitation, repeating the, by now, familiar mantra.

'Why didn't he tell me before the announcement? He must have known about it. Why couldn't he warn me in advance? Outrageous. What's so important about today? It could have waited till tomorrow. What's one day? He only ever thinks about himself and That Woman. I bet she wrote the bloody statement and she'll make damn sure she'll come out of it smelling sweeter than roses.

'Of course we're not important in his life now he's a minister.' Vanessa was winding herself up. 'They'll tell everyone how clever That Woman's been. Next to her I suppose I'll look useless and lazy and stupid. But I'll show them.'

Although she felt sympathy for her mother, Amy had been silent throughout this outpouring. The control of her shares seemed further away than ever. Everything had happened so fast, she hadn't had a chance to talk her father out of his foolhardy plan.

She loved her father and her mother and hated being stuck in the middle of their war zone.

Charlie groaned when she saw the digital display on the answering machine. There had been twelve calls since the nanny had switched it on at Miranda's bathtime.

'Darling, it's your turn to play the messages back,' she called out to Philip. 'They're probably all for you anyway. I want to see Miranda.'

But the calls were for both of them, mainly from a series of journalists from the *Chronicle* – the City editor, the newsdesk and then later the night editor sounding harassed. All mentioned the PA statement issued by Forrester's press office but said they needed a comment urgently from one or both of them about the story they intended to run concerning the fight between Charlotte Lockhart and Philip's former wife.

'I don't think we should make any comment at all,' Charlie said. 'In my experience, whatever we say will be twisted, especially by that rag.'

Philip looked at his watch. It was nearly seven o'clock. 'Surely things haven't become so bad they'll print the story if none of us has confirmed it happened?'

'They have a reliable informant,' she answered. 'Somebody obviously was listening because enough of the details Walter mentioned are accurate. They don't need confirmation from us. Now, shall we try to forget about all that and eat?'

Philip's face fell when he saw supper. During the quiet moments of the day he had visualised a night which included not only imaginative, long-lasting sex but one in which a juicy fillet steak, chunky chips and a bottle of decent Burgundy featured quite prominently. The reality was poached sole, sweated spinach with unadorned boiled potatoes and a salad with plain lemon-juice dressing. It was like having erotic fantasies about Claudia Schiffer and ending up with Roseanne Barr.

But Charlie was strong-minded about his health. Dr Murray had been insistent about the need to bring down Philip's cholesterol level and reduce stress. Philip had laughed at that. 'I'm a Member of Parliament, I thrive on stress.'

'Then you're a heart attack waiting to happen unless you take all this extremely seriously,' the medical man warned him.

Since then Charlie had watched her husband's diet assiduously and, though tonight's supper looked unlovely to him, Philip had to acknowledge it was a work of devotion, prepared with her own hands and exactly conforming to his doctor's dietary commands.

Charlie recognised his expression. 'Do you want to live to be a dirty old man or not? This is all on Doctor Murray's recipe list.'

'So if cholesterol doesn't get me, boredom will,' he retorted.

'Never mind.' She smiled lasciviously. 'Dessert is calorie-free.'

Outsiders often envied the glamorous lifestyle of the Lockharts, the flurries of embossed thick white card party invitations, Charlie's business trips to New York and the camaraderie Philip enjoyed with the great and good late at night in the Pugin Room at the House of Commons. They would have been less envious if they had appreciated how much the couple, particularly Charlie, coveted a simpler, quieter life.

They were living in two time zones. Charlie's job put her on transatlantic hours. This had advantages, in that she could occasionally spend the morning with Miranda before New York awoke, and then dash back in the late afternoon to put the baby to bed when New York was at lunch. This coincided with what Philip told the newspapers was 'golden time', the hour he had designated in his diary, before the seven o'clock vote, for Miranda. He had long since worked out that he would rather play with his daughter than attend another boring cocktail party. Having missed so much of his first family's childhood, he was quoted as saying, he would not make the same mistake again.

When Philip gave these interviews it did not occur to him that Amy and Louise would be deeply slighted when they read how he raved about the pleasures of fatherhood now.

Because Charlie returned to the office at seven for the New York afternoons and Philip went back to the House for the ten o'clock vote, weekday evenings alone were valued and rare.

As they finished supper, Philip returned to the subject of the row, wanting to hear every cough and splutter.

'But the physical stuff isn't true, is it? You didn't hit her?' he asked.

'I would have loved to, believe me,' Charlie answered then stopped. 'You know what we're doing, don't you? She's taking over this evening as she does all the time. We don't refer to her directly but we always end up dissecting, discussing, analysing or worrying about that woman. For God's sake can't we talk about something else?'

He gave her a wolfish grin. 'Talk?'

They started on the sofa to communicate in the oldest way since Adam and Eve when Walter Threadgold's anxious voice rumbled through the microphone of the answer machine. But by then they were far too engrossed in each other to stop and listen.

However often they made love, they never lost that sensation of sheer animal longing. It was exciting to want to make love so urgently they could not wait to take off their clothes.

Philip knelt on the carpet and bent over her while she stretched out in unselfconscious abandonment. His delight at the sight of her body had not diminished since they first met. There was no awkwardness, no inhibition, each knowing instinctively how to please the other with hands, lips and tongue. As he penetrated deeper and deeper inside her, their hips moved in a sexual choreography that was effortless. She began a slow murmuring which became louder as his movements grew more urgent.

Philip tried to think about the details of the Transport Bill in an effort to delay his climax. No use. As his body was overwhelmed by a surging wave he felt Charlie begin to shudder beneath him then, after a few seconds, slowly relax.

He rolled away gently, grateful that this intimate closeness smoothed over so many of the pressures in their lives, including today's.

Charlie kissed him softly on the mouth and traced a finger over his damp shoulder. 'Thank God Walter doesn't have a video telephone.'

'I don't know, I thought that was one of our better performances, worthy of a wider audience,' he teased. 'He might have learned something.' Walter was a widower and they had often conjectured about his sex life.

Gathering up her panties, stockings and skirt which were scattered all over the room, Charlie went into the hallway, wound back the tape and turned up the volume.

Philip stretched out languorously, a contented smile on his face which fast disappeared when he heard Walter's voice, giving an account of his conversation with the *Chronicle* City editor.

'I've left messages for you everywhere. I hope you pick this up. Unfortunately this story's going to be bigger than we thought. My contact's been told it's gone off her pages on to news. Looks like they're going to print a highly personalised account.'

Philip paced the room. 'If I get my hands on a first edition, maybe I could persuade Fergus to pull the story. I'll get our news editor to fax it here.'

'That means everybody on the *Citizen* will know we're worried. Not a good idea,' countered Charlie.

'OK, I'll go and buy one in Piccadilly.'

'You'll have to get a taxi. I told Helen she could use the car.' Charlie listened to the rain bouncing hard on the pavement and was glad she did not have to brave the weather.

She settled herself comfortably on the sofa. But when Philip reappeared in his coat, it occurred to her how unwise it would be for him to go out. Since he had become a Cabinet minister there had been photographs and profiles about him in the weekend press and on television and he was quickly becoming a well-known face. If someone spotted him prowling around Piccadilly waiting for the first edition, it would only add another dimension to the story.

Charlie sighed heavily and swung her bare legs back on to the floor. 'I'll have to go. All we need is for someone to see you. Nobody will notice me.'

'I suppose you're right though I hate letting you go out on a night like this by yourself. I'd better alert the Chief Whip to all of this. He's going to be thrilled.'

Once Charlie was out with the sleaze-by-nights who occupied Piccadilly Circus on a dank December evening she suddenly felt defenceless. Although she was surrounded by what were in the main non-threatening cinema and restaurant goers there was an aspect to the pre-Christmas crowds that reminded her of the bar scene in *Star Wars*, full of loudly laughing, eating and drinking animals. It had been years since she had felt so vulnerable.

Charlie had felt fear covering the mean streets of Detroit, with its armed drug runners, but she had coped. Likewise when she had to fly to Haiti as replacement for a sick colleague and when, on her return to Britain, she had covered the trouble spots of the Falls Road, Belfast. Here, on a well-lit, bustling corner of Piccadilly, waiting for the first edition of a newspaper which would say heaven knew what about her and Philip, she had the same feeling of apprehension as in those situations. She, more than most, understood what damage newspapers could do to a fledgling ministerial career.

Charlie was roused from her reverie by the squeal of brakes as a van hurtled round the corner and a man got out with a bundle of newspapers. While she waited for the first package to be untied, Charlie raged at the unfairness of it all. She was convinced she had done nothing wrong. She had asked for no shares. She did not want confrontation or publicity. Vanessa's self-indulgent emotions were, as usual, causing her and Philip more pain, embarrassment and disruption.

In other countries a dispute between two wives of a Cabinet minister over money might be ignored because of privacy laws, but in Britain it was big news. Politics, power and sex. A sensational mixture for the nation's tabloids, more especially for a paper with its own agenda for trying to bring down the government.

Charlie was first in line to buy a copy of the *Daily Chronicle*. On its front page was a glamorous picture of her and Philip taken at the recent Royal Society of Television Awards dinner. Alongside it was today's snatched picture of a startled-looking Vanessa.

Across the top the headline blared: 'First Wife Versus Second In Fight For Minister's Shares'. Inside the paper, two more pages were dedicated to the story. Across the centre spread the headline 'Battle of the Boardroom Beauties' screamed out at her.

Sheltering under a cinema canopy, Charlie read about herself in the usual terms employed by newspapers to portray successful women. The words 'ambitious', 'ruthless', 'determined' and 'tough' jumped out at her. Applied to men, the words were complimentary. But here, ascribed to her, they were definitely pejorative. How newspapers hated women who had done well. There was a lurid account of how she had apparently enticed Philip away from his happy home. The words 'temptress', 'love nest' and 'affair' insidiously peppered the paragraphs which were just this side of actionable libel. They did not use the word 'gold digger' in relation to the Forrester shares but the inference was there.

The powder room argument which the *Chronicle* labelled a 'cat fight' was described as if it was a world heavyweight title bout minus Queensberry rules. Her relationship with Vanessa was described as Round One, Round Two, Round Three and so on. The result was portrayed by the paper as a 'knockout win for Charlie' as she had, according to them, now snatched the shares of both of Vanessa's children.

Forrester's official statement was relegated to the bottom of the page and was given far less prominence than the come-on to readers which offered a financial reward for their own personal stories of first versus second wives.

The newspaper was equally insulting about Philip, accusing the new Secretary of State of being unable to keep 'his' wives in order and implying that if he could not control his women, how much less likely was he to be able to manage the nation's affairs.

Numb with cold, wet and miserable, it took Charlie twenty minutes to walk down the Haymarket, into the Mall past Buckingham Palace and into Birdcage Walk where she found a lonely taxi. She thought wrily what a contrast there was between her bedraggled, forlorn figure and the conquering cow described in the *Chronicle*. She was irritated that they had described Vanessa as someone akin to Mother Teresa, and, to add to her chagrin, the *Chronicle* had found pictures of her protagonist in which she looked like a young Grace Kelly. There was even one of her dancing cheek to cheek with Prince Charles, for God's sake.

As the taxi turned into their road, Charlie shuddered at the thought of the millions who would read this highly-coloured version of their lives over the breakfast table the next morning.

This time the poison from Vanessa was spreading far beyond their own family pond.

Chapter Twelve

For dozens of talk radio stations right across Britain, the front page of Wednesday's *Daily Chronicle* set the agenda for the day. The airwaves were full of indignant listeners, many purporting to be deeply offended, having enjoyed every word of the story.

This augmented the *Chronicle*'s readership which had already been bolstered by the kind of people in Vanessa's village who dismissed it as a paper they only glanced at 'when the nanny buys it.' The other newspapers steered clear of the personal muckraking. Mindful of the huge payouts awarded against the press in libel cases, they were careful of lifting this kind of story from a rival after the first edition. For them the Forrester story was mainly confined to the financial pages, except that one bright features editor had thrown out a lacklustre page and overnight inserted an article titled 'Bosses' wives in the boardroom', and another journal had done 'Nepotism in business'.

The American Broadcasting Network office was inundated with phone calls from TV, radio and press desperate for an interview with Charlie. The yellow post-its bearing names and numbers of callers mushroomed on her desk. The switchboard and the commissionaires had already complained to management before she arrived about having to deal with doorstepping reporters. Even long-suffering colleagues who were used to the methods of the press were irritated by the ceaseless intrusions to the business of the day.

At Number 10 the Prime Minister raised the subject with the Chief Whip towards the end of their breakfast session.

'How bad is this Lockhart story for us?' he asked.

'It's personal so the press love it,' was the reply, 'but I don't anticipate much follow-up or damage to the party.'

'I haven't met Philip's wife often.' The PM paused. 'Get them over for drinks early in the new session. See the press know about it.'

The Chief Whip deduced from this that the PM accepted that the political fallout would be negligible and the talk quickly turned to their mutual passion, the performance of England's rugby squad.

Walter Threadgold's reaction was a lot less sanguine. His most immediate concern was Vanessa. How would she respond?

As a Forrester employee of thirty years' standing, Walter had trodden a delicate path through the difficult months of the separation then the divorce of Philip and Vanessa. The second Mrs Lockhart was certainly a very different personality from the first. Charlie was always perfectly affable towards him but she had the confidence of a professional career woman which Walter found disconcerting; it was not something he had experienced at his level of management. He was more at ease discussing his garden and his dogs with a woman than the firm's profit and loss account.

Philip had assured him that Charlie's representing him on the board was a short-term arrangement, just until the next election. Walter's view, firmly expressed to Philip, was that it could only lead to trouble. It was the most he could say. Too proud to ask directly, he could not understand why Philip had not asked *him* to look after the shares.

He was not looking forward to the first board meeting. Nor, presumably, was Vanessa. Would she even attend, given the exaggerated rubbish in today's *Chronicle*?

Nervously he dialled her number.

'Oh Walter, you're the fifth person who's called this morning. Isn't it ghastly? And to resurrect all that stuff from the past, it can't do us any good, can it?'

'We must hope for the best,' he answered carefully.

'I'm dreading having to take Louise to her horse-riding lesson this afternoon,' she continued. 'You know what gossips they are around here.'

'Look, don't worry about it. It'll be a two-day wonder.' Privately he understood the reason for her loss of temper with Charlie but it was essential now to make it easier for her to face her rival at the board meetings, a rival who had so much power.

'Vanessa, board meetings are not going to be easy for you but we all have to work together for the good of the company. The important aspect of all this is the future of the Forrester Group.'

'That's easier said than done, Walter. You don't know how hard it is for me.'

'I do, my dear, I do. But don't you think that your grandfather would have wanted you to put the group before self?'

There was a pause.

'That's the only thing that would get me into the same room as That Woman.'

There was one more repercussion to the story. One of the millions who read the boardroom beauties disclosures was a penurious staff nurse in Edinburgh.

Like every British citizen aged over eighteen, she was well aware that some newspapers paid good money for bad stories. It had been a gloomy morning sifting through the bills which arrived with depressing regularity. The paper might pay her well for her information. She cut out the section that gave the contact numbers. She would phone the minute she came off duty.

She was nervous as she dialled the *Chronicle* that afternoon. Hesitantly she told the reporter who took her call, 'I know something about one of the Lockhart women that she's been keeping a secret.'

The reporter, who'd been sifting through a mountain of dross, recognised gold when he heard it. His was the sympathetic voice manning the line because, over the years, newspapers hunting for tip-offs were aware that careful handling was extremely important.

'Secret, eh? Yes, we're always interested in secrets. What's yours?'

'Not so fast. What are you prepared to pay?'

'Oh, we're very generous. It all depends what it is,' came the reply. 'I'll need a few details to whet my editor's appetite.'

'I'm not talking about it on the phone. I want the money in my hand first. But believe me, I'm sure your editor will be interested in what I have to tell him.'

An hour later the *Chronicle*'s man in Edinburgh was ordered to check out the nurse's tale.

Sixteen hard hats hung on pegs in a row. Below them was a plethora of poles and wooden trestle supports looking like giant tapers which had been dropped haphazardly. The walls were draped with bright green bunting and tinsel, and some wit had sprayed 'Happy Christmas To All Our Nags' in red across a bale of hay. Dorinda Cazalet was on her second glass of the weak mixture inaptly named pony punch served each year by the riding school mistress at the village Christmas gymkhana. She was bored. She had been here half an hour and although it was crowded, the large barn was cold. The eight- and ten-year-olds still had to show their paces. Her daughter, at twelve, was classed as a senior so there were still hours to go before watching her little darling on the Thelwell pony that appeared to eat five pound notes instead of oats.

Like many of the other parents, Dorinda had shown up to praise her daughter and see what justified the school's charge of fifteen pounds an hour. The riding school owner, mingling with her guests, had the satisfied expression of someone who was mentally counting up the money to be made from all those little bottoms on rotund ponies.

Vanessa hove into sight. Thank God, thought Dorinda. 'Ah, here's the tabloid star,' she greeted her friend. 'What's it like to be famous, darling?'

Vanessa made a face.

'They were wonderful pictures. You looked great in the arms of HRH.'

'Oh, Dorrie, I'm so miserable. It's awful.'

'Don't be daft, it'll be forgotten over Christmas.'

'The paper makes us sound like mad women. But it's not only that. I'm really terrified. Remember the interview I gave to Imogen Ferris? Now we're in the news she might do something about it, and I've a horrible feeling I let something slip.'

'What?'

'Let's get a drink. This is hardly the place but I must tell somebody otherwise I'll go off my head.'

Dorinda was delighted. There was nothing she liked better than secrets. 'OK, the girls are not on until after the juniors so let's go in that quiet little corner over there.'

Vanessa clasped and unclasped her fingers. 'I have to tell you something you don't know about me.' Dorinda leaned forward expectantly. 'That year when I left school so suddenly, in the summer . . . it was because I was pregnant.'

Dorinda gave a sharp intake of breath then tried her best to recover her equilibrium and not to overreact, fearing it would inhibit her friend. She touched Vanessa lightly on the shoulder. 'Oh Vee,' she said compassionately. 'Why did you never tell me? I would have helped you.'

'My mother made me swear I'd never tell anyone. So I didn't.' Vanessa could hear her mother's words as if it was yesterday: 'You will tell nobody. Nobody. Do you hear? Especially *him*.' She still remembered her mother's face contorted with hatred. 'I'd like to kill him.'

'But your mother's been dead for years,' countered Dorinda.

'Yes, but what was the point of telling you now? A few hours after I gave birth the baby was whisked away from me

128

and legally adopted. I was fifteen at the time and I've never seen him since.'

'Who's the father?'

'Who do you think? My mother was furious, of course, especially since she was terrified we'd marry as soon as I was sixteen. She always thought he was beneath me.'

'She would. It's just as well she's dead – your wedding would have killed her.'

Vanessa looked into the distance. 'We only did it twice, you know, Dorrie.'

'What bloody bad luck.'

'I know. I tried to ignore the whole thing which was easy because I didn't put on any weight in the beginning. By the time my mother found out, it was far too late for an abortion.' Vanessa's eyes clouded over. 'I still feel guilty about giving my son up so easily but my mother could always overwhelm me.'

She recounted to her friend how Mrs Forrester had made all the arrangements, booked the clinic in Edinburgh, contacted the private adoption agency and told Elliot that his granddaughter was being sent off to a school in Scotland to improve her marks.

When Vanessa reappeared months later, pale, thinner and withdrawn, her grandfather assumed the experiment had not been a success. She never returned to any scholastic training, all her old boyfriends seemed to have disappeared from her life. If Elliot noticed, he did not make any comment.

'Do you have any idea where the child is now?' Dorinda asked.

Vanessa shook her head emphatically. 'When you sign adoption papers, you sign away all your rights. After my mother died I did put my name down on the adoption register but I've heard nothing.' She gave a curious half-smile. 'I'd love to be able to talk to him, get to know him but that's not possible. It's something I've had to live with and, to be honest, I try not to think about him too often. And that's why I'm worried about that damn journalist. It was the boy's birthday the same day as the interview. I was depressed and I think I might have given the game away.'

'What did you say?'

'Oh, that the twentieth of December had special memories, that I always felt sad on that particular day, and later when she commented on some photograph or other, I told her I hadn't smiled for the whole of that year. If she puts two and two together . . .'

'She's quite sharp, that one,' Dorinda agreed.

'I know. I'm terrified it'll all come out. Think of the girls. And Philip.' Vanessa shuddered. 'Think what the papers would do with that. It'd make the thing with Charlie look like a tea party.'

'What do you want me to do? I'll help any way I can.'

'I'm not sure but you're a consulting social editor on that magazine, aren't you.'

'Leave it to me. I'm in an excellent position to read her story and find out what the bitch is up to.'

'What we need is a good war to break out,' Tony Burns told his news editor, only half-jokingly. 'Preferably before five o'clock.' Like many journalists he closed his mind to the human misery involved in such an event and only visualised the banner headlines which would attract more people to buy the paper.

He yawned as a head came round the door. 'Got a minute, boss?'

Tony beckoned to Kevin Jamieson, his frenetic chief reporter, limbs always moving, brain always scanning for stories, someone who never wasted his time.

'The Edinburgh correspondent's been to see that nurse, the one who phoned about Vanessa Lockhart.'

'What'd he get?'

'The nurse says the Lockhart woman had a baby at fifteen. She was working in the hospital and she says she recognised Vanessa from our pictures. She swears it's the same girl. She was with her for nearly a week.'

'Boy or girl?'

'Boy, she says.'

'What happened to the kid?'

'Adopted a few days after he was born. The nurse doesn't know where he is but she has someone she reckons can put us on the right track. She wants real money for this, boss.'

'What's she mean by "real money"?'

'I tried her on a couple of hundred but she just laughed. She hasn't said yet where and when the baby was born. We'll have to offer her more.'

If the nurse's story made the splash, Tony might have to pay thousands. A splash had no price tag. The money was not proportionate to how good the story was. Much depended on what else the newspaper had at the time, what they thought their rivals had, what season it was and whether the chairman had a bee in his bonnet about the same subject.

It was not an exact science. Every tipster thought their story should be big. But if the story was overtaken by a bigger one, it would be down-graded. In which case the final payout might be far less than the first one proffered. Newspaper lawyers were adept at let-out clauses in contracts.

Tony was not as impressed with the information as his chief reporter. Who cared about an illegitimate baby these days? Remembering the picture of Vanessa dancing with the heir to the throne, Tony joked, 'I'd only be interested if the father was the Prince of Wales.'

Kevin laughed. 'I'll ask him next time he pops into my pub. Come on, boss, it could be a great follow-up to the cat fight story and if the father's somebody interesting, all the better.'

Tony disagreed. 'She's only the ex-wife of a minister, for Christ's sake. Who gives a stuff?'

Kevin did not persist. When Tony said no, it stayed no.

Chapter Thirteen

Vanessa's secret fear had always been that once her daughters were old enough to choose, they would elect to live in the more exciting, glamorous London whirl with their father. So, in her wish to remain the centre of their world, she left no seasonal stone unturned.

By lunchtime on 24 December Amy and Louise had already been fully Christmassed. Stockings crammed with amusing little tokens plus the obligatory tangerine had been at the end of their beds that morning and they had each been encouraged to invite two friends for a special Christmas Eve lunch.

The meal, turkey with all the trimmings, had stretched on for a couple of hours with the obligatory crackers, pudding containing silver sixpences, and mince pies. The teenage guests agreed it had never been such fun.

A few minutes before the two girls had to depart for London, Vanessa produced two longed-for presents, a mountain bike for Louise and a coveted music centre for Amy. The girls had a tantalising few minutes salivating over these before they had to leave to visit their father. Stashed in the boot of the minicab were two more beautifully-wrapped gifts which, Vanessa ordered, were to be put under the tree and not to be opened till Christmas morning.

The long, emotional goodbyes with their mother ensured that the girls arrived too late to enjoy a bath and bedtime play with Miranda who was already fast asleep. The lavish Christmas Eve supper Charlie had prepared made them feel uncomfortable. Neither had any appetite after their huge Christmas lunch. Amy immediately excused herself and went to her room but Louise, trying to please, joined Philip and Charlie who was, as so often, feeling exhausted, at the table. Louise spent the rest of the evening feeling nauseous and had to go to bed early. She was up twice during the night to be sick, with Philip in anxious attendance.

The omens for a happy holiday were not good.

Christmas Day at 16 Chelsea Mansions started early and badly. Amy, used to sleeping till noon during the holiday, was roused by her half-sister next door crying at 6 a.m. for her breakfast. She tried to turn over, putting her head under her pillow. But a combination of anxiety about how she would tackle her father over her shares, an unfamiliar bed and the loud cooing from Miranda's room as her parents helped the little girl open her baby stocking made further sleep impossible.

Amy lay there feeling sorry for herself. Next year it could be worse. There might be another cot and another baby. Only last night Charlie had lamented that she was an only child, a fate she did not want to befall Miranda. Amy gave an involuntary grimace, recoiling from the thought of her father engaged in sexual activity. She loved Miranda, but wasn't he too old to produce more children?

The present-swapping was at best embarrassing. The girls

had not wanted to shop in Brighton for a gift for their stepmother and the quick dash to a supermarket on the way to London had produced indifferent bath salts and a box of cheap chocolates. Charlie did her best but her thank you sounded as false as Philip's repetition of 'Here we are, all together, isn't this wonderful, isn't it great?'

Their father's present of a thick volume of love poems to his wife made Louise giggle and Amy blush. The expensive gifts chosen for them by Charlie were completely eclipsed by those from their mother who knew well what both girls had been hoping for. Charlie could see that Amy hated the belt. The girl's half-hearted protestations when Charlie offered to exchange it flustered both of them.

Things did not improve. The girls were as tactful as they could be but Philip and Charlie still became aware that this Christmas turkey and pudding with its silver sixpences was the second such festive meal the girls had eaten in two days.

Later, simple tasks like unloading the dishwasher confirmed that this was a family of strangers. The girls were inhibited by having to ask where each dish was kept and they understood little of Charlie's habits or routines. She watched horrified as Louise swept into the bin all the surplus vegetables she had planned to use for soup on Boxing night. She could not suppress the thought that if this was how their mother lived it was no wonder she was always pleading poverty.

Matters did not improve when Miranda broke the horoscope mug Louise had carefully chosen for her father and paid for with her pocket money.

Everything conspired against them. Walks to relieve the tension were out of the question. It did not stop raining the entire visit. They were all invited to a neighbour's drinks party, a boring couple but they did live in the same block, and Philip agreed to go because they were promised a bevy of young people, none of whom materialised. Amy and Louise asked to be excused after twenty minutes. But it was another hour before Charlie and Philip were able to leave.

By the end of the evening, face aching from contrived gaiety, Charlie would have given a great deal to climb into the cot with Miranda. But when she saw Amy making the baby a pom-pom ball while Louise sang her a bedtime lullaby, she felt a small spark of optimism. Eventually, maybe, this would all work out.

Unexpectedly, Vanessa enjoyed her Christmas. No organising, no washing up and the Cazalets were excellent hosts.

At their lunchtime drinks party on Boxing Day, Dorinda cheered her with the news that she had been able to read the Imogen Ferris interview before publication. 'There's nothing remotely incriminating in it,' she assured Vanessa. 'Nothing nasty at all. I don't think you should worry about her. Now, enjoy yourself tonight. Let me introduce you to some people.'

It was day ten of Vanessa's new eating plan and she had managed to lose five whole pounds. She was wearing a red crepe two-piece which had not been out of its cleaning bag for a couple of years. The outfit seemed to be attracting the right attention though she was still nervous of being alone with anyone on the prowl.

'I hope you're not here with anyone.'

The man Dorinda had introduced her to leaned so close she could feel the outline of his jacket buttons against her nipples.

Vanessa shook her head, smiling politely.

'Good, because I have plans.'

She waited. This was unfamiliar territory and she did not know how to respond.

'You know what they say about voluptuous women like you, don't you?'

He was attractive, she could not deny it, and he seemed more sure of himself than the furtive local married men she usually encountered at parties. His Jermyn Street striped shirt moved closer as his beautifully modulated voice whispered, 'The bigger they are, the louder they shout.'

Vanessa was stunned. My God, she thought, do I seem that desperate for it?

He gave her a roguish wink, clearly thinking his crude approach had been successful. She pulled herself up to her full height and staring up at him retorted, 'I don't appreciate that kind of bar-room talk.'

He seemed unfazed. 'That's OK,' he said. 'I've done it in bars before now.'

'No, I'm sorry, I don't think so, thank you,' and she slid from under his arm which rested against the wall.

Damn it, she could not believe it, she had even said sorry. And why on earth had she thanked him? She felt his eyes on her retreating body as she moved across the room.

Dorinda was amused at her scandalised account of the attempted pick-up. 'That hearts and flowers stuff went out a long time ago, Vee. Welcome to the real world. You'll have to get used to the more direct approach.'

'I can't believe he's successful with women.'

'More than you'd think.'

'But he has no subtlety, in fact he's downright crude.'

Vanessa gazed across the room and sighed. 'Maybe I'm not ready for the real world.'

Although it was possibly the fortieth television showing of *Brief Encounter*, it was new to Amy and Louise and they were soon engrossed. Philip checked that Miranda was still fast asleep and then helped Charlie on with her coat.

A top executive from Charlie's New York office had arrived unexpectedly in London and suggested she and Philip join him for a drink at the Savoy. The girls had eagerly offered to babysit and Philip suspected they liked the idea of being in the flat on their own. He was amused that as he kissed Louise goodbye, she did not take her eyes off the screen as Trevor Howard took the speck of grit from Celia Johnson's eye. As they left he said loudly to Charlie, 'By the time they notice we've gone, we'll be back.'

The film had ended when Miranda, in the unpredictable way of toddlers, woke up unexpectedly and made it clear that she missed her parents. In spite of all attempts to divert her, she would not be comforted and screamed louder and louder. This made Louise decide the baby must be ill and she, too, became upset. Amy could not cope with both of them and became panicky. She tried to contact Charlie on the mobile but for some reason the number was unobtainable. In desperation she phoned her mother.

Vanessa had just got back from the Cazalets' party. All she could hear on the phone was the baby's howls and when, a few minutes later, Philip and Charlie walked through the door, she asked Amy to pass the receiver over to her ex-husband.

'How could you do that?' Philip could hear the strain in

Vanessa's voice. 'Leave all the children. And at Christmas time. After all the fuss you made to have them, you don't really care about them, it's just for your public image.'

Philip fought to keep his rage under control. 'Vanessa, why do you constantly put the worst connotation on everything? The girls were perfectly happy to be left in charge.'

'That's not true. Amy was quite scared. The poor kid doesn't know the first thing about babies and Miranda sounded hysterical. God knows what would have happened if you hadn't come back just then.'

Philip did his best to calm her down. When she asked to speak to Amy again, he handed the phone to his daughter and went to join Charlie who was in the kitchen with Miranda. The little girl was now happily eating a slice of tangerine.

The phone call had infuriated Charlie and started a row between her and Philip. She was particularly upset that in his efforts to calm Vanessa he had apologised for going out. She kept her voice low but her anger was obvious.

'Where those girls are concerned, you never back me up, you always take their part. When are you going to put Miranda and me first? When is it our turn? I'm exhausted and fed up with trying to please everyone.'

Her voice was cracking and Philip tried to take her in his arms. On the rare occasions she lost her temper she usually calmed down after a few moments but this time she was not to be placated.

He rubbed his hand across his forehead and felt an unexpected wave of resentment at the unfairness of it all. He was tired of feeling guilty – guilty about breaking up his first marriage, about leaving his two daughters, about not being around Miranda as often as he would have liked.

And then there was Charlie. Often there was too little time to make love in the leisurely way that they used to. Sometimes he would wonder if all marriages were the same. Did the excitement dribble out as the years ticked by? In the old days they would massage each other with aromatic oils and take long candlelit baths together. But he could not remember when they had last done that.

'Charlie, it's always your turn. I spend hours worrying about the effect my first family is having on you and Miranda. I wish you'd worry about the effect you are having on the girls rather than attacking me.'

Charlie turned away with the intractable expression that he knew from experience meant she was best left alone.

Philip sighed and went to see what his daughters were doing. There was silence as he opened the door to the television room. Amy was on the sofa, her arm round a quietly-weeping Louise.

'What's the matter, darling?' he asked, sinking to his knees and taking Louise's hand.

'She wants to go home. Now.'

'What? Why?'

'She doesn't want to stay here another night.'

'Louise, is that true, darling? What's happened?'

'Nothing. I miss Mummy. I want to go home.'

He turned to Amy. 'What's brought this on?'

She stared at him truculently. 'You know exactly what's brought it on. You two. You don't want us here, really. You couldn't wait to go and drink with people you didn't even know and only because Charlie wanted you to.'

'Hang on a minute, young lady. If you remember, you

both said you didn't mind because you wanted to watch that movie.'

'Only because we knew you wanted to go. Anyway, what else was there to do here?'

'We were bored,' said Louise tearfully.

'Bored?'

'None of our friends are here. And you can't go riding here. And I've got a mountain bike at home and I haven't had a go on it yet.'

Philip was incensed by her ingratitude but tried hard not to show it. He did not succeed and Louise abruptly left the room.

'I thought you were both enjoying yourselves here, Amy,' Philip said helplessly.

'Not particularly,' she replied tersely. 'Why must you always treat me like a child?'

'Darling, I don't mean to,' replied her father.

'If you ever bothered to come and see me in Cambridge, you'd know that I run my life very well.'

Philip realised with a pang that each time he planned to go, something cropped up that seemed to take priority. The one time he had managed it, his visit was sandwiched between two functions in the surrounding area. He and Amy had only had time for a snatched cup of coffee.

'You're quite right,' he said ruefully. 'You're a big girl now and I must start appreciating that.'

'Why don't you start with the shares?'

Philip was taken aback. This was the last thing on his mind. 'But darling, you can't do anything with your shares. Your grandfather said that in his will. Not until you're twenty-five.'

'Well, Grandfather died when I was little. He didn't know me.'

'Don't you think I'm looking out for your best interests?'

'But it's not you who is going to look after them, is it? I don't want Charlie to do it. I'd rather it was Mum or you.'

'Things are too complicated, darling. Lots of things are happening in the business that none of us understands, let alone your mother.'

'So how come Charlie understands?'

'Charlie has me to help her.' The moment the words left his mouth he regretted them.

Amy reared back as if she had been slapped and dashed out of the room.

For a terrible moment he waited to hear if she was going to walk out of the front door. When he heard her join Louise in her room, his shoulders sagged in relief.

He would have to make an effort with his older children and try to integrate them more with Charlie. Amy would not be so hostile to Charlie's guardianship of the shares if she knew her stepmother better. He accepted that Charlie could not be expected to love his daughters in the way he did. But as the girls grew older, surely things would improve.

There was only one thing for him to do now. He crossed to the drinks cabinet and poured himself an indecently large whisky.

Chapter Fourteen

Painfully Vanessa had to accept that she could do nothing to prevent Philip transferring his own shares to Charlie's control. But the trusteeship of the children's was a different matter. Elliot's will had been drawn up when there was no thought of divorce. Surely there would be a question mark over the suggestion that their birthright be handed over to this woman, against the wishes of Elliot's great-granddaughters? Amy was now a young adult and quite capable of making her own choices.

For a while, during her initial fury, Vanessa toyed with the idea of taking legal action, but she was reluctant to put the family or herself through such an ordeal. But Philip had acted in a most autocratic way. Loyalty, she believed, was still an important ingredient in the running of the Forrester business. Her only weapon now was to make allies of the board members and shame Philip into giving her control of the children's shares. Would this strategy work?

Vanessa conceded that if they saw the same woman before them they might not take her seriously. She had to show them she had changed, outwardly as well as inwardly.

This was the catalyst Vanessa needed to go on a programme of self-improvement. She needed to prove to the board that she was as well-informed as Charlie and worth listening to. She began reading board documents more assiduously. As she entered the dates of the year's board meetings in her diary, Vanessa glanced through the list of recipients. There was Charlie, Mrs P. Lockhart, and lower down the list, in alphabetical order, Mrs V. Lockhart. It was too hard.

Copies of the Forrester papers as well as their news magazine were now perused scrupulously. More importantly, so were the balance sheets.

Vanessa was doing something about her brain. It was time to do something about her body. Dressed in an old track suit that had belonged to Philip, Vanessa went for long daily walks. Never one to do anything by half, she had also signed up for step exercise classes in the village hall and kept rigorously to her low-fat diet.

She was determined there would be a different-looking Vanessa Lockhart at the next Forrester board meeting in four weeks' time.

Walter Threadgold was tanned and relaxed from two weeks ski-ing in Meribel and two weeks golfing in the Caribbean. He believed he looked all the fresher because he had been accompanied by a different woman in each place.

On a blindingly sunny tee at the eighteenth hole at the Royal Westmorland in Barbados, he decided his year was not going to be marred by the two Mrs Lockharts. He was not going to let this boardroom battle slide into a mess. They both had to be told to behave.

He had the share prices faxed daily to him. The fighting beauties stuff had done the company no good whatsoever. Charlie and Vanessa had to understand that people's mortgages and salaries were at stake. And it was his responsibility to point this out.

So it was with agreeable surprise that he greeted the news that both women would comply with his request to meet him privately half an hour before the first board meeting of the year. Philip had confided in him that as this would be the first time the two women had met since their row, Charlie was nervous about it.

She was the first to arrive but Walter did not detect any sign of tension. She looked wonderful yet businesslike. Neat and sexy. A vision in a pale grey suit, tights, shoes and handbag; even the rolled chrome watch matched perfectly.

As they waited for Vanessa, she opened a hand-tooled briefcase containing a thick file. 'Philip's given me a thorough briefing and we've worked out a strategy which I've put on slides. I understand there's a projector in the boardroom. I hope you'll give it the thumbs-up, Walter.'

He smiled, impressed by her composure. She looked as if she'd had a place at the top table all her life. He hoped Vanessa wouldn't feel intimidated.

A moment later he revised his thoughts as she entered. If Charlie had taken trouble with her appearance, so had Vanessa. She showed no signs of having failed to persuade colleagues to block Charlie's appointment to the board and she gave him such a dazzling smile that he felt she did not suspect how busy he had been pre-empting her efforts – it had been no problem for Walter to point out to City analysts

145

what a great asset Charlie's media knowledge would be to the board.

He stared at the first Mrs Lockhart. Vanessa was noticeably slimmer than at the last board meeting, her hair was different, bouncier somehow, and she had done something terrific to her eyes. Had she always had lashes that long? He had long admired her bosom and now that her waist had returned, the curves were far more pronounced.

Vanessa had opted for a close-fitting military-style suit in scarlet. She looked sensational. When she put her handbag firmly on the table and gave a general 'Good morning', she had the air of a woman who was going to take no prisoners.

Charlie drummed her manicured nails on her chair and responded softly to Vanessa's greeting. For the first time Walter saw what Philip had meant about Charlie being ill at ease.

He wasted no words on pleasantries and was abrupt to the point of rudeness. 'I don't know the truth of how this silly story came out in the press—'

Both women started to talk at once but he silenced them with a gesture. 'Ladies, please, let me finish. That little squabble of yours wiped nearly a million off the stock market value. Not particularly clever.'

They both tried giving their point of view. Again he stopped them.

'I trust all our board members to be utterly discreet but if there is any hint that we are still divided, it is bound to get out and could do even more damage. I propose we keep our private quarrels just that – private. May I also suggest we keep board discussions as businesslike as possible and allow nothing of a personal nature to intrude?'

They looked at him stony-faced then both nodded curtly.

With little confidence that his words had made any lasting impact, he took Vanessa's arm and ushered her into the Forrester boardroom. Charlie, as was the custom, had to wait outside until formally elected to the board.

Walter's appointment as the company's acting chief executive was waved through on the nod. Before taking the vote on the new board member, Walter reminded them that it would look much better in the minutes if the decision was unanimous.

There was only one abstention. By Vanessa. And from that moment the meeting went downhill for her.

Charlie was called into the room and seated herself in the only remaining empty chair, down table. But her triumph began when they reached the fourth item of the agenda. Until then she had behaved as a model first-time director, attentive but silent.

After the others had had their say on the future profitability of the group's local papers, Charlie asked for their indulgence. Despite being the new girl, she smiled charmingly, she thought it might be helpful to discuss her knowledge of the latest developments at local papers in America before the group made any decisions about research. She then asked permission to show them slides and data she had collated from the States.

Walter noticed Vanessa's discomfiture as Charlie pressed all the right buttons on the console to dim the lights, draw the curtains and lower the screen from the ceiling. It was obvious to them all that Charlie had been given a lesson from an expert on how the boardroom worked. No clues for guessing from whom.

Charlie proceeded to demonstrate how in the Boston area with which she was familiar, having studied at Harvard, local papers over the past six months had changed, softened, and deliberately become more women-friendly. As a consequence both their circulation and their advertising had increased.

'We all know that the future profitability of the *Citizen* and two of our local papers is some way off. Only this morning we've agreed on budgets which take account of increased newsprint costs and the enormous TV spend we will have to undertake later this year. But this is the time to revitalise our local press and make them yield more.'

There had been presentations to the board before but never from a non-executive director and the wife of the man whom they still regarded as the boss. And never, thought Walter, looking at the other male directors who were transfixed, from someone so easy on the eye.

Charlie used graphics to show how tightly-controlled experiments had revealed that when a paper involved itself in a local charity or a special school project, circulation and advertising profit levels increased. Her suggestion that the board should hire an events organiser who could work across the group's titles was greeted with enthusiasm. And when she proposed that the *Brighton Gazette* should be targeted as the paper to follow the Boston line first, the vote in favour was unanimous. Walter noticed that even Vanessa voiced no criticism. She had been outflanked and outclassed.

Charlie had won the first round.

Janice Gordon had never seen the Prime Minister undressed before and was doing her best not to appear to stare but she was transfixed by the sight of his old-fashioned mini trunks.

She was hot and frankly bothered. This was not what she had been led to expect. She fingered her blue serge skirt as she watched Edward Saunders, his deputy, the Chief Whip and the Party Chairman swim serenely up and down the length of the swimming pool at Chequers.

Heavy snow blanketed the southerly hills so the house party had decided to take its exercise indoors, following brandy and coffee in the study. Janice could imagine what her parents would think about the cost of heating the pool to this sultry temperature. It was more like Bahrain than Buckinghamshire.

She had been asked to bring in a telephone and spent as long as she dared checking that it was in working order so that she could have a good look around. The men were now talking animatedly at the shallow end. Reluctantly, for there was no one who relished insider gossip more than she did, Police Constable Gordon stopped fiddling with the telephone and left.

'Let's be realistic.' Edward Saunders looked intently at the Party Chairman. 'It'd be better to go to the country sooner rather than later, for all those reasons we've been through.' He was referring to the results of their own private polls, the two difficult by-elections coming up, problems with the new President of the USA, and the stalemate of the Irish talks, not yet made public.

The Deputy Prime Minister pulled himself out of the water and reached for a towelling robe. 'It would certainly give the Opposition a nasty surprise. They're not nearly ready.'

Saunders nodded. 'I don't need to point out to you that

this is all on a need-to-know basis. I haven't yet decided on an exact date and I'll have to go to Sandringham first anyway.'

'Surely if you do that, everyone will guess the plot,' said his deputy.

'Not necessarily. The autumn weekends that Avril and I have spent there and at Balmoral have gone so well I'm sure I can get permission to say there has been a longstanding invitation to go again in February to discuss the military career of the young prince. That would provide a good cover story.'

'It would,' agreed the Chairman, 'and that would certainly suit the Queen.'

The PM nodded. 'As you know, she doesn't like to be associated in any way with party politics.'

For reasons of his own, Edward Saunders did not confide in his colleagues that he had already decided on what he believed was the most propitious Thursday for their party. Elections always happened on Thursdays in Britain although no one understood why. If only the Prime Minister knew the actual date of the election, there was no one who could leak it. But he would put the inner Cabinet on a war footing at once.

Amy and her father had not spoken since Christmas. Still furious about his attitude over her shares, she refused all contact. She did not return Philip's calls and she did not answer his letter asking if he could meet her in Cambridge. Even Vanessa had tried to intercede on his behalf but to little avail. Louise spoke to her father a couple of times but Amy was obdurate.

Miranda's second birthday came and went. The girls sent a card but no present.

Then Vanessa received a call from Walter which presaged yet more unpleasantness. Walter was at Champneys, the luxurious health resort in Hertfordshire which he visited each year to be pampered and de-stressed, but nevertheless his voice was taut.

'Vanessa, I want to warn you. Next week's *Sunday Times* is doing a story about Forrester's.'

'Not more of that silly rubbish about me and Charlie, surely?'

'No, no, it's nothing personal.' Vanessa enjoyed a moment of relief before he went on, 'An American company called the Salter Foundation apparently wants to take us over.'

'But they can't do that if we don't want to sell, can they?'

'That depends,' answered Walter guardedly, 'on how many shareholders think it's a good idea.'

Vanessa experienced a wave of trepidation. 'I'm sure none of them will. You don't think it's a good idea, Walter, do you?' Her disquiet increased as Walter did not immediately reply. When he did, his words brought no comfort.

'Well, I can't dismiss it out of hand, my dear. As chairman and acting chief executive I have a duty to put the matter to the full board as soon as possible.'

Vanessa was appalled. 'Walter, we shouldn't consider it at all. That's not what Grandfather would have wanted. He told me often that Forrester's had to stay under family control.'

'That was some years ago, my dear, and Elliot was nothing if not a pragmatist. It's early days to get worked up about this. We've had nibbles before, as you know.'

'But then we all agreed it wasn't a good idea, so what makes this one different?'

Walter thought it injudicious to mention to Vanessa that he had already seen Kyle Salter's plans for the company and thought they merited further study.

Before booking in to the health spa, he had taken the precaution of seeking legal advice in his role as Forrester chairman and acting chief executive. His solicitor had quoted a 1902 House of Lords judgement, the case of Percival v. Wright, establishing that if a director told a white lie to another director to buy time, nothing could be done about it legally. The lawyer had quoted the judge: 'That matter lies not with the law but with God.' Walter's conscience could live with that ruling.

'The *Sunday Times* seems to think the Salter Foundation can count on the support of a sizeable proportion of our shares. I talked to the reporter and asked him what that meant but he wouldn't be drawn. If he's accurate, we have to take this bid seriously.'

'Which shareholders? No one's contacted me.' Everything's slipping out of my control, thought Vanessa. 'And it can't be done without my twenty-five per cent,' she retorted, 'and the children's . . .' She left the sentence hanging as her mind focused sharply on the person who now had power over her children's shares. Charlie.

She sank onto the hall chair. She was such a fool. Walter's tone should have warned her. I've been wrong to trust him, thought Vanessa. Rumours indeed. He was siding with Charlie. With Philip. As the realisation sank in, she recalled an uncharacteristically frank comment about Walter that her grandfather had once made to her: 'Walter's not a fighter, never has been. He'll tend to side with those he perceives to be the strongest. I'm not sure you'll always be able to rely on him.'

Her silence was making Walter feel uncomfortable. 'Vanessa, all I'm trying to do is prepare the family for the shock of seeing this story, however speculative, in print. We'll thrash it all out at the emergency meeting.'

Vanessa slumped in her seat.

Betrayal.

Walter called the specially convened board meeting to order. Speculation had turned into reality. On the table in front of each board member was a copy of the *Sunday Times* Business News with its page five story announcing the Salter Foundation's putative takeover bid.

The report also included a breakdown of the activities of the Salter business, together with profiles and large, prominent photographs of Paul Salter and his son. The paper had printed pictures of Philip and the two Mrs Lockharts, reproducing a tear-out of the battling boardroom beauties story. There had been a rash of follow-up stories in the Monday papers. There were cuttings from all of these.

Each board member also had a copy of the Salter Foundation's press release put out forty-eight hours after the story had appeared announcing their intention to bid plus a briefing paper.

On hearing the news from Walter, Vanessa had telephoned Philip at once. He had refused to discuss the story with her, saying that it would all be fully aired at the board meeting. 'We don't know the *Sunday Times* article is true,' was all he would be drawn into saying when she demanded to know what his intentions were.

Vanessa was determined not to give up without a fight. If she could not reason with Philip then she would try another tack. A psychological one. She had failed to persuade them to back her claim to the children's shares, but a takeover was a different matter. This affected their wallets and their future. So she had arranged a little shock for her fellow directors.

She had organised for the life-sized portrait of her grandfather to be transported from their Sussex office to the futuristic-looking boardroom in London's Docklands and had made a special trip to supervise the placing of the likeness so that it would dominate the room, the severe eyes directly facing the chairman. On the minimalist white walls, the painting, professionally lit, looked much more powerful than in the dark-panelled Sussex boardroom.

The effort had not been in vain. All of them, particularly those who had worked with Elliot, were surprised, but Vanessa was pleased to see one or two board members who had known him well looked discomfited, almost sheepish. It did not take them long to appreciate the significance of this gesture. Except for Charlie, who had never known Elliot Forrester.

Vanessa watched the expressions of Hugh Purcell and Anne Grover, trying to gauge their intentions. They both smiled back at her. She was encouraged. She did not think either of them had made up their minds. She wondered if they, too, had received a hand-written invitation to lunch from the Salter chairman and whether, like her, they had thrown it into the wastepaper basket. 'I've certainly no intention of consorting with the enemy,' she had told her daughter angrily. Amy had been distraught when Vanessa had informed her that the company might be taken over, and that there was nothing they could do if the board voted to accept the proposals and a majority of shareholders agreed.

On paper the proposed offer was extremely attractive, though the benefits would be long-term. The Salter Foundation was offering a generous investment commitment and a favourable exchange of Salter shares for Forrester holdings. This was welcomed by Charlie but Vanessa was quick to contradict her.

'Of course investment is essential but if the Salters think it's such a good bet, why don't we have some faith in the company? We should do what they intend to do and borrow to invest in ourselves. All the expertise we need is already in place.' Vanessa surprised herself with how forceful she sounded.

Hugh Purcell, the finance director, seemed to agree with her main point. 'If you remember,' he observed, 'I submitted a similar investment proposal two months ago which was handed to our financial consultants for analysis. I think their report should be due any time now.'

Vanessa could not resist a look of triumph in Charlie's direction.

'And then there's the family's reputation to be considered,' Vanessa continued. 'Forrester's has been in this part of the world for nearly a hundred years. We and the papers we run are part of the community. We mean something. Take our good name away and you have faceless bean counters. Don't be so quick to dispense with everything Elliot Forrester built up.'

'Well, that won't play in Tokyo,' Charlie countered.

'Surely the main advantage of this takeover would be our access to trans-global titles, finance and management. As we know, it's increasingly hard to compete against the international players when we have to restrict our operations to one country.'

There was a nodding of heads including, Vanessa saw angrily, that of the finance director.

Charlie felt some sympathy for Vanessa's wish to keep the family firm independent but why could the woman not see that Forrester's was bound to be swallowed up by some predator in the future who might not offer such favourable terms?

As the meeting ground on, Vanessa and Charlie disagreed on nearly every one of the takeover terms, and Vanessa was all too aware that she was also fighting Philip. Charlie made it clear that she and her husband were in total accord.

Before putting a formal proposal to the board that they should open a dialogue with the Americans, which drew a murmur of assent round the table, Walter briefly outlined the disposition of the company shares. Vanessa Lockhart held twenty-five per cent, while Charlotte Lockhart controlled her husband's eight per cent and the twenty-six per cent of the children, making a total of thirty-four.

Vanessa sat stony-faced under her grandfather's portrait. It was obvious that, in spite of her spirited efforts, the board was not averse to a takeover. She supposed Charlie could also count on the six per cent shared by Walter, Anne Grover, Hugh Purcell and two other absentee shareholders. Stalemate. Either side needed over fifty per cent to win. There was only one other shareholder Vanessa could approach personally. Elliot's daughter Cissi Toscani in

Cannes. Her twenty per cent holding was crucial to the vote. The remaining fifteen per cent were in the hands of the public and third-party institutions like pension funds.

'The more we know about this organisation and the principles involved, the more we'll know about how they operate and the better prepared we'll be to handle their bid.'

'Handle?' said Vanessa sharply. 'You mean "fight their bid", don't you? There's going to be no takeover, not if I can help it. We shouldn't consider it.'

'I don't agree,' said Charlie quietly. 'As a board it's our duty to discuss all its implications.'

'Don't lecture me on my duties as a board member.' Vanessa could not control the bitterness in her voice.

There were embarrassed coughs around the room and Walter interrupted to calm the atmosphere. 'Ladies, I don't think this is a fruitful avenue for discussion.' He thought it would be injudicious at that stage to reveal that he intended to seek Charlie's help in further discussions with the Salters.

The battle lines in the takeover were clear: first wife was pitted against her successor.

'A takeover, darling? How exciting,' rasped Cecily Toscani née Forrester, subsequently Countess Kulikowska, now widowed, from her penthouse eyrie in the Californie district of Cannes, Alpes Maritime.

Her voice was the product of Gitanes, Pernod and hundreds of late nights spent in a smoke-filled casino. Vanessa could picture the elegantly-coiffed, starved-size-six frame, beautifully covered in Chanel or Armani, depending on her mood.

'No, it isn't exciting, Aunt Cissi.' Vanessa was firm. 'The

deal doesn't mean more money, not for a long time.'

'No money? Then what on earth's the point?'

'Exactly. There's to be a battle for control. Charlie's using her votes in favour and I need you to help me defeat it.'

There was no hesitation. 'Well, we Forresters have to stick together. You can count on me, sweetie.'

Thank God, thought Vanessa. With forty-five per cent, she would need to pick up only another six per cent from those institutions who, in spite of everything, would still be loyal to the family. And she would win.

Chapter Fifteen

It was quite something when a son told a father what to do and the father did it, Paul Salter reflected wrily. He had been instructed by his son to fly over to London at once, 'have some fun and be there to sign the takeover contract'.

Trusting others was something Paul found difficult even when that other was his own child, but there was little point in putting his only son in charge of a deal like this and not following his instructions.

So, here he was, dressed up in dinner jacket and bow tie, sitting in a hired Rolls-Royce on his way to Pelham House deep in the Sussex countryside for a charity ball in aid of cancer research. Kyle had told him that it was one of the most important social events of the year, attended by Britain's 'A' list. 'You could be sitting at a table and be the only one there without a country. It's ex-King this and ex-Queen that. Every dame's a duchess.'

Paul was unimpressed. 'Just because you're dating Lady Henrietta and turned on by titles doesn't mean I am. New York's full of ex-countesses and Russian princesses and most of them are a waste of space. Anyway, I'm not sure this whole thing's going to work. Mrs Lockhart the First wouldn't see me for lunch anywhere, anytime. What makes you so sure she'll even speak to me tonight?'

'Dad, your table's right next to hers and you'll be sitting with some of the best known and most glamorous people there. She won't be able to ignore you. The actor who opened the Florida mall is over here promoting his latest movie and he remembers well the fee we paid him so he's pleased to come. We were lucky, there.'

That was no luck, thought Paul. Kyle must have been working hard and pulled more strings than Jascha Heifetz on a violin.

'And Joel Francis is in town, so is Tom Reeves,' continued Kyle. 'They're both coming with their wives. So's the guy from the Embassy and he's bringing his wife and daughter to make up the numbers. So you're a free agent. The table's been booked in his name and as all these guys have met HRH before there's no problem with security clearance. I fixed all that for you.'

This was the way his father liked to operate. The fifty-two-year-old self-made millionaire was loath to tailor his travel arrangements to anyone else's schedule. Paul was generous, warm and liked people but nowadays only when they fitted in with his time frame. He dreaded this evening, he hated posing, disliked small talk, and most of the people were strangers of no interest to him whatsoever but Kyle had sent him on a Mission. What the hell, it was only one night.

'All you have to do is concentrate on Mrs L,' his son had instructed gently. 'Get her to see you as a human being and not a marauding gangster.'

Paul laughed. 'I've told you, Kyle, never be too optimistic.'

'Well, if you can't persuade her with your legendary charm, sweep her off your feet with your wallet. My spy says she's real keen to beat last year's chairman's takings. These girls take it in turns to be chairman and underneath those fancy frocks they fight as hard as the chicks from the Bronx, Brooklyn and Queens'.'

If Kyle only realised how little he cared about this takeover, thought Paul as the car sped through the starlit night towards the eighteenth-century mansion, he would be horrified.

But his son was the only living soul who really mattered to Paul Salter. Kyle's mother had been out of his life for ten years. He had waited till Kyle went to university before foolishly following the example of a few of his friends and acquiring what he now saw was a trophy wife. Thank God that union did not produce children; the marriage had only lasted twenty-four months. That was a mistake he was determined never to make again. It had made him wary. These days the women in his life were no more than recreational light relief.

It was unfair but, rich or poor, men had their pick. For a man in his early fifties, to be single was a state close to heaven. For women of the same age, in spite of the progress of the liberation movement, Paul had heard it was hell. He was of the age to be unfamiliar with the concept that some of these women could exist quite happily without a man.

Vanessa Lockhart appeared self-assured and confident as she gamely went through the rituals of British upper-middle-class life, entertaining, organising these charity functions, but, according to the Deep Throat report, the truth was different and since her divorce she had had no real relationships.

Although Vanessa was nine years younger than he was, she was somewhat older than the women he had been seeing lately but she was not bad-looking judging from that picture in the papers that Kyle had sent him, although the photograph had been taken some time ago. Kyle had omitted to include the front-page picture of a worried-looking Vanessa taken before Christmas.

A veteran of many charity functions back home, some of which he attended because they were tax deductible, Paul well understood that the way to earn the admiration and gratitude of a charity organiser was to outbid everyone else in the room, however much it made you wince. This was one of the few occasions when there was no bottom line.

As the limousine glided up the long avenue of oak trees towards Pelham House, the grandest and largest stately home in Britain, rows of flickering torchères lit up the night sky, guiding the car to the main entrance. Nervously Paul noted the convoy of royal cars coming towards him.

Empty.

He was late. Paul was not easily wrong-footed but arriving after the royal party was bad form, even for an American. He took a deep breath and bounded athletically up the wide stone steps to the floodlit portico. His PR had ordered him to do this at all times, in case there were watching television cameras. 'Let's be honest, Paul,' she had instructed, 'you're over fifty. It's essential you look full of energy and vigour.' Now it had become a habit.

Striding briskly into the chandeliered hall, the thought of the long hours he would have to spend making small talk with strangers still irked the tall, wide-shouldered New Yorker.

He checked his cuffs. He had faced far more difficult challenges in his life than persuading Vanessa Lockhart to vote his way. It was all for a good cause. His own.

She was the first person he saw. Framed by the tall gilded archways, Vanessa was making her grand entrance with His Royal Highness into the Long Gallery. Not bad, he thought. Great cleavage. Breasts that reminded him of his first wife. He quickly put aside these thoughts. Kyle wanted him to charm this woman, not screw her.

It was hard to believe she was as vulnerable as Deep Throat claimed. The report had painted a picture of a rather downtrodden, suburban loser. But this woman with her dramatic blue gown, neck garlanded with pearls and diamonds which even at this distance Paul could see were no copies, looked totally in control. He sensed she would be no pushover.

As she was with royalty he could hardly introduce himself. Unusually for him, he dithered for a few seconds before pushing through the throng, searching for a familiar face.

Ranged along the walls of the gallery he saw sixteen top chefs resplendent in white toques and starched cotton aprons deftly turning delicate pieces of crab, lobster and king prawns over tiny lava rock grilles. Jugglers, conjurors, strolling minstrels wove in and out through the noisy, chattering crowd.

Across the room Paul saw three faces familiar not only to him but to cinema goers and sports fans throughout the world. The celebs were surrounded by admirers who did not know where to gawp first, at the stars or the royal personage.

163

He moved over to join the stars.

So far Kyle's organisation had been magnificent. With this crew at his table Vanessa would be sure to notice him. But halfway through the starter she still had not.

Delicately nibbling the elegant squares of filo pastry encasing beluga caviar, Vanessa sensed that someone was staring at her. Surreptitiously, without taking her eyes off the royal face, she felt the back of her gown to check that none of the bones in her bodice had slipped its moorings.

Etiquette decreed that the prince had to talk to the guest on his right during the first course before turning to his neighbour on the other side for the second course, alternating in this way throughout the meal. It was a neat and failsafe way to ensure that everyone had their share of the royal attention. It was Vanessa's turn at the moment so it was not until the plates were cleared to make way for the delicate slices of duckling, served slightly pink with a black cherry and wild honey sauce, and the royal guest had dutifully turned to his left, that Vanessa could slowly look round to see if her instincts were right.

After she had done a half-turn, her eyes locked on to those of a distinguished-looking man leaning back insouciantly in his chair. He was smiling lazily at her. He looked familiar and when he smiled again she responded faintly.

Then she recognised him from the large photograph in the *Sunday Times*. Paul Salter.

What was he doing here? How on earth had he wangled a table? She felt her cheeks redden as she nodded curtly and turned back to her table companions, angry and confused. Then she remembered the late table booking, the over-generous cheque from the American, which the committee had been so excited about. No wonder she had not spotted the name. The reservation had been made by a diplomat from the American Embassy, a barely remembered acquaintance of the charity secretary. Spending what to him were only a few dollars, Paul Salter had breached her defences totally.

Vanessa refused to look his way again.

An hour later she was forced to listen in mounting amazement as he outbid every other tycoon in the room for not just one but the top three auction prizes. After his successful and over-inflated bid for a holiday in Phuket, Vanessa noted that Dorinda, in her role as committee member, barely left his side as he did the same for the other two main prizes.

The atmosphere in the room was electric. When HRH asked to be introduced to the charity benefactor of the night and his film star friends, Vanessa was forced to walk over to Paul and make an introduction. When in the usual way Paul was tactfully moved along out of the royal presence, Vanessa stayed close to HRH's side. It might not be protocol but she was determined to avoid speaking to Paul Salter or giving him the opportunity to speak to her.

'Vanessa, my dear, hearty congratulations.' The charity's honorary treasurer was beaming at her, his eyes and bald head gleaming. 'You do realise, don't you, what you've done?'

She waited politely.

'By my reckoning you've tripled last year's takings. Jolly well done, my dear. I think it would be only right, don't you, to say your personal thank you to the man who made it possible?'

'Oh,' said Vanessa quickly, 'I think it would be so much better for the treasurer to do it.'

'No, no, it has to be the chairman, my dear. Come along, I'll take you over.'

Vanessa had no choice. She had been both conned and cornered. Fuelled by resentment, she moved towards her enemy in a flurry of satin and organza. 'Mr Salter, how very kind of you to grace our little charity and in such a generous way,' she said too sweetly.

'I'm delighted to have been able to help, Mrs Lockhart,' he replied, inclining his head in a slight bow.

'I hope,' Vanessa added, 'that such largesse will act as a spur to the guests you outbid.'

Paul looked at her quizzically. 'I guess that's Brit-speak for "You're verging on the vulgar". Did this boy from the colonies overdo the generosity thing?' Paul Salter seemed to be enjoying the charade.

'No, no,' the treasurer interrupted vehemently, 'absolutely not. We're delighted with your contribution. I don't know how we can thank you.'

'Oh, that's quite simple really.' Paul Salter smiled without taking his eyes from Vanessa's face. 'A dance with Mrs Lockhart will be thanks enough.'

The treasurer beamed. 'I'm sure Mrs Lockhart would be delighted to oblige.'

Now they were both looking at her. She was damned if she was going to dance with this man. 'I'm so sorry, I'm going to be too busy and now I have to dance with our guest of honour.' She turned away but Paul caught her wrist.

'If you're waltzing with a prince for the first dance,' he

said impudently, 'surely you can do the same with a frog for the second?'

Despite herself, Vanessa could not suppress her smile. She gave a barely perceptible nod.

When the first dance was over, Paul did not claim his dance with Vanessa. Instead he partnered Dorinda and then two of the grateful committee members. Had he forgotten his request? Vanessa was irritated that she felt a frisson of disappointment.

At last he caught her eye and began to stride purposefully towards her. With a sinking heart she heard the band strike up a samba.

'I'm terribly sorry, I'm not very good at this.' She was still apologising as he led her firmly on to the floor.

'Don't worry, Mrs Lockhart, hang on to me.'

To her relief Vanessa found it comparatively easy to follow his resolute lead. She was taken aback by the feel of his arms. His muscles were not those of a middle-aged businessman. He must work out.

For such a powerfully-built man he was surprisingly agile though Vanessa thought he held her a little too closely, using his hips too obviously to manipulate her over the floor. At one point he placed both hands on her waist as he pivoted her round. He was certainly making clear he was in charge of her body. But she felt she could hardly object as this was supposed to be the style of the dance.

It was a long time since she had been held close in a man's arms. Philip preferred talking to dancing. The way this man held her was bordering on the territorial but perversely it felt comfortable. They were a good fit, their bodies instinctively responding to each other's movement.

As they executed a sudden turn, Vanessa looked up at his face. He was absorbed, his eyes half-shut. It was obvious he was immersed in the dance, relishing every moment. In spite of her misgivings about him, Vanessa, too, began to enjoy herself.

She felt a spark of something which she had thought was dead, some flicker of animal interest. She could not help herself, she began to think the unthinkable. Of lying naked with this man, of being caressed and kissed. She dismissed these traitorous thoughts instantly but could not help smiling inwardly. Before she had lost some weight, it would have been unimaginable for her to have the confidence to undress in front of a strange man. Perhaps this arousal was her reward for those seemingly-endless weeks of self-discipline.

Vanessa looked up to see a small circle around them swaying and clapping admiringly. God, how embarrassing.

Over eggs *en cocotte* and dry toast at the Connaught, the Salter Foundation's Chairman and his number two were having an important conference. Having achieved a certain notoriety from the coverage of their takeover bid, they enjoyed being recognised. They had ascertained that in London's gossipy world it paid to be seen having a power breakfast in this, one of the haunts of the British establishment. Deals were not completed there but it was a good place to initiate them.

Paul passed his son a sheet of thick cream writing paper bearing the address of the Rectory in Pridlington. 'Read this before you accuse me of not working my butt off for you,' he said with a wry smile.

Kyle read Vanessa's florid scrawl. After thanking his

father for his support for her charity, the last line of the message was explicit: 'As I said at the ball, I am unable to lunch nor can I see a time when I will be free to do so.'

'Even the flowers were returned to sender,' said Paul. 'I give up.' But the feel of her scented body pressing against his as they danced lingered disturbingly. He shook himself. This was business, damn it.

Kyle was silent for a moment. 'We can't give up, Dad. And we're paying for advice so I consulted our girl.'

'How are you getting on with your Deep Throat?'

'On a personal level? No dice, I'm afraid. Such a body but no vibes in my direction. Tragic. But she's come up with some orders for you. Turn up on Vanessa's doorstep with flowers and she says the woman will be too embarrassed to send you away.'

'No way,' Paul protested. 'You're not asking me to chase that woman again, are you? Go down to some God-forsaken spot in Sussex to sweeten her up?'

'Dad,' said Kyle, 'did you or did you not promise that when you came over here you'd do anything to help me, anything at all, to clinch my first deal? Then when I ask you to do the smallest little favour . . .'

They both started to laugh.

'When I made that promise I thought you wanted my mind not my body.' Paul shook his head. 'I'm glad there's only one of you.' He thought again of his dance with Vanessa. She was certainly a challenge.

They were still smiling when the waiter showed their guest to the table. As Anne Grover, Forrester's financial secretary and member of the board, took her seat, Paul was amused to note that his son's hangover seemed to vanish.

Anne did not seem Kyle's type, but he could see the attraction for him as the woman hit the button in the figure department.

All discussion of Vanessa Lockhart ceased.

Chapter Sixteen

Paul knocked on the door of the Rectory with a certain amount of trepidation.

A young girl ushered him into the hallway. It was the nearest thing to the Ralph Lauren shop on Madison Avenue Paul had encountered in Britain, only much untidier. There were sweaters piled on a chair, a riding coat slung over the banister and a spaniel surveying the world from a circular ottoman in a corner of the hall.

Vanessa's expression when she saw him made it clear she was annoyed at his sudden appearance.

He put on a sheepish smile. 'I happened to be in the area and I couldn't resist seeing if you were at home.' He did not know that often, when she was alone, she would, for reasons of economy, have an early bath, so that the hot water could be turned off, and then curl up in a track suit or pyjamas with Louise to watch television.

'I wish you'd phoned in advance,' she said, conscious that she was barely being civil, aware of the shapeless jeans and old sweater she was wearing.

He looked at her with the same penetrating intensity as he had after that disconcerting samba and she coloured appealingly. Legendary British good manners struggled to the surface, exactly as Deep Throat had predicted, and she offered him a drink, albeit unenthusiastically.

Paul had planned his first sentence carefully. Somewhere he had read that Ronald Reagan restarted the Reykjavik peace talks with President Gorbachev by saying, 'Hi, I'm Ron. This isn't going very well. Let's start again.'

It seemed appropriate.

'Hi, I'm Paul. This hasn't gone very well so far. Let's start again.' He held out his hand.

Louise, in tartan pyjamas and dressing gown, watched from the sofa with interest as her mother shook the man's hand perfunctorily and showed him into the room. It was quite tidy if you did not count a gymkhana rosette on the seat of the armchair, the opened pin of which nearly punctured Paul's trousers, or the two large empty but useful cardboard boxes that she had been hoarding to use at the village fête.

Paul smiled at Louise. 'Hi,' he said easily.

He soon established that Louise was horse mad. One thing Paul Salter knew a great deal about was horses and ponies from his losses at Kentucky and Kyle's modest wins at the Westport and Bridgehampton Horse Shows. By the time Vanessa pushed the boxes into the snug and returned with the drinks tray, Louise was entertaining their guest with a virtual monologue involving tack, jumps and rosettes.

She was his passport to dinner. Paul had a fleeting thought that this guileless young girl might be in trouble later, for it was obvious her spontaneous invitation did not best please her mother.

The dinner was not a success. As a cholesterol-aware,

non-smoking, non-drinking, non-fat-eating svelte New Yorker, Paul could not believe that middle-class Britain still ate this way. In America, women on high-rolling alimony, back on the marriage market, did not serve huge dollops of calorific shepherd's pie made of non-lean mince topped with mashed potato, not to mention the bottle of red wine which accompanied it. The small salad drenched in a delicious but dangerous oil-rich vinaigrette made him shudder. As did the fact that Vanessa remonstrated only half-heartedly with Louise when she fed the dog from her plate.

Once the talk veered away from horses, Louise's attention wandered and she quickly excused herself to disappear to her bedroom.

Vanessa put down her glass when she realised she was the only one drinking. She was still trying to lose weight but, like tonight, the diet did sometimes slip. In spite of eating sensibly most of the time, her thighs still felt uncomfortable inside her gardening jeans. She did not in any way look like the Vanessa Paul had first seen, corseted as she was in an evening gown. She wondered miserably if Cinderella looked fatter as well as poorer when she met her Prince after the ball.

They moved with their coffee from the dining room into the snug sitting room with its log fire. Vanessa tried to kick the damn cardboard boxes behind the chair.

'Hey, don't do that,' Paul said. 'Those are good strong boxes. When I started out in high school delivering groceries I'd have given anything for two like those.'

'Would you like to take them back with you?'

'Yeah I would, thanks.'

They both laughed and Vanessa indicated a chair on one

side of the fireplace. She struck a match and watched the kindling light before positioning herself in the opposite chair.

'God, when I think of the things we used to get up to in those days,' said Paul, leaning comfortably into the chair. 'I rarely go back, I think it's because I still can't look at some of my customers in the eye. In those days I was always ravenously hungry. I bet Mrs John Graham still doesn't realise that her regular order of plums was always a couple short and the same went for Mrs Purdy's frankfurters.'

'You think they never found out?' inquired Vanessa.

'I hope not but, you know, they were kind people and, boy, was I skinny in those days. Then of course there were the times I was in a hurry and roped in my little brother to deliver my orders. I discovered later that he'd get kinda tired halfway and never get to some places but, hey, I was sixteen with raging hormones and I had a hot date.'

Over a glass of brandy, as the fire slowly came to life, both of them forgot the outside world for a while. There was no stopping him now and, like all men, he was enjoying making her smile.

'Once when I went to the prom, the corsage which I couldn't afford was courtesy of Mrs Sager. A dozen roses, ten roses, who checked?'

Vanessa caught his mood and recounted the time her grandfather was delighted to get what he thought was a bargain price for newsprint only to find when it arrived that they had become the yellow press, literally.

'When we were starting the *Brighton Gazette* I helped out in editorial for a short time until,' she pushed her hands through her hair, laughing at the memory, 'I made a mistake with the weekly knitting pattern. The instructions were for a chunky polo-neck sweater but the photograph I chose showed a slinky V-neck. I wasn't a knitter so I didn't spot anything was wrong and it was only when readers got to the neckline that they realised they were in serious trouble. Then came all the calls. Mind you, I thought I should have been congratulated, it showed how popular that section was.'

They matched each other's stories and her face was animated as she remembered the start of Forrester Newspapers, long before she was married. She had not thought about those days for many years.

As the room grew warmer, Paul stood up and removed his jacket and while his eyes were momentarily off her, she forced herself to analyse why he had come all the way from London to see her.

Silly, silly cow. She was not the magnet. It was, as always, the company. She *had* to keep remembering that. His tactic was to disarm her, to make her see him not as a formidable business operator but as a friend. All that cosy talk about his youth, his poverty, his skinniness, it was merely a ploy.

Well, if Paul Salter was using her, she would use the same strategy. Now, when he was so relaxed, seemed a good opportunity to try and raise doubts in his mind about the takeover, explain how important it was to her that the business stayed in the family.

Vanessa was attempting to find a way to introduce the subject when he flummoxed her by asking, 'How do you like living in such a small village?'

'Oh, my family's lived here for generations.'

'Yes, but that's not what I asked. How do *you* like living here?'

'I don't know. People are really friendly.' She laughed. 'We all know each other's business.'

'So? Are you happy here?'

'I've never really thought about it.' She could not keep the note of surprise from her voice.

'I asked because I come from a small town not unlike this one. My folks were amazed when I said I needed to get out of a place where I was Dorothy's eldest or Henry's brother.' He smiled at her, his eyes bright. Why did he unsettle her so? 'Mom said I'd stand one day in Times Square New York and be sick that no living soul around me knew my name. But you know what? It's never happened.'

'I understand what you're saying but . . .'

'But?'

'I couldn't leave. There's the children, you see.'

'Vanessa, I'm talking to you as a person, a woman, not as a mother.'

It was so unusual for someone to ask about her feelings she was momentarily disconcerted and to cover her confusion she blustered, 'Too many problems. And, of course, there's Forrester's.'

'Why don't you let me take care of that for you? It'd be one problem less, wouldn't it?'

She looked up sharply, then saw the twinkle in his eye and his smile. 'You'd like that, wouldn't you?' She tried to match his light tone. 'If I caved in with my paws in the air.' Then she turned solemn. 'Well, I won't. I never will and you'd better understand that.'

He raised his palms. 'Listen, I'm no thief. We're making a good offer and all we want you to do is to leave emotion out of this and just consider it. We're also a family, not so different from the Forresters. We've also worked hard to make a success of our business. We're not Neanderthal foreigners moving in for the kill. You have legitimate concerns about the takeover,' he went on. 'I can understand that. All I'm saying is, let's talk about the deal.'

Vanessa felt a swift burst of anger. 'The deal.' Her eyes were blazing. 'That's all you Americans are interested in. You don't care about tradition, family, staff who've been there for years. All you care about is the almighty dollar.'

'Whoa, steady there, lady. Don't dismiss millions of people because you don't like the methods of one American.'

She stood up, her face turned away. 'I don't see much point in discussing the company with you. It's rather late and you've a long way to go. I think it's best that you leave now. Please.'

On the way back to London Paul ruminated on what he could report to his son. Precious little. He had not managed to change her mind at all. But despite the nuisance her opposition was causing him, Paul could not help but admire the passion she felt for her company and the people in it. In the soft light from the chintz-covered lampshade, Vanessa, a glint of determination in her eyes, had looked extremely attractive and he had to admit he was intrigued by her and sorry when she firmly brought the evening to a close.

With some surprise he realised he had enjoyed talking to a grown-up woman, one who did not aspire to baubles, bangles or babies.

Chapter Seventeen

The phone had rung five times that evening but Vanessa had made no move to pick it up. It was always for the girls. So she was surprised when Louise called down the stairs, 'Mum, it's for you.'

The husky voice was instantly recognisable and filled Vanessa with unease. This could only mean trouble.

'Darling, I'm giving you a little tinkle about this takeover business.'

Vanessa was guarded. 'What do you mean, Aunt?'

'Plee-ase,' admonished Cissi, 'don't call me that. You know how ancient it makes me feel and I'm not looking that bad since I had the Brazilian face lift. I wanted to tell you the other side's been in contact, a nice man called Paul Salter. He has spoken to me once or twice actually. Quite charming. Do you know him?' In Cissi style, she did not wait for a reply.

'Darling, the deal doesn't sound half as black as you painted it. Are you sure you've really understood all the nuances? Only, since we took over that wretched news magazine, there's been virtually no dividend at all. How's a poor girl like me going to manage? If this takeover goes

179

through, it might be exactly what you need, darling. In fact, I was discussing this very thing with Paul Salter today.'

Alarm bells clanged, whistles blew, drums banged.

Mentally Vanessa kicked herself. The Salters were serious about taking over Forrester's, they were bound to lobby all the main shareholders. Paul Salter was just the kind of rich man Cissi admired. If he put half the effort into wooing her aunt that he had put into the charity ball and his visit to the Rectory, Cissi's shares were lost.

Vanessa betrayed no sign of her inner turmoil. 'But Cissi,' she countered, 'you made me a promise. You agreed that we would fight these foreigners and keep Grandfather's company in the family.'

'Yes, I admit I did, darling. But now that I've had time to think about it, I realise I'm not involved in quite the same way with the company any more. Perhaps it's time for a new broom. Oh, I don't know. My head aches from all of this, it's so complicated. And the stock market has not been kind to me.'

Despite her apprehension, Vanessa could not suppress a wry smile. Cissi had been the beneficiary of one generous divorce settlement and one will. Her apartment alone, overlooking the Croisette and the Mediterranean, was worth a cool million. Pounds sterling.

'What exactly did that man tell you?'

'He said I'd receive fat dividends regularly. Supermarkets are so much more reliable than newspapers, darling. And now that Philip's left us, we need a strong man in charge. Not that I'm saying a word against dear Walter but if only you and Philip had stayed together. Any company needs a strong man. Just like any woman, darling.'

Vanessa raised her eyes skywards. She knew what was coming. If only she had not, in Cissi's phrase, 'let herself go', and had devoted herself totally to Philip's needs, he might not have strayed.

'I've always looked after myself . . .'

Yes, thought Vanessa, you and the hairdresser, couturier, beautician, manicurist, personal trainer and masseur, not to mention the planet's finest cosmetic surgeons.

'. . . None of my husbands ever left me.'

Vanessa cut in urgently. 'Your shares are pivotal to defeating the takeover. I want you to promise me again that you won't agree to anything, sign anything or do anything with them before I see you.'

'When will I see you, darling? You know how much I hate Britain when the tourists are there.'

'I know.' Vanessa made a swift decision. Nice was only two hours away. 'I'll come over to you.'

'Lovely, darling. The Forbes-Robertsons are coming to dinner next week. I'm sure they'd love to see you again.'

'Not next week. Tomorrow.'

Three hours after this conversation took place, Paul Salter learned of Vanessa's plans from Deep Throat. As her British Airways scheduled flight out of Heathrow rumbled down the runway, the Salter chartered Lear jet was already halfway to Nice Airport.

Vanessa was determined to nip in the bud this nonsense between Paul and her aunt. She had to convince Cissi that the *Citizen* would be a drain on the company for only a little while longer, that a short-term loss was quite common when national titles were being re-launched. The years of neglect had to be overcome, but there would be fat dividends again, and the board was now looking at other ways to attract investment into the company without diluting the shareholding. All Cissi had to do was to have faith.

These days Vanessa was unused to unplanned trips abroad and initially she thought of economising by staying in a small hotel in the rue d'Antibes. It was only when Amy reminded her that Charlie always stayed at the five-star Carlton when she covered the Cannes Film Festival and other trade conferences on the Côte d'Azur that she decided to switch.

The white seafront hotel, with what Jean Cocteau called its breasted cupolas at each side and wrought-iron lace-patterned balconies facing the Mediterranean, welcomed her as only such a grand hotel can.

Her bedroom was a vast eau de nil suite filled with flowers. A waiter in a white uniform so stiffly starched that she wondered how he could possibly bend opened the waiting bottle of champagne with a small flourish.

The champagne in its silver bucket had been up to its neck in ice and bedded right down next to it was a tall fluted glass. Deftly the waiter filled the cold glass, which frosted as the liquid came into contact with it. It was the most enticing glass of champagne Vanessa had been offered for years.

She looked quizzically at the waiter. Did the Carlton welcome all their guests in this fashion?

He smiled. 'With our chairman's compliments, madame. He never forgets your grandfather.'

Ah yes, Elliot had loved this coastline. Vanessa, too, loved the French Riviera. She had persuaded her grandfather to bring her and the children here year after year. Sometimes

Philip had come too, but often only for the weekend.

The only time her grandfather really seemed to relax was when he was enjoying himself with the girls – buying them ice creams in the back streets of Nice, taking them all for leisurely walks in the hills behind the town or for picnics in the forests near Mougins. He could only bear to be away from his business for four days at a time and he and Philip would alternate so one of them was always on duty at home.

Vanessa had wondered since if Philip had been faithful to her then. He had often, so often, assured her he had been and she could still remember the enthusiasm of those first nights when he would bounce off the plane and into her arms.

The enthusiasm and the love.

They had things in common then. The business, the choice of direction to take. The struggles. He was really involved with the children, too, and so doted on Amy that Vanessa had to be doubly nice to Louise to make up for it.

Amy was more his type of child. She was tall and intense like him. She was easily bored with small talk, with detail, with girlish things. She matched her father stride for stride when he went on what he called his 'hikes'. He had always needed to exhaust himself physically. When he had a knotty problem to solve, he would walk for a good two or three hours to clear his head. Given the choice, Amy would go with him. From about nine, she was determined to keep up with his long legs. Louise did not bother. She dimpled and charmed him when she needed to. Her mother was her refuge, everything from being a hole-in-the-wall money machine to sorting out her pony.

Philip had taken the girls to the Hotel Bel Air at Cap Ferrat to learn to swim under the guidance of the charming

183

French instructor. He persuaded them to immerse their heads in a huge clear plastic bowl of water and learn to open their eyes underwater and conserve their breath. Their confidence grew and soon they were both fearless in the water and strong swimmers. Philip hired a speedboat and they would zip round to St Tropez to the beachside cafes or, occasionally, to quiet coves further afield.

Happy days. Had she valued those moments enough?

The last time Vanessa had walked into the Carlton dining room she had been part of a family. Today she was alone and felt self-consciously conspicuous, but it was late and there were only two lone women in the room, elderly ones at that.

Vanessa would have chosen a corner table but Cissi had opted for one in the centre of the room. Her aunt was dressed to perfection, looking for all the world like a valuable antique laid out for sale. She had glints everywhere, on her pale blonde hair, her long pale fingers, her narrow wrists, on the slim belt buckle that looped over her cream cashmere sweater, on the buckles on her shoes, the clasp of her lizard handbag. And in her eyes as she surveyed her niece.

This was not, thought Vanessa, going to be an easy lunch.

When Cissi had consumed four lettuce leaves and announced herself 'entirely full', and after everything from her latest beautician to her stepchildren had been discussed, they finally got round to the problem of the shares and the Salters.

Vanessa was taken aback when her aunt broke the news that Paul Salter was already in Cannes.

'What a coincidence. Did he know I was coming?'

'I don't know, darling. He phoned me and charmingly

asked if I wished to join him for dinner tonight. He knows all the best places, of course. Naturally I accepted. After all, he's paying.'

'Why meet him?' asked Vanessa. 'He's only going to confuse the issue. All you have to ask yourself is would Elliot have agreed to a takeover of the company? You know he wouldn't.'

But Cissi wanted to meet the man who had been so 'charming' to her on the phone and Vanessa suddenly saw behind the façade. Her aunt who maintained she had such a fabulous Riviera social life was lonely. She should have come earlier and often, Vanessa chastised herself. The truth was, Cissi was looking forward to having dinner out alone with a younger man.

Cissi looked at her elegant gold watch. It was three thirty. 'I really should be going now, dear. It wouldn't be fair after Mr Salter's come all this way not to make adequate preparations. I must pop into the beauty salon.' Cissi smiled skittishly at Vanessa. 'It's really my duty to hear what he has to say face to face.'

Cissi's girlish manner belied the expert financial brain of a woman who had picked over two rich men and their pockets. It was clear she could barely wait for lunch to be over and she was only mildly put out when her niece finally grew angry with her. In Cissi's eyes, women did not really count. She was off to be massaged before an afternoon nap, refreshed for her dinner with an attractive man. That was what was important.

All Vanessa could manage was to make her aunt swear not to commit herself to anything that night. They arranged to meet the following day at Cissi's flat.

As many rich women would, Cissi left Vanessa to pay the bill. As her aunt walked briskly away from the table, Vanessa noted that from behind her aunt could be in her twenties. And she was most agreeable when she made an effort. Paul Salter would probably end up as husband number three! She should never have let him invite himself to supper at the Rectory. Probably he was about to entertain Cissi with the same amusing stories.

Vanessa had not returned Paul's subsequent phone calls, aware that her resistance might not survive his humour, his warmth and, damn it, his looks. And she would not talk to him on the phone either. The new answer machine installed at the company's expense had been helpful in avoiding his calls but she rebuked herself for re-playing his amusing messages when she was on her own. His voice made her smile.

After lunch Vanessa decided to take a leaf out of her aunt's book. She took a brisk walk in the bright sunshine down to the Palm Beach summer casino before spending two hours in the beauty shop. It helped clear her thoughts. She spent so much money in the local boutiques that she decided to stay in her room and skip dinner.

She went to bed with thoughts of Paul and Cissi filling her brain. When she finally drifted off, she dreamed Paul Salter was sitting behind her grandfather's desk. She woke with a start. It was still only eleven o'clock and she decided she could not wait until morning to find out what had happened at the dinner. She phoned Cissi but there was no answer. They were still out.

Now Vanessa visualised another scene. Paul and her aunt in bed. Would Paul go that far? Was it such a ridiculous

thought? Maybe he genuinely liked Cissi. Thin and sophisticated, she was probably much more his type.

Did she care?

She gave this some thought. About a nanosecond.

Yes.

She missed sex, a man's arms round her, someone stroking her spine and massaging her shoulders, kissing the nape
of her neck and the shadow between her shoulder blades.

She shook herself. The dream had nothing to do with the
real Paul. He would only be interested in Cissi because of
the business; exactly the same reason he was interested in
her.

Vanessa stood by the big balcony window and gazed out
to sea. The Mediterranean looked like a pond in the moonlight. The swaying trunks of the palm trees were ringed with
small white lights. It was late and there were few cars on the
road and fewer people walking. She decided that what she
needed to ease the tension was a scented bubble bath.

She had just settled back in the foam when the phone
rang. What a treat to have a phone at her right hand. Who
could be phoning so late? She picked up the receiver.

Silence. Then a sigh, then his voice. 'No, don't tell me. I
woke you.'

'Not at all,' she replied coolly. 'I've just come in.' She was
not going to let him know she had been alone in the suite
while he had been out gallivanting with her aunt.

'I've had a most entertaining evening,' he told her. 'Are all
your family so interesting on the female side?'

What a heavy-footed smoothie. 'My aunt has had a varied
life,' Vanessa managed to say drily.

'I'll say.' He laughed then stopped abruptly. 'Look, I know

it's late but could we please talk?' Before she could say no, he continued, 'I'm emotionally attached to this part of the world. I did my first real deal here.' She heard the chuckle in his voice. 'I was nine, she was ten. I wanted her bucket and spade like crazy. It was the only time we ever came to Europe, the only year my dad made money. He went bust the next year and that was that.'

He did not pause.

'It's such a waste both of us being here and not talking.' His speech was rapid, he was almost tripping over his words. 'Look, it's a beautiful night. I'll be outside on the Carlton beach pontoon in five minutes. I'll wait for fifteen.' The phone clicked.

Should she talk to him? There was nothing, no premium he could offer, which would change her mind. It was madness to go out now. She was bound to say the wrong thing. It could only help him and not her.

A few minutes later, still wrapped in her bath towel, she looked out of her window. Paul Salter was sitting at the end of the wooden jetty, gazing out to sea. Behind him was an array of white night-light candles on a tray, flickering in the dark. They had been placed in the shape of the letter V.

Fifteen minutes? She shrugged on a pair of French-cut jeans newly bought from a boutique that afternoon. She could not have worn them a month ago. Days of feeling hungry had been worth it. The boring hours on the treadmill were at last beginning to make inroads into the extensive layers of undulating fat. Vanessa had long thought that the best contraceptive was an inability to imagine taking clothes off a highly imperfect body in front of a strange man. Even with the few opportunities she had

had, all with married men, this fear had overtaken almost every spasm of lust.

She paired the pale blue jeans with a ruinously expensive sweater which the sales girl swore she would never regret buying. She barely had time to comb her still-damp hair and apply some blusher and mascara before the fifteen minutes were up. The simplicity of this look gave her a more youthful appearance which pleased her enormously.

Why am I worrying about what I look like? I'm going to see my enemy.

The fifteen minutes had stretched to twenty. It had been a long time since a man had waited for her. She had to go.

Paul was looking at his watch and as she walked towards him, heels clicking on the wooden planks, she was perversely pleased that he had waited ten minutes past the allotted time.

For a second she surrendered to the sensations of a girl on a date, excitement, nervousness, anticipation. Below her feet the vanilla-coloured sand floated into the silver Mediterranean with its rows of boat lights, a line of perfectly-spaced fairy dots, street lights edging the romantic coastline. It was an unseasonably warm night. She could smell the jasmine in the light breeze.

The instant he heard her, he stood up, revealing another tray holding a bottle of champagne and two glasses. A sizeable cashmere rug was carefully laid out over the wooden slats.

He had clearly taken a great deal of trouble and he looked somewhat sheepish. It was, she thought, so at odds with his machismo image.

'I'd nearly given up on you.' He pointed to the rug lying on the ground. 'Be my guest.'

For the first time since she had met him, Paul Salter seemed to be discomfited. She immediately felt more at ease and sank down on the rug.

It was all so romantic. Boy meets girl. Girl meets boy.

Boy wants girl's shares, Vanessa reminded herself.

He chivalrously put out an arm to help her sit down and she felt the softness of the hair on his muscular hands. Careful, she thought. This was a man who always got exactly what he wanted.

'I'd like you to think I always greet ladies with candles on the beach at midnight,' he said, 'but truly I've never done this before. Well, to be honest, Pierre the maître d' fixed it. Thank God your name doesn't begin with a W, we'd have run out of candles.' Paul's grin showed he was ridiculously pleased to see her.

'I'm impressed at your way of doing business,' she murmured, sipping appreciatively at the ice-cold bubbles.

'I was worried you wouldn't come.'

She looked around. 'Well, it's a little ridiculous, isn't it?'

'Sitting on a pontoon in the middle of the Mediterranean? What's so bad about that? When do people like us ever get the chance to do something silly?'

His remarks disarmed her but she steeled herself against his charm, saying, 'I suppose you do this for all your takeover prospects?'

Again his reply surprised her. 'Not really.' He leaned towards her. 'I'm beginning to think it must be something to do with you.'

Careful, she thought.

'You're different. Peculiar.'

'Thanks very much.'

'No, I mean I've been trying to work you out. It's not just because you're British, I rejected that idea a week or so ago.'

He's been thinking about me.

'You care about abstracts. Most women only care about things. That's quite right, of course, it's how children get raised and homes stay together and I'm not saying that's not part of your make-up but I find you more complex than that. You're motivated by this idea, this loyalty, this dynastic vision.'

She hugged this to herself. The Vanessa he was describing sounded impressive.

'It's inspirational.' He turned to look straight at her. 'But I have to tell you, for the latter half of the twentieth century, it's out of date. More champagne?'

Vanessa held out her glass. The dark made it hard to decipher his expression. 'Old-fashioned it may be but it's what I believe in and,' she added firmly, 'champagne and candles won't make me change my mind.'

Paul touched her arm. Involuntarily she shivered. 'One thing I've learned in business, Vanessa, is never close the door entirely. Always leave a little chink open for future negotiations. You never know where they may lead. In different circumstances you and I might have been quite close.'

How was she to take that? Was she so out of practice that she did not recognise a flirt? Maybe this was not about the business. Maybe it was because it was late at night, he was away from home and he was one of those men who regarded it as a wasted night if there was no soft body in bed with him. Any body. Especially a protagonist like her. For a man like Paul, sated with any girl money could attract, it might be a real turn-on. The thought made her chuckle.

'What's so funny?'

'I don't know you well enough to tell you.'

'That can be remedied, can't it?'

Vanessa watched fascinated as, with deliberation, Paul balanced his champagne glass carefully on the pontoon. She knew what was about to follow. If she was going to resist, now was the moment.

He was going slowly enough for her to stop him whenever she wanted but as she felt herself being drawn towards him, the sensation was so pleasurable she could not find the willpower to pull away.

His lips pressed strongly against hers and Vanessa relaxed into a kiss which was surprisingly tender and prolonged. She had to resist the impulse to put her arms round him. That would be a submission but her lips told him the truth. She wanted him.

Her skin seemed to burn wherever he touched and his hands seemed everywhere and nowhere, tracing a finger down the back of her neck, the hollow of her shoulders, before clasping her round the waist to draw her closer. Once again, when their bodies were close, as they had been at the ball, the chemistry between them ignited.

He was the first to draw away.

Quietly he murmured, 'Believe me, this was not part of the takeover plan.'

At that moment Vanessa did not care if it was, but she could not tell him that.

'Aren't you merely trying to soften me up?'

'Yes, I can't resist it,' he said with great seriousness.

As Vanessa parted her lips to respond, she found he was kissing her again. He covered her eyelids, her cheeks with urgent lips. He groaned and involuntarily she pulled her hands through the thick roughness of his hair.

The mocking wolfish yells of young boys watching them from the promenade broke the spell. Vanessa pulled away and jumped up.

Cheeks aflame, all she could whisper was, 'I'm sorry, I'm sorry, I must go.'

If she expected him to persuade her to stay, she was disappointed. Paul made a deprecatory gesture with his hands and in silence watched her walk off, her footsteps clattering on the wooden boards of the jetty.

He stood gazing up at the gleaming white hotel for a long time and worked out which of the balconies was hers. A light flicked on in her window on the sixth floor. He stayed motionless until it switched off. Two kisses had turned him into a nervous schoolboy, he thought. This was nuts. But it would pass.

He would never admit any of this to Kyle.

Chapter Eighteen

Vanessa was barely through the Rectory door from the airport when her daughter phoned and dropped her bombshell. She had consulted a top legal expert in her law faculty at Cambridge about the shares and he had advised her she could make out a good case to try and overturn the terms of her grandfather's will.

'Well, I understand why you've done it but I wish you'd talked about it to me first.'

'Mum, you were out of the country.'

'You could have waited till I returned.'

Amy was unrepentant. 'It was you who said we should fight, and as I'm surrounded by the best legal brains in the country it seemed madness not to use them. Especially since the lawyer's promised to keep the bill down as I'm a student. He says the advantage of threatening to go to court is that even if I don't win, any potential legal complication would stop the takeover dead. And that'll make you happy, won't it?'

'Yes, it will, but I suppose I never thought you'd go this far.'

'That's the trouble,' said Amy. 'No one thinks I have a

mind of my own. You still all treat me like a child.'

'But have you thought it through? How it will affect your father?'

'Mum, of course I have. Thoroughly.' Vanessa could hear her daughter's exasperation. 'There's no point in shouting at him, I wanted to do something concrete. Show him we mean action.'

'Yes, but when it comes out that you're suing your father in court, the press will go on the rampage. It'll be a scandal.'

'Well, it's up to him, isn't it? He knows what to do. It serves him right. He should give me control of my own shares.'

Vanessa sat by the phone mulling over what her daughter had said. Philip had to know at once about her threat and she had to be the one to tell him. This was not something she could discuss on the phone. It had to be done face to face.

Philip's new personal assistant at the Department of Transport was not persuaded that the former Mrs Lockhart needed to see the Secretary of State that day. Unknown to Vanessa, the girl's briefing had included a warning that her boss's first wife was in the habit of involving him in any domestic problem, however minor. 'When she says it's ultra-important it probably means the pony's got loose again,' Philip's former secretary, Maggie, had told her.

'I'm afraid the Secretary of State has a full list of engagements today,' she told Vanessa frostily. 'I can't see any way he could fit you in, Mrs Lockhart, but I will tell him you phoned. Thank you, goodbye.'

Vanessa took little notice of the secretary's lack of enthusiasm. She was disconcerted but only for a moment. Of course she had no intention of phoning Philip at home where it was almost always That Woman who answered. This was something Vanessa needed to talk over with Philip before he had a chance to tell his wife. How much she resented That Woman's involvement in her life. There was nothing for it, she would just have to go to the House and track him down herself. She understood well how the place worked so it should not be too difficult.

On the train up to London she thought back to the beach at Cannes. It was a long time since she had been sexually roused by a man and she cursed the fact that it was someone who was intent on using her. She could still almost sense the pressure of his lips and she could not resist luxuriating in the idea that maybe there was something about her that he found attractive. She could not remember the last time she had been with a man who really wanted her. Not since the early days of her marriage.

Since the divorce, Vanessa had had one affair with an opportunistic married man. But she could see that the so-called romance was going nowhere, it had to be furtive and circumspect. And once she had met his wife, she thought, I'm no better than Charlotte the Harlot. After a short time she broke off the relationship.

Was she giving too much importance to a few kisses on a beach?

As the train pulled into Victoria station, Vanessa turned her mind to more immediate concerns – the difficult discussion she would have to have with Philip. A court confrontation with his daughter would be disastrous. Vanessa shuddered at the prospect of more press intrusion into her life and her family's. The Forrester Group would be badly damaged, Philip's career would be lucky to survive and, more important than any of this, the rift between Amy and her father would be total and irretrievable. Amy might not think so now, but control of her shares could never make up for the complete loss of the close relationship she used to have with her father.

Vanessa felt confident she would be able to locate Philip. She would use the same method as a constituent, filling in the green card available in the Central Lobby and giving it to the attendant on duty. If the minister was in the Chamber, he would be passed the card at once. If he was not, she would first try his press spokesman or the Whip's Office. Somebody would know where he was.

Vanessa hoped she would not have to use the tactics of one parliamentary wife who, desperate to talk to her husband, a new MP, queued at his constituency advice bureau. When at last she was ushered in and he politely asked her what she wanted, she told him it was the only way she could gain his attention to discuss the pros and cons of whooping cough injections for their baby.

Vanessa smiled wrily at the memory of the story, though it had led to another bitter quarrel between her and Philip.

'I know how she felt. I wish you'd give me a small part of the time and trouble you give to constituents,' she had lamented. 'You're hardly ever home and even when you are, you're so distant, working on your papers, thinking about other things. I might as well not be here for all the notice you take of me.'

He had been furious, lambasting her for not understanding the pressures of his job, never taking the slightest interest in it – worse, never offering him any help. They had not spoken again that evening.

Vanessa halted the taxi at the St Stephen's entrance to the House of Commons. Walking in through the door, overtaking the line of tourists queuing for that day's passes to the Stranger's Gallery, her path was blocked by a blue serge uniform.

'Sorry, madam, the queue's along there.'

She smiled up at him. 'I'm here to see my ex-husband, Philip Lockhart, the Secretary of State for Transport.'

The young policeman was scrupulously polite. 'May I see your Commons pass, please, madam?'

'Er, I haven't got one. Well, not any more.'

'Do you have an appointment?'

'No, but I'm sure he'll see me. It's really important.'

The policeman pointed impassively towards the waiting line. 'I'm sorry, madam, everyone who comes here has to join the queue. Security, you know.'

Vanessa's cheeks reddened as she was again reminded by a stranger that she had no status in Philip's parliamentary life now. Having his children and being a loyal wife for twenty years did not count here.

For half an hour, as she filed slowly up towards the security scanners, she was conscious that the waistband of the suit she had not been able to fit into for five years was still too tight. At least she was able to wear it, although with the top button unfastened.

Vanessa again rehearsed how she would break the news of the impending legal action to Philip. He would be shocked, bitter and extremely angry but this, she would tell him, was no time for recriminations. What she had to get across to him was how they could divert their daughter from her intended path. There was only one way, and that was to allow Amy to take control of her own shares not when she was twenty-five years old but now.

A Japanese visitor ahead of her was holding up the queue as officials wearily explained why they had to search her briefcase after the scanner had sounded its alarm signal.

While she waited for the search to finish, Vanessa looked down at the medieval splendour of Westminster Hall. This was the part of the ancient building Philip most enjoyed showing his guests. There had been some happy times here. She had enjoyed watching and listening to him as he told visitors that this hall had been centre stage for some of Britain's most historic moments. Then he would lead them to the brass plaque embedded in the flagstones marking the spot on which Charles I had stood as he was tried and condemned to death. She remembered with a twinge of sadness how they had once discussed renewing their marriage vows in the underground crypt to the right of Westminster Hall.

She passed through the scanners and was turning to pick up her handbag when she noticed two people below examining the brass plaque which commemorated the lying-in-state of Sir Winston Churchill. The woman's face was very close to her attentive companion's thick head of greying hair. He appeared absorbed in their conversation. They began to make their way up the stairs in Vanessa's direction, talking animatedly. As the woman linked her arm through his, she gesticulated with her other hand to emphasise a point. Vanessa stared, rooted to the spot. That expressive hand gesture was one with which she was all too familiar.

She was appalled to see these two, of all people, together. As she seized her handbag off the scanner's conveyor, she saw Philip emerge from a door tucked in the corner of Westminster Hall and stride briskly towards the couple. The woman saw him too and instantly removed her arm.

Vanessa watched aghast as Philip greeted Paul Salter warmly and kissed Charlie on the cheek.

They must not catch sight of her. Wheeling round, Vanessa half ran back down the corridor towards the exit. She had been right to be suspicious of Paul Salter and his honeyed words. Thank God I didn't sleep with him in Cannes, she thought. She realised how close she had been. What a fool. They were probably having a good laugh at her expense.

And what of Philip? He had to be in on the conspiracy. Why else would Paul be at the Commons if not at his invitation? Did he know how familiar his wife was with the American? Paul Salter was playing a very nasty game.

Damn him. Damn Charlie and damn Paul Salter. They were all plotting against her.

Rain was bouncing off the pavements and Vanessa hovered in the porchway of the House of Commons, unwilling to expose her suit and hair to the unfriendly elements. Taxis always seem to disappear at the first sign of a shower. Just then the Right Honourable Patrick Forbes, MP for a neighbouring constituency and a man she had known for a number of years, hurried in shaking his umbrella. Vanessa smiled at him, wondering if she had the courage to ask to borrow his umbrella. He had no idea of his colleagues' nickname for him, the 'Standing Member', a reference to his predilection for sexy encounters behind closed doors at lunchtimes with a succession of personal secretaries. Vanessa caught his eye and was about to say hello when his gaze swivelled and he walked on. She was crestfallen. Once again the message was rammed home. She was invisible without Philip.

She struggled down Victoria Street towards the station and was soon drenched, feet wet, shoes pinching, hair lankly clinging to her face and neck. When she finally arrived at the station platform, she could not find the return half of her rail ticket.

In her preoccupation she did not see the newsvendor changing his poster. 'PM calls snap election' it announced.

At last she found her ticket and was able to sink into the haven of an empty first-class compartment, flustered and embarrassed at having held up a queue of impatient commuters. She spent the entire journey not, to her disgust, worrying about the takeover or Amy's legal threat but wondering just how close the relationship was between Paul and Charlie.

In the pouring rain it took an age to get the Volvo estate out of Brighton station's car park and into the tentative traffic. Vanessa inched her way forward to the roundabout and spotting a gap shot across like a get-away car. Beyond the roundabout the matinée crowd from the Theatre Royal was holding things up. The elderly patrons could not make up their minds whether or not to make a dash for the other side or wait for the next courteous motorist to slow down at the zebra crossing. One octogenarian held up a peremptory hand as he and a dozen other pedestrians trailed across the road. Frustrated commuters hooted and gesticulated at Vanessa's seeming slowness. She was tempted to climb out of her car and hit the driver behind her.

This was madness. She had to calm down. Vanessa

switched on one of the new talk radio programmes which gave local traffic reports.

She was only half-listening when a woman's laughing voice penetrated her mind. 'If my vibrator could kill spiders in the bath I wouldn't need a man.'

Despite her troubled thoughts, Vanessa could not suppress a smile. Who needed Paul Salter?

When she examined her life, she had to admit there was an up side to divorce. Able to please herself, she had become selfish. Her TV viewing was often in the bedroom now, something Philip had frowned on. She never had to worry that the house was a little untidy on Fridays when he was coming home. If she was honest, Philip now provided her with many of the cushions of marriage without the inconveniences – money, a man to call on in emergencies but with no dirty socks to wash.

Vanessa was pleasantly surprised. This was the first really honest chat she had had with herself. It took a nightmare like this to clear away the debris.

All her life she had relied on other people for support, approval and decisions. No longer. Though nervous of throwing away the crutches of the past, she determined to start to live as an emotionally independent woman. From now on she would try to sort out her own mistakes and her own problems. She felt a small surge of optimism, immediately dampened when once more she pictured Paul and Charlie together, convinced they were laughing at her futile efforts to hang on to her heritage.

Her hands tightened on the wheel. It was still raining heavily, the clouds were darkening as she came to the B road leading to Pridlington. As she pressed the accelerator,

Vanessa did not see the small grey Escort van turning across her path into the neighbouring farm.

There was a squeal of brakes as both drivers frantically tried to take evasive action. The last thing Vanessa saw as her seat belt slackened then locked was the terrified face of a young man through the windscreen. Her head was thrown back and then jerked forward as, with a sickening crack, she hit the safety glass of the toughened windscreen.

It was nearly six o'clock when Tony Burns, the Assistant Editor News of the *Daily Chronicle*, was told that the paper needed to firm up its election coverage. He would be expected to have a planning dinner on the ninth floor in the boardroom dining room rather than at the flat of his new tumble, Imogen Ferris.

Tony checked out his appearance. His suit was fine and he always kept a spare shirt and a lot of aftershave in his office for emergencies. Then he phoned Imogen. Though deeply disappointed, she pretended that his non-arrival had barely dented her evening's plans. The fact that she had spent the lunch hour belting around two delicatessens to produce the perfect meal was not mentioned. Nor that she had bought new sheets and a bath towel big enough for two. But she did get an unexpected treat.

'If you could wait for me to get round after the dinner, I could probably convince everyone at home that I need to stay in town all night. It's an emergency, isn't it? That's showbiz, know what I mean?' He laughed.

Imogen was thrilled. Who cared about dinner if she could have him all night and especially in the morning? After all her exertions, she would make him desperate to give her a job and so have her on tap all the time.

'I'll wait up until whenever, don't worry,' she told him.

It did not take Tony long to square his wife. The election was the sort of heaven-sent opportunity that a man of his talent could turn into a legover situation without breaking sweat. His wife, bored by the lies but pleased Tony still cared enough to tell them, was mollified by a promise from her husband that he would drive them up north to visit her parents at the weekend.

All three thanked the PM for this surprising bonus.

The hospital found Amy's name in Vanessa's wallet as next of kin, but it was still an hour before she could be tracked down and told about her mother's accident and a further three before her arrival at the hospital from Cambridge.

In the absence of a more senior member of the family, the doctor on duty quietly took her aside to explain that they would be detaining her mother in hospital for observation as she had been unconscious far longer than was usual after such a comparatively light head injury.

He saw her alarmed expression and said quickly, 'Don't worry, Miss Lockhart, we're just being cautious. We want to keep an eye on her.'

Amy was shocked to see her mother looking so vulnerable. In the white hospital gown, Vanessa's face in repose seemed older, sadder. Though she was still woozy, her first question when she saw the doctor and Amy was about the condition of the young man in the Escort. The doctor assured her that his injuries were minor. He had suffered a fracture in the left femur and slight concussion. Vanessa was highly relieved to be told he would make a full recovery.

When the doctor had left the room, she told Amy about her trip to London and what she had seen in Westminster Hall.

'How very, very cosy,' said Amy softly, trying to hide her fury from her mother. From the beginning her father had been lying to them. Her anger was fuelled by the guilt she felt that she was indirectly responsible for the accident. If her mother had not gone to London to intercede on her behalf, she would still be safely at home.

Amy went back to the Rectory. She would stay for a few days, until she was sure her mother was all right, before going back to Cambridge. She did not return her father's calls and so was unaware that, having been assured by the hospital that Vanessa was in no danger, he intended to visit at the weekend. This necessitated some elaborate re-scheduling as the government embarked on a highly volatile election campaign. Charlie immediately offered to have the girls to stay. But when Philip managed to speak to Louise, she refused. As usual when Vanessa was not there, Mrs Prescott would stay over.

Amy felt she was right to have broken off relations with her father. What sort of hypocrite was he to stand up day after day in the House of Commons dealing with the business of state when he could not even deal honestly with his own family's affairs?

Chapter Nineteen

The *Chronicle* made no secret of its wish to get this government out. There was almost a sense of jubilation on the news floor as the first eight pages were turned round to accommodate features on the three party leaders and their wives, a story on other unexpected elections, who had called them and why, and views on the election's outcome. The front page splash summed up the *Chronicle*'s preferences. 'Good Riddance to Bad Rubbish' the headline screamed. 'No more nice-guy stuff,' Fergus Canefield had told them. 'The way I see it, if we don't get this government out now we'll have no one to blame but ourselves.'

It was exciting. It was the chance to be in the kind of ringside seat of history which had lured many of them into the profession in the first place. Tonight, agendas would be set, careers would be built, things would change. When news of the Lockhart car crash came in Tony made it his business to deal with it himself. He was developing a special interest in this family. Maybe now was the time to look again at the Scottish nurse's claim about Vanessa Lockhart having had a love child, he mused. Now the election was on, there might be an angle to the story which could embarrass the Secretary of State for Transport. He decided to put Kevin Jamieson back on to it as soon as possible.

It was 1 a.m. when Tony finally found himself on the street. He easily justified his adulterous behaviour because he was going off to see someone who might help stand up his one slender lead. He would ask Imogen Ferris to have another attempt at finding out about Vanessa Lockhart's background. In this way he persuaded himself he was obeying His Master's voice without delay. And performing the task would rarely be more pleasurable.

The *Chronicle*'s account of the accident was not the only one to note pointedly that it had taken place after lunch and to wonder if the minister's ex-wife would be prosecuted for dangerous driving. The party's chief spin doctor advised Philip not to wait till the weekend to visit his ex-wife but to go to the hospital as soon as possible.

Philip was halfway to Brighton when his driver passed him the car phone and he heard his eldest daughter's clipped voice.

'Dad?'

'Oh darling, I'm glad you phoned. I've been trying to get through to you. I've left lots of messages and I wanted to send a car to Cambridge to pick you up.'

She made no comment.

'I'm on my way to visit Mum right now.'

'Dad, I have just one message from me, Louise and Mum. Don't bother. It will be less embarrassing for all of us if you turned round and went back to London.'

'I'm halfway down the motorway,' Philip protested. 'I'll be there in an hour.'

The line went dead.

Philip tried to contact Vanessa in the hospital but he was told that she did not want to receive any visitors or calls. Nervous of creating a scene there, Philip instructed his driver to return to London. If the driver was surprised, he did not show it, trained as he was never to react.

Philip thought wrily that those who needed to know what was happening at the heart of government talked not to civil servants but to ministerial drivers. He hoped this one would be loyal to him and keep his mouth shut.

When her mother was comfortably settled back at home, Amy went up to the Inner Temple, a world not unfamiliar to her after the years of wrangling between her parents during the divorce. She and her sister had provided affidavits, the contents carefully rehearsed in advance, to be used as evidence during the acrimonious court case discussing cus-tody arrangements. On this occasion she was to meet her tutor's contact at Frobisher & Co., one of London's top family law specialists, for the next step in the battle for her shares.

She stayed with her legal adviser for an hour.

Further down the river at the *Chronicle*'s Docklands offices Tony Burns and Kevin Jamieson were also closeted with their lawyers. As a result, Kevin picked up the over-night bag he always kept at the ready and rushed to the airport to catch the Edinburgh shuttle.

A few days later one of Philip's secretaries from the Ministry of Transport arrived at Chelsea Mansions with a pile of mail marked personal.

Philip had asked Charlie to open up his letters while he was away on the hustings. 'Darling, we've no secrets between us, have we?'

'Not on my side,' she laughed.

Today, however, Philip was due home after midnight from the BBC's *Newsnight* studio so she left the mail unopened on the kitchen table.

The letters were still there, untouched, when they sat down to breakfast. Charlie worked out that this was the first time the three of them had eaten a meal together for nearly two weeks. They would have two precious hours before they were all due to set off for a photo call at the street market in the constituency.

Framed in the bright morning light streaming through the large balcony windows, Charlie thought Philip looked grey and tired. The polls were running neck and neck on this, the last weekend before the election, and he was constantly having to attend strategy meetings with the Prime Minister and his hierarchy. The newspapers were more hostile than ever, picking up on anything and everything that could damage politicians, little heeding how the criticisms and barbs, whether about a speech or a hairdo, could wound.

Whenever she could, at evenings and weekends, Charlie was out there supporting Philip. She had seen more of British trains, had shaken more hands and pounded more pavements than she ever wanted to again. Their usually perfectly organised flat looked like hell. Only this morning Charlie had thrown out a vase of dead flowers and all the nanny seemed to do these days was moan about the 'ridiculously long' hours she was working. Charlie had assured her that things would return to normal after the election but this did not seem to mollify the girl. Charlie paid her extra for overtime, hoping to mitigate the sulky attitude and the effect it might have on Miranda. Once the election was over, Helen would have to be replaced.

Philip was going desultorily through his mail, bills to one side, letters to the other, while playing peep-a-boo with Miranda in her high chair next to him. After opening the thick envelope with the name Frobisher & Co. printed on the flap, the game suddenly stopped. His face crumpled, registering disbelief, and without a word he handed Charlie the letter. He stood up and stared aimlessly out of the window.

The letter was succinct. Their client Amy Elliot Lockhart had instructed them to take action in the matter of Lockhart v. Lockhart. There would be a preliminary hearing in the Chancery Division of the High Court. They would contact him about the date.

That thoughtless child, was Charlie's first reaction. But she restricted herself to saying, 'I wish she had come to you first before taking it this far.'

'It's my fault, Charlie. This election has taken my mind off the share business. I knew she was upset, she told me her views at Christmas. That poor girl. I didn't appreciate how strongly she felt.'

'Philip, please try not to let it upset you. Is there anything I can do?'

'I don't feel like talking about this. Not now, Charlie. I want to think it through. I'm not sure this whole business is worth it if this is where it leads to with my daughter.' He picked up the letter and went into his study.

Charlie could only wait in frustrated silence as she heard him trying to contact Amy. Having established that she was not at the Rectory, he fruitlessly telephoned the porter's lodge at her college.

Charlie stayed by his side as much as she could that weekend, behaving more like a solicitous nurse than a wife. Her heart felt heavy as she watched him play-act with constituents, press and local party luminaries.

Philip was aware of her concern but was unable to share his thoughts, some of which would cause her more pain. He thought in terms of Biblical retribution, that his firstborn could only speak to him through the law courts. How had he managed to make them all so unhappy? Vanessa, the girls, and now even Charlie? Had being an MP ruined his marriage to Vanessa? Had becoming a Cabinet minister destroyed his relationship with Amy? He had not given priority to discussing the problem with Amy, to explain the reasons for his decision to transfer her shares to Charlie. He had failed to take his daughter into his confidence, never seeing her as the intelligent, self-sufficient young woman she had indisputably become.

There was so much of her life he knew nothing about. Where was she now, for example? Philip felt a sense of shame. He had no idea who her new friends at university were, which societies she had joined, how she spent her leisure time, anything.

It occurred to him that perhaps he should inform the Chief Whip of the letter. There was a real danger that when the court actions were posted, a journalist would pick out his name. But he did not have the stomach for that yet. What mattered now was to get hold of Amy. They had to discuss this problem between them and bridge the deepening rift.

He recognised he was being unfair to Charlie, shutting her out, but until he had his thoughts in order, he felt it was wiser to keep his own counsel. He was afraid that anything he might say could wound her more than his silence. Right now he needed to examine his priorities.

He spent most of Sunday in his study, unreachable. Early on Monday morning, before she was up, Charlie heard him talking yet again to the porter at Amy's college. By now he was on first-name terms with the man. Still no sign of Amy. She feigned sleep until she heard the intercom buzzer announce the arrival of his car.

Philip came into the bedroom and leaned over to kiss her forehead. 'I'm sorry about all this, darling. I'll phone you later.'

Before he left she heard him go into Miranda's room. He stayed there for what seemed a long time.

She had been awake most of the night debating whether she had the courage to intervene. Philip had not asked for her help. But then he had hardly said a word to her all weekend. God knew what he was thinking. On the one hand she was frightened that if she interfered, the whole thing could blow up in her face. But she needed to do something. Philip might give way to his daughter's emotional blackmail and change his mind about the takeover. That would be disastrous, both for the future of the company and for his health.

She finally decided she could not sit back and do nothing, she had to intervene. Philip would strongly disapprove but she felt she had to give it a chance. Amy was not heartless. If she could only get to the girl and explain why she had accepted the shares and why a court case could so damage her father, surely Amy would change her mind about taking legal action?

★ ★ ★

Kevin Jamieson's arrival at SRN Fiona McKellar's Edinburgh flat coincided with the latest demand from her building society. It wanted to discuss the irregularity of her mortgage repayments. Urgently.

All uneasiness at becoming involved with newspapers was banished as she and the *Chronicle*'s chief reporter discussed how valuable it would be to the newspaper and how grateful they would be if Fiona could remember any more details of the Lockhart baby. Wasn't it fortunate she had seen that paper on that particular day?

Nurse McKellar wanted to know exactly how grateful they would be. In pounds and pence.

Kevin procrastinated and they agreed to discuss the matter with the editor. But she could trust him, Kevin assured her. The paper would be generous. He mentioned four figures to start, more if her tip yielded a front page story. Added to the money she had already been promised, this ensured the nurse's full co-operation.

A rummage through some files produced the name of the head of the adoption agency that had handled the Lockhart case. Kevin asked the local correspondent to establish that she was still alive. He phoned with the information in an agreeably short time. She was resident in the same block of flats in Edinburgh she had lived in for the last thirty years.

It was with great difficulty that Kevin managed to persuade her to see him. On the phone she was curt. At his second attempt he changed his voice and his story, claiming to be one of the children she had placed for adoption. She then did agree to see him, but only in the corridor outside her flat.

The trim, grey-haired woman, in her late sixties, was clearly deeply suspicious of Kevin's story and, deciding that he had little to lose by being straightforward, he identified himself as a reporter from the *Daily Chronicle*, up from London. He confessed that he was searching for a boy born twenty-seven years ago.

She was furious at being deceived.

'I know that your work was confidential and I don't expect you to give me his name or his whereabouts,' Kevin persisted. 'But there's a substantial sum of money due to him if he can give us some small assistance with a story we're working on at the moment. I thought you might contact him and give him the opportunity to talk to me and earn some money.'

There was a long silence which Kevin's years of experience had taught him not to fill. A woman like this would not be easily persuaded.

Her answer, when it came, was unequivocal. 'No.' She moved towards her front door.

Kevin thought rapidly. 'Are you sure you have the right to deprive this young man of a great deal of money? Especially since we know who he is,' he added. 'We have a copy of the birth certificate. We know the baby's mother is Vanessa Forrester but we would rather not involve her at this stage if we don't have to. Our business is with her son. That's why we need your co-operation.'

There was no change in her hostile expression.

Shit.

The adrenaline drained away. Instinct told him this woman was never going to crack. As she quietly closed her front door, Kevin made one last desperate attempt to get her to co-operate: 'You know, we will find him. With or without your help,' he shouted.

Her door remained firmly shut. OK, he'd have to do it the hard way. Nine times out of ten they reached for the phone to warn the victim at a time like this. It would take him only a few hours with his telecommunications chum to get all the numbers she dialled from now on.

He was right. Before Kevin had returned to the Edinburgh office, the woman had looked through her old files and picked up the phone. She understood how persistent and powerful these newspaper people were. Reluctantly she had decided it would be best if she got to the family before they did.

An hour later, through his telephone exchange contact, Kevin picked up the itemised list of calls she had made. To each number he pretended to be a contest organiser offering those between twenty-one and twenty-five the chance to win a convertible. By this process of elimination he tracked down his quarry.

Chapter Twenty

This was going to be the most difficult thing Muriel McKinnon had ever done. She was whisking eggs in preparation for a surge of sponge-making. She found the motion most therapeutic when she was troubled and Angus loved having cake for his tea.

After the phone call which had so agitated her, Muriel had found it hard to concentrate on her domestic duties. The woman from the adoption agency had said that she would never normally break a confidence, but in the sad circumstances she thought it only right that Muriel should know that a newspaper reporter was trying to track down Angus and knew the name of his natural mother. She did not know what the reporter planned to do next but it might be best if Angus was forewarned.

A bewildered Muriel thanked her.

She had always said that it was God's will that Angus should be told the truth, that he was adopted, but not by her, and not in these circumstances. Not now when Angus had just lost the two people he had known and loved as his parents. They weren't even buried yet. The funeral was on Wednesday.

Muriel sat down and wiped her eyes. Angus had lost his parents in the car accident and she had lost her dear brother and sister-in-law. Apart from her nephew Angus, she had no other family now. She had never married.

She heard the front door letter box rattle and thought it must be her nephew but when she went into the hall she saw that someone had pushed a letter through. She picked it up. It was addressed to Angus.

Muriel went back to the kitchen and finished preparing Angus's tea. She had moved into the family home temporarily until the funeral. Her nervousness made her over-enthusiastic so by the time Angus arrived the polished walnut table was barely visible beneath the profusion of plates filled with her legendary high tea – miniature game pies, quarter wedges of Scottish Cheddar cheese sandwiches and thick rashers of ham, alongside her famous apple and clove tart and cream sponge.

As she poured the strong dark tea, she nodded approvingly as Angus heaped his plate, her intelligent brown eyes searching his face. She could see he had no real appetite, he was only trying to please her.

'Auntie, how are you bearing up?'

She hesitated. 'I haven't been able to cry, not properly. I still can't believe your parents have gone. I keep expecting them to walk in any minute.' The tears glistened on her eyelashes as she busied herself with the teapot.

'I know what you mean,' said Angus sombrely. 'It's the suddenness of it I can't cope with. One minute I picture them both sitting here with you, laughing and chatting, and the next minute . . .'

Her aunt put her head in her hands and Angus went to her.

'They were very good to me, Angus. Always welcomed me to their home. They were there whenever I needed help or advice.' She sighed. 'At least helping you to organise the funeral has kept me going. I've contacted all the people on your list. Most of them are going to be there. I'm glad you're going to be able to take a few days off afterwards. It'll do you good.'

They discussed the hymns to be sung, the people they would ask to speak during the service and the sleeping arrangements for some of the guests.

'And I've arranged for Morag to stay next door,' his aunt concluded.

Although he had shared a flat in Edinburgh for two years with his girlfriend, when they stayed with the family it was understood that no unmarried couple could be in the same bedroom.

Muriel looked at her nephew with a smile. 'It will be different when she's family.'

'I'm not sure she's going to be,' replied Angus. 'I'm not sure about anything now. You'd think that grief would have brought us closer but I think it's having the opposite effect. I think we've been together a little too long.'

Good, thought his aunt, and wondered whether she should be frank. But this was not the time.

'It's early days, Angus. My advice is not to make any decisions at the moment.'

Her task was going to be hard but she stiffened her shoulders. She had to do it now or she never would. But it was difficult to find a way to broach the subject.

'More tea?' she prevaricated.

'No thanks. As it is I've had to let out my belt.'

'You do need fattening up, my boy. You're too thin.'

They both smiled. She always said the same thing although the shape of his six-foot-two frame had not changed since his teens.

She looked at him levelly. 'There's something you should have been told years ago and I've been wrestling with my conscience because I'm finding it quite hard.'

He smiled. 'Dad always told me it's best to come right out with anything that's bothering you. Come on, it can't be as bad as all that.'

'Angus,' she said tenderly, 'I know this will come as a great shock to you but,' she inhaled deeply, 'your mother and your father were not your real parents.'

'What!'

'They adopted you when you were only a few hours old.'

He just stared at her. It never crossed his mind to question or contradict his aunt. He accepted at once that what she told him was true.

Nervously she continued, 'They wanted children so badly, they tried everything. When the doctor told them they could never have a child of their own and they had the chance of a private adoption, they didn't hesitate. Believe me, they wanted you very much. You couldn't have been more wanted if you had been in your mother's womb.'

Angus was stunned. 'Why didn't they tell me? Why did it have to wait till they were both dead?'

Muriel brushed at some crumbs on the table. 'I can't answer that. Angus dear, I urged them time and time again to tell you. But they so much wanted you to be their own, their very own, that after a while I think they convinced themselves that you had been born to them. They were afraid that if you knew the truth you might leave them some day.' She clasped her hands over his.

'Oh Angus, I wish you could be spared this. I would never have dreamed of breaking their confidence but I don't have any option. A journalist from London has contacted the adoption agency about you. The woman who was in charge is retired now but she warned me that the reporter had come up here from London and is nosing around. She doesn't know why. And this letter came through the door this afternoon.' She handed Angus the envelope bearing his name.

The letter, on *Daily Chronicle* letterhead, was from Kevin Jamieson. It was brief and to the point, requesting an interview urgently in connection with a story the newspaper was working on. This concerned the woman mentioned on the copy of the birth certificate (attached). There would be a sum of money involved if Angus co-operated.

After studying the certificate intently, Angus passed it across to his aunt. She felt compassion at the sight of his stricken face.

'So that's her name. Vanessa Forrester.'

Angus flushed. 'Did you ever meet her?'

Muriel shook her head.

'What do you know about her?'

Muriel sighed. 'Not much. She came from a village in Sussex. All the midwife said at the time was that the girl came from a good family and because she was only fifteen she wasn't able to keep you.'

'But she's never tried to find me since?'

His aunt explained to him gently. 'The terms of the adoption were strict. Once the agreement was signed, there was to be no contact from either side. The papers are all upstairs.'

'What about my ... father? Is anything known about him?'

'Nothing at all, and as you can see, his name isn't on the birth certificate. Oh Angus, Andrew and Rosalie were your parents. All these years they brought you up and thought about you and worried over you and prayed for you. You were their son in every sense of the word. I didn't want to tell you this, certainly not so soon after your sad loss, but hearing about the newspaper reporter gave me no choice.'

Angus was puzzled. 'I don't understand why he should be interested in me. If he has come all this way for a story, it must be pretty important. It has to involve my ...' he found himself unable to use the word, 'the woman who gave birth to me.'

'I don't know,' replied his aunt. 'But I couldn't let you find out about your adoption from a stranger.' She paused. 'Did I do right in telling you, Angus? Should I have kept quiet?'

Angus stood up and put his hands on her shoulders. 'I don't know. I have to go and think it all out. It's been such a tremendous shock.' He shook his head as if trying to clear away his thoughts.

Muriel tried to comfort him in the only way she knew. 'Angus, you've been given a lot to think about. Have another cup of tea.'

'No thanks ... I'm sorry, will you excuse me? I need to be on my own for a while.'

As she watched his tall frame walk slowly up the stairs to the bedroom his parents had so recently occupied, Muriel

McKinnon felt uneasy. Angus's parents had often fretted about their son's impetuousness. 'Doing before thinking' was how his father put it. Now she was the one left to cope with his reaction to the cataclysmic information he was trying to absorb. She took her coat from the cupboard, went outside and began walking towards the tiny church nearby.

The bedroom was as Angus had always remembered it. Nothing had changed for years.

He looked sadly round at the faded cream walls, past his mother's walnut dressing table to the bedside table where his father kept his Bible.

Under the bed was an aged suitcase, cracked and coming unstitched, in which they kept all their precious documents. It did not take him long to find the faded manila envelope, creases deeply etched on the yellowing document. Their copy of his birth certificate. The space allowed for the father's name was blank but the registrar's neat handwriting gave his place of birth as a hospital only seven miles away. The building had long since been demolished and the hospital amalgamated with a nearby infirmary. The newspaper's copy was identical.

Angus stretched out on the bed and laid his head on his father's pillow. He could almost smell his aftershave. His throat constricted as his eyes roamed the walls where a row of certificates proclaimed his triumphs at school and university over the years. They had been so proud of him.

He thought of something positive he could do right then. He would phone Morag and cancel supper so that he could go through the papers thoroughly.

The suitcase was filled with old bills, out-of-date contracts and the family's personal papers. He would look through every scrap for other clues to his background. Although he had no firm plan, Angus wanted to find out who his real parents were and why the reporter should be so interested.

Was this being disloyal to his parents' memory? He did not know. A short while ago everything had seemed so ordinary, so settled. Though he had loved his parents dearly, he had recognised that they were different in personality, style, and temperament to him. He had been puzzled that he did not physically resemble either of them. His hair was much darker, thicker and curlier than theirs and he used to joke about how much taller and more angular he was than his father. But like most of his generation who towered over their parents, he had explained this to himself as being due to better nutrition and a vigorous exercise routine. His grandparents were unknown to him, both sets having died before he was born. Was that true? He had to question everything now.

Angus and his parents differed in their interests, too. He was sporty, they were not, and secretly he wished he had inherited their ability to play several musical instruments – they had met as members of the college orchestra. He was tone deaf, and he attributed this deficiency to a genetic and tuneless throwback.

His had been an uncomplicated life: assiduous student, a Fine Arts graduate of Glasgow University and now at twenty-seven number two in an advertising agency's graphic design department. In his spare time he developed his talent for portraits in oils.

Now he could not be sure of who he really was. Angus turned over and shielded his eyes with his forearm. At last they came. Deep, wracking, wrenching sobs.

★ ★ ★

Imogen was still breathing heavily after some very strenuous exertion. She had practised everything on him, everything she had ever learned or read in sex manuals. And it seemed to be having the desired effect.

Inspired by her efforts, Tony gave a groan, rolled off her and said, 'I could give you some more work for the *Chronicle*.'

To Imogen this was almost as desirable as love talk.

'We had a bit of luck after your catfight story,' he told her. 'Some nurse from Edinburgh tipped us off how naughty Vanessa Lockhart had been when she was a schoolgirl.'

Imogen raised herself up on her elbow. 'What do you mean, naughty?'

Quickly Tony told her about the lovechild, the discovery of the birth certificate and Kevin's success in tracking Angus down.

'Why didn't you tell me this before?' Imogen was pained.

'Well, you weren't authorised to know at that level.' He grinned mischievously and she squeezed his ear till he gave a mock yowl.

'It's all hands on deck now the election's on,' he said as he tapped a cigarette out of his pack. 'Top priority is to find out who the father is, particularly since Vanessa was under age when she had it.'

Imogen was overjoyed to be at the centre of a national newspaper investigation. She could almost see herself in a job in the capital.

What was it Vanessa had told her? 'I don't remember smiling that whole year.' It all made sense now. 'I bet you the baby was born on December the twentieth,' she told Tony triumphantly, recounting how melancholy Vanessa had been on the day of their interview and how she had commented that the date always marked a sad anniversary.

'You're right. If you'd told me that before we'd have saved a lot of time,' said Tony. 'Maybe you should go and dig around that village she lives in. Try and find out who she hung around with at that time.'

So it was that the following day an exhilarated Imogen found herself in Pridlington, a small village where she assumed everyone knew each other's business and where Vanessa had lived all her life.

Imogen spent hours trawling round the cobblestoned streets talking to people in the pub, the garden centre and the garage. No one seemed to know about Vanessa's past boyfriends. Most had only ever seen her with her ex-husband.

But an interview with one of the local residents, Vanessa Lockhart's board colleague Anne Grover, was more helpful. On the pretext of adding to her magazine profile, it had been surprisingly easy to lead the woman round to discussing Vanessa's love life.

'Such a shame Vanessa hasn't married again,' Imogen said, trying to sound disingenuous.

'I know,' agreed Anne, 'but there's only ever been one man for her, more's the pity.'

'She's an attractive woman, I can't believe there weren't plenty of suitors in her past,' Imogen probed.

'As far as I know there's only ever been Philip. I never heard her talk about anyone else. Then or now.'

Imogen remained silent.

'Let me give you a refill.' Anne poured more coffee.

'Vanessa told me years ago that her mother even sent her off to boarding school to try and break them up but they got back together after her mother died.'

'How old was she when she was sent away?' Imogen asked casually.

Anne looked at her sharply. 'I've no idea. That's not important to your article, is it?'

Anne Grover would not be drawn further and Imogen, aware that she must not arouse suspicion, backed off. For the moment.

She reported her findings to Tony immediately.

'By God, Imogen, you're a lucky girl.' Tony sounded pleased. 'All the best journos are.' But he was already planning to send another, tougher interviewer to grill Anne Grover. 'Leave it to me now. I'll get back to you.'

'When are we going to meet again?'

Women. They could never leave their emotions out of business. 'I'll call you.'

Chapter Twenty-One

Vanessa was hungry. She had already consumed her ration of two ounces of unsugared oats, a slice of melon and a cup of black coffee an hour earlier. All she could think about was what else she could eat without wrecking her diet.

She was sore and bruised after the accident. But it had provided one small advantage. She had lost another five pounds during the hospital stay.

Her post was the usual collection of junk mail and brown envelopes containing bills. Nothing interesting. She threw out the amazing competition prizes and once-in-a-lifetime offers, put the brown envelopes aside to be dealt with later, and hurriedly slit open the only white envelope addressed in unfamiliar handwriting to Vanessa Forrester. It was a long while since she had been called that. Vanessa was intrigued by the Edinburgh postmark. Who did she know in Scotland?

As she unfolded the one-page letter with its perfect fountain-penned script, one short sentence leapt out at her: 'I believe I am your son.'

Hands trembling, she re-read the letter twice before she could fully absorb the message, all thoughts of food forgotten.

She stared at the signature again with a mixture of apprehension and excitement.

Vanessa closed her eyes, picturing the small hospital room, the intense pain, then the joy when they put him in her arms and the anguish when, that night, her baby was taken away. She had been allowed only a brief glimpse of his reddened crying face topped by downy black hair before they whisked him into a side ward.

A day later a probationer nurse, moved by her tears, had brought her own Polaroid camera into the hospital and secretly took the baby's photograph for her. But the picture had long since faded. The other nurses had been efficient but there was a dour, censorious air about most of them. Vanessa was never sure whether it was because her mother had persuaded them it was their duty to 'punish' her or in deference to her sorrow at the loss of her baby that they were so monosyllabic.

Vanessa read the letter again, slowly. Angus McKinnon. So that was what they had named him. He wanted to meet her.

In the early years she had regularly taken out the fading photograph on his birthday, an emotional exercise which always led to speculation about what he looked like now, where he was, what he was doing. It ended up far too often with Vanessa seeking the consolation of too many glasses of wine.

Now he was asking to see her – because of the newspaper's intervention, it was true. Despite all the upheaval it would cause, she was glad. She had dreamed of this for so long. Part of her had always hoped it would happen. What would he be like? What would he think of her? How would he react when they met?

Vanessa was in turmoil and the thought of explaining Angus McKinnon to her daughters filled her with dread. She had talked to them many times about the dangers of having sex before they were ready. They would never understand about Angus. And they would not be the only ones. What about her friends on the charity committees? The other members of the Forrester board? The people in the village? No, she did not want to share this secret with anyone. Only Dorinda was aware of the child and she would never betray that confidence.

Vanessa stood up, shivering, and crossed the well-worn flagstones. She had taken succour from the many people who thought of her as the injured party in the divorce, the woman who had seemingly done no wrong. 'You have nothing to reproach yourself for,' was the constant refrain when news leaked out that Philip had left her for another woman. How would they react once they heard she had had sex at fourteen?

But it was Philip's secret too. Angus McKinnon would want to know who his father was. If she told him, what would he do with the information? 'I would not have contacted you,' he wrote, 'but the *Daily Chronicle* have sent me a copy of my birth certificate bearing your maiden name. The adoption register gave me your last known address and, hopefully, you are still in the same area.'

It did not sound as if he wanted to co-operate with the *Chronicle*, but how could she be sure? She had given him up for adoption as soon as he was born. He owed no allegiance to her, or to Philip.

How had the *Chronicle* made the connection? Her mind raced through all the possibilities. It had to be something she had said to Imogen Ferris. Why had she not been more careful?

Impulsively she dialled Imogen's office but as the switch-board answered, Vanessa quickly replaced the receiver. No, the idea of trying to find out what Imogen suspected was far too dangerous. Her grandfather had always cautioned her against anticipating problems before they happened. 'You're inclined to cross bridges before you even reach the field the river runs through. The clever solution is to take evasive action when you know the extent of the problem, not when you can see it in the distance.'

Head in hands, Vanessa turned over all the permutations. The press was only interested because Philip was a member of the government. It would not take the paper long to establish that she and Philip had been close friends since their early teens. If she told them he was not Angus's father she could imagine the response: 'Well, you would say that, wouldn't you?' Or the trickier question, 'Who is the father?'

She ought to warn Philip. They could deflect the press more effectively if they combined their efforts. But instinc-tively she recoiled at the thought of contacting him. She had not spoken to him since before the accident and by now he would have heard from the solicitors acting for Amy.

Vanessa sat up and straightened her shoulders. She was once again crossing bridges before she had reached them. The press had no hard evidence to implicate Philip. She would not give it to them, nor would Philip, with or without forewarning, and Angus was in no position to. For all she knew, he might not give a damn who his father was. It seemed unlikely, but until she met him she had no way of knowing and no way of assessing what he might do. Really, she had nothing useful to say to Philip. And with a sudden surge of anger Vanessa recalled what had happened last time she had tried to help her ex-husband with a forewarning. An image of Charlie and Paul Salter, arms linked, heads close together, and then a smiling Philip joining them, flashed into her mind.

No, she would not contact Philip. She would meet her son, something she wanted to do more than anything else at that moment, whatever the consequences, and only then would she decide on her next step.

Vanessa could hardly absorb what Angus was saying. She was so focused on the way he looked, his wavy brown hair springing in an unruly forelock. He bore a striking resemblance to Philip's father.

What a nice-looking young man. He has the same intense blue of my eyes, she thought with a stab of pride.

They had arranged to meet in London, in a hotel near King's Cross station. Vanessa had stared at him with instant recognition the moment he walked into the lobby. Her instinct had been to fling her arms round him but she was unsure how he would react. He appeared to be as nervous as she was. Instead, she led the way self-consciously into the lounge and ordered coffee.

He had clearly taken a great deal of care with his appearance, wearing a well-cut navy-blue suit with a crisp white shirt and silk tie which he fingered nervously. She had discarded three outfits before choosing a black suit then, at the last minute, abandoning the jacket for a less formidable dark green one.

As they sat down, she was overwhelmed by a wave of

love and she could tell from his flushed face and shining eyes that he, too, was emotional.

Angus's manner was direct. 'You know I didn't seek you out because I wanted to. I would never have known I was adopted if that newspaper hadn't decided to take an interest. But for that, you and I would never have met.'

'In that case I'm glad it happened.' Vanessa gave a timid smile. 'I've wanted to meet you for a long time.' She looked at him. There was one question she had to ask him. 'Do your parents know you're here, with me?' She saw the pain in his eyes before he looked away.

'They died in a car accident. Quite recently,' he said, his voice tight.

Vanessa paled with shock. 'Oh Angus. I'm so sorry.' Her heart went out to him. She wanted to reach out and comfort him.

Angus was silent for a moment. When he spoke, his tone was brisk. 'How did the *Chronicle* get on to this story? How did they trace me? Do you have any idea?'

'No, I don't,' Vanessa said quietly.

'It wasn't the adoption agency,' Angus told her. 'They tried that route and failed. The woman who used to run it alerted my aunt. But they still managed to discover my parents' address and my name, and it didn't take them long. They know where I work now, too, and they're quite persistent.'

Vanessa wondered uneasily how he had dealt with their persistence. 'They won't be easy to shake off,' she said. 'But the fact is, all they have is a birth certificate, my name and your name. It's not much of a story on its own and they'll have a difficult time making it run if we refuse to say a word.

Absolutely nothing, not even a "no comment".'

Angus only nodded.

'I'm assuming,' she added carefully, 'that you don't want to co-operate with the press.'

He looked at her sharply. 'I would feel I was being disloyal to my parents' memory.'

Vanessa's relief was apparent but she warned, 'They won't be easy to shake off. They'll try and get you or your aunt to the phone by pretending to be someone else. They'll tell her it's you. They'll tell you it's her. They'll certainly go round all the people at your office and try and put words in their mouths. It doesn't matter if your friends tell them nothing. Some reporters will make up quotes. But eventually when they can't get anything, they'll drop it. After all, they're not interested in either you or me. It's my connection to Philip Lockhart. That's who they're trying to wound. They're hoping this will give them a stick with which to beat the government now there's an election underway.

'But the birth certificate doesn't name the father and it would be a foolhardy editor who tried to implicate Philip on the basis that I knew him in my early teens. That's not enough.'

Angus nodded. He seemed reassured by her analysis of the situation which was a combination of some knowledge of the way the media worked and common sense.

Vanessa wished she could ask him about himself, his life, his interests. Did he have a girlfriend? Was he married? But she knew she couldn't. Not yet. His outward composure barely covered his grief and confusion. All she could do was try and help him to understand.

'You know your parents had no choice but to keep the

secret,' she said. 'It was one of the terms of the adoption.' Embarrassed, Vanessa hurried on. 'Over the years I thought of you often. I was always miserable around your birthday. I used to sit and imagine what you were doing, how you would turn out and whether you were happy. That's all I could do,' she said hoarsely, 'since I was legally bound not to interfere in your life.'

'If you felt like that, why did you allow me to be adopted in the first place?' Angus's voice sounded critical.

Vanessa knew she was being assessed. It was impossible to tell from his expression what he thought of her. His gaze was steady as he waited for her reply.

'Angus, I was only fifteen when you were born, a very young, unworldly fifteen at that. The moral climate was antediluvian – at least it was in the village I lived in. As soon as my mother found out I was pregnant, she took charge of everything. She arranged for me to go to Scotland, sorted out the adoption and made me swear that I would never tell anyone. She told me that no man would ever want me if he knew about the baby and I believed her.'

Vanessa felt ashamed. It was one thing to rationalise this to herself over the years, another to say it to the consequences of her schoolgirl passion.

'I know it sounds pathetic now but she was a domineering woman and in those days I would never have dreamed of disobeying her. And I was frightened about what would happen if she left me to cope on my own.'

Still Angus gave no hint of what he was feeling. Finally, he said brusquely, 'And what about my father? Did he know?'

'He didn't know I was pregnant.'

'The newspaper people think Philip Lockhart is my father,' Angus said bluntly. 'They've been badgering my aunt and told her that's why they're interested in me.'

Oh God, thought Vanessa. Here it comes. She ran her fingers nervously through her hair. 'I can see why they think so because he's the only serious boyfriend I'd ever had so they would assume . . .' Her voice trailed off.

'And they'd be right to assume that. Wouldn't they?' Urgently he leaned forward, his body tense.

'They have no right to assume anything,' Vanessa prevaricated.

'That's not what I asked you.' There was an angry edge to his voice now, which alarmed Vanessa.

She took a deep breath. 'Angus, you have every right to know who your father is. But I think your father has rights too. He doesn't know I'm meeting you. He has no idea that the press are interested. If his name ever comes out, it could do him a lot of damage, and I'm not just talking about embarrassment. Remember, I was under age when you were conceived. I must talk to him first.'

Anger and disappointment flickered across Angus's face. 'When?' he asked curtly. 'I'd like to know now. It's the least you can do.'

'It's not easy,' she said quickly. 'We haven't spoken . . .' Vanessa faltered under her son's unflinching gaze.

Angus moved nearer. 'If it's Philip Lockhart, I won't do anything, I won't tell anyone. I need to know,' he said forcefully.

For an instant Vanessa was tempted but she stopped herself. 'As soon as I get home, I will contact you directly after I've spoken to him.'

'I suppose I'll have to be satisfied with that,' Angus said, obviously disappointed. He looked at his watch. It was time to catch the train back to Edinburgh. Stiffly, he said goodbye and left.

Vanessa was close to tears as she watched his tall figure leave the restaurant. Would she ever see him again? She had so wanted to earn his trust and get to know him. Damn and blast the *Chronicle*. There was no question in her mind that she had to get hold of Philip as soon as possible. The task filled her with dread.

She would have been even more apprehensive if she had known that Angus, still angry at not finding out the name of his father, had on impulse caught a taxi at King's Cross station instead of his train and was on his way to Philip's constituency.

The party HQ was situated at the wrong end of the High Street in Heathgate, furthest away from the big shops and the motorway.

Originally an attractive Georgian double-fronted house, it could have been improved with an industrial clean, thought Angus with his artist's eye when he arrived. Its handsome front door, opening right on to the pavement, had not seen a lick of paint for many years. Inside, the décor had been woefully neglected, a disregard which continued throughout the building.

As Angus entered the hallway, a short, compact woman greeted him. She was immaculately though plainly dressed, her neat grey hair setting off rather fine, dark brown eyes. Her smooth skin belied her sixty-odd years.

She introduced herself as Wyn Stevens, provider of teas,

coffees, homemade biscuits and tender loving care at election time for the parliamentary candidate and her co-workers.

Angus told her he wanted to help the campaign and asked when the MP was due to arrive. Wyn, used to volunteers wanting to meet the star, said vaguely that he was expected later. 'Poor lamb, he's so busy. The local paper's waiting to take a picture of him and Miranda. And Mrs Lockhart, of course. But I don't think he'll have time for that today.'

Angus was uncertain what to do next. He was not used to play-acting and was unsure whether he could keep up the pretence of eager volunteer but Wyn seemed preoccupied with her own problems and ushered him into a large, draughty hall without asking any further questions.

Several lines of trestle tables were set out as if for a meal but instead of cutlery and flowers, leaflets showing Philip Lockhart's face exhorting the voters of Heathgate to re-elect the 'man they can trust' smiled across every available surface. Volunteers were filling envelopes.

Wyn showed him the most efficient way to insert a leaflet into an envelope and left him to it.

Sensing an appreciative audience, she also told him about some of the tactics used in the past to shoehorn voters out of cosy homes and into the polling stations. 'One of our blokes was told by this woman that she couldn't go out to vote because she couldn't find her false teeth. Well, he simply took out his own and said, "Here, missus, use mine." ' Angus could not believe it had happened but she laughed and insisted it was true.

For two hours Angus worked steadily, waiting for Philip to turn up. Finally, stiff from sitting so long, he decided to stretch his cramped legs. In the hallway, Wyn came up to him.

'I know you were keen to meet Philip but I've just had him on the phone. He has to write a speech for a rally tonight so he's decided not to come here today. He sounded tired. But he might pop in tomorrow.'

Angus sighed to himself. He looked past her into Philip's office and, following his eyes, Wyn smiled. It was clear she greatly admired 'my Member', as she called Philip. 'A lot of people respect him. Would you like to see a photograph of him taken when he first came here? I had someone take it for me as a souvenir.'

She led him into a small waiting room.

'I've hung it in here,' she said. She took the picture off the wall and handed it to Angus. 'I'm on the left,' she said proudly. 'That's Vanessa, his first wife, with their two daughters. Amy, on the right, was about nine or ten, and there's little Louise. Next to Philip is his father. Such a nice man. See how proud he looks?'

Angus stared at the photograph. It was like looking into a mirror. He was the image of Philip's father. There could be no mistake. The angle of the head, the same brow. And he could recognise himself in the young Louise, a typical tomboy with shorn hair and a devilish grin.

The evidence was in front of him. Angus was as certain as he could be that Philip Lockhart was his natural father.

Wyn did not seem to notice his silence, and when he suddenly made an excuse to leave, she did not appear to mind. Cheerfully she bade him goodbye, saying she would see him tomorrow.

As soon as she had left the hallway, Angus darted back

into the waiting room and lifted the photograph off the wall.

He hurried from the building, angry and hurt. Vanessa had painted a picture of a young girl facing disgrace alone, forbidden ever to see her lover, threatened with a life of lonely spinsterhood if she disobeyed her mother. It was all lies. She had not only seen her lover, she had married him – Philip Lockhart, his father. They had deserted him, packed him off to strangers at the other end of the country, not because it was in his interests but because it suited them and their ambitions.

Angus made his way to the party's election head-quarters. The staff there were only too pleased to give him details about public meetings he could attend. He quickly discovered that the rally Philip Lockhart was due to address that night was at the International Convention Centre in Birmingham.

Angus made up his mind what to do.

In the train en route to Birmingham, Angus stared at Wyn's photograph. It was ten years old and faded but he remembered photographs of himself at Amy's age. It was like looking at his twin. He scoured that morning's papers. Two of them had pictures of Philip at a rally the day before but any likeness between him and the minister was not obvious from the photographs.

The train was late and by the time Angus arrived at the huge hall in the impressive Convention Centre, the only seats vacant were in the balcony.

Campaign posters picturing the Prime Minister lined the walls. Television arc lights illuminated the platform where the local MP was already speaking and trying to whip up the crowd's enthusiasm. This was Angus's first political meeting and the fervour of the audience surprised him. The atmosphere was more redolent of a rock concert or an evangelical meeting.

Often he had accompanied his father – his adoptive father – on church business, for he was an elder of the kirk. They had discussed what it was that urged certain personalities to seek the limelight. 'Anyone who needs such public approbation, and I'm including elders in that,' his father used to say, only half-jokingly, 'is probably covering up deep insecurities. However self-assured they look up there on the stage, likely as not they're a mass of quivering jelly inside.'

Angus found this hard to believe as he watched the confident-looking, arm-waving party official build up to a crescendo of praise to introduce the star speaker of the evening.

'... The man who was catapulted into the Cabinet because he's what this country needs. Fresh ideas, energy,' the announcer thumped the air with his fist, 'action to take this great country of ours onwards into the next century. Ladies and gentlemen, Philip Lockhart.'

The television cameras swung round to the side door as the audience stood up, stamping their feet, and clapping till their hands stung, shouting 'Yeah, yeah . . .'

Angus found himself on his feet too, caught up in the passion of the crowd. The inspirational election anthem played at full blast and TV and press people surged towards the platform where a tall, square-shouldered man raised his hand in salute to the crowd.

Angus's breathing was shallow as he set eyes on the man he now firmly believed was his father. Philip Lockhart was beaming delightedly at the ecstatic reception and went into his speech full throttle.

Angus was too far away to see his features clearly but instinctively, like the rest of the audience, he responded to his warmth. Philip Lockhart was a passionate proponent of his beliefs and ideals, and the vigour with which he put his arguments was impressive. For nearly an hour he spoke without notes and for the most part the audience was rapt, enthralled.

As Philip acknowledged the standing ovation of the euphoric crowd, Angus battled his way to the side door and waited for him to emerge. A line of cars, engines running, was ready to take the entourage to their hotel for the night.

Philip was first through the door and was immediately surrounded by throngs of wellwishers. Angus was one of the dozens who proffered their hands over the heads of the crowd.

Shouting above the din, he tried to catch Philip's eye. 'Excuse me, Mr Lockhart . . .'

The MP flashed his brilliant smile and reached for Angus's hand. But it was grabbed by a party zealot who gushed, 'Wonderful speech, Mr Lockhart. An inspiration.'

'Thank you. Thank you.' Philip was moving through the crowd, adhering to the politician's motto of 'If it moves, shake its hand; if it doesn't, stick a poster on it.' Angus was uncertain whether or not to be more assertive when security men hustled in front of him, pushing him aside. Within seconds Philip was inside the waiting black Rover and the car moved off.

Angus followed the hordes of media to Philip's hotel where the candidates were due to have dinner but his entrance was barred by the uniformed doorman because he could produce no accreditation.

'Sorry, sir. Security's tight tonight.'

Angus's instinct was to try and make an ally of the doorman. 'I want to see Mr Lockhart on personal business,' he told the thickset six-footer. 'I'm related to him and I'm sure he'll see me when he knows I'm here.'

'Well, I'd like to take your word for it, sir,' was the reply in a thick Brummie accent, 'but it's more than me job's worth to let you in.'

Angus thought for a moment. 'Could you get a message to him then?'

'That I could, sir. Why don't you write a little note. I'll see it gets to the right quarters. But I go off duty in fifteen minutes so don't be long.'

In the pub opposite, the barman only had till receipts and a green ballpoint. It would have to do.

Angus sat in a corner of the crowded pub trying to find the right words. In the end his letter was short and to the point. 'Dear Mr Lockhart, I hope this will not come as too much of a shock, but I think you are my father. I was born in Edinburgh twenty-seven years ago and only recently discovered I was adopted. There is a particular reason why I need to speak to you urgently.' He underlined the word 'particular'. 'I will call at your hotel later this evening and look forward to meeting you then.' He signed the letter carefully, making sure his signature was legible, and then, as an afterthought, underlined the word 'later'.

The doorman was most obliging, especially when he saw the twenty-pound note Angus proffered. With a sleight of hand any magician would envy, it instantly disappeared into his pocket. He promised that the letter would be delivered to Philip Lockhart's suite immediately.

Angus went off to find a bed for the night, hopeful that Philip would know of his existence within a few hours. He would not have been so confident if he had been able to see into the doorman's hatch inside the hotel lobby and overhear him reading the contents of his letter down the phone to the *Daily Chronicle*'s newsdesk.

The doorman was well satisfied with the promise of an extra fee on top of his monthly retainer, a reward for alerting the *Chronicle* gossip columnist to the hotel's high-profile guests. Many politicians used the hotel as they criss-crossed the country in the hunt for votes. The doorman was one of those targeted by the paper after the election was announced. At the newsdesk's request, he faxed Angus's one-page letter to their London office and, just to be on the safe side, repeated the same exercise with the *Daily Despatch* before re-sealing it and handing it over to Philip's chief aide. Two payments for the same information was good.

At the *Chronicle*, an excited news editor read out the contents of Angus's letter to Tony Burns.

'That's the guy we're after. We'd better get someone up there,' he ordered. 'Concentrate your fire on finding Angus McKinnon. We must get him to talk before Lockhart shuts him up. He says he's going back to the hotel so get your butt over there *toute suite* and sign him up.'

Although Angus had marked his envelope 'Confidential' and 'Personal', all mail at election time, home or away, was screened before being handed to a politician. Elections attracted all kinds of unwanted letters, ranging from those sent by militant activists to the green-ink missives from what the MP's entourage called the 'fruitcake brigade'.

Sadly for Angus, letters claiming close kinship with people in the public eye were not unknown. His political adviser, Chris Bennett, noted that the handwriting was evidently that of an educated man but those telltale signs, green ink, heavy underlining and scruffy paper, persuaded him not to bother the Secretary of State in the midst of a gruelling election campaign.

'Battiness comes from every quarter,' he thought ruefully as he put Angus's letter in a bag earmarked for party headquarters and eventual filing with other unwanted correspondence.

When Angus presented himself back at the hotel, he was told brusquely by the receptionist that he could not enter without the right security pass. She had no knowledge of any letter and the Secretary of State had left strict instructions that he was not to be disturbed. Had Vanessa tipped off his father? It was clear he did not wish to see him. Angus left in deep depression.

By the time the *Chronicle* reporter had been roused from a well-earned dinner after following the political circus all day, Angus had been and gone. Tony told his reporter that he would be facing a job hunt next week if he had not tracked down Angus McKinnon by morning. So began the wearisome task of phoning the many hundreds of hotels and guest houses in the city.

Tony took down a copy of that year's *Who's Who* from his bookshelf. What he saw pleased him and he pressed the intercom buzzer to summon his chief reporter.

After explaining his strategy he instructed, 'Get up to Edinburgh and squeeze that nurse like a lemon.' He leaned forward. 'And Kevin, this is where you justify some of the cash you've splurged on those expensive lunches. Ring your credit card guy and find out where our mysterious McKinnon's been spending money lately.'

Tony and Kevin were treading a well-rewarded path. Thanks to the credit card ploy the *Chronicle* had been able to publish the first exclusive photograph of Princess Diana's alleged lover, who was using his credit card all over America as he fled press attention when his royal romance hit the headlines.

'You'll find McKinnon's been in Birmingham.'

'How the hell do you know that?'

Tony tapped his nose.

'It's called journalism, my son. That's why I'm here and you're there.'

Chapter Twenty-Two

Angus's gaze wandered forlornly round his drab hotel room with its dung-coloured curtains which did not quite meet in the centre and the burn in the carpet where a previous occupant had casually lobbed a cigarette.

He sighed heavily. He had just been speaking to a distressed Aunt Muriel who had complained that a *Chronicle* reporter was still camped outside her front door after she refused to talk to him. 'I've not told him anything but he says he won't go away till you speak to the paper. But don't worry about me. He'll get fed up before I do.'

Angus's pent-up anger erupted. How dare these damned reporters threaten to splash their names across the newspaper, and for what? To titillate readers for a day or two. He and his aunt were pawns in an odious little game.

He told his aunt how Vanessa had tried to fob him off with a sob story about how young and isolated she had been when he was born, and how she had refused to name his father. Even now she was still putting her and Philip Lockhart's interests first, he said bitterly.

Muriel tried to soothe him. 'Leave well alone, Angus,' she counselled. 'Come home.' But she could hear the determination in his voice as he vowed not to return before establishing exactly who he was and where he came from.

Angus lay on the bed and stared at the ceiling. He would have to get a message to Philip Lockhart at his home – and deliver it personally this time. How could he find his private address? The *Chronicle* would know how, no trouble, he thought wrily. He could not go back to Heathgate and try his luck at the constituency office. Party headquarters certainly would not help. As he wracked his brains, he suddenly had an idea. He would look up Lockhart in *Who's Who*. He was sure Cabinet ministers did not usually give their home addresses, but Philip Lockhart had only recently been promoted. It was worth a try.

The disinterested hotel receptionist gave him directions to the nearest public library and soon Angus was leafing through the pages of the latest edition of *Who's Who*.

Philip's lengthy entry listed all his achievements but Angus was only interested in his personal details: 'Married 1st,' he read, 'to Vanessa (née Forrester) 2 d; 2nd Charlotte Gabrielle (née Mills) 1d.' It seemed he had two sisters and a half-sister. And he was in luck. There at the end of the entry was the Lockharts' London address.

Carefully Angus wrote down the details. Where the hell was Pimlico?

Charlie was finding it hard to concentrate on the station's editorial news conference.

Such a lot was resting on her impending lunch with Amy. If anything went wrong when they met, Philip would find it hard to forgive her interference. As it was, she had not told him what she was doing.

It had not been easy to arrange the lunch. Amy never returned her calls and in the end she had written to her at Cambridge, a brief but urgent note, sent by special delivery, asking her, please, to respond. Next time Charlie phoned, Amy spoke to her and, to Charlie's relief, agreed to meet her. I must have sounded really desperate, Charlie reflected. That girl has a will of iron. This was the first time Charlie had ever interposed herself between father and daughter but it was unthinkable that they should find themselves confronting each other in the High Court. She had to prevent it.

Charlie's mood was not improved by Tom Levin's sniping. He was number two in the London office of ABN. It had been getting worse since the election was called. As a Brit educated in America she had been put in charge of their British election specials and he resented this. He maintained that it was only because of her marriage to a British Cabinet minister that she was the pivot of the channel's election coverage. He chose to ignore, although her bosses had not, how well she had handled her first British election campaign, long before she had married Philip but at the time of their romance.

Charlie was finding this campaign exhausting. On top of her work she had to deal with a baby, a nanny and the greater demands made on both her and Philip because of his Cabinet position. She had to show her face at many weekend and evening rallies, and Philip was hardly ever at home.

As a minister Philip was usually chauffeured to some hotel for the night, leaving Charlie to make her own way next day by train or drive herself. Not the most pleasant of pastimes in an already crowded schedule. Last night Philip was in Birmingham and tonight there was to be a huge rally in Manchester. Charlie had been given a personal invitation to attend dinner afterwards with the Prime Minister, a command performance, Philip had told her. There was no possibility of her getting home. She and Philip would have to stay in some impersonal hotel. Charlie hated sleeping in a strange bed and, worse, spending a night away from Miranda. She only did it when forced. She had already packed her overnight bag to make a quick dash to Euston station. If everything went to schedule, maybe there would be time to rush home for a quick cuddle with Miranda.

Helen, the nanny, had been sullen at having to give up yet another evening to care for the toddler. What was the point of coming all the way from Waikato, New Zealand, she complained, if she had to spend evenings the same way she did at home? Charlie had been uncharacteristically sharp with the girl.

She tried to shake these worries from her mind and pay attention to what was being discussed.

'We're giving this election far too much coverage.' It was Tom Levin sounding off again. 'Last night we sent over five minutes of the stuff in our package. New York used thirty seconds of it. The cables had only a tiny mention and CNN had it at number eight. Back home they think it's boring. If you think my mother in Peoria cares about this election here, you're wrong. There isn't anyone sexy in it, or anyone they recognise. At least Thatcher was exciting and everyone was aware of who she was.' Tom was looking straight at Charlie. None of this was new to her but she wished today of all days he would shut up.

'I take my orders from the political bureau in New York, Tom, not you,' she said, gathering her papers. On the wall were clocks showing the times at the various ABN bureaux around the world. London time was twelve thirty. She was due to meet Amy for a late lunch.

She tried to concentrate on work. The video tapes she was waiting for arrived at that moment and she asked the editor to come in and watch them with her. As Charlie slipped on the earphones she entered another world. Twenty minutes later she took advantage of a lull while New York discussed her ideas to phone the nanny on her mobile to make her peace.

That irritating message again. 'The number you have dialled may be switched off. Please try again later.' Damn that nanny. She was always blaming the battery for break-downs but Charlie was beginning to suspect it suited Helen to turn it off.

For the first time that day, Charlie looked outside at the sky and realised how blue it was, a bright, perfect spring day. Helen must have gone with the nanny mafia to the park. Charlie felt a wave of envy at the thought of Helen walking leisurely through their pretty neighbourhood park. A few Sundays ago it had been her and Philip with their daughter among the daffodils, feeding the ducks, with a gurgling Miranda attempting to throw breadcrumbs somewhere in the direction of the brooding mallards. If only that could happen more often.

Charlie checked her screen for messages. There was nothing from Helen but this office was notoriously lax about passing on information about personal calls. She made an effort to sound cheerful on her home answering machine, leaving a brisk message asking the nanny to phone her at the office the minute she returned.

Charlie looked at her watch. It was time to go and face Amy.

Charlie perused the menu for the third time. Amy was twenty-five minutes late and she had convinced herself that her stepdaughter was not going to turn up. Part of her sympathised with Amy. Being an MP's child was often a handicap. There was too much early attention at play group and school, when everyone knew who you were. Then you had to try to live up to the well-known parent while observing what a lonely, frustrating life it might be for the other parent. Weekends were often filled with photo-opportunities, fêtes and fund-raising sales. If the MP were really successful he – or she – might become a minister. Then not only local papers but nationals too would wait for the child to put a foot wrong so they could splash its misdemeanours on the front pages.

In some ways Philip's remarriage had taken the spotlight off Amy and Louise. Charlie did not know the statistics concerning the offspring of politicians whose children had disappointed lives and occasional premature deaths, but she was determined that this would not be the fate of Miranda even if it meant sacrificing her own career.

Charlie was about to leave the restaurant when a tall, windblown figure, pale face atop a swathe of black cotton layers of varying thicknesses, appeared in the doorway.

On reaching the table Amy mumbled hello and shook out a tumble of long dark hair, uncombed since the bicycle ride from Trinity to Cambridge station.

After waving away the menu and ordering a plate of stir-fried vegetables, she announced pejoratively, 'I think there are better ways to spend money than to patronise places like this.'

This was not a great start but Charlie decided to ignore her rudeness.

'I want you to promise not to tell your father about this meeting. Nor anyone else.' Charlie's face was strained.

Amy stared at her, her head held slightly to the side. 'I can't possibly promise that unless I know what all this is about.'

Charlie hesitated. 'Your father had a nasty fright last summer. He collapsed and I had to take him to hospital. They told him it was his high blood pressure and when we came home he went to his own doctor. After various tests, he was told that too much stress would be extremely dangerous.'

Amy's response was still quite hostile. 'If it's so serious, why doesn't he give up politics?'

Despite herself, Charlie could not prevent a wry smile. 'Do you think I haven't asked him? Repeatedly. Don't you think Dr Murray hasn't suggested it? I was horrified when he told me about his Cabinet job. But your father thinks that if he takes things a little bit easier, cuts down on alcohol and watches his diet, that'll be enough. He's kidding himself. He's quite forgotten that visit to the hospital.'

Still Amy did not react. How was she ever going to get through to this recalcitrant girl? While Amy picked at her meal, Charlie forced herself to continue the one-sided conversation. This was her one opportunity to convince Amy of the seriousness of the situation.

'I wouldn't blame you for thinking that I'm being alarm-ist, that I'm exaggerating everything to stop you taking your father to court.'

'Isn't that what you are doing?' Amy's tone was caustic.

'Amy, I know you love him as much as I do. You have to believe I would never lie about your father's health. I want you to be under no illusions,' Charlie emphasised the words, 'that I would do anything, absolutely anything to protect your father. It's why I'm always trying to persuade him to cut down on his commitments.'

'Is that why he hasn't come to see me once in Cambridge except when he was in the area for a speech?'

The two women stared at each other. 'Look,' said Charlie after a while, 'parents make mistakes. We're not perfect. You and I haven't got on very well but can't we try and make a new start? Your father is miserable without you and Louise. He misses you terribly and the one thing he wants most in the world is for you all to be friends again. You can't be happy about this situation. Can you?'

Amy looked into the distance and shook her head.

'Please think about what I've said and the effect your legal action will have on your father.'

When they parted, Amy had not given Charlie any hint by expression or word of what she intended to do.

The New York bureau kept Charlie so busy with queries about arrangements for a new camera crew that she had little time to reflect on anything when she got back from lunch. It was more than an hour before she looked at the clock and realised there had been no call from the nanny.

Like most working mothers, Charlie took comfort in

knowing precisely what her daughter was doing when she was at work; it made her feel less cut off from Miranda's life. She and Philip had been delighted when Miranda had come to recognise their voices on the phone although, in quieter moments, Charlie felt sad that this precocious ability was too often the main communication with their child these days.

Charlie was adept at disguising how much she allowed her domestic arrangements to intrude into the office routine. Her colleagues were unaware of the extent of the phone calls needed to organise the nanny, the baby, the flat and social engagements. When she was ordering the delivery of groceries for a dinner party her demeanour was the same as if she were questioning a prospective interview subject for the nightly bulletin. She had become skilled at that.

The sky began to darken and she could see from the barometer that the outside temperature had fallen to a chilly twelve degrees. She dialled her home number.

Damn the girl. Still the answer machine. How often had she impressed upon Helen that it was vital to tell her in advance about any change in routine?

Nowadays this was not merely to assuage her guilt at being a working mother. Shortly after Philip's promotion they had been visited by a Special Branch officer who had stressed the importance of at least one member of the family knowing the movements of the others throughout the day, and at the start of the election campaign Cabinet ministers and their families had been given special briefings about the increased need for vigilance.

'Don't open packages you have not ordered,' they were told. 'Be safe rather than sorry, call us immediately. In the unlikely event of an undesirable getting hold of your private phone number, tell us at once. If they are on tape, do not wipe it until we have checked it out.' The danger was not from criminals but more from obsessives demanding action for their own particular hobby horse, and an election campaign tended to bring them out. Charlie had painstakingly transmitted the Special Branch advice to Helen.

Although she wanted to believe there was a good reason why the nanny had stayed out so long, instinct told her something was wrong. She tried to reassure herself. Helen was probably having tea with one of the other nannies she met almost every day. Maybe she was with the girl who had charge of those lovely twin boys in Paget Street. What was their surname? Gregg? No, Gregson. Luckily they were not ex-directory and Charlie found them in the telephone book.

But Mrs Gregson's nanny had not seen Helen. Not that day. Not any day. Two other neighbourhood nannies said the same. In the five months Helen had been looking after Miranda, she had never brought her charge to the local park with them. No, they had no idea where she took Miranda each day.

Feverishly Charlie tried to remember the exact words Helen had used to explain her movements. No, she was not mistaken. Helen had given the definite impression that she met the nanny mafia on Tuesdays and Thursdays. Why would she lie?

Charlie had a sudden picture of the packet of condoms in the kitchen. I should have trusted my instincts and asked her about them. At least let her know that I was aware of them. Where on earth could she have taken Miranda for this long?

Helen had been out of contact since before eleven that morning.

The sky had deepened to navy blue by now and Charlie pressed the Home button on her desk console and activated the remote control function. The first voice she heard was her mother's. She was looking forward to seeing them all next Sunday. The next message confirmed an appointment with the central heating engineer. Then followed calls which were work-related, two of which Charlie had already dealt with, and a friend from the States asking plaintively, 'Am I going to see you before I fly home?'

No message from Helen.

There was a second message from the central heating engineer, now sounding annoyed, complaining that he could get no answer at the flat although he had an appointment. There would be a call-out fee to pay, he warned.

The next was from a man with a soft Scottish accent. 'This is a message for Philip Lockhart. I called at your home earlier to discuss something personal but as you were not there I'm forced to communicate with you through this machine.'

What was all this about? That question was quickly followed by the unpalatable thought that the man had been there, at their flat.

The voice went on, 'My name is Angus McKinnon and I've just met my mother, Vanessa Lockhart, for the first time.'

Vanessa? His mother? What was he talking about? And what did it have to do with Philip?

Haltingly the man continued, 'I tried to find out from her who my father was and she wouldn't tell me. I am very angry about that.'

259

For a second Charlie thought that was the end of the tape. But the voice went on, 'That's why I came to your home earlier. I am desperate to talk to you because I believe you are my father.'

Philip? His father? The man must be deranged.

There was a longer pause as the voice hesitated. 'I wish I didn't have to leave such a personal message on your answer machine but you leave me no choice since you've ignored my letter. But I've met Miranda and Helen,' Charlie listened in mounting panic, 'and I'm with them now.'

There was a silence on the tape before he added, 'I'll be in contact later.' Then the line went dead.

Charlie's heart stopped and her mouth went dry. She pressed the remote control button and waited for the message tape to rewind. Listening again to the man's words, she strained her ears for any sound of Miranda. There was none.

'What's the matter?' asked the vision mixer, seeing all colour drain from her face.

'Miranda's disappeared,' Charlie blurted out. 'And this strange man on the answer machine says he's got her.'

'Oh my God.' His face mirrored her terror. 'What can I do to help?' he asked. 'Phone the police?'

'I don't know. I must get hold of Philip.' She tugged nervously at her hair. Who the hell was this man? Apparently he had met Helen. Was he a friend of hers?

Charlie grabbed her mobile and her coat, and raced to the stairs, dialling Philip's number.

Chapter Twenty-Three

Philip was spending the afternoon inspecting a new range of catalytic converters being manufactured by a factory in a marginal constituency near Plymouth. Party strategists had targeted the area as one of those they had to hold if the government was to be re-elected. A visit from a high-profile, well-liked Cabinet minister might swing a few of the wavering votes and tip the balance their way.

Philip's mobile was answered by his political adviser Chris Bennett.

'Who's that?' asked Charlie agitatedly, expecting the personal phone to be answered by her husband.

Chris recognised her voice at once. 'Sorry, Mrs Lockhart, it's Chris Bennett. The minister gave me his mobile as he is touring a factory at the moment.'

'Oh God, I must speak to him now. It's urgent.'

He picked up the panic in her voice. 'He's not in my sight right now; they're looking at some sensitive equipment. Is there anything I can do?'

She hesitated, torn between trying to be discreet and communicating the urgency of the situation. Since the story of her row with Vanessa had appeared in print, she had become very cautious.

Maternal anxiety overcame professional caution. 'Miranda's disappeared and there's a message on the answer machine from a man called Angus McKinnon. I think he's kidnapped her.'

It was then that the political adviser justified his top-grade rating. His tone switched from placating wife-of-Cabinet-minister mode to handling emergencies.

'Do you know him?'

'I've never heard the name but he says he's Philip's son and he's met Vanessa.'

'Tell me his exact words.'

When she repeated Angus McKinnon's message: 'I am desperate to talk to you because I believe you are my father', a warning bell sounded in Chris Bennett's brain.

Christ, he thought. The hotel, the letter. He had not mentioned it to Philip. He was damned if he could remember the name. What if it was the same person? What had he done with that letter? Yes, that's right, he had sent it on to party headquarters.

Given Charlie's state of mind, he thought it wiser not to mention the letter at this stage. If it was written by the same person, it would show premeditation. Dangerous.

Charlie's voice was almost inaudible. 'This man says he tried to find out from Vanessa Lockhart who his father was and she wouldn't tell him. He said he was angry about that.' She began to cry. 'Chris, do you think he'll take it out on the baby?'

'No, no, of course not.' Chris tried to sound more reassuring than he felt. 'Try not to worry. I'll get your husband to call you at once and I'll alert the police. Why don't you go home in case he rings again and we'll contact you there?'

Chris put his sluggardly weekly training run round the park to good use and ran over to the laboratory block in seconds. I'd better cover my back, he thought. He laboured for breath. I'd better check that letter in case this thing develops.

The factory's managing director did not attempt to disguise his extreme irritation at being interrupted when he was in full flow burdening the minister with an account of government regulations which were 'strangling the industry and making it impossible for us to compete with the Koreans'. Ignoring his angry stare, Chris took Philip aside, his face impassive, his voice betraying no sense of urgency.

'Minister, you're needed back in London at once. I'm afraid we'll have to cut short this visit. Your wife called. There's a problem.'

By his tone Philip knew at once something terrible had happened.

The MD's fury increased when he learned that the minister would miss the expensively catered lunch, the informal chat with the workforce and, much worse, the valuable photo opportunity. He thought with chagrin of the bragging he had done at the nineteenth hole of his golf club. Graciously he had invited a couple of his golfing buddies to the reception. Well, this government had lost his vote.

As Philip was making his apologies, Chris walked towards the ministerial car. He was already on his mobile phone to party headquarters. 'There's a real emergency here. I want you to organise a helicopter now, I would guess the nearest one's in Plymouth, to return Philip Lockhart to

London. I'll ring you from a more secure place en route.' Then he rang the police.

As the car pulled away, Philip's politician's smile switched off instantly and he turned anxiously towards Chris.

'Minister, your baby and the nanny have been out of contact since around eleven this morning.' Chris chose his words carefully. 'And there's a rather odd message on your machine at home from a man who says he's with Miranda.' Chris saw Philip's hands clench. 'He says his name is Angus McKinnon.'

Philip shrugged. 'The name means nothing to me. What else did he say?'

'He seems to be under the impression he's your son.'

Philip's expression changed. He seemed to be stunned. Chris waited.

Eventually Philip said, 'Vanessa and I did have a baby, a boy, a long, long time ago, years before we married. He was adopted and as we couldn't trace him, I had to put it out of my mind. I'll have to talk to my ex-wife.'

Good God, thought Chris, careful to keep his face expressionless. How many more skeletons did this man have in his cupboard? Chris served the Prime Minister and the government as a whole before any individual member of it. He wasted no time on platitudes or questions.

'This must not come out, Minister,' he said firmly. 'It would be highly damaging.'

Philip was aghast at this reaction. 'What are you saying? I don't care about publicity now, not if it's going to help my child. To hell with my career, to hell with everything. This is far more important than politics.' He reached for the car phone. 'I must talk to Charlie.'

★ ★ ★

Charlie was in a taxi on her way home. The bureau chief had prevented her from driving because she was in too emotional a state. She had refused his offer for someone from the office to accompany her and had sworn both him and the vision mixer to secrecy.

The bureau chief, a normally undemonstrative American, saw her into the cab and flung money at the driver to ensure a faster than usual journey. But outside the Tate Gallery the traffic gridlocked. Charlie thought she would scream. This turned to a wail when Philip at last reached her on her mobile.

'I'm on my way home, darling,' he said. 'Any more news? Has the man phoned again?'

'No,' she cried, 'and I'm stuck in traffic. Oh Philip, you don't think anything's happened to Miranda, do you?'

'No, I don't. Helen's a sensible girl. I'm sure they'll be all right. Hang on, Chris is speaking.'

There was a slight pause.

'The police have been informed.'

'No, no, no,' shouted Charlie. 'Maybe this man's after money and if he thinks we've told anyone he might . . .' Her voice broke.

'Try not to worry about that. There will be a total news blackout. Nobody will know the police are involved. They are on their way to you. They'll want to listen to the tape and get a full description and photo of Helen and the baby. I should be home within two hours. Darling, Miranda's going to be all right. I love you.'

He was relieved Charlie had not asked him outright about Angus McKinnon on the phone. If she knew that the man

265

could indeed be his son, it would only add to her fears. She would have to know soon enough.

He dialled Vanessa's number. When he heard the engaged signal, he gave a tut of exasperation and as the driver negotiated the narrow Devonshire roads at over seventy miles per hour, he pressed the redial button constantly. The speedometer slowly crept up to ninety. Still Vanessa was talking as they reached the Plymouth base.

The Royal Air Force pilot was already warming up the engine of the Puma in readiness for his VIP passenger and the two-hour helicopter flight to London.

When she heard Charlie's voice, Vanessa nearly put down the phone.

'Hello? Hello?' Charlie was getting desperate. 'Vanessa? It's Charlotte Lockhart.'

For a second Vanessa wondered if she dared pretend she was Amy or the daily or anybody. This was the first time she had ever taken a phone call from Charlie.

'This is an emergency,' Charlie said quickly when Vanessa answered at last. 'Have you heard of a man called Angus McKinnon?'

'What?' Vanessa was startled. This was the last name she expected to hear from Charlie. Where the hell had she got it from? She played for time. 'What do you mean, Angus McKinnon?'

'Don't play games, I think he's kidnapped my baby.'

'Kidnapped? That's ridiculous.'

'It's not!' Charlie tried not to shout. She did not want the driver to hear. The more secret she could keep it, the safer her baby. 'This Angus McKinnon left a message on the answer machine saying he's got the baby and the nanny. There's definitely something wrong otherwise I'd have heard from Helen.'

'Oh my God.' Could it be true? Vanessa was panic-stricken.

'He says he's your son. Is he?'

Vanessa was uncertain how to answer. Philip had obviously not told Charlie, even now.

'Vanessa.' Charlie was getting hysterical. 'This McKinnon says you're his mother. Do you know him? Is he your son?'

In a voice little more than a whisper, Vanessa replied, 'Yes, he is.'

'For God's sake, Vanessa. He's gone off with my baby and he says you've met him. Is that true?'

There was a long silence before Vanessa finally answered. 'Yes. Once. But I can't think why he would do something like this.'

'Well, I bloody can. He has a crazy idea that he's Philip's son.'

Vanessa felt sick. How had he found out? 'Well, he didn't get that from me,' she said warily.

'Why the hell couldn't you tell him who his father was? If you'd had the decency to level with him, he wouldn't have been angry, he wouldn't have jumped to conclusions and he wouldn't have gone off with my baby.' Charlie was beside herself with fear and rage. She hardly knew what she was saying.

Her words made Vanessa flinch, but it was not for her to tell Charlie that Philip was Angus's father. 'I'm so very sorry about all this,' she said. 'I didn't tell anybody about him because I couldn't see how it would involve anyone else.'

'Well, now it bloody does. Is this man so angry that he'll harm my baby? Does he want money?' Her voice rose. 'Vanessa, what's he going to do to Miranda?'

'I'm sorry, Charlie, I can't help you. He seemed normal when I met him.'

'Normal? My God.' Vanessa could hear her breathing hard. 'Now look, you're the only one of us who's set eyes on him,' Charlie said finally. 'I want you to talk to the police now and give them as much information as you can.'

Vanessa's response was instant. 'Of course I will. I'll help in any way—'

'If anything happens to Miranda,' Charlie cut in, 'I'll never forgive you. Never.'

Vanessa could hardly bear to listen to the torment in Charlie's voice. However much she disliked her, she would not wish this pain on anyone.

She heard the click as the phone was switched off and put her head in her hands. Miranda missing, Angus implicated. Vanessa groaned. After the divorce she did not think life could get any worse. But it had.

The flat was in darkness. Charlie raced from room to room looking for signs of life, a note, anything.

Nothing. It was exactly as their daily had left it. No one had used the kitchen or the bathroom.

Charlie ran downstairs to talk to the porter but he could offer no clues. Scratching his head he pondered while Charlie moved around agitatedly.

'Yes, I'm sure they left a little before twelve or it may have been eleven. I remember I hadn't had my sandwiches. I usually eat about noon because it gets so busy with—'

'Think, Robert. This is very, very important. Were they with anybody?'

'No, I don't think so. But your car's not in the garage so she must be using it.' He looked at her agitated face. 'Is there something wrong, Mrs Lockhart?'

'Yes, I think so, Robert.'

Ignoring the lift she dashed back up the stairs. Charlie wracked her brains to think of anyone who could shed light on where Helen had gone. She realised she knew virtually nothing about the girl's private life. She had never brought a visitor home. Charlie had rarely heard her make a phone call. Surely Helen had talked to someone, sometime.

The phone bill.

Feverishly she went through Philip's meticulous filing and found the itemised accounts for the previous quarter. In her state, all the numbers looked unfamiliar. Oh God. She would phone Helen's previous employers, the Lawsons. Perhaps they would know something about Helen that could help.

The Lawsons said she was a quiet, reserved kind of girl. She did go out regularly but she would never say where. Since Helen seemed content and only went out after their youngest had started school, they did not like to pry.

Charlie was sitting at the kitchen table amidst a heap of phone bills, head in hands, when she was startled by the sound of the intercom buzzer.

Thank God, they were back. Helen had forgotten her key.

But it was only the voice of the porter announcing the arrival of Detective Superintendent Peter Goddard and his team.

They took over the flat. The tape was listened to several times while a detective took copious notes. Then it was carefully extracted from the answer machine, bagged and sent off by despatch rider for a transcript and voice analysis.

'In your experience, could there be some innocent explanation for this?' Charlie asked the superintendent.

'At this stage, no one can be sure,' Goddard answered carefully. 'We're always concerned about any young child who goes missing in unusual circumstances. Now,' he went on, 'who is Vanessa Lockhart?'

Charlie told the police all the relevant details about her husband's first wife, giving him a full account of her phone conversation about Angus McKinnon with Vanessa.

'Do you think this man is her son?' asked the officer.

Charlie was cautious. 'I don't know for certain but it's hardly something she would make up.'

If the policeman was intrigued by this information about the ex-wife of the Secretary of State for Transport, he did not show it. He spoke to his opposite number in Brighton and asked him to despatch a car to take Vanessa to the local station so she could be interviewed about the personality and character of Angus McKinnon and brief the police Identikit artist.

Philip's study was commandeered as an interview room. The porter's memory was dredged for information about Helen's habits and clues as to her possible whereabouts. He revealed a disturbing pattern of nocturnal outings by the nanny. Since Charlie's anguished questions he had concentrated on remembering more about the nanny's movements.

'You see, what used to happen was that the Lockharts would usually come back around six, you know, for the baby's bathtime and all that,' said Robert, happy to have a legitimate reason to gossip about his tenants. 'Then on the nights Mr Lockhart had to get back to the House of Commons and Mrs Lockhart to her office – she worked far too long hours, in my opinion – this girl would go out, taking the baby with her. I thought it was strange, much too late to keep a baby out, but it wasn't any of my business, was it?'

Charlie was horrified when Goddard communicated this information to her. As Helen was always back by the time she or Philip returned, they had had no idea she was in the habit of going out. When they phoned home and found the answer machine on, Helen would say she had switched off the bell so she could get a good night's sleep.

Among the police team was a woman officer who had been involved with several child abduction cases. Her attitude was so sympathetic it had the effect of frightening Charlie rather than reassuring her. But the only time she broke down during the entire recital of events was when she had to go into Miranda's room to fetch a recent photograph.

Helen's room surrendered very little information. There were no address books, very little reading matter, few clothes, for that matter. It was unnatural really, for such a young woman. Charlie had ascribed this austerity to Helen's having come from a Calvinist background and to her travelling light in preparation for the usual backpacking journey round Europe before returning home to New Zealand. The Lawsons had never found fault with her in the two years she worked for them, although they did mention Helen was reserved. That seemed to Charlie at the time to be an asset for anyone who had to share the flat with them.

The police were as puzzled as Charlie had been by the condoms she had found in the kitchen.

'Before Christmas I heard Helen talking on the phone about some party,' Charlie told them, 'but I could never draw her out about her friends or what she did in her spare time. She never mentioned a boyfriend, didn't seem interested in men at all.' She remembered the phone bills and handed them over.

The focus of the questioning switched back to Angus. What power could he exercise over the nanny? Charlie speculated whether Helen was being held against her will by Angus or even that Helen had run away with him taking Miranda with her.

'We can't dismiss any theory at this stage,' was all the superintendent could be drawn into saying.

As Philip had said, a news blackout was immediately enforced. Police press officers began phoning editors of all the country's national newspapers. News blackouts were reserved for emergencies where the safety of an individual was dependent on absolute secrecy. This procedure had started twenty years ago after the kidnap of the wife of an oil magnate. The police enquiries were conducted under such a ferocious media spotlight that it had pushed the kidnappers over the edge and frightened them into killing their victim rather than holding out for the ransom.

Protected by this blackout, details of the missing baby and her buggy, the nanny plus a description of her suspected abductor were circulated. Within minutes, through a message switch system into the main computer, the information had reached all police stations, airports, ferry ports and railway stations, including the Channel link. Hospital admissions had been checked. So had all charge sheets in police stations listing those arrested throughout Britain that day.

Charlie was sitting rigid by the phone, willing it to ring. Both times it did so, she and her two police minders jumped. On neither occasion was it Angus McKinnon and she cut short her American friend who had left a message earlier, and also her mother, without alerting her to the drama. She had been warned not to talk about Miranda's disappearance to anyone and to keep the line as free as possible in case the man made contact again.

At the same time Philip's pilot was looking for the beacon on the outskirts of London which would guide him to the Battersea heliport.

Though as emotional as Charlie, the Minister was having to be more controlled. Having automatically been offered the headphones that bypassed the pilot, he and his aide were able to discuss whether everything that could be done, had been done, including calls to his daughters, his constituency agent and the Prime Minister.

Though extremely concerned, the Prime Minister had instantly decided the sympathy vote might help his party's electoral chances so long, he told the Chief Whip later, as the whole saga did not overshadow polling day itself. It was imperative at this stage that no media emphasis should be taken away from his electoral message.

The news blackout did not stop certain policemen continuing to moonlight as newspaper spies. Less than half an hour after the clampdown, in common with other papers, the *Daily Chronicle* was contacted by its informant and given a transcript of Angus McKinnon's message.

Tony was exhilarated. A Cabinet minister in a kidnap story just before election day? And the great twist was that his illegitimate son was the suspected kidnapper. Couldn't be better.

The story that he thought had died was coming alive again. With bells on. He could hardly contain his excitement until Kevin Jamieson, summoned on a pager, walked into his den. Tony closed the door, a sign to Kevin that something big was about to break.

'That Lockhart story looks as though it has legs. My contact at Snow Hill tells me Philip Lockhart's kid has been snatched. And get this. Who do you think's done it? Our Houdini of the north. The one we're tracking.'

'That McKinnon guy?'

'The one and very same.'

'Bloody hell.'

'Where was the last time he used his credit card?'

'New Street station, Birmingham. He took an Inter-city to London.'

Tony briefed his chief reporter on what his police contact had told him. 'What none of the other buggers will know is that our up and coming new Cabinet minister was giving Vanessa one when he was seventeen and she was fourteen.'

'You're going for the under-age-sex angle?' Kevin brightened. 'That's more like it.'

'Yeah,' chortled Tony. 'It's still against the law, never mind that half Britain's schoolkids are at it. But won't their mums and dads be scandalised?'

'I don't suppose the PM and the party will be thrilled either,' added Kevin.

They allowed themselves a small smile.

'Our proprietor's going to be pleased if we pull this one off,' said Tony. 'Right. Now the blackout's on, we need another source. The Anne Grover woman refused to talk to our guy and I doubt she'll give anything to us. So here's what we do. Write the story up with everything we have. We'll concentrate on the one person who knows for sure why McKinnon's done this. Get yourself down to Brighton with a snapper. I'll get Duncan to have another go at the guy's aunt in Edinburgh.' Tony swivelled in his chair. 'No need to mention this story yet to our revered editor, Kev.'

His colleague understood. Tony had been at odds with the editor ever since her appointment and never lost an opportunity to gain points with the proprietor.

'Now get going,' Tony told his chief reporter. 'Keep in touch every half-hour.'

Tony looked at his watch. He wondered if he would get anything for tonight's paper. Probably not. It depended on how long they maintained the blackout. But it would be hard for the powers-that-be to keep a lid on this story until after the election.

Not if he could help it they wouldn't.

Chapter Twenty-Four

Philip could not imagine being more miserable. His baby daughter was still missing and now he had a task even an experienced politician would baulk at. How would he tell his wife that the man who had taken their child was his illegitimate son, a son she knew nothing about?

All he could do, Philip decided, was to tell the truth and hope that was good enough.

When he had arrived home, he and Charlie had been united in their grief and did their best to comfort each other. 'Darling, they can't disappear into thin air,' he said as he hugged her. 'Someone will spot them. The police are being brilliant. They've put a lot of people on it. We'll have Miranda back in no time.' He tried to sound confident. All the way home he had been worrying about how to confess to Charlie that he was Angus's father. He had to tell her – and also the police – without delay.

There was little privacy in the flat. In the drawing room policemen with tapes and tracers surrounded the telephone. Chris Bennett and a newly-arrived elder statesman of the party were closeted in the study. The fingerprint experts were roaming from room to room. The only place free of investigators was the bathroom and so it was that Philip found himself sitting on the edge of the bath as he tried to find the right words to make his confession to his distraught wife.

He took her hands in his and squeezed them tightly. 'I've something I must tell you and there's no easy way of softening it. Angus McKinnon was telling the truth. He is my son. Mine and Vanessa's.'

'Oh Philip.' Charlie seemed to crumple. Her voice was little more than a whisper. 'Why on earth didn't you tell me before now? How could you keep such a thing secret from me?'

Her voice was cracking and Philip pulled her close. 'I've never set eyes on him. He had been adopted by the time I knew about his existence. Vanessa was insistent that I tell no one even after we split up and especially not you. She made me swear to that.'

'But why? Why did it matter if I knew or not?'

'Because of the girls. She was paranoid about them ever finding out.'

'I wouldn't have told them.'

'I know that but she didn't want to take any chances and it was pretty emotional at the time. I thought it was the least I could do for her. I can appreciate how you're feeling but can you imagine how I felt when I found out?'

'When was that?'

'She told me when we were just engaged. One evening she suggested going to the summerhouse in the Rectory, said there was something she needed to confess and hoped it wouldn't affect our engagement. Of course I was intrigued but I thought it was some affair she'd had. I didn't take it too seriously.'

Philip thought back to the darkness of that summer night, the quiet garden and Vanessa sitting next to him in the hammock swing, motionless, as she told him she had given birth to a boy and that she had given him up for adoption.

A look of pain flickered over his face and he went on, 'She looked at me and said, "You're the father of the boy, Philip. He's yours and mine. Our son." '

'My God,' said Charlie. 'And you had no idea?'

'None.'

'How did you feel?'

He smiled wrily. 'Quite icy and calm. In moments of high drama I tend to be at my most pragmatic and prosaic, as you know. At that moment I felt detached, almost as if the whole thing was happening to someone else. It took me some time to accept what she'd told me. And it was weird knowing that somewhere there was a little boy running around with my genes, who perhaps looked like me. I couldn't believe Vanessa had kept him secret from me for so long. I was furious that I'd been left out of all the decisions. I should have been told. I still think so. Vanessa was crying, saying how sorry she was, asking my forgiveness.'

'What did you do?'

'What could I do? The boy had been adopted, to a good home, and we couldn't get him back. *Fait accompli.* Later she put her name down on the adoption register but the boy was then six years old. It all seemed pretty pointless.'

Charlie momentarily forgot her misery and clasped her husband's hand.

'Then she asked if I wanted to be released from our engagement and, truthfully, I did think about it. Vanessa said she didn't want me marrying her out of pity or guilt. I did

279

feel sorry for her having had to go through all that and I suppose there was some degree of guilt on my part. But I said it made no difference.'

'Did it?'

'I don't think so. We used to speculate now and again about how the boy looked and what he was doing. She used to get melancholy around his birthday but after a while it all seemed unreal and I didn't think about him at all, and I haven't for many years. Until now.'

Charlie was still feeling hurt. 'I can't get over the fact that you've kept it from me all these years.'

'We never expected the boy to come into our lives.'

'Well, he has. With a bloody vengeance.'

He tried to calm her. 'Vanessa's trying her best to help now. She's down at Brighton police station giving them a description.'

Charlie couldn't help her bitterness. 'If she had told you at once that he wanted to meet you, Miranda wouldn't have gone missing.'

It was with a great sense of relief that Amy saw on her return from London that the house was in darkness. It would give her time to collect her thoughts and decide what to tell her mother after her lunch with Charlie.

She was still digesting the worrying news about her father's health. It had never occurred to her that he could be ill. He always appeared to be so energetic and robust and she found it painful to contemplate that, according to Charlie, her legal action and the stress it would cause might result in a heart attack. She had always considered her stepmother to be the original Miss Cool, Calm and Collected; her anxious manner had convinced Amy that she was not exaggerating.

Charlie had not pushed her to make a decision about the legal battle, which was clever of her. Before Amy did anything else impetuous, she had to think it all through and discuss her plan of action with her mother and Louise.

There was a note from her mother on the hall table. 'Back in an hour. It's vital,' underlined four times, 'that you keep the phone free. I'll explain when I get back.' Was this anything to do with her father?

Amy was filling the kettle when the phone rang.

'Dad?'

It was the first time father and daughter had talked since Christmas. After so many weeks of no contact, Amy felt awkward, almost embarrassed. But it did not sound like him. His voice was unsteady. So Charlie was right. He really was ill.

'Darling, is your mother back?'

'No. Back from where?'

'She's at Brighton police station helping the police. Something terrible's happened,' he said. 'Miranda has disappeared and the police are looking for a man who says he has her.'

Amy gave an anguished cry. 'Why would he take Miranda?'

'We're not sure but he seems to be angry and bitter. It's urgent that I talk to your mother.'

'What's she got to do with it?'

A pause. 'The police think she's met this man and she's giving them his description. Please ask her to call me the minute she gets home, will you?'

'Of course. Dad, Miranda's going to be all right, I know she is.'

'I'm sure you're right.'

Amy heard the break in his voice, an emotion-filled sound she had never heard before, not even at the time of the divorce. Take legal action against her father? How could she inflict more pain on him now? There had to be another way to resolve the problem between them.

'Dad, I'm sorry about the letter,' she blurted out, 'and don't worry, I've no intention of taking legal action against you or anyone. We must be able to sort it out some other way.'

'Thank you, Amy. I'm sure we can,' he replied. 'Goodbye, I'll let you know the second we hear any news.'

For over an hour Vanessa, pale and shaky, was questioned at the local police station by skilled detectives who coaxed from her every last detail of her meeting and contact with Angus McKinnon. She had given them Angus's letter and through the address on it they had tracked down a distraught Muriel McKinnon.

Vanessa was exhausted. She felt intensely guilty that she had unwittingly exposed an innocent child to danger. Her sympathy for Charlie overrode all her hostility for That Woman. She and Philip would be going through hell and Vanessa offered a fervent prayer for the child's safe return.

As the police car swooped round the village green towards the Rectory, she saw both her daughters in the porchway.

'Have they found her?' the girls cried out in unison.

Vanessa told them that Miranda was still missing but that the police were confident she would be found soon.

'Why Miranda?' asked Louise, podgy-eyed from crying.

'Is it because Dad's a politician and this man thinks they're rich?'

'Is he some kind of crank?' Amy's eyes reflected her doubts. 'Dad says he's angry. What about? And how did you get involved with him?'

'It's a long story,' Vanessa said, leading them into the kitchen where they had shared so much emotion during the depressing, drawn-out months of the divorce. But this time she found it hard to be honest with her daughters. She had half hoped that they need never know the full truth but that was out of the question now. Slowly, painfully, choosing her words with care, she told her daughters about her past.

She was surprised by their reaction. Her constant fear that they would regard her with scorn seemed unfounded. They accepted what she had to say apparently without censure for her or Philip. They peppered her with questions, some of them embarrassingly personal.

'How often did you do it?' asked Amy, not the least abashed.

Vanessa decided she had to be completely open. This was no time for being coy. 'Only twice,' she said. 'I became frightened after that so we didn't do it again.'

'Were you in love with Dad?' asked Louise.

'I thought so at the time but I was very young. And once I found out that I was expecting a baby, I wasn't allowed to see your father.'

She made them understand that it was because of what had happened to her that she had been so strict about not allowing them to go to overnight parties. Why she was so much more uncompromising than other mothers. Despite tantrums, pleadings, tears and sulks she would never budge and all through their puberty she had been insistent on warning them against the advances of their boyfriends. It had been like a mantra throughout their teenage years. 'In these days, when sex is apparently on tap, don't think if you're easy game that the boys don't swap names,' she would tell them. 'They do. And think of the consequences of getting pregnant. I couldn't bear the thought of either of you two going through all that trauma.'

Now she looked at the two girls fondly. 'I thought you'd be so shocked by all of this,' she confessed. 'I was really worried.'

'Oh Mum, you must have gone through hell,' said Amy. 'It doesn't make any difference to how we feel about you, does it, Louise?'

The younger girl shook her head vigorously and hugged Vanessa.

'How did this Angus person find out you were his mother?' Amy asked.

'The *Daily Chronicle* told him,' Vanessa said bitterly. 'Don't ask me how they got on to the story, I have no idea, but it seems that the business over the Forrester shares whetted their appetite for more damaging exposures, particularly now, with an election due.'

Amy thought guiltily of her own actions over the shares. It all seemed so petty now.

'When this young man asked me who his father was,' Vanessa went on, 'I said I couldn't tell him until I had spoken to his father, that it wasn't my secret alone. He was obviously disappointed but I thought he'd accepted my reasons for asking him to be patient. I was wrong. I don't know what convinced him that your father is his father too but I think he's taken Miranda to try and force public recognition. I blame myself for what's happened. He told me his adoptive parents had just recently been killed in a car crash. On top of that he had to cope with discovering – through the tabloid press, what's more – that they were not his true parents. I should have realised how much strain he was under but he seemed so composed. My refusal to trust him with the name of his father must have been the last straw.

'He is so angry now. So very angry. I blame myself for what's happened.'

Muriel McKinnon collapsed when confronted with the news that her nephew appeared to be involved in the abduction of Philip Lockhart's young daughter.

From the start it was apparent to the two detectives that she had been completely unaware of her nephew's intentions. She could offer no explanation for his behaviour. When she uttered the standard comment of the relatives of mass murderers, serial rapists and other miscreants, 'He wouldn't hurt a fly,' they did not respond.

However Muriel did admit, when pressed by the sympathetic though insistent officers, that Angus was in emotional turmoil. She explained the reasons and described his phone call to her. 'I've never heard him so deeply angry and hurt,' she told them, her disquiet apparent.

Muriel was able to supply a recent photograph of her nephew taken on holiday but could offer no clue to his whereabouts. He had told her he was moving from his hotel and would contact her soon. But he had not done so.

'Why on earth hasn't that man rung again?' Charlie burst out to no one in particular. 'He said he would.'

She started each time the door was opened and each time the phone rang. It was never the call they were expecting and there was still no news from any quarter about Miranda's whereabouts.

Superintendent Goddard had persuaded Charlie it would be best, since Angus McKinnon wanted to speak to his father, if Philip was the person to pick up the receiver. The strategy was to keep McKinnon talking so that the intercept on the phone could track him down.

Charlie and Philip were lying on the bed trying to conserve their energy for the long night ahead when they were interrupted by a soft tap on the bedroom door.

'Minister, could you spare a moment?'

Chris Bennett led Philip into the study and handed him a scruffy-looking letter.

'This will answer a few questions.' He sounded defensive. 'It was delivered to your hotel room after the Birmingham meeting. I didn't bother you with it at the time because I thought it was the usual obsessive eccentric, and passed it straight to security at party headquarters, but it's from the same man. The signature is quite clear. I wish I'd taken it more seriously. I can't say how sorry I am, sir.'

Philip could hardly rebuke the man. What he had done was standard practice and this was no time for recriminations.

Apprehensively, Philip read the short letter. Chris's eyes did not leave his face. When Philip had finished reading, he commented, 'There was nothing in that which would ring alarm bells for you, Chris. It's the kind of letter they tend to write.'

'The police believe this letter throws a different light on the search.' Chris did not add that the police graphologist had been concerned that the pressure on the paper indicated that the person who wrote it had been extremely overwrought at the time. 'We'll have to face up to the fact that the action was premeditated rather than spontaneous. The police want to lift the blackout and broadcast a description on television and radio of Miranda, the nanny and McKinnon.'

Philip saw the sense of this but did not mention what was also in his mind. That it would not take the papers long to discover that McKinnon was his illegitimate son, the product of under-age sex, with all the consequences such a scandalous story would bring to him and his family. He had to face the unpalatable fact that his political career could well come to an end.

When Philip showed Charlie the letter, she was furious it had been ignored. 'The least they could have done was to go and see the man. What if he'd been waiting outside with a gun?'

'The police want to make an appeal on television and radio,' Philip told her.

Charlie cried out in alarm. 'If they do that he'll know the police are on to him. That could frighten him into making a run for it and,' her voice caught, 'he wouldn't want to take a child with him.' Her self-control, perilously thin, evaporated and Philip rocked her in his arms until her tears subsided.

He tried to persuade her that without the help of the public, the police had few clues to track down the missing threesome. In similar cases there had by now been a demand for a ransom. The police psychologist had produced a psychiatric profile which indicated that Miranda's disappearance had far more to do with the man's need for family recognition than financial reward. And because the nanny was assumed to be with him, possibly held against her will, Miranda would probably be well cared for.

Reluctantly, Charlie agreed that the police needed new clues and fast.

Superintendent Goddard summed up the situation for the anxious parents. 'At this stage we've no idea whether your nanny is a willing accomplice. We've phoned her family in New Zealand, the agency and her previous employers and they all say snatching a baby would be entirely out of character. Of course that's exactly what Angus McKinnon's aunt and work colleagues say about him. So we've a rather sensitive suggestion to make.'

Philip and Charlie listened to his argument in favour of bringing Vanessa to the flat. They felt it would be more effective if she could be there to apologise if and when Angus McKinnon made contact. The police psychologist had been adamant. 'There has been no request for money so it is imperative that we keep negotiations as amicable as possible. If we can persuade his mother to apologise to him and reassure him that she does want him to be part of her family in the future, you may find he would respond more positively.'

Philip could hardly imagine a worse situation than Charlie and his ex-wife in the same flat and in such harrowing circumstances. But he was never more proud of his wife than when she told the police with quiet dignity that she would make Vanessa welcome.

'I'll try anything and everything to get my baby back,' she said softly.

The Press Association statement was stark. It asked only if members of the public could help trace the whereabouts of Helen Brickhill and her charge, Miranda Lockhart, aged two, daughter of the Secretary of State for Transport. They mentioned that the pair might be with a young man, Angus McKinnon, whom they wanted to come forward to help with their inquiries. Television stations would be showing the relevant photographs on their next news bulletin. The statement finished with the note that the police and the Lockhart family wanted to thank the press and electronic media for maintaining that day's silence.

Tony Burns reckoned the *Chronicle* was still way ahead of the pack. He doubted if the rest would make the connection between Angus McKinnon and Philip Lockhart from the bald statement issued by the police. It made no mention of the fact that Vanessa Lockhart was McKinnon's mother.

'Have a word with our guy at Scotland Yard,' he instructed the news editor. 'We've paid him enough over the years. Vanessa Lockhart was picked up from her home twenty minutes ago. I want to know where they're taking her and what they know about McKinnon.'

As the blackout restrictions now did not apply, a four-man team was ordered to Pimlico to wait outside Chelsea Mansions. Within half an hour they had been joined by a gaggle of reporters from rival papers, and a forest of aluminium ladders to accommodate the assembled photographers sprouted opposite the mansion block's front door.

Tony strode out to the newsroom. 'The other papers will

be going apeshit trying to find out why the nanny's run off with the new boyfriend, so we're ahead on that fucking score at least,' he said. 'Can't let the rest of Fleet Street get to the auntie. Ask Duncan if he's bought up the McKinnon aunt yet,' he ordered. 'The police must be freaking out to lift the blackout so early in the game. Of course he's a Cabinet minister so they're pulling out all the stops.'

Vanessa's mouth was dry and she tried to steady her trembling hands as the police officer rang the doorbell of the Lockhart flat. She was determined not to show how apprehensive she was.

Philip's face was impassive as he opened the door. There was no welcoming smile, simply a curt, 'Thank you for coming up from Brighton.'

She recognised this mood. Whenever there had been a crisis in their lives, Philip's response was always supremely practical and icy rather than sympathetic. He maintained that emotions only hindered effective action and could be gratified when the crisis was over. This difference of approach had been a source of constant friction between them. When the newly-born Louise had been diagnosed as severely jaundiced, Philip's response had been to discuss the baby's symptoms with the doctor, not comfort his distressed wife.

Why had this come back to her so vividly now? For the first time since their break-up, she was pleased he was no longer her husband.

'The TV appeal is about to start,' Philip said. 'They're going to show Miranda's photograph. I think it's best if you watch in another room from us.'

He led Vanessa and her police escort into the study where

he adjusted the controls of the small set before leaving. She noticed little details around the room, family photographs which rang bells from the past, reminding her of days when she had been happy. There was one of Louise holding up her first rosette and Amy clutching Tansy on the day they had first brought the dog home. Vanessa wondered if she would ever be that happy again.

'You'd think he'd offer us a cup of tea,' complained the police officer.

Vanessa said nothing. This treatment was part of her punishment.

In the next room, a few minutes before the broadcast, Charlie was so overwrought that Goddard advised against her watching the television appeal but she was vehement.

'I don't care how painful it is. I need to see what's happening.'

The BBC news led on the sensational item about the Secretary of State's missing child. The studio announcer launched into a résumé of the day's other events before showing stills of Miranda, Angus, the nanny, a similar model of their baby buggy followed by a picture of a red Ford Fiesta with their registration number. There was, of course, no mention of Angus McKinnon's connection to Philip. Nor any mention of Vanessa.

Philip felt Charlie's hand tighten in his as Miranda's smiling face filled the screen.

'Oh Philip,' she sobbed helplessly. 'Will we ever get her back?'

Quietly, Superintendent Goddard closed the door as he left them.

Charlie buried her head in Philip's chest and for the first

time since the trauma began he allowed his anguish to show.
'Darling, she's going to be all right,' he murmured repeatedly. 'Nobody could hurt a dear little thing like Miranda.'
Vanessa would have found it hard to recognise her former
husband in this gentle, sympathetic individual who was
giving such comfort to his distraught wife, a man able to
share his suffering.

The announcer gave a phone number and asked anyone
with information about the whereabouts of Miranda Lockhart to contact the police urgently. A minute or two later
Chris Bennett appeared at the door.

'The police think that went rather well,' he remarked,
feigning cheerfulness. 'They're pretty confident that it did
the job it was supposed to. And the Prime Minister has asked
me to let you know that he's thinking of you both and not to
worry about anything else.'

Philip had forgotten he and Charlie were due to be with
the PM at a rally that evening in Manchester. It, indeed the
whole election, seemed so unimportant now.

Goddard reported that calls were flooding into the police
nerve centre. 'We're checking them out, every one of them.
We'll let you know the minute there's anything concrete.'

Privately he had warned his team that although publicising the disappearance was still the best way to obtain recent
sightings, the bulletin was bound to flush out dozens of
mentally disturbed people who would claim to have the
child. Happily, they usually backed off when asked for their
address.

Now he needed to brief Philip and the two women about
how to handle the phone call. If and when it came. He asked
to have a private word with Philip.

★ ★ ★

As the TV news started, the *Chronicle*'s picture editor punched the video-grab screen machine attached to the computer which registered the six hundred and twenty-five lines of the television picture. It would record every fleeting nanosecond of the bulletin and using an electronic filter they could later isolate each frame. This was used to great effect in the criminal trial of O.J. Simpson when it caught the smirk after the not guilty verdict; the picture was featured on the front pages of most of the world's newspapers.

Tony switched back into action, barking orders. 'Tell me the minute we've bought up Muriel McKinnon. That's vital, otherwise everyone might get an up-to-date photo of Angus. We already have some great pictures and background stuff but we can't say that this McKinnon is Lockhart's son.' Tony stroked his chin. 'We'll call it a riddle.'

The front-page splash shouted: 'Minister's Baby Snatched By Ex-Wife's Son' above a white on black strapline. 'Battling "boardroom beauty" in under-age sex scandal'. Inside, the word 'Kidnap' was blown across six columns with the strapline 'Minister's baby in hostage riddle. Who is the father?' A strip of pictures showed a youthful Vanessa with various escorts including Philip Lockhart and the Prince of Wales. Angus's birth certificate was blown up to show the blank space where the father's name should have been.

The *Chronicle*'s detail about Vanessa and the birth certificate could not be matched by their rivals. Tony was triumphant. Taking her cue from the mood of the assembled company, the editor issued an edict, smiling, 'Champagne in my office in five minutes.'

But as he was taking his first sip, the newsroom secretary

took Tony aside and told him that Muriel McKinnon had been spirited away by their arch rivals, the *Daily Despatch*.

'Whaaat?' Tony was incredulous. 'How could that happen?'

'Our cop says they conned her with some cock and bull story about taking her to Angus to help them out. They didn't get far with her but we can't get near her now. The local police have put a man outside her home.'

'How did they know to go for her?'

'Apparently they got the same note as us, the one he sent Lockhart in Birmingham. They're using it on page one.'

They were both silent as they absorbed the consequences of losing McKinnon's aunt.

Behind him, Tony could hear the happy buzz of his colleagues clinking glasses and making mutually congratulatory quips.

The fizz turned sour in his mouth.

'Darling, the police want us to talk to Vanessa.'

Charlie's clear, frightened gaze was unnerving. 'Why? It's bad enough she's in my home. Why do I have to see her?'

'They want to brief us together so we can decide exactly what Vanessa should say when McKinnon does ring again.'

Vanessa was sitting at the study desk, lost in thought and seemingly oblivious of her surroundings. She was wearing the white jumper, navy blazer and jeans she had put on when she was first taken to Brighton police station.

The sight of the woman who had caused her so much grief over the years and who she felt was largely responsible for the situation they were now in made Charlie long to give vent to her rage and frustration. She felt as though her nerve endings were outside her skin, the inactivity of the day exacerbating her tension. But a wrong word now could send Vanessa marching out of the house. Or, worse, unnerve her so she made mistakes during that vital phone call.

Vanessa had never shown herself as anything but an enemy and Charlie could not remember when they had last exchanged a civil word. It took all her self-discipline to quell these feelings of enmity and bitterness at the situation in which Vanessa had placed them. Unused to the role of supplicant, she made a great effort to sound noncombative.

'These are not the circumstances under which either of us would choose to meet,' she said levelly. 'Let's hope McKinnon phones soon.'

Vanessa nodded and replied hesitantly, 'May I explain why I didn't contact you when I received the letter from Angus McKinnon? If you remember we were not communicating because of the takeover business and as I thought it was my problem, I wanted to handle it on my own.'

She added ruefully, 'I didn't make too good a job of it, did I?'

Charlie dearly wanted to agree but Philip, almost as if he were reading her mind, interrupted, saying that it was little use to flagellate themselves about the past. What was needed now was a united approach in dealing with the abductor.

The police psychologist took over. 'When this man phones, I suggest you both speak from the heart. Try to forget we're all listening in. Mr Lockhart, he's expecting to talk to you but I wouldn't mention the child at first, unless he does. Start by trying to gain his trust. Explain that you did not receive the letter he wrote in Birmingham so you were not ignoring him. What I think he also wants is some sort of apology from his mother. Acknowledge this and suggest he speaks to her himself.

'Then, Mrs Lockhart,' Charlie could not control her start of irritation at being reminded that she was the second woman to hold this title, 'I suggest the first thing you do is confirm who his father is, if he hasn't already asked the question, and apologise for not telling him when you met. If you want him to be part of your family . . .'

'Yes, I do,' said Vanessa quickly. 'I'm sure he wouldn't be in this position if it wasn't for me.'

'Then now is the time to say that. I think that's what he's really after. There's been no mention of a ransom, which is a good sign. If he does demand money then I suggest you hand him back to his father. Mr Lockhart, agree at once and take as long as you can to discuss the arrangements. By then we should have tracked down his whereabouts anyway.'

'Now all we have to do is wait,' said Superintendent Goddard sombrely.

Half an hour later there was no further news. A white-faced Charlie was staring into the fire, a blanket over her shoulders, a cup of untouched tea at her side.

'Philip, I swear that when we get Miranda back I'm never going to let anyone else look after her. Never.'

He squeezed her hand, glad she was talking about a future for their baby. Unlike him. He could not put the thought out of his mind that Miranda might never come back.

Chapter Twenty-Five

At the Bayswater Court Hotel, the bored receptionist, a young man recently arrived from abroad, watched idly as the news item came on television. He turned up the sound.

The newscaster's face was replaced with a photograph of a young baby, followed by a fuzzy picture of an unsmiling, tousled-haired man. The receptionist did not fully understand the English, it was spoken too quickly for him, and he called over to the chambermaid.

'What they say?' he asked.

She put down the towels she was carrying and looked at the television where a photograph of Helen was now smiling at her. 'Bloody hell, it's that girl,' she exclaimed. 'The one with the bloke and the baby – they were here this afternoon. You must ring the police. They're wanted.'

'Police?' He reared back in alarm. His father had arranged his entry into Great Britain and not through the usual channels. 'No. No police. You go back work. You not say anything otherwise no job, no job.' He waved his finger at her threateningly.

The girl retreated, red-faced. Who was this foreign pipsqueak to tell her what to do? He was only here because of his father. He treated her like a slave since she had refused to go to his bedroom one evening. She was looking for another job anyway; his father had refused to hand over the overtime due to her last week.

Three minutes later, West End Central police station received an anonymous phone call from a woman. 'That baby on the television. Ask at the Bayswater Court Hotel, they were there this afternoon,' she said before slamming down the receiver.

Even in the congested Bayswater Road, it took the special patrol car only seven minutes to halt outside the revolving door of the hotel. The receptionist, terrified he had been identified as an illegal alien, made a rush for the kitchen. His exit was quickly blocked.

The policemen were quiet but menacing. 'Where are they?' asked the senior of the three as his colleagues strode through the lobby and waited at the foot of the stairs.

'What you talk about?'

'Come on, we know the child's here. Where is she?'

Relieved that he was not the subject of their hunt, the receptionist relaxed slightly. 'Oh, the baby. With the man and woman. They go out.'

'Shit.' The officer grabbed the cowering young man by the lapels and hauled him to the door. 'Which way?'

The receptionist stabbed a quivering finger in the direction of Hyde Park.

'When?'

'Hour. I don't know. I not see.'

While two officers hurried back out, the third and fourth stayed behind to take statements from the staff and to check all the rooms. It did not take long to establish that

Angus McKinnon was indeed staying at the hotel. The nervous receptionist unlocked the six by nine foot cubicle of a bedroom which was advertised to gullible visitors as 'a luxury overnight stay in the heart of the nation's capital'. On a small side table alongside Angus's small suitcase was an artist's sketchpad. The policeman opened the front cover to reveal a charming pencil drawing of a smiling little girl.

Miranda Lockhart.

Charlie sagged in relief at the news that her baby had been seen that afternoon. Then she began firing questions at the young policewoman who had brought the message.

The officer could add little more. 'All we know so far is that the baby was wheeled out of the hotel in a buggy. We have no other details at present. I'm sorry.'

Charlie's euphoria evaporated. She forced herself to ask the unthinkable. 'Did anyone see if Miranda was moving?' she asked.

In the tension-filled silence, Philip walked swiftly across to his wife.

'Answer me.' She was almost shouting.

'Mrs Lockhart, our information is limited at the moment. Your nanny and the child and Mr McKinnon were sighted at an hotel on the other side of Hyde Park in the late afternoon. The hotel staff are being questioned at the moment. We'll bring you more details as soon as we have them.'

Charlie turned a desperate face to her husband. 'Can't we go to this hotel? We might get something out of them that the police miss.'

'Darling, we have to stay here,' he said firmly. 'We need

to be at the end of the phone in case Angus McKinnon tries to contact us.'

She nodded but her despair was palpable and turning to the policewoman she said in a voice which sounded so unlike her that Philip recognised she was at the end of her tether, 'I want to be told everything, whatever it is. Don't hold anything back. I can only cope if I know the truth.' Her voice was breaking. 'Promise me you'll tell me everything. Please?'

The policewoman, as near to tears as she had been in her job, nodded. 'I promise,' she answered huskily, fervently hoping that if there was bad news she would not be the one who had to give it.

In Downing Street the Chief Whip snapped off the television set. Lockhart was becoming a bloody nuisance but he was too experienced to share his opinion with the Prime Minister.

Edward Saunders looked exhausted. Earlier he had been interviewed by the *Chronicle*'s editor. She had been no pushover. After that he had been grilled by the BBC's main presenter for an election special. Asked about the missing baby, the PM had said in no uncertain terms that electoral matters had to take second place if a baby's life was in danger. But he had returned from the interview in a different mood.

'Christ, this is a nightmare. The public's had its eye taken off the ball,' he exclaimed to the assembled company. 'And,' he added, 'my information is that we're partly to blame.'

His colleagues looked startled.

'While Philip was campaigning, this young man – his son,

I suppose we'll have to call him – wrote to him and when the letter was opened his PA thought it was from a nutter. It's been sitting at party HQ for nearly twenty-four hours. Think what fun the media would have with that.'

'I don't think Philip's played this ball as cleverly as he could have,' said the Home Secretary.

'He's been a trifle accident-prone, if you ask me,' murmured the party's millionaire pollster softly. Then, louder, 'Of course it's all a terrible business. I'm just sorry for the lovely girl he's married to.'

'What are we going to do about it?' asked the Prime Minister peremptorily.

One of the party's most experienced spin doctors, famed for his lack of sentiment even by the cynical standards of this circle, commented, 'You can't be seen to be uncaring. Once the public sniff you're insincere, your ratings will go down at least two points, maybe three. We can't afford that at this stage of the campaign, especially in the marginals.' His busy mind had already formulated a damage limitation scenario. 'Sir, what's your schedule in the next twenty-four hours?'

The Chief Whip reeled off a list of the PM's appointments.

'Right,' said the spin doctor decisively. 'I suggest you make time, sir, to squeeze in a visit to the Lockharts.'

The PM frowned. 'Bit intrusive, don't you think? They'll hardly be in a fit state.'

'You have a point.' The spin doctor seemed pleased with himself. 'Then how about going to the West End police station handling the case? We can get a crowd up. You can press some flesh, express quiet confidence, that sort of thing.'

'Smart thinking.' The Chief Whip nodded.

'We'll alert the papers and the TV. You'll be quoted as saying everyone most concerned blah blah, understand can't comment on what's going on blah blah, prayers, thoughts are with the parents, the usual.'

The PM frowned at this but justified the operation by consoling himself that he was fond of Philip Lockhart. He well remembered how frightened he and his wife had been when the IRA and other terrorist groups had threatened their own children while he was in the Cabinet, and throughout the evening he asked for regular updates. At first he had been convinced that the Lockhart abduction was political. As with many successful and powerful men, life only meant anything to him when he, or at worst the party he led, was centre stage. When the police had told him it was a 'domestic', he had almost been disappointed.

'Your visit'll make a great splash in tomorrow's papers,' added his aide.

'Yes,' said the spin doctor, who was interested only in television, 'but if we get our skates on you'll be in time for News At Ten.' As he nodded, the Chief Whip held up his palm.

'Prime Minister, there is something else you should bear in mind.' His expression was stern. 'I've done some calculations and it seems that, admittedly twenty-odd years ago, the Secretary of State for Transport was sexually active with an under-aged schoolgirl.'

Silence.

'Well, no paper's going to write that while the baby's still missing,' said the spin doctor. 'Of course, if she's found alive and well, that's different.' His voice tailed off.

No one dared voice what many of them were thinking. If the baby was not found until after the polling booths closed, the safer the secret would be. Even the normally outspoken Chief Whip did not dare articulate his venal thought that the government would be blamed by the fickle electorate if the child was harmed. They would say the police were under-funded and hence undermanned. But if the child was found quickly, alive and safe, the feel-good factor should last until the polling booths closed at 10 p.m. on Thursday. And, if handled properly, the problem of the minister's under-age sex all those years ago might not upset voters – well, not the younger ones anyway.

As he left for his office at Number 12 Downing Street, the Chief Whip was praying almost as hard as her parents for the safe return of Miranda Lockhart.

Paul Salter had been appalled by the bulletin which led the BBC news. The Lockhart baby kidnapped? What more could happen to that family? Philip's new job seemed to have brought bad luck. Deep Throat had reported Amy's threat of legal action. And now this.

The lawyers were ready to finalise the takeover documents but were the Salters right to become involved with this family? In Paul's opinion there were lucky people, and then there were the others.

Vanessa was a separate issue. He had been surprised at how often he had found himself thinking about her since returning from the South of France. God knew she was not his type. Older than the women he was used to nowadays and much less sassy. But no coyness, no games. A grown-up. Good sense of humour. Well, she had laughed at his stories.

And boy, something was switched on when they kissed.

He paced restlessly. He was reluctant to contact her again with the takeover in its final stages, but maybe this was a good excuse to offer some moral support.

A policewoman answered his call. She was taking messages for Vanessa who was not to be disturbed. The information that Vanessa had been taken to London to the Lockhart home was known only to a restricted circle although the same newspapers, including the *Daily Chronicle*, had been tipped by their police contacts already.

Yes, Mrs Lockhart would be told as soon as possible that Mr Salter had phoned. The police officer took a careful note of the spelling of his name. She thanked him and sounded as if she meant it.

Paul Salter was intrigued by the notion of himself as a knight on a white charger. That had not happened for eight years and he had married the woman.

The press army on the hoof was not an elegant sight. Based on the premise that they had to be ready to make a dash for it, they had to travel light and fast, so kept nothing extraneous in their pockets or in their camera cases.

Within an hour and a half, they had managed to transform the refined Victorian crescent with its white painted stucco and crocus-filled window boxes into an urban tip. Tiny discarded black film cans by the hundred nestled between Pimlico's ornamental bay trees in their cemented-down tubs, early editions of evening newspapers were strewn around the wrought-iron railings, empty Coke cans sprouted among the ivy-trailing terracotta pots.

The local police had already had complaints about the

disturbance and the mess from a High Court judge, the president of the Red Cross and a Miss Backlash, the dominatrix who ran a discreet service to the repressed gentry of Westminster, all of whom lived within a few yards of the Lockharts. The most strategically placed neighbours had been approached by representatives of the Fourth Estate offering instant cash if they and their cameras could have access to the windows opposite 16 Chelsea Mansions.

Since the broadcast, Charlie, oblivious of the presence of the press pack, had sat listlessly in her bedroom with Philip. Occasionally he would check with the police on what was happening, while she absent-mindedly clutched her baby's favourite teddy bear in her arms. The only time she managed to rouse herself was to search relentlessly through the channels for repeats of the appeal, finding them on Sky News, several of the cable stations, Channel Four and ITV.

Each time the phone rang the police instructed Philip to pick it up in the study where Vanessa was waiting. The two women had not been in the same room since the briefing.

Charlie stared pensively out of the bedroom window. 'It's much worse, with her here. I feel trapped, not able to walk around my own home.'

'She hasn't moved from the study since she arrived,' Philip replied.

'I don't want to take the risk of bumping into her. I couldn't bear to see her face.' Charlie stood up and walked to the window. As she did so she saw the flashes of what looked like lights exploding across the road. Philip knew in an instant what they were.

'The bastards. Get back from that window,' he directed. As he drew the curtains, shutting out the street lights, he cursed again and allowed the anger inside him to erupt. 'Bloody photographers. Have they no decency? No wonder everyone hates them. This isn't doing a job, it's hounding. I'll ask the police to sort the buggers out.'

In the small study where the thick curtains had been closed, Vanessa felt claustrophobic. Like Charlie, she was imprisoned in this room, intimidated by the thought of venturing outside, of seeing Charlie's reproachful face. Unable to eat, she sipped a lukewarm cup of coffee and wondered when her ordeal would end. She felt drained and helpless and as the seconds dragged by, she was beginning to lose hope that Angus would phone, that Miranda would ever be found.

West End Central police station was working at full stretch as it dealt with a flood of calls from a concerned public who liked to play detective, especially in the case of a missing child. People phoned in who thought they had sighted Angus, Miranda and the nanny on top of buses, at the seaside, in the cinema. A young couple, travelling with their toddler on the Intercity between London and Liverpool, were startled when, after an unscheduled stop, two plainclothes officers boarded the train and asked them for proof of identity. Sadly for the Lockharts, this couple was simply taking a twenty-month-old toddler to be introduced to her great-aunt.

Then there was information from what the police called the grudgers, women mainly, who had such violent feuds with their neighbours or relatives that they rang up to blame them for every publicised crime.

Each call had to be checked out in the remote possibility that it could be valid.

And there were the lonelyhearts, so disturbed that simply knowing someone would talk to them was satisfaction enough. In most cases it soon became apparent they were time-wasters but it still snarled up the lines and used up police hours. It did not help that Ford Fiestas had apparently had a successful year, particularly red ones. The car manufacturer had confirmed that two million were on the road and there were thousands with the prefix H15.

The officer in charge groaned. He was in for a heavy night. Why didn't these Cabinet ministers have any style? If the nanny had the use of a Ford GTI they would have had a lot less bother tracing it.

In Heathgate, the broadcast brought a steady stream of sympathisers to the constituency office. Philip's misfortune had assured him of a record number of volunteers to help get him re-elected.

Police were still waiting at the hotel in case Angus McKinnon returned. Forensic experts had combed every centimetre of his room to see if there was anything that could yield a clue. Anything at all.

The *Chronicle* reporter who had been waiting outside the lounge ever since a policeman's tip-off, had been warned there would be trouble if it was discovered he had been in position before the blackout was officially lifted.

'They're really pushing the boat out on this one,' he remarked to his snapper as they watched squads of police trudge through the hotel door.

'Are you kidding? A Cabinet minister's baby and just before an election? They'll be pulling up the tarmac before they're finished.'

The photographer, veteran of many a stake-out and front-ups, was wearing a special photographic jacket. At the touch of the lapel button it set off a mini camera in the breast pocket. He was also equipped with an infra-red camera. They usually produced lousy pictures but they were better than nothing if he could not use his flash.

He was heartened to see there were no rivals around, although it was less fun. Everyone must be down at the Lockhart place. He supposed the office knew what it was doing.

Chapter Twenty-Six

It was nearly two o'clock in the morning and every available patrol car and police officer on the beat had been marshalled to search for the red Ford Fiesta, registration number H15 WJL. After the Lockharts' huge phone bill had been scrutinised, the only unfamiliar number was traced to a phone box in the Hammersmith area. A street-by-street search had been organised, with each patrol car being given a separate zone.

Detectives in charge of the search took the gamble that because of the 'nosy neighbour syndrome' the car would have been spotted in a built-up area. So they ordered their forces to concentrate on those areas which were a mixture of light industry or sparsely populated residential areas.

In the end it was not any of the hi-tech wizardry of which Her Majesty's police force were so proud that brought about the breakthrough they were all waiting for. It was shoe leather and a beam from a Maglite torch wielded by a bobby on the beat that revealed the number plate of the car.

He had been warned to keep a low profile so he whispered into his radio, 'I've found the car you're looking for but I've no idea which house the driver could be in.'

An unmarked van containing a six-strong specialist team

of undercover detectives, expert in covert surveillance techniques, soon arrived in the dimly-lit side street in South London. The van was fully equipped with listening devices, one-way windscreens, tracking and bugging equipment.

The Ford Fiesta was outside number 31; the house was in total darkness.

The van cruised slowly up and down the road, beaming the radio antennae towards the buildings in all directions around the parked car. Every sigh, snore or whisper within a radius of a few metres would be picked up by the powerful listening devices. Then they trained heat-seeking cameras, able to scan through bricks and mortar, on to number 31. This revealed two occupants, in separate bedrooms. One man and one woman, judging from their body mass. Their breathing level indicated they had been asleep for several hours. There was no baby in the house.

Nor in any of the adjacent houses. It took another precious seventeen minutes to monitor the rest of the terrace. The team was about to cross into the next road when the camera operator spotted a light in the upstairs window of the corner shop.

The radio operator gave a thumbs-up when the microphones picked up the resonance of several voices. He saw the gleam of his colleague's teeth as he grinned in silent congratulation.

'Good God,' exclaimed the other operator as his heat-seeking scanner registered a confusing mass of body heat. 'They're having fun in there.'

'Any young kid?' asked the detective inspector in charge of the squad.

'It's hard to tell, sir.'

A collapsible ladder was brought from the van. Its rubber-tipped legs made no sound as it was gently placed underneath the first-floor window. A nimble policewoman tiptoed up the rails to operate a noiseless drill. This would create a hole, no bigger than a pinhead, through which they could thread the fibre optics that fed the tiny but powerful video camera.

The monitor inside the van showed a floor of seething limbs.

'They're having a bloody orgy, boss,' said the policeman watching the monitor. 'There's about twenty of them, all heaped together.'

'It's going to be pretty bloody difficult to spot the nanny among that lot.'

'There are several backs-of-bums that could be her,' said the operator prosaically, after scanning the room. 'But until they turn round there's no chance of a definite ID.'

The heat-seeking camera then picked out the sleeping bodies of two children in the next room. From their body mass they appeared to be quite young.

'We'll have to get a camera into that bedroom. Hudson, back on the ladder.'

The camera probe was so delicate it was able to pierce the fabric of the building up to the outside of the wallpaper. The room was in darkness but there was enough light from the open door of the adjoining hall to illuminate the bodies of the young children. In one corner was a child's buggy. The camera zoomed in.

'That certainly looks like the buggy the kid was in when she disappeared. Can you hear any breathing?'

There was a pause.

'Sorry, chief, there's such moaning and groaning from those sex maniacs in the next room that I can't get a fix. Hang on.' He raised his hand for silence, his face intent as he listened through the earphones.

The detective inspector radioed in to West End Central. They gave him his orders.

'We're going in the quick way.' His voice was quiet. 'Take no chances. We've got to get those kids first.'

The team surrounded the building, all wearing connecting earpieces. Burly officers in riot gear, each holding up a two-foot hydraulically-operated steel battering ram, got ready to break down the door.

From the van came the command: 'Strike, strike, strike.'

The normally imperturbable Superintendent Goddard was devastated that Helen Brickhill's arrest did not lead to the discovery of Miranda Lockhart.

Two young children were taken from what his officers described as 'that fucking den', but Miranda was not one of them. The children, whisked off to a temporary foster home, belonged to one of the writhing couples all now herded into a mini-van on their way to the police station.

Goddard had taken the sensitive decision, approved by his superiors at the police station, that it would serve no useful purpose to tell the Lockharts of the nanny's arrest, whatever the consequences later. He would supervise the interrogation of the nanny himself and until they shook the truth out of her there was no point in adding to the Lockharts' suffering.

It was now approaching three in the morning, a time when people were at their lowest ebb; the couple had given up all attempts to keep each other cheerful.

Outside Chelsea Mansions, the street was deserted but inside the cars, parked bumper to bumper, the red tips of glowing cigarettes were visible as the press corps waited for news.

Helen Brickhill had been inside police stations before. Hundreds of them. Most often with Clint Eastwood, Marlon Brando or Sylvester Stallone but nothing prepared her for the real thing. It was less frenetic, less well lit, bleaker. And the people were not half so attractive as they were in the movies.

They bustled her, hastily dressed and red-faced, into a sparsely-furnished interview cubicle. Above her winked a surveillance camera. One wall was covered by a large sheet of glass which she supposed from her television viewing concealed a two-way mirror. Policemen were probably watching her now, assessing her.

The demeanour of the unsmiling police guard, silent, menacing, and the harsh lighting from fluorescent strips were calculated to intimidate the suspect.

As the girl from New Zealand waited trembling, the door opened with such force that it banged against the wall and Superintendent Peter Goddard walked with measured steps towards her.

'Where is Miranda Lockhart?' he asked without preamble.

Inside Chelsea Mansions the phone rang. Seconds afterwards, a police officer tapped at the door of the Lockharts' bedroom.

'Superintendent Goddard's phoned. I'm happy to tell you your baby's been found.'

'Thank God.' Charlie stood up.

'Is she all right?' asked Philip as he squeezed Charlie's arm fiercely.

'I was told she was fast asleep and seemed fine, Minister,' was the careful reply.

Charlie's maternal antennae were aroused. 'Seemed?'

The police officer looked uncomfortable. 'I understand the doctor's on the way to examine her and I'm told she appears to be sleeping soundly.'

'A doctor? Why does she need a doctor?'

'Purely routine, Mrs Lockhart,' the policeman replied. 'We'll take you to her right now.'

Charlie was at the door almost before the words were out. The policeman put out a restraining hand. 'If you would give us one minute, Mrs Lockhart, it'll make things faster in the end.'

Charlie looked at him impatiently. 'Where is she?'

'At West End Central. If we allow the press to follow you, they'll clog everything up. We're about to block off the end of the road.'

'How long will that take?'

He listened to his two-way radio. 'No time at all.' As the officer spoke, Charlie heard the piercing whine of a police siren. 'We have the lift waiting and the patrol car's arrived. I suggest you ignore the press, Minister, and that you, Mrs Lockhart, get straight into the nearside door. You go round, sir, and sit next to your wife and I'll be in the front.'

Chris Bennett, smiling for the first time for many hours, agreed with Philip that he would stay in the flat to look after Vanessa and answer the phones.

As Charlie reached the lift, she asked the policeman

fearfully, 'You're quite sure she hasn't been harmed?'

'That's my information.'

Charlie felt instinctively that he was holding something back. 'I said early on that nothing was to be kept from us. I want to know what you know, however upsetting you think it's going to be.'

'Until the doctor arrives, they can't say anything more about the baby than I have told you.'

Philip put a comforting arm round his trembling wife. 'Darling, we'll be there in a few minutes. We can see for ourselves. Don't torture yourself with speculation.'

There was near bedlam as they walked the short distance from the front of the mansion block and climbed into the police car. The press had been herded into a small section of the pavement opposite, flanked by police. The second they saw the couple, the yelling started. Suddenly bedroom lights switched on all along the street as residents, woken by the noise, appeared at their windows to discover what the latest commotion was about.

The questions from the frenzied journalists ranged from the obvious to the crass.

'Have they found her?'

'Is your baby alive?'

'Have you paid a ransom?'

All the while, photographers were trying to get the couple to face their cameras.

'Over here, Mrs Lockhart.'

'Minister, Minister.'

As soon as the car door closed, the view of Charlie and Philip through the window was blocked by a police outrider. They could hear the sounds of photographers racing behind the car, camera motors whirring as they continued to bang off pictures, hoping that later, in the darkroom, there would be a surprise shot showing the couple either kissing or crying through the back window.

One enterprising photographer was already astride his Harley Davidson before they reached the end of the road but his path was blocked by a burly, rugby-playing policeman who ponderously booked him for riding on the pavement.

The traffic, such as it was, parted like the Red Sea. This was royal treatment. Red lights did not merit a change of pace and the twenty-minute journey from Pimlico to Mayfair took only seven.

Vanessa had been roused from her fitful doze by the sound of voices, the flurry of activity. She raced to the front door only to see Philip and Charlie disappearing towards the lift.

'What's happening?' she asked as Chris Bennett came back into the flat.

'Good news. Miranda's been found.'

He had to support Vanessa as she sagged in relief. He led her into the lounge.

'What about Angus?'

'Yes, he was with her.'

'Where were they found? Why did he take her? Why didn't he phone?' The questions poured out.

Chris sat down beside her on the sofa. 'Look, we haven't been told anything. They've gone off to pick up Miranda.'

'So Angus is at the police station now?'

'Yes, I think so.'

'Well, I'm going to him.'

'With respect, I don't think that's a good idea.' The

usually impassive Chris was panicked at the thought and did not choose his words with his customary care. 'In fact, I forbid you to go.'

She reared up. All her life Vanessa had been told what to do by others and generally obeyed them. Often it had not been in her best interests. She had never trusted her instincts until lately when she had vowed to take more control over her life.

This was one of those times.

'Forbid? How dare you? You have no jurisdiction over me.' She stood up. 'I'm going to see my son now and there's not a thing you can do about it.'

Charlie had no recollection of arriving at the police station, being shown the way to a small anteroom.

Her heart was pounding as a policewoman tapped softly on the door. There in the corner with the police doctor was her baby. Miranda was lying inert, stretched out in the buggy, her podgy arms above her head, in a deep sleep.

'I assume one of you will be happy to identify this young lady as Miranda Gabrielle Lockhart.' The policewoman smiled.

Charlie's eyes filled with tears and she clutched Philip's hand. They stared down in silence at their slumbering child.

'Philip, I really thought we'd lost her.'

'Darling, so did I.' Philip's voice was breaking.

Charlie bent to undo the safety straps and gently cradled her child in her arms. 'Miranda,' she said softly. 'Wake up, sweetheart.'

Philip repeated her name.

No response.

'She doesn't normally sleep so soundly, what's the matter with her?' Charlie felt a stab of unease.

The police doctor was noncommittal. 'I've examined your daughter briefly but I'd like the paediatrician to have a look at her in hospital. I presume you'll give your permission.' She looked at their stricken faces and added, 'It's simply routine. She's sleeping heavily but otherwise I can't find anything amiss. But I would like to keep her under observation overnight.'

'Why?' Charlie felt alarmed and looked anxiously down at Miranda. 'Has she been drugged?'

'We think she may have been given some sort of tranquilliser. I've sent for an ambulance because we can't give any treatment until we identify it.'

Charlie's face was tense.

'Don't distress yourself,' the doctor told her. 'I'm sure it's not serious. Her pulse is normal. Her heart sounds fine. But you would want us to be completely sure she's all right.'

Charlie gazed at the rosy-cheeked face she had studied so many times since she was born. Miranda was breathing evenly, her face was serene. Surely if there was something wrong she, above all, would be able to spot the signs. One thing was certain. She would not leave her baby's side.

'We'd both like to stay with Miranda,' Philip said swiftly.

'That's no problem. The hospital has all the facilities. They'll sort it out.'

Superintendent Goddard came into the room. He had admired the way the Lockharts had coped with the traumatic situation. As the hours dragged by, there had been times when he had been pessimistic about the outcome. So it was particularly satisfying to be in at the finish, to see the family reunited. So far it was a good result, as his desk sergeant was fond of saying.

'Well, that little lady seems to have had quite an adventure.' He was beaming, exhaustion forgotten.

'We're waiting for the ambulance,' said the doctor, 'then it's over to you.'

'Superintendent, I want to thank you and your force very much indeed.' Philip had difficulty controlling his voice.

Charlie was unable to speak. She took Goddard's arm and he patted her hand gently. 'It's going to be all right.'

He told them that the nanny and Angus were being interviewed separately and would be held until their stories could be checked out.

Philip cleared his throat. 'Do you know why the two of them did it?'

'We don't, not yet. Mr McKinnon does keep asking to see you but that won't be possible because identification will be a factor in any court proceedings.'

When Charlie asked exactly where and how her baby had been found, the superintendent was interested to see that the anguished woman of a few hours ago had turned into a resolute terrier. He was relieved that procedures did not allow him to tell her about the sex orgy and the reason, he supposed, that her daughter had been drugged.

He looked at them sympathetically. 'Look, you've both had a terrible time. I suggest we put everything except your baby's welfare on the back burner until you've had some rest.'

The interrogation of Helen Brickhill took three hours. Her account of the time spent with Angus McKinnon differed in

319

one important detail from his. She blamed him entirely for Miranda's disappearance.

When she wanted to return home with the toddler, she said, her kind heart had been softened by the story of his rejection by his father. Now she realised he had manipulated her into using the baby as blackmail to strike back at his parents.

The party was only a few streets away from her boyfriend's flat where Angus and the baby were sleeping, and as she expected the minister and his wife to be away overnight, she had believed her absence would not be noticed anyway. She said she had every intention of returning home well before the Lockharts next morning. In any case, she had watched Angus dial the Lockhart number to leave a message explaining his plans but she did not hear everything he said as she was outside the phone box with Miranda.

When pressed further, Helen admitted that she had gone along with his scheme because she very much wanted to go to the party. And, she pointed out, there was nothing illegal about being at a party, even one which had developed into a sexual orgy. Group sex among consenting adults in private was not against the law.

Helen agreed that her actions were a breach of the Lockharts' trust. She had not seen the television appeal and apologised sincerely for any anxiety she had caused.

The only moment she lost her composure was when questioned about Miranda's drugged state. She vehemently denied all knowledge of any tranquilliser, though by then it had shown up in the baby's blood sample. 'He must have given it to her,' she asserted. 'I take my professional duties seriously,' she insisted. 'Check that with any previous employer of mine. Certainly the Lockharts have never before questioned my handling of their daughter.'

Helen stuck to this story throughout the hours of intense interrogation and refused all offers of legal assistance as she felt she had done nothing criminal.

She was still being interviewed when Vanessa walked into the police station.

Chris Bennett had phoned ahead to warn the desk sergeant of her impending arrival. He was scrupulously polite but unyielding. Under no circumstances would she be allowed to see or talk to any of the suspects until they were either charged or allowed bail and released.

Undaunted, Vanessa announced her intention of staying in the front hall until she was allowed to talk to her son.

It took over three tense hours before the worst effects of the sedative wore off and Miranda's china-blue eyes slowly opened. She was soon alert and babbling to the nurses. After watching her demolish scrambled eggs and toast, the doctor pronounced Miranda fit and able to be taken home by her relieved parents. The sympathetic staff showed the tired Lockharts how to escape through an underground archway to avoid the attentions of the waiting press.

Those outside Chelsea Mansions, who had patiently waited through the long hours of the night, received their reward with a brief but happy photograph of the reunited trio.

When Philip walked in with a beaming Charlie, carrying Miranda, Chris Bennett was waiting to welcome them. No one could mistake the delight and relief on a face grey with fatigue.

Charlie disappeared with Miranda into her bedroom and Philip took his aide aside. 'Where's Vanessa?'

'She left some time ago.'

'Where did she go? The trains to Brighton don't start running till six.'

'She wanted to go to the police station. To see Angus.'

'That's not on, Chris. Didn't you tell her it wouldn't be possible?'

'I went further than that, sir. I forbade her to go. But she told me I had no jurisdiction over her, that she was going to see her son and that I couldn't stop her.'

'Vanessa said that?' Philip asked with raised eyebrows. 'Good God, that's most unlike her. Usually she . . .' He stopped. 'Ah well, we'll have to let the police sort that one out. Now I've a phone call or two to make.'

The receiver was snatched up after one ring by an anxious Amy. He heard her relay the news of Miranda's safe return to Louise, before she said, 'Oh Dad, it's wonderful, I'm so happy . . .' Unable to continue she passed the phone to Louise.

'Give her a big kiss from us and an even bigger hug and, oh Dad, I thought . . .'

'I know,' Philip interrupted, 'but it's going to be fine now. What about coming up for an early lunch to see for yourself how well Miranda is?'

Their excited assent told him that all past enmity had been forgotten. Philip then made a few more calls, to Charlie's mother, the Chief Whip (who had already heard the news from Chris) and a few close friends, taking pleasure from the fervour of their response.

Seconds before drifting off alongside his sleeping wife

and baby Philip tried to imagine Vanessa standing up to the formidable Chris Bennett. She was always telling him she had changed. Maybe she had.

As he had promised, Superintendent Goddard, freshly showered but heavy-eyed, called round a few hours later to give Philip a personal briefing. Chris Bennett was fielding dozens of calls from newspapers in the study and Philip guided the officer to the sitting room, offering his wife's apologies for not being there. 'She doesn't want to leave Miranda for a minute even while she's asleep. It's going to take us a long time to forget this,' he commented. 'We're certainly changing our priorities.'

The policeman nodded. 'Understandably so.'

'What have you found out?' asked Philip.

'Both McKinnon and Brickhill agree they spent a happy afternoon feeding the ducks in Hyde Park. Then they went back to his hotel for him to do the portrait. Mr McKinnon genuinely believes he is your son and wanted to give you the sketch of Miranda to prove he was with her. Basically, he wants your attention.'

'Well, his method of getting it is unfortunate, to put it mildly.'

Goddard continued, 'Helen Brickhill claims that since the election campaign was called, neither of you has been home before eight in the evening at the earliest. And that night, she claims, you told her you were both to be away overnight in Manchester. Is that true?'

Philip confirmed it was. 'It was only when my wife decided to see Miranda before leaving London that she became alarmed at their disappearance.'

Goddard hesitated slightly. 'Miss Brickhill says it was McKinnon's idea that they stay out overnight, to alert you to his presence after you seemingly ignored all his attempts to contact you. But we don't think that's true. We have interviewed her boyfriend and he told us that this young woman used every opportunity when you and your wife were out to take the baby and spend time with him. As far as we can make out, she's stayed overnight with Miranda at least once, possibly twice before.'

'What? We never knew anything about that.' Philip was incredulous. 'That was highly irresponsible of her,' he continued harshly, 'particularly when we and the security people had drummed into her how important it was to stay in contact.'

'I agree,' said Goddard. 'None of them saw the television appeal so they didn't know there was a search on for them. When we caught up with Angus McKinnon in the boyfriend's flat, my officers tell me he did not act in a guilty manner. He claims the nanny told him it would be a waste of time phoning you again since you were both away.'

'Do you believe him?'

'On balance, I think so. He's genuinely appalled at the distress he's caused whereas Brickhill's pushing all the blame on to McKinnon. Under that girl's submissive appearance I suspect lies someone determined to get her own way. She is certainly not the demure child-carer she purports to be.' Goddard went on to describe to a shocked Philip the circumstances in which Miranda had been found.

Philip could hardly bring himself to ask the question. 'Did they involve my baby in their activities?'

'No. She was safely asleep in the boyfriend's house a few

streets away with McKinnon. Miranda was sedated to ensure that there was no disturbance from her.'

There was silence while the policeman waited for Philip to regain his composure.

'From what we can gather, your nanny is infatuated with her boyfriend. He doesn't do any paid work that we could establish and she pays most of his expenses. In return he seems to have introduced her to sex and by the look of her dilated pupils, she's on something more potent than coffee.'

Goddard looked at Philip's stunned face and said quickly, 'She was clever and until recently she appears to have been a model citizen. Certainly her previous employer was as taken aback as you are to hear about the sex and drugs. I would guess that this boyfriend of hers, a most undesirable type, has been instrumental in her education.'

'But I still don't understand. What was Angus thinking about?'

'I suspect there are many things unresolved within that young man. But the sequence of events is quite simple to piece together. As soon as Helen Brickhill gave us the address where Miranda was, we sent a team to pick her up. McKinnon had to be roused from a heavy sleep in an armchair in front of an electric fire. Helen Brickhill had persuaded him to babysit for an hour or so, he said, while she and the boyfriend popped into the party. He didn't realise how long she'd been away until our boys woke him up.'

'What happens now?' asked Philip.

'Well, a report will have to go to the Crown Prosecution Service. But unless you plan to press charges we will release them on police bail.'

Philip cleared his throat. 'Superintendent, how much of this has to be made public?'

'I'm afraid it might have to come out as evidence.'

Both men looked at each other.

'Is there any way we can avoid that?'

Goddard considered for a moment. 'It all depends on whether the Crown Prosecution Service looks upon this as the actions of a feckless nanny rather than a pre-meditated act which endangered a minor. A skilful lawyer could argue that as Miranda was kept separate from the nanny's activities that night, she was in no danger, moral or otherwise. In that case the nanny would be guilty only of failing to keep in touch with her employer, not a criminal offence, or guilty of administering an unlawful substance to a minor. But the analysts have identified the substance as a sedative commonly found in medication for, say, flu symptoms, available without prescription over the chemist's counter. Incidentally, there were none of McKinnon's fingerprints on the bottle.' He looked down at his hands and added slowly, 'If the CPS don't do anything, you or your wife could of course press a civil charge against the nanny.' He looked inquiringly at Philip.

There was only the smallest of pauses before Philip said resolutely, 'I think, Superintendent, in the circumstances, you can take it that we will not be pressing charges.' Philip paused. 'I have talked to my wife about this and she agrees that this whole business won't really be laid to rest until we meet Angus McKinnon before he leaves London, if only to reassure ourselves that he won't go off the rails again. If he goes straight back to Scotland, we'll always wonder whether he's taken his anger with him. If I write a note to him, asking him if he would come here and meet us when he's released, would you give it to him?'

Goddard nodded. 'Good idea. If he agrees to come, I'll have someone ring you to let you know, and we'll arrange transport.'

'Many thanks, Superintendent.'

Philip went to Charlie and filled her in on his conversation with Goddard, then he went back to the bedroom to collect his thoughts and try to sleep. How would the Prime Minister react to all this?

The calls from reporters had been relentless and were stepped up when the *Chronicle* and the *Despatch* were seen by their rivals. 'Can we get a comment from the minister on the rumour that Angus McKinnon is his illegitimate son?' Chris Bennett, keeping vigil in Philip's study while the minister slept, had given them short shrift, but he knew he was only buying time.

He sent out for the early editions and with deepening gloom read the screaming *Chronicle* headline, 'Who Is The Father?' Poor sod, he thought. Who could expect a fuck at seventeen to wreck a career twenty-odd years later?

On the right-hand side of the front page they ran the kidnap story, on the other were two photographs, one of Angus McKinnon, flanked by one of Philip and Vanessa. Chris scanned the accompanying story which, though it did not actually offer proof that Vanessa and Philip were Angus McKinnon's parents, built up a convincing picture of a teenage couple in love, then separated when Vanessa was sent away to Scotland ostensibly 'to study' at the age of fifteen. 'She told me she could not remember ever smiling that year' an unnamed friend was quoted as saying, adding that December 20th was always a depressing day for Vanessa. 'Angus McKinnon was born on December 20,' ended the *Chronicle* story.

The *Despatch* had somehow got hold of the letter that Chris had sent to Party HQ. He was furious, realising that for the newspapers to be so well-informed so early, not just about the family but about the kidnap – there was even a photograph of the Bayswater Hotel on an inside page of the *Chronicle* – meant there must have been leaks. Where? One of the policemen? Maybe even a member of his own staff? He would probably never find out.

Chris forced himself to concentrate on the real problem in hand: how to dampen down the story. His agile mind went through all the possibilities. Finally he decided that Philip had to be made to roll over and admit he was Angus McKinnon's father. His admission of the truth would cut short the inevitable endless speculation. The PM would have to be consulted, of course, and there would have to be an official statement. Thanks to Miranda's safe return, the under-age story might be buried.

If it was not, Philip would have to be dumped.

Miranda's cot had been moved from her own room to the foot of her parents' bed. She had fallen asleep as soon as they arrived back from the hospital and had not stirred since then. The doctors expected the sedative to wear off completely within the next twenty-four hours and had advised she should be roused every two or three hours during the day.

Charlie had been unable even in her exhausted state to sleep for long. The traumatic events of the night had brought to a head a question she had wrestled with many times before: did she have the courage to change the direction of her life? ABN was an important part of it, but for some time she had felt that it was not only Miranda who suffered from the hours she had to work. So did her marriage. Now she had to face the fact that if she had been looking after Miranda herself, her daughter would never have been put at risk. And it was not as if this was the only time the nanny had abused her position. Charlie shuddered. She loved Miranda and Philip so much she did not know what she would do if anything happened to either of them.

Since Dr Murray had delivered his warning about Philip's health, Charlie had often lain awake at night, not, as her husband might have thought, worrying about her job but listening to the sound of his breathing. The strain of the last terrible hours would have taken its toll.

Miranda was growing up so fast, too. One incident in particular had pinpointed what continuing in full-time work could mean. Two nights ago Charlie had come home to find her baby as usual sitting on the nanny's lap, all cuddly and warm after a bath. But instead of handing over the baby to her mother, Helen had said, 'Miranda, sweetheart, be a good girl. Say hello to Mummy.'

Her own child, being instructed to 'say hello to Mummy'. That sentence had nearly broken Charlie's heart. All the talk about quality time with children was piffle, she thought. It was quantity time Miranda needed. And so did she.

She stretched out her hand towards the bedside phone and, keeping her voice low so as not to alert Philip who was talking to Chris Bennett in the next room, she spoke to her station boss and told him she wished to resign her job. 'I've made up my mind, Jack,' she said. 'No. There's nothing you can say. What'll change in a few weeks' time?'

Again she listened to his entreaties.

'I've told you. There's nothing to think about. Well, all right. That's up to you, but I'm telling you this is final.'

As she went into the kitchen to make herself a cup of coffee, Charlie felt a wave of apprehension. She had been working ever since she had left university and this was unknown territory.

She took her coffee back to the bedroom. Jack had said she was still in shock and it was not the time to make life-changing decisions. Of course she enjoyed having a successful career but she was lucky enough to have a choice. Yes, they would miss her salary. It would be a struggle to meet Vanessa's alimony payments without it. So what? Money was unimportant after what they had been through and they would have to manage somehow. Other people did on much less. Maybe she could persuade the Salters to keep her on as a consultant when the takeover went through.

As she was washing up her coffee cup, Charlie felt Philip's arms enfold her. He turned her round to face him and kissed her gently. 'Chris Bennett has gone. He'll bring the PM up to date and get back to me.' This was not the moment to add that he would probably have to make a public statement acknowledging Angus as his illegitimate son. 'How are you feeling, darling?'

She chewed her bottom lip, a habit since childhood when she was stressed, and told him she had resigned her job.

'Charlie, my love,' Philip said gently, 'we've been through the most traumatic time of our lives. Is it wise to make such a momentous decision when you're still so overwrought?'

Sceptical that such a high-powered racehorse would be content to minister to a baby and husband day after day, he was nevertheless aware that she had been feeling like this for some months. He surmised that what had happened to Miranda had put everything into context.

'It seems the right time to start a different chapter in my life,' she said, 'and you know I want another baby.'

He did not attempt to dissuade her. If this was what she wanted, how could he stand in her way? She looked so woebegone, he kissed the tip of her nose. 'OK, but I've been married to a housewife before. I didn't like it.'

'You're a self-centred, egotistical shit.' Another kiss, then a sigh. 'But you're *my* egotistical shit.'

This time the kiss was so fervent, Philip was emboldened to suggest, 'How long do you think Miranda will stay asleep?' And when she made no reply, added, 'Is dancing under the duvet out of the question?'

'Oh, all right then, you smooth-talking bastard.' Charlie took his hand and led him smiling into the spare bedroom.

Chapter Twenty-Seven

Vanessa's vigil finally ended just before eleven o'clock when the desk sergeant told her Angus was to be released.

Cold and cramped after spending half the night and most of the morning sitting on an uncomfortable bench, Vanessa asked if she could talk to her son privately. But Angus sent a message that he did not want to talk to her.

The desk sergeant, who had been on duty all night, took pity on her. He suggested she accompany him down a corridor where it was just possible she might bump into her son as he was being released.

Angus appeared in the doorway with two officers and, recognising her, tried to brush past. She blocked his path.

'Angus, I'm really sorry about what's happened.'

He stared at her mutely.

'I can see that you think it was all my fault and I agree. I've made it clear to the Lockharts and the police that I was totally to blame for everything that happened last night. At least give me the chance to explain. Can't we go somewhere just for a few minutes to talk?'

'No, I don't think so,' he said shortly. 'I've nothing to say to you. I don't need you.'

Vanessa looked at her son sadly. 'But I need you. Please?'

The policemen, embarrassed, stepped back to give the pair some privacy.

Angus hesitated. 'I really haven't the time now.'

'Look, I'm really sorry I upset you so much. I was wrong not to tell you what you wanted to know but I'd only just met you and I was afraid.'

He rubbed his brow wearily. 'I can't talk about this now. You'll have to give me a bit of time. Right now I want to go and meet my father.'

Vanessa's eyes filled with tears and she watched dejectedly as he disappeared down the corridor with his police escort.

Angus had his first taste of life as the son of a Cabinet minister by being smuggled out of the back entrance of the police station to avoid the hordes of photographers anticipating his release. And then once more he found himself in a speeding patrol car, this time as a passenger of status rather than a suspect.

As the vehicle transported him towards Chelsea Mansions, Angus tried to think what he would say when he was face to face with Miranda's parents.

When Chris Bennett returned to Pimlico to discuss what he felt was the real business of the day, Philip saw at once that this was a different Chris Bennett, stern-faced, unemotional and brusque, quite unlike the concerned adviser of last night.

'I've spoken to the PM,' he said flatly.

Philip felt a frisson of anxiety.

'He believes that somebody has to take the heat out of the problems surrounding your son.'

Philip had been expecting this. 'That somebody should be me,' he said resolutely.

'I'm glad you see it that way, Minister, and I've taken the liberty of jotting down a few notes.' Chris pulled out a sheet of paper from his briefcase. 'I've cleared the words with everyone from the boss down.'

If Chris Bennett had cleared the words with the PM, this was more than a 'few notes', it was a finalised press statement. Philip was enough of a politician not to show surprise but even he was taken aback by the slickness of this Machiavellian operation. Once again his family was being railroaded for the convenience of his career and his party's fortunes. This statement was something he should have written himself.

The statement left little unsaid: 'In the hope of clearing up any misunderstandings regarding the events of the last twenty-four hours I would like to announce that Angus McKinnon is my son. His mother is my first wife Vanessa Lockhart. He was born when we were both very young and before we were married. I did not know of his existence at the time of his birth but as soon as she could my former wife put her name on the adoption register to try and find him. But because in this country the adoption laws are designed to protect the child, we were unable to contact him. We are proud to have him in our family now though we pay tribute to his adoptive parents, Andrew and Rosalie McKinnon, who sadly died in a car accident recently.

'I am happy to say that my daughter Miranda is safe and well. There will be no charges in connection with her temporary disappearance and my family and I deeply regret the inconvenience it has caused. I want to thank the police for their efforts, support and patience, and the media, too, for respecting the blackout. I and my family would like to make it clear that there will be no additions whatsoever to this statement, not now, not ever.'

Philip was impressed in spite of himself. He could not have bettered the statement.

Chris informed him that the PM's advisers had pointed out that the return of Miranda only a day before the polling stations opened was a heaven-sent photo opportunity. 'They believe that a photo of the PM with all of you will show the media you have his full confidence.' Chris looked at him steadily.

Philip shook his head. 'The timing's all wrong here, Chris. My wife and I have been through hell. My daughters are due from Brighton any moment to see Miranda, and Angus McKinnon is coming here as well to meet us all.'

'Be that as it may, Minister, this must take precedence. The press office is at this moment trying to re-work the PM's schedule.'

Philip was extremely irritated. 'I can go along with the personal statement but having to drag my family into a photo call at such short notice is too intrusive.'

Chris shrugged. The PM's suggestions were his commands. That went for Philip too. The unspoken code between minister and adviser was that the former would be jettisoned from the Cabinet if he embarrassed or disobeyed the party.

Amy was enjoying the drive to London. She had not been behind the wheel for some weeks as undergraduates were discouraged from taking cars to Cambridge; driving was a rare treat. Her pleasure was only marred by concern over the brief phone call she had received early this morning from her mother. She had sounded so tired and upset. She gave no details but said she hoped to be home by the early afternoon, she wasn't sure exactly when. She was subdued when Amy told her she and Louise would be in London to see Miranda then. She said only, 'In that case I'll probably be asleep when you get back but wake me up and we'll talk then.'

The car was packed with presents for Miranda, and Amy and Louise had included beloved old toys of their own childhood to give to their half-sister.

Outside Chelsea Mansions police were keeping a swarm of weary-looking press people away from number 16. As their car approached the block, the girls could hear shouts of recognition from some of the photographers and a scuffle broke out as the police barred them from the entrance to the flats while they escorted the girls inside.

'It's like being a film star,' giggled Louise as they dashed into the building. Amy only wished she had taken more trouble with her make-up.

Philip opened his arms wide as the girls ran to him. It was the first time they had seen him since Christmas. Miranda squealed with delight at the sight of her two half-sisters.

'Oh, haven't you grown?' both girls said at once as a beaming Charlie put her on the ground. She toddled towards them to play a well-loved game, the 'Miranda sandwich' which involved the two girls kneeling down and planting a kiss on each of her cheeks.

It was a joyous moment in the Lockhart household. Miranda, infected by the atmosphere, was giggling with delight and Charlie felt for the first time that she was included in their warmth.

When the initial excitement had died down, Philip dropped his bombshell. 'We have a visitor arriving any moment.'

There was a chorus of disapproval.

'Oh Dad, not today,' said Amy disappointedly.

'We've only just arrived here ourselves,' added Louise. 'We don't want to meet any of your boring political people.'

'Oh, I think you'll want to meet this person. It's Angus McKinnon, your brother.'

There was a silence.

'I don't want to see him. Ever.' Louise's voice was defiant. 'He took Miranda away.'

Charlie intervened. 'I don't want him here either, Louise, but your father is convinced he was being used by the nanny and wasn't to blame.'

Philip explained that the police would drop charges against Angus but there were still questions about the nanny's behaviour. 'The main thing is that Miranda's back home and unharmed. And although I take Charlie's point, there have been too many rifts in this family and I think we should make the young man welcome.'

Charlie and Amy exchanged looks.

'Some of those rifts have been sorted out, Dad,' said Amy. Philip raised an eyebrow. 'Charlie, has Dad told you I'm dropping the court case?'

Charlie gave her stepdaughter a smile of pure pleasure and said simply, 'No, he hasn't, but I'm really pleased. I'm sure you won't regret doing that.'

'I thought the picture of Angus McKinnon they showed

on television made him look like Grandpa,' Amy remarked.

'I think so too,' said Philip. 'Apparently both his adoptive parents died recently in a car crash so I think he may need us.' He ruffled Amy's hair. 'I've learned something in the last few days about needing a family,' he said gently.

The girls spent the next quarter of an hour hovering at the window overlooking the front entrance, waiting for Angus's arrival. Suddenly, they saw photographers racing towards a police car as it braked heavily in front of the entrance.

'He's here, he's here,' shouted Louise, and Philip rushed to watch as the police linked arms to hold back the press.

A pair of long, denimed legs swung on to the pavement. The girls could hear the shouts of 'Hello, Angus' as the photographers tried to attract his attention. He turned round in response to the call, which gave the cameramen an excellent opportunity to record his face.

The young man who stepped out of the lift looked so like his own father at that age that Philip took an involuntary breath. The family jawline, those same hooded eyes.

Angus McKinnon. His son.

He had always longed for a son. Would it have made a difference to his marriage to Vanessa? The disloyal thought slid into his mind and was instantly dismissed.

Amy had restrained Louise as she was about to rush out of the front door. It seemed only right that Angus should have a few moments alone with his father.

British phlegmatic reserve vanished. Father and son embraced.

'I never thought this would ever happen.' Philip was close to tears as he gazed into Angus's face.

Angus seemed unable to say anything.

'Come in. Come in,' said Philip quickly. 'I think you could do with a strong cup of coffee.'

Ill at ease, Angus nodded. 'I'm really sorry for the trouble I caused,' he said quietly.

'No, no,' protested Philip, 'don't let's talk about that now. Come in and meet your family.'

'Amy, Louise, this is Angus.'

Louise smiled shyly and Amy, trying to cover her nervousness, said, 'I suppose I'll have to learn to think of you as my big brother.'

Angus smiled diffidently.

As he was introduced to Charlie, holding a squirming Miranda, he coloured and said, 'I don't know what to say to you.'

'There's nothing you can say,' she said abruptly. 'It's over now.'

There was an awkward silence until Miranda, recognising her friend and squealing with pleasure, steadied herself against his knee. At once Angus bent down to the little girl's level and Charlie's hostility lessened on seeing the rapport between the two. Those hours her child had spent with him must have formed a bond between them.

Angus seemed to gain courage from Miranda's welcome and blurted out, 'I must explain. I thought that going along with Helen was wrong but she provided a heaven-sent opportunity to meet you. After all, I hadn't had much luck on my own. I didn't say anything or call you because part of me wanted to get back at you,' Angus went on, looking directly at his father. 'Despite what Helen said, I knew you'd both worry about the baby not going back home so you can't blame her for everything. I had the strong belief you didn't know anything about Miranda sleeping at the boyfriend's flat.'

'You're right, we didn't,' admitted Philip.

'I can't excuse myself but something in me wanted to punish you so I didn't tell her I thought it was wrong. When she asked to go to the party just for an hour, I still didn't object. She disappeared for ages and I didn't know where she was. In the end I fell asleep. The rest you know.'

Charlie looked at him reflectively. 'You've been frank and I'll be frank back. We went through hell yesterday and it won't be easy to forget that. You'll have to give us, well, me anyway, some time to get over it. But I'm glad you said what you did.'

Philip shepherded them all into the kitchen where coffee was percolating. He squeezed his wife's shoulder. 'Dull it ain't,' he whispered.

There was not enough suitable food in the fridge to feed several voracious appetites, sharpened by the all-night vigil. Louise and Amy volunteered to go shopping but their father vetoed the idea. He was well aware of the dangers of snatched pictures and regretfully he knew he would have to use them for the well-structured, stage-managed photo call. The police came to their rescue and while Charlie briefed them on what was needed for a traditional English breakfast, Philip took Angus aside.

'Have you spoken to your mother since you were released?'

Angus nodded. 'Briefly.' He did not elaborate.

'Give her another chance, Angus. Please. Rightly or wrongly, she was only trying to protect me. The one thing this hideous experience has taught me is to forget misunderstandings and arguments. What's important is the family, the people who care for you. I know Vanessa cares for you.'

His son did not dissent and Philip added, 'At least think about it.'

Angus asked whether he might use the phone to call his aunt, after which they settled down to an extended brunch and Angus was coaxed into talking about his upbringing in Scotland, his love for his adoptive parents and the shock of being told he was adopted.

After the meal, Charlie excused herself and disappeared into the bedroom with Miranda. The rest of the family were comfortably installed in the living room when the phone rang. It was Chris Bennett. The Prime Minister would be at Chelsea Mansions for a photo call in one hour's time. Chris himself would be there in about half an hour. The media was notified at the same time as the Secretary of State for Transport. Number 10's press officers emphasised that it was for pictures only and that no questions, absolutely none, would be countenanced.

Philip entered the bedroom quietly. His wife and child were in a deep sleep. As gently as he could, he stroked Charlie's cheek. She stirred and he told her the Prime Minister was on his way. He felt extremely guilty. She and their baby daughter had been through so much and needed to rest.

Charlie groaned and Miranda wailed when Philip picked her up. Nothing they could do or say would placate her. She was still distressed when Chris Bennett arrived.

'Perhaps the PM will be able to cheer her up,' Philip told his disconcerted aide.

Fifteen minutes before the PM's arrival, the girls had done and re-done their make-up. Initially reluctant to be photographed, Angus had needed to be persuaded that the photo call would help deflect publicity from him later on. 'By doing this photo call we appear not to be hiding anything so you become less interesting to the media,' Philip told him. 'That's the theory anyway.'

Once he had agreed, Angus entered into the excited preparations. Unused to sisters, he seemed amused at the trouble they took choosing one of Philip's ties for him, protesting that he rarely wore one anyway.

As the appointed time came and went, Charlie's irritation at this political interruption increased. Miranda was still bad-tempered and unhappy, despite all attempts to divert her. At ten-minute intervals, they were given reports of the prime ministerial progress. 'He's on his way. He's on his way. He's running late.'

Philip observed the interaction between his four children and watched them, adrenaline ebbing, slowly lose their sparkle. They were tired. So was he. He had had little sleep over the last twenty-four hours and he was exhausted physically and mentally.

When the PM eventually arrived, Philip watched the magic happen. He had seen it a thousand times. People forgot their irritation, how long they had been kept waiting, all the inconvenience. They were in the Presence and that was all that mattered.

Though the Prime Minister had been briefed, he was curious to know the circumstances in which the baby had been found.

'The police say Miranda's been to places they can only

guess at,' commented Charlie. 'If only she could talk, who knows what kind of secret life she's led?'

'Just like my backbenchers,' remarked the PM.

The picture that appeared on most front pages the next day showed the ensuing laugh. There was a broadly-beaming Angus next to his father holding Miranda, flanked by Charlie, Amy and Louise. The Prime Minister was centre stage. The photographers felt that the long wait had eventually been worthwhile.

As the PM was about to sweep off, Philip asked for a private word and was given a choice. Next week in Number 10 – 'or the leader of the Opposition's office,' he joked – or now in his car, en route for his next, late appointment. Philip chose the car.

As the Jaguar pulled away, Philip waved and saw the crestfallen faces of his children through the window. How many times had he been there only to disappear without warning? And how had he never noticed before? It made him more resolute about the difficult conversation that lay ahead.

'Prime Minister,' he began, 'this business with Miranda has brought my priorities into perspective and, with regret, I feel I have to resign from your Cabinet.'

'Philip, Philip,' replied Edward Saunders, completely unfazed. 'Of course you feel like that now. Take a week off after the election and we'll have another talk.'

'I've made up my mind, sir.'

'Well, I refuse to accept your resignation.' The PM became steely. 'You're making an understandable but purely emotional decision. And you're not looking at the broad picture. If we win tomorrow, I'll need you and so will the country. We still have immense problems to solve.' The

Prime Minister turned so he was facing Philip. 'Over these few weeks you've had a number of difficulties and I've supported you one hundred per cent.' He paused and said with emphasis, 'Now I expect that same degree of support from you.'

Extricating himself from the prime ministerial entourage proved difficult but Philip eventually walked through his front door an hour later. He could hear an animated buzz of conversation coming from the sitting room and quickly joined his family.

'I tried telling the PM that, win or lose, I wanted to give up my Cabinet job,' he said as soon as he had sat down. 'I told him it takes up too much extra time which I want to spend with my wife and children. But he refused to accept my resignation.'

Charlie was as good an actress as anyone but he could hardly miss her indrawn breath. Amy and Louise's startled expressions also showed their surprise.

Philip looked at Charlie. 'You're upset with me.' It was more a statement than a question.

She shook her head decisively. 'No. I'm glad you thought of it. But why did you do it without talking to me first?'

'Snap.'

'All right, I'm sorry I didn't discuss my decision with you but there's a difference. I'm reasonably certain I can get my job back at some stage.'

'Well, I wasn't sure exactly what I wanted,' said Philip slowly, 'but in the last twenty-four hours I realised how self-obsessed I've become. In this kind of job it's almost obligatory. What happened to Miranda was a nightmare but we've been lucky. I've been given the chance to put things right before it's too late and whatever happens in the future, I'm determined not to neglect you again.' He gave Angus a broad smile. 'I know all this must seem unreal but you and I have twenty-four years to catch up on.'

His son seemed uncertain and appeared to be about to speak when Amy interjected, 'Dad, I wish you'd give up being an MP altogether. If you went back to running Forrester's, you could show Angus and me how the place works. We could take over from you when you retire.'

Philip started to laugh. 'Don't get me out of the way so soon, young lady. Let's talk about it, but we have an election to worry about first.'

'And I have a job I love.' Angus smiled at his sister.

Then Philip mimicked the famous cry of the Speaker of the House of Commons, 'Order, order.' He went on, 'Win, draw or lose for the party, I'd still like to achieve the biggest majority I've ever had. There's a great deal of work to be done in the constituency and only a few hours to do it. We need people to knock on doors, ferry voters to the polling stations, make tea, help Wyn and, most important of all, smile at photographers and say wonderful things about me at all times.' He glanced affectionately at them. 'So if it's at all possible, even though some of us have had virtually no sleep, I'd like a full turnout of the Lockhart army.'

There was a hum of excitement as they agreed enthusiastically.

They were a family. Almost.

Chapter Twenty-Eight

The news of a government election win on the bedside clock radio aroused Vanessa from a half sleep. Edward Saunders's party had a majority of only five but he was already doing deals with the minor parties.

Political pundits dubbed the finding of the missing baby on the eve of poll a 'womb trembler'. They felt it had undoubtedly influenced women voters to go out and vote for 'Steady Eddie', which had definitely had an effect on the result of the election.

Philip would be the golden boy now and if the political commentators were right, he was certain to go back into the Cabinet. Damn. Vanessa had been hoping that if Philip's party lost, he would return to the back benches and resume his position as chief executive of Forrester's.

The girls had left a loving message on the answer machine saying they were staying in London with their new brother. He, too, had left a brief postscript saying he looked forward to seeing her soon.

Her three children.

She had never said it to herself before. It was a wonderful thought, to imagine them all with her at the Rectory. But when would things ever return to normal? Following the banner headlines in all the newspapers, Superintendent Goddard had asked the local police to maintain a presence outside the Rectory to keep the reporters and curious onlookers at bay. It rankled that some of the gawpers flattening the dandelions on the kerbside and turning the early grass to mulch were her neighbours. She was trapped by them all.

The answer machine was another intrusion but she had turned it down to such a low volume she could hardly hear the frequent calls from the press and television news channels requesting interviews with the mother of Angus McKinnon. Philip's statement had not deterred the media from doing what it saw as its duty, to pursue every member of the Lockhart family in the hopes they could persuade them to tell their story.

Vanessa was alarmed by a loud insistent knocking on the front door but when she peered through the spy hole it was to see a strikingly glamorous Dorinda carrying the biggest box of food Vanessa had seen outside Fortnum's.

'Well, if you're going to be holed up here, I thought you might as well do it in style,' her friend said after a reassuring hug.

'Why are you so dolled up?' asked Vanessa. 'Which man are you lunching with today?' She made a valiant attempt to sound welcoming. She took in the carefully teased, wild-thing hair, buttock-hugging jeans, tight black body under a skimpy jacket and the pale ready-for-bed make-up. So this was how a lunchtime mistress prepared herself.

'None. I'm having lunch with you. I made a special effort because I realised our local celeb would be surrounded by the paparazzi today and I thought I might as well look the business if I'm going to be photographed front, back and sideways.' She held out her arms to hug her friend again. 'I came to make sure you ate something nourishing and relaxed in a nice, soothing bath. Look.' She held up a bottle of Laura Biagiotti bath oil.

The eclectic mix of bottled peaches in champagne, game pâté, home-cured ham and thin water biscuits was quickly unloaded into various cupboards and the fridge. Dorinda knew this kitchen almost as well as her own and began to prepare a cafetière of freshly-brewed coffee.

Yesterday's *Daily Chronicle* was still on the kitchen table. Dorinda glanced at the pictures on the front page.

'So your dear friend Imogen did do the dirty on you after all,' she said, pouring the coffee. ' "December twentieth has such unhappy memories for her," eh? Bitch.'

'Even if she hadn't it would've all come out anyway,' replied Vanessa. 'I was pretty devastated when they told me about that statement but apparently Philip had no choice. The PM insisted on it, and you know when the Master calls . . .'

She sat with her head in her hands. 'Can you imagine what the people round here will think of me? Having a child at fifteen.'

'Come on, darling, they've just got away with it. The people who love you don't care about that.' She looked at her friend sympathetically.

'What I hated more than that was seeing the photo of my three children with Charlie.'

'*Three* children. I bet that's the first time you've said that to another person.'

Vanessa smiled. 'It's good to include him at last. That picture with the grinning idiot Edward Saunders was so posed, so phoney. Damn it, our private affairs should be of no interest to anyone else outside the family.'

'Oh, Vee, you forfeited your privacy once Philip became a politician.'

Vanessa pulled her ear lobe reflectively. 'I suppose so. Honestly, Dorrie, anyone who wants to be famous must be deranged. I never want to see my name in print or mentioned on radio or television ever again.' She drained her cup. 'And these press people outside are driving me mad. They'll follow me wherever I go, you know. I feel like a prisoner. God knows what they're doing to Angus.'

'Have you heard from him?'

'One phone call. Quite brief.'

'Did he sound friendly?'

'Fairly. There's still a barrier, but that's only to be expected. He has to go back to Edinburgh but I've invited him to come and stay in a few weeks when everything should've calmed down. I'm hoping we can at least become friends. I'd like that very much.'

'Will he come?'

'I think so. He said he would.'

Just then the phone rang and Dorinda picked it up before Vanessa could warn her that the answer machine was on. She listened briefly before turning to Vanessa who was backing away, shaking her head.

It was Paul Salter.

Vanessa's pulse quickened. 'My God, that man is certainly persistent,' she said angrily. Dorinda quickly covered the mouthpiece with her hand. 'Kidnap, scandal,

total mayhem in my life – nothing puts him off his stride.'
Vanessa could still visualise the easy way Charlie had slid
her arm through his in Westminster Hall and the quick
way she withdrew it when her husband appeared. She took
the phone from Dorinda.

'What do you want?' she said brusquely.

Paul Salter was taken aback by Vanessa's hostile tone. His
last memory of her was an electric kiss on the Riviera
seafront. Here he was phoning up to ask her to lunch and,
God damn it, nervous about it, and was the woman pleased?
The hell she was.

When Vanessa put the phone down, Dorinda was grinning
from ear to ear. Vanessa pointed an accusing finger at her
friend. 'You can wipe that smile off your face, Dorrie. The
threat of the takeover hasn't gone away, you know. I only
agreed to see him to hear what he has to say. It must be
important,' she went on quickly before Dorinda could inter-
rupt, 'because he's sending a helicopter to pick me up,' and
Vanessa gave a loud laugh as Dorinda's jaw dropped.

'I'm impressed,' she chuckled. 'But let's check into Hotel
Reality here, Vee. This isn't just business on your side, is it?
You fancy him. Admit it.'

Vanessa was indignant. 'Don't be ridiculous. It's not that
at all.'

'Come on, Vee. It's me you're talking to.'

'It *is* just business.'

Dorinda guffawed. 'Now, what are you going to wear?'

'Oh, something comfortable. A blazer and skirt, I
thought.'

' "Comfortable"? No, no. Not the right attitude at all.
Let's see.'

Dorinda bulldozed her into trying on a rarely-worn aqua-marine crepe frock. The zip would still not quite close across her back. She ordered her friend to take off her bra and lean over, so that the extra centimetre gained made the fastening possible. The midriff-hugging dress would give all the support necessary.

Dorinda also insisted on two coats of mascara, perfume sprayed behind the knees and the back-combing of Vanessa's hair into a less extravagant version of her own style.

'This is a mistake,' wailed Vanessa.

'Look, you said you don't fancy him,' said Dorinda with a wicked gleam in her eye. 'It's only a lunch, for heaven's sake.'

A few minutes later, downstairs, dressed and waiting, Vanessa began to fidget nervously. Dorinda diverted her with the suggestion of a drink.

'Oh, I never touch the stuff before six in the evening these days.' A pause. 'What's the time now?'

'Nearly eleven.'

'Close enough.'

Aware that she was looking better than she had done for years, Vanessa began entering into the spirit of things. The wine exercised its customary influence on an empty stomach and she brandished her glass in the air.

Maybe it was misplaced but she had a surge of optimism that the Salter takeover would not be a walkover.

'It's my duty to go,' she said playfully.

Dorinda imitated her action and they downed another glass.

'It's in my children's interests to go.' Vanessa waved her glass in a toast. 'And it's in a helicopter.'

Another clink.

'You'll be the talk of the village, Vee.'

'I already am.'

Their laughter stopped abruptly when they detected the faint whirr of rotor blades as the helicopter ventured towards its landing place in the paddock behind the house.

Dorinda hustled Vanessa out through the French windows into the garden, the anguished yells of frustrated photographers held back by police ringing sweetly in their ears.

As Vanessa dodged under the blades to reach the steps, she gave Dorinda a mock Royal wave.

My God, thought Dorinda. She doesn't half scrub up well.

Paul seemed to be as nervous as she was. He was pacing up and down the elegant stretch of Persian carpet in the suite in The Ritz when she arrived. He had opened the bottle of champagne with a fair degree of skill but had then forgotten to pour it out.

Vanessa sat wordless, pressing her knees together so that her tight skirt did not ride too far up her legs.

'I'm glad you came,' he said abruptly, looking out of the window. There was a strained silence.

'This is very difficult for me,' Paul ventured at last.

'I can't believe that. You still think you're going to win, don't you?'

'This has nothing to do with winning, Vanessa,' he said emphatically. 'It's more personal. I couldn't wait until after the takeover in case you refused to see me.' He began walking round the sofa. Vanessa was forced to turn her body to follow his route. 'It's crazy but I have to tell you that I've been thinking about you ever since Cannes.'

She looked at him in disbelief but he was too wound up to notice.

'I wake up in the night and you're still on my mind. And I'm not a man who does this, you know. It's not what I do. I don't get emotionally involved, it's not worth it. When I want to be romantic I pay the maître d' to organise it. When I want to give a woman a gift, I have the best secretary in the world, who knows exactly what to choose.'

'What did she buy for Charlie?'

He looked genuinely puzzled. 'What are you talking about?'

'I think there's something between you.'

'You're wrong. I've never been alone with Charlie.' He thought hard. 'I'm certain I never have.'

Silence again.

'I can't get you out of my head.'

'I suppose all this guff impresses most women.' Vanessa's tone was disdainful.

'Are you crazy? I don't say this stuff to anybody. Nowadays, let me tell you, you don't have to. I can't believe I'm saying it now.'

Vanessa was beginning to feel unnerved and said defensively, 'You must want my shares really badly.' There was only a week to go before the crucial board meeting that would decide the fate of Forrester's.

Paul exploded. 'Don't you understand anything? I don't want to talk about takeovers. That was a ruse to get you here. I don't want to talk about shares. I want to talk about you and me.'

Her eyes widened.

'Don't you see what I'm getting at here? I can't help

354

myself and all you think I'm after are a few lousy shares. I suppose that just shows,' he said ruminatively, 'what kind of a man you think I am.'

'A very clever one.' She was still far from convinced. 'I nearly fell for all that sweet talk in Cannes.'

The soft burr of the phone intruded.

'Oh hell,' he cursed, picking up the receiver. 'Yes,' he said to the caller, 'I see, hang on a minute, I'll take it in the other room.' He looked across at Vanessa with embarrassment. 'It's business. I won't be a minute.'

Vanessa did not believe him. He was so discomfited she was sure this was no business call. She was certain it was another woman.

She never again wanted to be deceived as Philip had deceived her. Curiosity overcame caution and she gingerly lifted up the phone. She put her hand over the mouthpiece to muffle the sound of her breathing, something she had done many times when she was trying to get evidence of Philip's infidelity.

Vanessa recognised the voice at once. Charlie.

She railed against her own stupidity and weakness in allowing her emotional guard to slip even for a moment. She had almost been ready to believe Paul's blandishments. What a fool to fall for such a well-honed seduction exercise.

As she listened, she heard Charlie assuring Paul that Miranda had emerged from the ordeal relatively unscathed. The nanny was still at the police station and Angus was there with them, getting to know his new family.

Vanessa felt a stab of anguish.

The hated voice continued, 'Look, Paul, I can't get hold of Kyle and this is urgent. I thought you should know that Amy

Lockhart has decided to drop her legal action.'

Paul sounded happy. 'Good, that's the final problem solved. It makes it easier for us to go ahead and win. Kyle will be pleased.'

Vanessa tightened her grip on the receiver to still the tremble in her hand. She was afraid Paul would hear the sound of her quickened breathing.

Charlotte Lockhart was spying for the Salters.

She would bet money that Philip did not know his wife was giving sensitive information to the other side in the takeover. How could he have been duped by this woman? Charlie had double-crossed her and now she was doing the same to her own husband.

Charlotte the Harlot? No. Judas.

'Yes, but I think we ought to meet,' Charlie was saying, but Vanessa did not wait to hear any more of the conversation. Replacing the receiver softly, she grabbed her handbag, and walked quickly out of the suite.

Vanessa sat in the Rectory gazing at the last photograph of her grandfather Elliot Forrester, taken with herself and her daughters.

Slowly she turned the remaining pages of the photograph album, flicking through a history of her family. There she was, with the Princess of Wales opening the new building. Next to them was a beaming Elliot holding a pair of scissors which the Princess used later to cut the red ribbon at the entrance to the foyer. She remembered the reception afterwards where Elliot had talked so movingly about the company and the loyalty of the employees.

Vanessa sat up. Loyalty.

She snapped the album shut with a thump. Charlotte Lockhart did not know the meaning of the word. No wonder the Salter camp had always been one step ahead. Even when she went to Cannes to persuade Cissi to vote her way, Paul Salter had already been warned to put his oar in. It was clear from their every move that the Salters were aware of all the Forrester Group's strategy and thinking.

She decided her grandfather's company was worth one last fight. Surely it would make a difference to the vote if the board knew about the treacherous behaviour of their newest recruit.

Chapter Twenty-Nine

As board members gathered for coffee in the anteroom, Vanessa garnered her courage and walked up to her rival who was talking to Hugh Purcell. It was the first time the two women had been face to face since Miranda's disappearance and Charlie could not disguise her surprise.

'Hugh, would you excuse us, please?' Vanessa said sweetly.

Hugh disappeared with alacrity.

Vanessa turned to Charlie. 'I've something I want to talk to you about and I'd prefer to do it in private.' Seeing the look of alarm on the other woman's face, she added quickly, 'Oh, you needn't worry, I'm quite calm. It's just that I want you to hear what I have to say before the meeting.'

Charlie was still reluctant. 'I really would prefer it if you could say what you have to say in public.'

'I don't think you will,' responded Vanessa emphatically. 'I suggest you come with me to the office next door.' And she walked off.

After a brief hesitation, Charlie followed, conscious of the murmurs of surprise as she left the room.

'Well? What's all this about?' Charlie looked composed.

Even now I can't rattle her, thought Vanessa. She plunged straight in. 'You've been spying for the Salter organisation. Don't bother denying it. You've been undermining us from the beginning.'

Vanessa was taken aback by Charlie's reaction. There was no hesitation, no denial. Her tone was assertive. 'I've never made any secret of the fact that I wanted the takeover to succeed,' she retorted hotly. 'I don't deny that I was helping the Salters but I had a good reason. Philip's health.'

Vanessa looked sceptical.

'I know he looks well but his doctor has warned him that unless he drastically cuts down his work schedule and stress levels, he'll get ill again.'

'Ill? He's never had a day's illness in his life.'

'Last summer he collapsed on holiday and I had to take him to hospital. He has high blood pressure and he could have a heart attack if he's not careful. It's why I agreed to go on the board and it's the reason I've been helping the Salters with the takeover. If the company were out of Philip's life, it would remove one huge worry from his shoulders.'

'That doesn't make sense. If he needs to reduce his workload why did he take a job in the Cabinet?'

'Oh, come on, you know Philip as well as I do.'

'All right. But whether the reason was good or bad, I think it's outrageous to work with our enemy. More than that, it's unethical and I believe the board will agree with me.' She hoped her voice sounded as resolute as she felt. 'I intend to tell them about it. Unless you vote with me.'

There was a long pause.

'That sounds like blackmail.'

'If you like to put it that way.' Vanessa was pleased at how in control she felt. 'I'm quite sure Philip would never approve of how you tried to win and I'm certain you never intended him to find out. Did you?'

Charlie looked out of the window, turning her face away so that Vanessa could not see her expression. For the first time in their relationship, Vanessa thought she was making things happen rather than reacting to them. She waited for Charlie to respond but before she did, Walter Threadgold's head appeared round the door.

'The meeting was due to start ten minutes ago,' he said. 'We must get started right now. Shall we go?'

As he ushered them towards the boardroom, Walter hoped they were not going to have one of those interesting afternoons.

Every face in the boardroom was tense. Hugh Purcell was tapping his pen in rhythm with the tick-tock of the grandfather clock.

'Ladies and gentlemen,' Walter was at his most formal, 'we have an important decision to make today.' He looked over his half-moon glasses at each of them in turn. 'I need hardly say it is one which will affect all of us most profoundly. In front of you is written confirmation from the Salter organisation of their takeover bid, details of which you have already seen. Let us waste no further time and move to the vote.'

'Mr Chairman?'

Walter looked up, irritated. 'Mrs Lockhart, I thought we'd finished with questions.'

'Yes, I'm sorry, but there's something I'd like to say which I believe is relevant to the vote.' She cleared her throat. In spite of the chairman's strictures she did not intend to be harried. 'Mr Chairman, you're right. The offer before us is attractive in the long term but I believe we could safeguard the company's interests better if we do not agree to this takeover.'

Against the buzz of surprise from the rest of the board, Charlie was the focus of every eye. She looked across at the first Mrs Lockhart. No one else noticed the imperceptible nods they exchanged.

The deal was done. No one need ever know about Deep Throat.

However, the Salter Foundation had one more task for Deep Throat to perform. Paul asked if she could arrange for him to meet Vanessa, ostensibly by chance. Charlie, unaware that his direct approaches had been unsuccessful, assumed there was some leftover business to do with the failed takeover. During Louise's next visit, she discovered when Vanessa was going to be in town.

The annual general meeting of the Harlequin Charity, to which the public was admitted, was always held in a big meeting room at the Reform Club. On the platform as part of the committee, Vanessa was on automatic pilot. She had won the takeover and Forrester's was safe, so why did she feel so dispirited? She had to stop fooling herself. It was Paul Salter. She missed him.

So when he walked in just after the meeting started she thought it was one of her daydreams come to life. He sat down without taking his eyes off her. The rest of the meeting passed in a blur. After she came down from the platform, Paul immediately made his way towards her. Unsmiling, without preamble and to the bemusement of the startled onlookers, he steered her into the nearest anteroom and then kissed her. As soon as he touched her, she was lost.

Later, lying at his side, she thought it was true what they said. Lovemaking was like cycling. You never forgot how to do it.

Paul was tracing a lazy finger across her cheek and down her shoulder as they lay in companionable silence. The sex had been amazing. He had been so sensitive, so gentle, realising how nervous she was. She did not know that in the original report compiled by Deep Throat, she had been portrayed as an insecure, vulnerable, discarded wife who had made no new relationships since the divorce. Without asking, Paul had half-drawn the curtains against the pale spring sun. And he had whispered over and over again how sensuous she made him feel and how lovely she was until there came a time when she lost all inhibition. She felt desirable. This man made no secret that he lusted after her. She gave him pleasure.

'I'm glad I persuaded you to come back here,' he said.

'You're lucky I even spoke to you. Imagine, getting Charlie to spy on us.'

'That's what you do in a takeover. You find someone inside the camp so you're always one step ahead of the game. It's elementary.'

'Underhand.'

'Necessary.'

Vanessa began to get up, pulling the top sheet over her breasts. Paul gently pulled her back.

'Not so fast. I haven't finished with you yet.' He began caressing her spine slowly, up and down, with his index finger. 'Do you remember our first meeting at the ball?' he asked hoarsely. 'You were such a bitch to me. But I guess I like challenges.'

Vanessa could feel her body respond again.

'I didn't get the company but you might say this is the ultimate reverse takeover,' he whispered softly in her ear. 'And this isn't so bad, is it?'

Was it possible that Paul Salter, the tycoon who could have any woman he wanted, needed reassurance of his abilities as a lover?

Vanessa recognised this as a pivotal moment. She recalled one of Dorinda's favourite sayings: 'There are only two things a man always wants to know. First, that he's a good lover. And a close second, that he's a good driver. But remember, when you think you're overdoing the praise, you're only just beginning to get through.'

Vanessa shelved her British reserve and took a deep breath. 'It's wonderful. Sex may always be like this for you, it's never been like this for me. Ever. When we first met we were enemies,' she murmured, 'but we don't have that to hold us together any more, do we?'

'No. We don't need it,' he mumbled, his lips against her warm skin. 'Not when we have this . . . and this . . . and this . . .'

Epilogue

Dearest Dorinda,

Couldn't get you on the phone before I left so Paul's driver will fax this when we land at JFK. Fantastic news. Cissi phoned to tell me he's proposed. Husband number three, can you believe it? She's already been given the ring. Trust Cissi. A three-carat whopper. The wedding is being arranged in a hurry for next month. Well, the bridegroom is a young seventy-eight! All this courtesy of Paul who introduced them in the Hamptons this summer. That woman's amazing!

Louise is furious that she's been left behind this trip. She's devoted to Paul, they've taken to going to the racetrack together. She's hinting she wouldn't say no to a school in America. Isn't that a come-up for the books? Do you know why Amy's work experience at Forrester's during the holiday was such a great success? I've found out. She's very keen on the new right-hand man. I think he's a bit old for her but at least he's not married.

Incidentally, we had a family pow-wow and I nearly had egg on my face because I found out that Charlie and Philip had already decided to back me to ditch the takeover! If I'd eavesdropped a little longer at the hotel, I would've heard her arrange to meet Paul and Kyle to tell them she was withdrawing her support. Kyle went ballistic, apparently, and Paul, who was never that keen on the takeover, was furious on his behalf. He still is! I didn't need to threaten to tell everyone about Charlie's spying activities. Paul told me her motive was never financial. All she wanted was to influence the proceedings and, as she didn't ask for a penny, he must be right. Thank God I kept my mouth shut at the board meeting. And I'd stake my life that Charlie has never mentioned Deep Throat to Philip. He told me that their ordeal, waiting for Miranda to be found, made them re-examine many things in their lives. And it convinced them of the importance of families, of continuity and tradition.

Philip's certainly taken all this family business to heart. He's keener than I am about Forrester's and talks about the kids taking over one day. And he seems to be spending much more time with the girls, even took Louise and Miranda to Cambridge last week! Also, he's agreed that Amy should have her shares earlier than twenty-five. We're trying to organise it in time for her twenty-first. She's very happy about it, of course.

Had another call from Forrester's new chief executive. I think he'll turn out to be sound, as they say in the City. Like all new brooms he's reorganising everything and he's suggested I become a two day a week consultant. He seems to think I'll be helpful on the PR front. They're paying me, too. Not much, but Dorrie, it'll be the first time I've earned my own money since I married. Wonderful thought.

Such a lot's been happening to me lately. Watch out for some pictures in the *Sunday Chronicle*'s colour supplement.

It's called 'Board Women' and Imogen Ferris has been made their new features editor. She interviewed me last week. But I'm smarter now. Instead of inviting her home I talked to her over lunch at San Lorenzo and I watched my tongue. Still no man in her life but she mentioned her new boss a lot. Tony someone or other. I think something must be going on there. I'm still suspicious about that woman and how the story about Charlie and me came out. I can't prove it but it seems too much of a coincidence that Imogen was at the Christmas party and now she's on the staff of the *Chronicle*. Be warned.

By the way, tell Peter to buy United shares. Kyle's going for it and from what I hear he has a good chance. I'm pleased because if they're successful, Paul will have to spend far more time in Britain.

I've just looked up at the TV news and guess who I saw? The Secretary of State for Education at some school function. Poor Philip, I thought he was looking rather old. He was pleased to be given Education in the Cabinet reshuffle, but the job seems to be taking its toll. I hope he's sticking to his special diet. His health's still a worry, I gather. Mind you, last time I saw him – we had lunch, with Angus and his aunt, at the House of Commons – he told me he has to get up whenever Miranda wakes because Charlie's having such a difficult pregnancy. Dorinda, Amy says she's huge and looks far more than six months. That'll be baby number five for Philip! Angus looked well and seems happy. We keep in touch. His Aunt Muriel is a dear.

Louise says that Miranda is at the 'terrible twos' stage. Apparently Philip took her out shopping the other day (miracle of miracles) and she had a mega tantrum. From what I gather, Charlie's finding it difficult to cope without a nanny. (The horrible one who caused all that trouble has disappeared, they think back to New Zealand.) If Charlie hasn't discovered already, she'll soon learn that looking after a child at home is much more stressful than swanning off to an office! Maybe that's the reason she had her old boss to dinner the other night. I bet she's angling to get a part-time job. Watch this space!

Isn't it extraordinary how Miranda's disappearance has affected all of us? I've spent a lot of time thinking about how my life has changed, too. It's been nearly nine months since that dreadful Forrester Christmas party. Isn't it ironic that just when Charlie's given up her job, I'm becoming a bit of a career woman? Odd to think of us swapping roles.

That last board meeting was pivotal. I think we both realised we had to forge some kind of truce, mainly because of the children. I can't imagine us ever being bosom friends, but then again I can't see us ever being such bosom enemies.

You were asking about how it is with Paul and me. Well, he's exciting to be with and I love flying to America. I've just organised all the curtains for the new Knightsbridge house. He finally got rid of the suite at The Ritz. Last night on the phone he actually mentioned the M-word! But Dorrie, I changed the subject. That surprises you, doesn't it? And, perversely, it's made him more keen! But I've learned so much about myself these past months, mainly that I'm not ready to get married again. This is the way I see it now. The divorce wasn't all Philip's fault – I have to take some of the blame. I had talents which I never developed. I allowed others to take charge of my life – my mother, my grand-father, then Philip. All I ever did was complain about my lack of independence. No wonder I had no confidence.

The hardest lesson I've had to learn is that unless I'm happy with myself, I can never be happy with a man. I may have lost a husband but I've gained something better. Me.

In the meantime, I love being with the guy. It's true what you always say – sex really *is* good for you!

Much love,

Vanessa.

Splash

Val Corbett, Joyce Hopkirk, Eve Pollard

'Bold, bubbly and deliciously bitchy. From three
women who have seen and probably done it all'
Michael Dobbs, author of *House of Cards*

Katya, Liz and Joanna have been friends for years;
closer even than sisters, they have always shared
everything – except men. They have always supported each other on their way to the best jobs in a
world dominated by men, acquiring the trappings
and luxuries of authority that are the envy of other
women. Nothing could drive them apart – or could it?

Now they're coping with new pressures. Katya is
breaking all her own rules, for her new lover is
married and she won't tell even her closest friends
who it is. As the Television News Personality of the
Year, Katya is a front page story waiting to happen –
and the news, much more sensational than mere
adultery, is beginning to break. It's just the story Liz
needs for Page One to clinch her appointment as first
woman editor of a British national daily newspaper.
Their friend Joanna, editor of a glossy women's magazine, argues no story is worth destroying a friendship
for – but how can Liz resist the splash of the year?

SPLASH is the story of power struggles between men
and women, of unexpected love and the hurt of
betrayal. Above all, it is the story of a friendship. No
woman who has ever had – or been – a friend should
miss it.

0 7472 4889 3

HEADLINE

Going Too Far

Catherine Alliott

From the bestselling author of The Old Girl Network;
*'[An] addictive cocktail of wit, frivolity and madcap
romance'* Time Out

*'You've gone all fat and complacent because you've got
your man, haven't you?'*

There are some things only your best friend can tell
you but this outrageous suggestion is met with indig-
nation from Polly Penhalligan, who is recently
married, trying for a baby and blissfully happy in her
beautiful manor farmhouse in Cornwall. At least, she
was, until Pippa's unfortunate remark forces her to
realise that her idyllic life of gorging on chocolate
biscuits, counting her seemingly endless blessings
and not getting dressed until lunchtime could be
having a few unwelcome side-effects.

So Polly decides to razz things up a bit – and agrees
to allow her home to be used as a location for a com-
mercial. Having a glamorous film crew around
should certainly put something of a bomb under rural
life, shouldn't it? But even before the cameras are set
up and the stars released from their kennels, Polly's
life and marriage have been turned upside down.
This time, it seems, she's gone too far . . .

0 7472 4607 6

HEADLINE

If you enjoyed this book here is a selection of other bestselling titles from Headline

LIVERPOOL LAMPLIGHT	Lyn Andrews	£5.99 ☐
A MERSEY DUET	Anne Baker	£5.99 ☐
THE SATURDAY GIRL	Tessa Barclay	£5.99 ☐
DOWN MILLDYKE WAY	Harry Bowling	£5.99 ☐
PORTHELLIS	Gloria Cook	£5.99 ☐
A TIME FOR US	Josephine Cox	£5.99 ☐
YESTERDAY'S FRIENDS	Pamela Evans	£5.99 ☐
RETURN TO MOONDANCE	Anne Goring	£5.99 ☐
SWEET ROSIE O'GRADY	Joan Jonker	£5.99 ☐
THE SILENT WAR	Victor Pemberton	£5.99 ☐
KITTY RAINBOW	Wendy Robertson	£5.99 ☐
ELLIE OF ELMLEIGH SQUARE	Dee Williams	£5.99 ☐

Headline books are available at your local bookshop or newsagent. Alternatively, books can be ordered direct from the publisher. Just tick the titles you want and fill in the form below. Prices and availability subject to change without notice.

Buy four books from the selection above and get free postage and packaging and delivery within 48 hours. Just send a cheque or postal order made payable to Bookpoint Ltd to the value of the total cover price of the four books. Alternatively, if you wish to buy fewer than four books the following postage and packaging applies:

UK and BFPO £4.30 for one book; £6.30 for two books; £8.30 for three books.

Overseas and Eire: £4.80 for one book; £7.10 for 2 or 3 books (surface mail)

Please enclose a cheque or postal order made payable to *Bookpoint Limited*, and send to: Headline Publishing Ltd, 39 Milton Park, Abingdon, OXON OX14 4TD, UK.
Email Address: orders@bookpoint.co.uk

If you would prefer to pay by credit card, our call team would be delighted to take your order by telephone. Our direct line 01235 400 414 (lines open 9.00 am–6.00 pm Monday to Saturday 24 hour message answering service). Alternatively you can send a fax on 01235 400 454.

Name   ....

Address ....

....

....

If you would prefer to pay by credit card, please complete:
Please debit my Visa/Access/Diner's Card/American Express (delete as applicable) card number:

Signature .... Expiry Date ....